Samuel Smiles

George Moore, merchant and philanthropist

Samuel Smiles

George Moore, merchant and philanthropist

ISBN/EAN: 9783337729011

Printed in Europe, USA, Canada, Australia, Japan

Cover: Foto ©Andreas Hilbeck / pixelio.de

More available books at **www.hansebooks.com**

By SAMUEL SMILES, LL.D.

AUTHOR OF "LIVES OF THE ENGINEERS,"

SELF-HELP," "THRIFT," ETC.

WITH A PORTRAIT.

LONDON

GEORGE ROUTLEDGE AND SONS

BROADWAY, LUDGATE HILL

NEW YORK : 416, BROOME STREET

1879

PREFACE.

I HAVE written this book at the earnest request of Mrs. Moore.

The subject was brought under my notice by the late Mr. William Longman and Mr. Murray, at the instance of Mrs. Moore. They both recommended me to write the book, though neither of them was to publish it.

I was at first unwilling to undertake the Life; the state of my health not permitting me to undertake much brain-work. Besides, I was far advanced with another book which had been advertised, and which I was unwilling to postpone.

I knew a great deal about Mr. Moore's benevolence towards the poor, the helpless, and the orphans; but I thought that some other person, who had know Mr. Moore intimately, might have done greater justice to the subject.

I called upon a leading City merchant to ask his opinion. He thought it impossible for anything interesting to be written about George Moore. As to his munificence, there were hundreds of men in London

as good as he! "What *can* you make," he asked,
"out of the life of a London warehouseman?" This
statement discouraged me, and I felt disposed to return
to my former work.

It was not until Dr. Percival, Head Master of Clifton
College, called upon me, that I ascertained something
of the actual life and character of George Moore. He
spoke of the Man, and not of the Warehouseman.
He said, in a letter which I afterwards received from
him,—"There is so much genuine character in the
Cumberland Folk, that I feel sure you will be attracted
by them; and I hope you will find that the incidents
of Mr. Moore's boyhood and early life are sufficiently
characteristic to enable you to use some of the excellent
material furnished by the habits and traditions of the
district. Then, I hope you may find sufficient illustra-
tions in his middle life, of his really splendid pluck and
energy; and again in his later life, of his rare liberality.
This last trait ought to be very instructive, because of
its extreme rarity among men who have had to struggle
as he did. I don't think I have come across any other
self-made man who had so entirely 'got the chill of
poverty out of his bones.'"

I was also encouraged by the Rev. G. C. Bell, Master
of Marlborough College, who wrote to Mrs. Moore as
follows:—"I am rejoiced to hear that a memoir of
your husband is to be published; for the example of
his life, with its combination of 'self-help' and unselfish-
ness, well deserves a permanent record; and it may
be full of stimulus and encouragement to many. I

had indeed," he added, "good reason to be grateful to him for many substantial kindnesses, made all the more precious by the kind of fatherly interest that he took in those he cared for. He was, in truth, a large-hearted man, whose like I never knew."

This was, indeed, encouragement enough. I accordingly went down to Whitehall, George Moore's country seat in Cumberland, to look over his papers. I there found a story, a romance, followed, alas! by a tragedy. Mr. Moore had written out an account of his early life, which I have introduced in the course of the following pages. He had also left a Diary, containing a daily entry during the last twenty years of his life. These, together with his numerous papers, have furnished abundant information for his history from its beginning to its end.

Biographers, like portrait-painters, are sometimes suspected of painting men as they ought to be, rather than as they are. To avoid this objection, I have quoted George Moore's own words from his Autobiographic Notes, and from his Diary ; and thus enabled the story to be told as much as possible in his own words and in his own way.

I have said that I began this work with unwillingness ; but I can add that as I wrote I felt that I had to do with the life of no ordinary man. George Moore, in some ways, stands apart from other men. He yielded to no hindrances ; he was overcome by no difficulties ; he was consistent in his aims, in all the good work that he did. This the story of his life will fully show.

I need scarcely say that I have been greatly helped by Mrs. Moore, who has furnished all the necessary information, and supplied many of the most interesting descriptions in the book.

I have also been much indebted to the Rev. W. M. Gunson, Cambridge; the Rev. Alfred Oates, Maryport; James Cropper, Esq., Ellergreen, Kendal; Alfred Chapman, Esq., and many others, for the information they have communicated as to the life, habits, manners, and character of their deceased friend.

It has been the one wish of Mrs. Moore's heart that a proper memorial of her husband's life should be placed on permanent record. I hope that I have gratified her wish, and that the public will be satisfied with the result.

S. S.

LONDON, *May* 1878.

CONTENTS.

CHAPTER IV.

IN LONDON.

CHAPTER V.

COMMERCIAL TRAVELLER.

CHAPTER VI.

PARTNER AND TRAVELLER.

CHAPTER VII.

TRIP TO AMERICA—HUNTING.

CHAPTER VIII.

SAFETY VALVES.

CHAPTER IX.

VISITS TO CUMBERLAND.

CHAPTER X.

WORK IN CUMBERLAND.

CONTENTS.

CHAPTER XXII.

LATER WORKS OF BENEVOLENCE.

CHAPTER XXIII.

GOOD WORKS DONE IN SECRET.

CHAPTER XXIV.

THE END OF GEORGE MOORE'S LIFE.

CHAPTER XXV.

GEORGE MOORE'S CHARACTER.

GEORGE MOORE.

CHAPTER I.

THE MOORES—OLD TIMES IN CUMBERLAND.

GEORGE MOORE was born at Mealsgate, Cumberland, on the 9th of April, 1806. He was the third of a family of five. He had two brothers, Thomas and William, and two sisters, Sarah and Mary.

George's father, John Moore, was a man of ancient descent, though of moderate means. He belonged to the rank of Statesman—a title held in as high regard in the North as that of the Order of the Garter. "I am prouder," says a well-known scholar, "of being a Cumberland Statesman than a Cambridge Don!" But the Cumberland statesmen, like the English yeomen, are fast passing away.

The old Moores lived at their paternal estate at Overgates for more than three hundred years. Overgates is in the parish of Torpenhow, a few miles to the south-west of the market-town of Wigton. The village of Torpenhow consists of a straggling street of little old houses, grey or whitewashed. The ancient church, dedicated to St. Michael, stands at the east end of the village. The "pellitory from out the wall"

B

of Shakespeare grows luxuriantly near the churchyard gate. People still come from long distances to gather it for medicinal purposes.

Inside the churchyard we come upon the resting-places of the old Moores. There they lie, generation after generation. The Moores of Overgates; the Moores of Bothel; the Moores of Highwood Nook; the Moores of Kirkland, and the Moores of Mealsgate. They seem to have been a long-lived race. Many of them lived to eighty and upwards. Thomas Moore of Mealsgate, grandfather of George Moore, was buried among his fathers in Torpenhow Churchyard, aged seventy-eight.

Torpenhow parish is situated on the south bank of the river Ellen. The land rises gradually from the river until it reaches its highest points at Camphill, Caermote, and Binsey. From the high grounds a splendid view is obtained, southward, of the Cumberland mountains, Skiddaw towering high above all. Bassenthwaite Water lies quietly sleeping under the shadow of the majestic hills which surround it.

The high lands from which we look down remain very much as nature left them. The country hereabouts is wild and lonely. Scarcely a house or a person is to be seen. The land is poor and uncultivated. It is half moor, half inclosed pasture. A few Fell sheep and black Scotch cattle grub for grass among the roots of the whins and heather. Yet it is not without its beauties for the lover of nature. The glorious mountains, the far-off sweeps of gorse, the wild smell of the heather, the sea air from the west blowing fresh against your face, the large purple shadows dropped by the passing clouds upon the moor, the lark singing over-head, the bumble-bee humming close by; and above all, the infinite silence! That indeed is a picture to be remembered.

Looking towards the north, over Torpenhow, the view is altogether different. In the bottom of the valley lies the river Ellen. You see the little farmstead of Overgates, the original home of the Moores. Far away,—over woods and pastures and cornfields, —over grassy knolls and winding valleys,—over clusters of farmhouses half hid in clumps of sycamores,—over villages, mere specks of whiteness nestling among green fields,—over stately homes and ruined castles,—you see the northern border of Cumberland. In the distance the Solway lies in the sunlight like a silver strip of brightness. Beyond the Firth, the lowlands of Dumfries and Kircudbright stretch away glimmering through the sunshine. Above and beyond them the Scottish mountains are seen,—Criffel standing out boldly and alone.

The Solway Firth extends inland, between Scotland and England, from Maryport to Carlisle. It is in many places about twelve miles across. The tide runs up and down with great force, especially at spring tides. The Solway might be thought a sufficient protection for Cumberland during the troublous times which preceded the union of the crowns of England and Scotland. But it was no such protection against hungry and warlike people. The Solway can be crossed at low tide by horsemen who know the secrets of its depths and eddies. For this reason, amongst others, the northern part of Cumberland was constantly exposed to the depredations of the Scots. They waded the Solway, pillaged the villages and farmsteadings, and carried off to Annandale and Nithsdale all the cattle they could seize and drive before them.

For this reason the people of Cumberland, a few hundred years ago, always stood at arms. The entrances to the villages were defended by a double ditch, and by gates fastened with an iron chain. This was the case at Wigton. Those who could, fortified their houses, and left a space beneath into which their cattle might be driven at night. A little beneath Overgates, in the valley of the Ellen, there are two border castles, or Peel towers, which afford a good example of the fortified houses of these days. One of these is called Harbybrow, now in ruins, and the other is Whitehall, recently renovated and enlarged,—the country-seat of the subject of this story. These border castles stand about a mile from each other. It is said that there was once an underground road between them.

The original towers are lofty, square, and massive. The walls at the lower part are about nine feet thick. They are divided into three stories. Harbybrow remains very much as it was. It has an arched chamber underneath—the old cattle keep. During the Scottish raids, the men and the cattle entered the tower by the same door. The cattle were driven into the arched chamber, while the men fastened the door and mounted to the higher stories. If assailed, they stood to arms, threw down huge stones, or poured boiling water or lead upon those who ventured to assail the little garrison. But when the cattle were secured, that was rarely done. The mosstroopers had no means of laying siege to fortified places.

In the meantime the country was up. During the border raids, people were stationed on the higher grounds to keep a strict look out. The names of "Watch-hill" and "Beacon-top" still point to such localities.[1] The church towers were also used for the

---

[1] The Cumberland beacons that were lighted up to assemble the surrounding population to arms were Blackcombe, Muncaster Fell, St. Bees Head, Workington Hill, Moothay, Skiddaw, Sandale Head End, Carlisle

same purpose. The country was apt to be ravaged for twenty miles along the border. The tenants of the manors were obliged, by the firing of the beacons, to attend their lords in their border service. If requisite, their attendance might be prolonged for forty days. There was little or no cultivation of the land at that time. Indeed payment of rent was scarcely known until after the Union. All that the landlord gained from those residing upon his estate was personal service in battle or in pursuit, and perhaps a share of the spoil taken by rapine from the Scotch side of the border.

The morality of those days was of a very wild description. Freebooting was considered a respectable profession on both sides of the border. It was like piracy at sea, of which neither Raleigh nor Drake were ashamed. To be a freebooter or a mosstrooper was not considered a term of reproach. The free-booter did not keep a "gig," but he kept a pricker, on which he scoured the neighbouring county for plunder. Every man fought for his own hand, like Harry-o'-the-Wynd. If they could not steal from the neighbouring border, they stole from each other.[1] They were quite as dangerous to their neighbours as to their enemies. They were very valiant men too. Many were the instances of dash and daring among them. The Elliots, Armstrongs, and Scotts were as daring on the one side, as the Græmes, Rutledges, and Howards were on the other. Their names have been alike immortalised in the ballad lore of the border.

The Scotch were, however, the hungriest of the two.

Castle, Lingy-close Head, Beacon Hill, Penrith, Dale Raughton, Brampton Mote, and Spade-adam Top.

[1] There is a wild path across the mountains, far south in Cumberland, very unlikely to be disturbed by the Scotch mosstroopers, for it is between Borrowdale and Ravenglass,—still called "The Thieves' Road." It must have been so called from the Lancashire and Cumberland reivers.

Whenever their food fell short, they determined on a
raid. Though they were ready, as the Armstrongs were,
to rob each other, they preferred harrying their neighbours across the border.[1] They could then combine
their personal views of plunder with something like a
spirit of patriotism. There was a portion of land
between the two countries which was long known as the
Debatable Land. It was long a source of contention.
It was situated north of Carlisle, between the rivers
Esk and Sark. It belonged neither to England nor
Scotland. The land was infested by thieves and ban-
ditti, to whom, in its mossy, boggy, and uncultivated
state, it afforded a desirable refuge. They robbed alike
the English and the Scotch. Once, when a battle was
going on, some of the men succeeded in robbing their
fellow-troopers of their horses. The inhabitants of the
Middle or Western Marches were unrestrained mosstroopers and cattle-stealers, "having no measure of law,"
says Camden, "but the length of their swords." When
caught by their enemies, they were dealt with by
Jeddart justice,—that is, they were first hanged and
then tried.

The Græmes were among the chief occupants of the
Debatable Land. A document quoted in the *History
of Cumberland* says, concerning the Græmes of Netherby
and others of that clan, "They were all stark mosstroopers and arrant thieves, both to England and Scotland outlawed; yet sometimes connived at, because
they gave intelligence forth of Scotland, and would
raise four hundred horse at any time upon a raid of the

---

[1] A saying is recorded of a Border mother to her son, "*Ride, Roley,
ride, the last hough's i' the pot*"—meaning that the last leg of beef was
being boiled, and that it was high time for him to go and fetch more. An
equally good story is told of a Cumberland matron. So long as her provisions lasted she set them regularly on the table, but as soon as they were
finished, she brought forth two pairs of spurs and said, "Sons, I have no
meat for you; go, seek for your dinner."

English into Scotland." And so it was of the Elliots and Armstrongs on the northern side of the border, which led to the popular saying,—" Elliots and Armstrongs,[1] ride thieves all." From these grim borderers have descended General Elliot, who so bravely defended Gibraltar; Sir James Graham, one of our greatest statesmen; and Sir William Armstrong, the inventor of the Armstrong gun.

When the hungry Scots prepared to make a raid southward, they mounted their wiry horses, met at their appointed places, and either waded the Solway or forded the Liddel or the Esk. They crossed the border by secret by-ways known only to themselves. They knew every road across the mosses, and every ford across the rivers. They also knew every channel of escape from Cumberland to the north. The men were armed with long spears, a two-handed sword, a battle-axe or a Jedburgh staff, and latterly with dags or pistols. Each trooper carried his own provisions, which consisted for the most part of a bag of oatmeal. They trusted to the booty they seized for eking out their meals.

So soon as it was known that the reivers were abroad —that they had crossed the Solway from Annandale, or come down from Eskdale or Liddesdale—all Cumberland was roused. The beacons blazed out at Carlisle, Watch-hill, Torpenhow, Sandale Head End, Beacon-hill, and Skiddaw. The mounted troopers gathered at the appointed places, harnessed in jacks, and armed with spears and swords. Away they went in *hot-trod!* So soon as they came upon the mosstroopers the sleuth-hounds[2] were set upon their track, and wherever they

[1] In the sixteenth century the Armstrong clan, under the command of the English chief, Sir Ralph Evans ravaged almost the whole of the west border of Scotland.

[2] As late as 1616 there was an order from the King's Commissioners of the Northern counties that a certain number of sleuth-hounds (so called

went they blew their horns to summon their countrymen to their help. They also carried a burning wisp of
straw or wood at their spears' point;[1] and raised a cry
similar to that of the Indian warwhoop. It appears
that those who heard this cry were bound to join in the
chase under penalty of death.

The pursuit might last for days or for weeks. The
regulations of the barony of Gilsland, still preserved by
the Earl of Carlisle, show the nature of the border-
service of the tenants. Every tenant was required to
keep a good, able, and sufficient horse—"such a nagge
as is able at anye tyme to beare a manne twentie miles
within Scotlande and backe againe without a baite."
They were to be provided with a "jacke, steale-cap,
sword, bowe, or speare," and were to be ready "to serve
the Lord Warden or their officers upon sixe houres
warninge, in anye place where they shall be appointed
to serve." They were also required to appoint a watch
over their farms by day and by night ; and, when a foray
occurred at night, "the partie that is harried to keepe a
beaken burning of some height, of intente that not-
withstandinge all the country be in a fraye the fier may
be a token where the hurt is done, that all menne may
know which way to drawe."[2]

The old statesmen held their lands by border service,
as appears from the old title-deeds. They were required
to be ready to follow the fray when the mosstroopers
were abroad. They must be armed, horsed, and ready
to fight. In the recital attached to a decree in the

from their quality of tracing the *slot*, or track of men and animals) should
be maintained in every district in Cumberland bordering on Scotland. The
breed of this sagacious dog is nearly extinct.

[1] A practice borrowed from the Norsemen, who formed large settlements
roun l the Solway Firth, as is still indicated by the names of places, and
especially of headlan ls. The Highlanders also borrowed their fiery cross
from the Norsemen, many of whom became chiefs of the Highland clans.

[2] LY(s's *Magn t Britannia*, vol. iv., Cumberland xi. xii.

Court of Chancery[1] relating to the Woodvilles or Woodhalls, of Waterend, near Cockermouth, it is stated that the " plaintiffs (the statesmen) and the other tenants there, or their assigns, had *time out of mind* been seized to them and their heirs, by and according to the ancient and laudable custom of tenant-right then used, being within the West Marches of England over against Scotland ; " and further that they held "their several tenements by serving upon the said borders of England over against Scotland, at their own proper costs and charges, within the said West Marches, then and so often as thereunto they should be required by the Lord Warden of the said West Marches, for the time being, or his sufficient deputy or deputies, as well as defending the frontiers of the said Marches, as in offending the opposite Marches as occasion served."

The freebooting raids between the borderers of the two countries continued long after the union of the crowns.   Shortly after James I. came to the throne of England, he set up a claim to all the small estates in Cumberland and Westmoreland, on the plea that the statesmen were merely the tenants of the crown.   The statesmen met to the number of two thousand, at Ratten Heath, between Kendal and Stavely, where they came to the resolution that " they had won their lands by the sword, and were able to hold them by the same."   After that meeting no further claim was made to their estates on the part of the crown.

But freebooting had not yet come to an end.   The disposition to plunder had become part of the borderers' nature.   Mosstrooping continued during the English Revolution and the Commonwealth ; and after the Restoration it reached to such a height that it was found necessary to enact laws of great severity for the protec-

[1] Dated the 25th April, 1597.   LONSDALE'S *Worthies of Cumberland:* " Memoir of Dr. Woodville," p. 231.

tion of the more peaceful bordermen. The magistrates were authorised to raise bodies of armed men for the defence of property and order; and provision was made for supporting them by local taxation. Bloodhounds were again used to track the mosstroopers to their retreats among the hills. These measures, in course of time, had their due effect. Yet it was not until some time after the union of England and Scotland, in Queen Anne's reign, that the border hostilities died away, and the inhabitants were left to cultivate their land in peace.

Yet cattle-stealing, and sheep-stealing—the survivals of the old freebooting system—still continued to be carried on. Juries were never found wanting when a cattle-stealer was to be tried. The punishment was short and sharp—hanging by the neck. Even in modern times it is difficult to induce a Carlisle jury to convict a man of murder; but when the offence is sheep-stealing, the conviction is certain. When Baron Martin crossed Shapfell, on his Northern Circuit, he used to say, "Now we have got into Cumberland, where we can scarcely get a jury to convict a man of murder, even though he has killed his mother; but they will hang a man for sheep-stealing!"

The story is told of a stranger who visited Bewcastle—formerly the centre of a wild district—for the purpose of examining the Runic pillar in the churchyard. On looking round among the tombstones, he was surprised to find that they commemorated none but female deaths. He made a remark to this effect to the old woman who accompanied him: "Ou, Sir, do ye no ken what for? They're a' buried at that weary Caerl!" He found, in fact, that the male inhabitants of the district had either been transported or hanged at Carlisle!

The modern Cumberland Statesmen are the northern yeomen of England. They are men who work hard, live frugally, and enjoy an honest independence. They are neither squires nor labourers. They stand betwixt both. They till their own soil and consume their own produce. They sell the cattle and corn which they do not require, to buy the household articles which they cannot produce. They used to weave their own cloth. In olden times, the " Grey coats of Cumberland " was a common phrase. But all this has passed away ; and statesmen are now sinking into the class of ordinary farmers, or even labourers.

The statesmen of the mountain districts—so many of them as still remain—are a very primitive class of people. They know nothing of the rate of discount or the price of gold. They have enough of the world's gear to serve their purpose. They are uncorrupted by modern luxury. They are content ; and happy to enjoy the golden mean of Agur. They pass a simple and inoffensive life amidst the lonely hills which surround them. "Go," said one of these statesmen to a tourist, "go to the vale on the other side of yon mountain. You will find a house ; enter it, and say that you came from me. I know him not, but he will receive you kindly, for *our sheep mingle upon the mountains !* "

These men have no inclination to change, either in their life and customs, or in their sheep-farming. "At Penruddock," says an agricultural report on Cumberland, " we observed some singularly rough-legged, ill-formed sheep, and on asking an old farmer where the breed came from, he replied, 'They are sic as God set upon the land : we never change them !' " These are the people whom Wordsworth—himself a Cumberland man—has described with so much character and feeling.[1]

---

[1] Close upon the border, the Cumberland men are rougher and readier than those towards the south. They have scarcely outgrown the moss trooping life of their forefathers. Many of them are "Bworder Cowpers," dealing in horses and cattle. One of them tried to recommend himself to a travelling Scotsman by claiming kindred, affirming that he was a Border

The statesmen of the low-lying districts towards the
north are of a sturdier character. They have more
mother wit and back-bone. Their forefathers being
constantly on the alert to resist the inroads of the Scots,
have handed down to their sons their fearless resolution
and undaunted courage. They bear the greatest fatigue
with patience. They live contented on humble fare,
though their hospitality to strangers is open-handed
and liberal. Though not rich in money or land, they
are rich in character and healthful contentment. They
are satisfied with their social position, and are even proud
of it. To be "an able and honest statesman" used to
be one of the highest titles in Cumberland.

The statesman's household was a school of thrift and
industry. The clothing was made at home. The
women wore linsey-wolsey cloth of their own making.
The young men and lads thought themselves well clad
if they went to kirk in homespun hodden-gray. Stalwart
sons and comely maidens were brought up on porridge,
oatcakes, and milk ; in fact there could be no better
food. These were occasionally varied with barley ban-
nocks, Whillimer cheese, potato-pot, a bit of bacon, and
an occasional slice of salt-beef or mutton in winter.
What could they require more? Their sharpness of
appetite was whetted by the keen atmosphere of the
mountain air.

"Come in," said a tenant to his landlord one day,
" an hev a bit o' dinner afwore ye gang." The landlord
went in amongst the family, the servants, and the
labourers, who were about to " set to." Near the end
of the table was a large hot-pot, containing beef or
mutton, cut into pieces, and put into a large dish along
with potatoes, onions, pepper and salt. This was the
famous Cumberland "taty-pot." The farmer, after help-

Scot. "Gude faith, I dinna doubt it," quoth the other ; "for the selvage
is aye the warst part o' the web!"

ing himself, thrust the dish towards the landlord, and said, "Noo ye man help yersel, and *howk in !* Theer's plenty meat at bottom, but its rayther het !"

Nor does this food disagree with the well-appetised Cumbrians. They are for the most part men of large stature. They are big-boned and broad-chested. Their firm muscles, well-knit joints, and vigorous hands give them great advantage as wrestlers. What they want in agility and suppleness they make up for in strength.

Although the Statesman worked hard and lived on humble fare, his wife was a Dame ; his eldest son was the Laird ; and when there was no son, his eldest daughter was the Lady. Thus, while the statesman himself was at the plough, the laird was driving the cattle to market, and the lady was working at the churn. Getting up in the morning was a great point. The Cumberland ballad-maker, when deploring the introduction of new customs fifty years ago, when the country was " puzzened round wi' preyde," goes on to say—

> " We used to gan ta bed at dark,
>   An' rose agean at four or five ;
>   The mworn's the only time for wark,
>   If fwok are healthy and wad thrive."

The difference between one statesman and another consisted principally in character. Where the statesman was slow, sluggish, and inert, he gravitated rapidly downwards. No changes were made in the improvement of the farm. The old hive became filled with drones. The sons dropped down to the condition of farm servants and day-labourers. When the statesman borrowed money and got into the hands of the lawyers, he never got out of them until the land was sold.

On the other hand, another statesman, of a better sort, would keep the rooftree up by dint of energy and forethought. He would give his sons a fair education,

set before them a good example, instil into them principles of independence and self-help, and send them
into the world braced with courage and the spirit of
duty. The eldest son became the statesman, like his
father before him. The second son sometimes became
a "priest"—the ordinary name for a clergyman in
Cumberland,—while the others emigrated to the colonies,
or entered into the various avenues of business life at
home.

On the whole, however, it must be confessed that the
statesmen of Cumberland, like the yeomanry of England, have been rapidly disappearing during the last
century. Sir James Graham spoke of the cavalcade of
mounted statesmen who accompanied Mr. Blamire into
Carlisle, on his appointment as High Sheriff in 1828, as
"a body of men who could not be matched in any other
part of the kingdom. The sight they had seen that day
was such as they could never forget. The yeomanry of
Cumberland were the finest and purest specimens of a
set of men, who in all periods of its history had been the
strength and pride of their country." But the fifty years
that have passed away since then have seen great changes.
Wealth is everywhere absorbing landed property. Small
holdings are disappearing ; small estates are blotted out ;
and the Cumberland statesman is already becoming a
thing of the past.[1]

---

[1] "One thing," says Dr. Lonsdale, "is manifest in the history of the
yeomen, and that is, their gradual decadence, especially during the last
thirty years. Many a 'canny house,' where yeomen had for centuries kept
their yule, taught their sons and grandsons the traditions of their home, no
longer shelter 'the weel kent folk o' ither days.' Even the names of their
founders are forgotten. This disappearance of names, if not of habitation,
in many rural districts, brings about reflections of by no means an agreeable
kind. Among many changes affecting both men and interests in these
northern counties, there is no change more marked than that arising from
the purchasing of real estate and the absorption of small holdings of a few
potato fields or share of pasturage, once the pride of decent folk content in
their changeless life, by larger landed proprietors.

'Ill fares the land, to hastening ills a prey,
Where Wealth accumulates and Men decay.'"

During the long period that George Moore's fore-elders lived at Overgates, few records of their lives have been preserved. They had their part in the border raids. They were always ready to join in the fray when the mosstroopers were abroad. At the western end of Overgates house, there was a con-cealed place in which a nag or charger was kept; for in those days a nag was almost as good as a man. When the war-cry of " Snaffle, spur, and spear ! " was raised, the Moores of Overgates mounted like the rest, and galloped off to the meeting-place. The border towers and the cattle-keeps were in the valley below, almost within sight of the homestead ; and when the muster took place, away they went after the " ruffian Scots."

Thus the Moores lived until the troublous times had passed away, and peace fell upon the border-lands. The young men and women intermarried with the sons and daughters of the neighbouring statesmen. For the most part they settled near the paternal home. Thus there were the Moores of Bothel, the Moores of Highwood-Nook, and the Moores of Kirkland—all in the parish of Torpenhow. In the churchyard we read the names of the forgotten dead—sometimes on a broken gravestone covered with grey lichens. None· of them seem to have come to any fame in the world's history. It was a little circle they lived in. Anxious thrift and carefulness were their portion. They lived their lives of joy and sorrow, of homely experience and of daily work,—little heedful of the troubles and turmoils of the outer world. They did their duty, and then they went to rest.

Thomas Moore, a younger son of the statesman at Overgates, was born in 1733. He went to Bothel in his youth to assist his brother in the work of the farm. In 1773 he went to Mealsgate, where he

purchased a farm of sixty acres, recited in the deeds
as "the Mealsgate tenement in the parishes of Bolton
or Allhallows." There he lived a careful, frugal, and
industrious life. Fair, market, and church, were the
only little breaks in his life of daily toil. He married,
and had an only son—John Moore, the father of George.
John did not marry until he was thirty-five. We learn
from the Family Bible that on the 15th of February,
1800, he brought home Peggy Lowes, the daughter of
a neighbouring statesman, as his wife. The register
goes on to say that Thomas Moore was born on the
27th of January, 1802; Sarah on the 17th of January,
1804; George on the 9th of April, 1806; Mary on
the 5th of March, 1808; and William on the 30th of
March, 1810. Thomas Moore was now an old man.
He lived to see all his grandchildren born. Then
he passed away and was laid amongst his forefathers
in Torpenhow church-yard, at the ripe age of seventy-
eight.

The house at Mealsgate lies on the main road between Wigton and Cockermouth. It is a house of two
stories, standing a little back from the road. A brook
runs through the orchard before the house. It wanders
along the valley through the Whitehall estate, and
runs into the river Ellen, near Harbybrow. A few
scattered cottages lie about the place, constituting the
village of Mealsgate.

On entering the Moores' dwelling, you pass at once
from the outer door into the general sitting-room. This,
in Cumberland phrase, is known as "The House." A
large old-fashioned fireplace occupies one end—the
"ingle neuk,"—round which the family held their general conclave and told stories of the olden time during
the winter evenings. At the other end of the room,
opposite the fireplace, is the Parlour, which is usually
appropriated as a bedroom by the married pair. Behind

is the kitchen and the other offices.   A staircase of the simplest kind leads up to the four small low-roofed bed-rooms above.

Such is the house at Mealsgate in which the subject of the following story was born and brought up.

CHAPTER II.

GEORGE MOORE'S BOYHOOD.

AFTER the birth, the christening. George Moore of Bothel was to "stand for" the child. He was an old bachelor, a man of good means, and he meant to "do something" for his godson. A large party of Moores assembled at Mealsgate on the christening morning. It must have been regarded as a matter of considerable importance. A chaise was brought from Wigton to convey the mother and child up the hill to Bolton Church.

Chaises were very uncommon in Cumberland in those days. The roads were unsuitable for wheeled carriages. Chaises were called those " queer trundlin' kists on't roads." Horseback was the usual method of convey-ance ; and women rode on pack-saddles. But on this occasion, as the mother was delicate and the child was young, a post-chaise was brought from Wigton to convey them to Church. The child was baptized in the name of his great-uncle and godfather, George Moore. His father afterwards said of him that "he had begun the world with a chaise, and he was likely to end it with a chaise."

Old George Moore of Bothel, the godfather of the child, was as good as his word. When he died, in 1817, at the ripe age of seventy-two, he left his godson a legacy of 100*l.*, together with a big hair-trunk. The 100*l.* was to be paid to him when he reached the age of twenty-one; but by the time it was paid it amounted, with accumulations of interest, to about 170*l.* It was then found very useful. The hair-trunk also had its history. It had the letters " G. M." marked in brass nails on the top. The hair-trunk went to Wigton, to London, to America, and is still in the possession of the family at Mealsgate. It is more than 150 years old.

The earliest recollection of George Moore was a very painful one. He was about six years old when his mother died. She was laid in the parlour, next to the room known as " the house." The boy turned into the parlour as usual, went up to his mother, touched her, but she did not move! He saw the cold pale face, and the shrouded body. This was his first idea of Death, and it left a startling impression on his mind. He saw his mother taken away by men in black, followed by a long train of mourners; and he saw her no more.

The same night he was taken by his father to sleep with him in the same bed from which his mother had been taken in the morning. The boy was frightened, startled, almost horror-struck. He did not sleep; he was thinking of his departed mother. The recollection of that day and of that night haunted him all his life. It left in his mind a morbid horror of death. It was so strong that he could never afterwards see a dead person. His intense vitality recoiled from the terrible accompaniments of that mystery which we call Death.

And yet he had nearly his whole life before him. Such losses as these must soon be forgotten, or remembered only with sorrow; otherwise life would be intolerable. It might be thought that John Moore, who took his boy to sleep with him that night, was a hard and unfeeling man. But this was not the case. Let George

Moore himself speak of his father's character. " My father," he says, "was a fine specimen of the North Country yeoman, whose fore-elders had lived at the same place for generations. His integrity, generosity, and love of truth left influences on my life and character for which I can never be too thankful. I have often said that I think he never told a lie in his life. The only time he flogged me was for telling a lie ; and I never felt so sorry for anything as to have grieved him.

"His great failing was in believing others too implicitly. His generosity got the better of his judgment. He lost a great deal of money by becoming bound for friends at public sales of cattle. The purchaser being unable to pay, my father had to find the money. Very often it was never repaid. Had it not been for the thrifty and careful habits of the family, our estate would long ago have passed into strange hands. At the same time, my father was one of the most straightforward of men. He had as great a moral courage as any man I ever knew. I can well remember his ordering a man out of his house who came in drunk, and reprimanding others who had done some bad deed. John Moore of Mealsgate was indeed a terror to evil-doers."

Some five years after his wife's death, John Moore married again. The children were growing up untrained and ill-tended. There wanted some clever woman about the house to look after the bairns while John was afield at his work. The consequence was that he married Mary Pattinson, sister of the Rev. Mr. Pattinson, of Caldbeck. She proved an active and managing house-mate. She was a good wife as regarded her husband ; but she did not get on very well with the elder children. They regarded her as an intruder, and were predisposed to resist her authority. " My stepmother," says George Moore, "was invariably kind to me, but the elder children probably had a strong prejudice against her.

At all events, as regarded the family, she did not add to the happiness of our household."

At the age of eight, George Moore was sent to school. The school to which he went was situated at Boltongate, about two miles from Mealsgate. It used to lie at the corner of Bolton churchyard, separated from the church itself by the parish burying-ground. It has recently been pulled down to make room for more graves. To that school George Moore walked daily, wet or dry, to receive his miserable quotum of "education."

Very little provision was made in those days for the education of the rising generation. Cumberland was no better than the other English counties. Any man who had a stick-leg, or a club-foot, or a claw-hand, thought himself fit to be a teacher. The three R's formed the amount of the accomplishment given. The teaching was altogether lifeless and humdrum. What was knocked into the boys was done for the most part by caning and whipping. In George Moore's case the teaching was given by a man addicted to drink. His name was Blackbird Wilson. He was called Blackbird because he could imitate the singing of any bird in the neighbourhood, and especially of the blackbird. Here is George Moore's account of him :

"The master, Blackbird Wilson, was an old man, fond of drink. The scholars were sent out to fetch it for him three or four times a day. He used to drive the learning into us with a thick ruler, which he brought down sharply upon our backs. He often sent the ruler flying amongst our heads. The wonder is that he did not break our skulls. Perhaps he calculated on their thickness. His rule was to drive reading, writing, and arithmetic into us by brute force. He never attempted to make learning attractive. He did not cultivate the understanding or endeavour to teach us the good of knowledge. Such being the case, I was never fond of school. I often played the truant, and rambled about whenever I could get away. Indeed I should have been much oftener absent, had it not been for the dread of the terrible floggings which were then as common in Cumberland as elsewhere. My determination not to study followed me through my school-days ; and often, indeed, have I repented of my folly in not learning as much as I could when at school, for I have often felt the mortification of being ignorant. My faults were those of an energetic and wayward disposition, unhelped by a mother's sympathy and solace."

When Blackbird Wilson retired from the office of schoolmaster, he was succeeded by Mr. Allison, a humaner and better teacher. The Rev. W. M. Gunson, M.A., has furnished the following information as to the teaching and routine of the school while he attended it. He says, "Dull tradition and immobility are very conservative in isolated country places like Bolton ; and I believe that an account of my school-time will accurately represent that of George Moore's. The curriculum consisted of the three R's, with spelling. I have no recollection of learning anything like grammar or parsing. One other thing, however, was carefully taught, the Church Catechism. In Lent, every year, we spent much time in committing it to memory, and on the afternoon of Easter Sunday we were publicly examined in it by the clergyman in the church, in presence of the largest congregation that assembled on any day of the year ; for the parents were there, wishing to hear their children acquit themselves well.

"The arrangements of the school itself were rude and rough enough. The fire was lighted in the mornings, and the school swept out by two of the boys in turn, specially told off for the purpose. Their duty lasted for a week, at the end of which they had the privilege of naming their successors for the following week. When coals were wanted, the money to buy them was raised by levying a tax of twopence or three-half-pence each on all the scholars. Many of the children, who came from a distance, brought a cold dinner with them, and ate it in the school. The time that remained at the midday interval was mostly spent in bathing in the river Ellen, which runs about half a mile from the school. This contributed to cleanliness and health, and gave the boys a love of cold water which clung to them through life.

"One of the holidays occurred in harvest time. It was secured by a process of *barring t' maister oot*. As soon as any of the scholars announced that they had seen t' first stook,[1] a conspiracy was entered into; and during the midday interval the boys shut themselves up in the school, and barricaded the door and windows against outsiders. On the master returning from his dinner, entrance was denied him. He generally made a *show* of violence to break in, but of course he never succeeded. When he found his efforts vain, he called a parley. The first condition the boys insisted on was freedom from punishment for the *barring oot;* and when that was promised, they then proceeded to negotiate as to the length of the holiday that was to be given. Their rebellion being always successful, was, like other successful rebellions in wider spheres of action, regarded as an act of schoolboy loyalty and patriotism, and when it was over, all alike enjoyed its successful results."

The amusements of the boys during play-hours were in some respects peculiar to the district. Wrestling, or worsling, was their most famous sport. The boys tried their strength with each other. They got to know the best way of *takin' hod;* the chips and the hypes; the buttocks and cross-buttocks; the back-heeling, the hank and the click inside. The wrestling of Cumberland and

---

[1] The earliest shock of corn cut.

Westmoreland is well known. The game, as practised there, is not so savage as that of Cornwall. There is no hard kicking of the shins or legs, and the boys or men who have thrown each other continue the same good friends as ever. Men of all classes wrestle,—statesmen, ploughmen, cobblers, labourers, and even clergymen. One of the most noted wrestlers in Cumberland was a curate—the Rev. Abraham Brown. William Richardson of Caldbeck, and George Irving, the publican at Bolton-gate (whose whisky Blackbird Wilson so much relished), were the most noted wrestlers in the neighbourhood.   .

The boys began to try their physical powers early. They wrestled with each other on the village greens. George Moore, like his schoolfellows, often tried his hand. He was strong and wiry; tenacious and persevering. He learnt the various tricks of the art; and before he left school there were few boys who could stand before him.

Another game of the schoolboys was *Scots and English*. This was doubtless a survival of the old border warfare. The boys form two parties, which respectively represent the Scots and English. They fix upon two strongholds, at the distance of from sixty to a hundred yards apart. A boundary line is drawn, and each party deposits their coats, waistcoats, and bonnets at the proper hold. The sport then begins. The boys run across the line, and endeavour to make prisoners of each other, at the same time that they plunder the enemy in the most dexterous manner, without becoming prisoners. If they are taken prisoners they are carried to a supposed place of confinement, though sometimes the prisoners are mutually permitted to pillage for the conquerors. The same game is played, with some slight variations, on the Scottish side of the Border.

Among George Moore's other amusements was that of bird-nesting. He was accustomed with other boys to search the bushes which overhung the Dowbeck burn and the trees which skirted the river Ellen. He climbed trees that no one else dared to climb. He searched the Peel Towers of Whitehall and Harbybrow. They were haunted by jackdaws, whose eggs he wished to secure. They built their nests in the old wide chimneys of the towers. With his usual daring, he had himself let down by ropes from the top of the towers to the places where the nests were built. Thus he brought home lots of eggs, and when he had blown them and strung them, he hung them in long rows over the mantelpiece at Mealsgate.

George Moore was an excellent player at marbles. He was so successful, that the other boys thought that the merit was due to the marbles and not to the player. They consequently bought his marbles for a penny apiece, though they cost him only five for a halfpenny. As he was not allowed any pocket-money, the money thus earned was sometimes found very useful.

For instance, on one occasion, when eleven years old, he went from Mealsgate to Carlisle to see a man hanged who had passed a forged Scotch note. He was accompanied by another boy. They started early in the morning, and made their way to Carlisle, walking a distance of seventeen miles. They reached the Sands, where the execution was to take place. But the boys, being so little, could scarcely see over the heads of the people who crowded round the gallows. George, with his usual resolution, determined to push himself forward, and got as near to the gallows as possible. He pushed through amongst the people's legs, and when he got to the troop of dragoons who surrounded the scaffold, he passed under the horses' legs, and thus got to the front rank. He saw all that happened. When the man was hanged, George swooned away. When he came to himself, he found that some hot coffee was being poured into his mouth. He could never afterwards bear the taste of coffee. After the execution, he walked home again ; thus doing thirty-four miles walking in a day— a remarkable proof of strength in so young a boy.

George Moore, though an unwilling scholar, enjoyed his truant days and his holidays very much. "Being passionately fond of horses," he says, "whenever I escaped from school I spent the time in leading the horses with the carts of some farmer in the neighbour-hood." He had also the ambition of following the hounds. One day he got hold of his father's half-blind mare and mounted her barebacked. He could not take the saddle, for that might be missed. But away he went in search of John Peel and his hounds, which he understood were to hunt that day over the adjoining fells :

D'ye ken John Peel with his coat so gray ?
D'ye ken John Peel at the break of day ?
D'ye ken John Peel when he's far, far away,
　With his hounds and his horn in the morning ?
　　'Twas the sound of his horn brought me from my bed,
　　An' the cry of his hounds has me ofttimes led ;
　　For Peel's view-holloa would 'waken the dead,
　　Or a fox from his lair in the morning.

John Peel was an enthusiastic and hair-brained fox-hunter. His name was very widely known. The song from which the above verses are taken is known all over the world, wherever English hunters have penetrated. It was heard in the soldiers' camps at the siege of Lucknow. It is well known in America. Boys whistle the tune, or sing the song, all over Cumberland.[1]

---

[1] John Woodcock Graves, the author of *D'ye ken John Peel*, gives the following account of its composition :—" Nearly forty years have passed since John Peel and I sat in a snug parlour at Caldbeck among the Cumbrian mountains. We were then both in the heyday of manhood, and

John Peel lived at Uldale, near Caldbeck, between
Brocklebank Fell and the High Pike, not far from
Bolton church. Everybody knew him and his hounds.
They knew where he was to meet and where he was to
hunt. He had a rare mongrel pack of hounds. They
were of all sorts and sizes, yet they were good hunters.
He had an immense affection for his dogs, as they had
for him. A mutual feeling seemed to exist between
them. One who knew him said, that if he threatened,
or even spoke sharply to a dog, he would be found
wandering and hiding for two or three days together,
unless he had previously expressed his always returning
kindness. Whenever they came to a dead-lock he was
sure to be found talking to some favourite hound as if it
had been a human being. The dogs seemed to know
all that he said relative to hunting as well as the best
sportsman in the field.

John Peel hunted everything, from a rabbit to a fox.
Even the sheep were not secure against his hounds.
Boys used to assemble from all quarters to see the hunt
start, and to follow it on foot as far as they could.
Happy were they who, like George Moore, could obtain
a barebacked horse. For this they would endure any
punishment. The first hunt of George Moore's with
John Peel's hounds occurred about the year 1816;

hunters of the older fashion ; meeting the night before to arrange the earth-
stopping, and in the morning to take the best part of the hunt—the drag
over the mountains in the mist—while fashionable hunters still lay in their
blankets. Large flakes of snow fell that evening. We sat by the fireside
hunting over again many a good run, and recalling the feats of each particular hound, or narrow breakneck escapes, when a flaxen-haired daughter
of mine came in, saying, ' Father, what do you say to what Grannie sings ?'
Grannie was singing to sleep my eldest son—now a leading barrister in
Hobart-town—with an old rant called *Bonnie Annie*. The pen and ink
for hunting appointments being on the table, the idea of writing a song to
the old air forced itself upon me, and thus was produced impromptu, *D'ye
ken John Peel with his coat so gray?* Immediately after, I sang it to poor
Peel, who smiled through a stream of tears which fell down his manly
cheeks : and I well remember saying to him in a joking style, ' By Jove,
Peel, you'll be sung when we're both run to earth ! ' "—*Songs and Ballads
of Cumberland and the Lake Country*, by S. GILPIN.

though the famous old huntsman lived on till 1854, and died full of honours at the ripe age of seventy-eight.[1]

There was another sort of hunt in which George Moore took a still keener interest than in the hunt with John Peel on a barebacked horse. This was a day with the Dalesmen, who are all keen hunters. The shepherds look upon the fox as their natural enemy. They are not like the low-country hunters, who cherish the fox, find covers for him, and regard the unhallowed man who kills him as a vulpicide. In Cumberland and West-moreland the fox, in lambing time, takes to the hills. On his way he robs some auld wife's henroost: and when he reaches the higher grounds he begins to worry the lambs. The hue-and-cry is got up against him. The shepherds collect their collies, and determine to hunt the fox and destroy him.

The cry goes abroad that there is to be a hunt. All the runners in the neighbourhood join the shepherds. They bring dogs of all sorts, Scotch terriers, retrievers, Dandie Dinmonts, Bedlington terriers, bulldogs, grey-hounds, foxhounds, and everything that will run. All is done on foot, so that the fleetest is in at the death. The shepherds soon find out the fox. They know where he is by the remains of his last lamb-feast. They track him to the adjoining holes, and his smell soon betrays where he is. Sometimes he is drawn like a badger; and then he is worried where he is. At other times he hears the yelping of the dogs and the noise of his pursuers, and hastens away. "There he is! Yoicks!" There is a terrible run; up hill and down dale; through bogs

---

[1] John Peel possessed a small estate near Caldbeck. He spent the greater part of his fortune in keeping up his hounds and harriers. He used to sell a bit of his land from time to time to carry on the hunt. At length he became much embarrassed. The Cumberland hunters then called a meet, and before parting they sang *John Peel* in full chorus, presenting him with a handsome gratuity, which enabled him to shake off his encumbrances and to die in peace and quiet.

and marshes; over the fell and down into the hollow
beyond,—where the fox is lost in some " borrant." But
the shepherds are out again next day, and they never
cease their efforts until they have killed the fox or
driven him away from the sheepwalks.

George Moore's school-days were not yet over. Though
fond of fun, frolic, wrestling, bird-nesting, and hunting,
he was yet a general favourite. He was such a helpsome
boy. He thought nothing of getting up early in the
morning and walking nine or ten miles over the Fells to
Over Water to get a basket of fish for the family. In
the autumn, he would walk a long way up Binsey Hill
for blackberries. During the war time, the necessaries
of life were very dear. Everything was taxed to the
uttermost. Poor people could scarcely live. Salt was
sixteen shillings a stone. This told very heavily on the
statesmen; for salt was necessary for many things connected with farming and cattle-keeping.

"I was much delighted," says George Moore in his
autobiography, "when the harvest holidays came. As
my brother did not pay me any wages, and as I only
had my meat and clothes, I hired myself out, when the
home fields were cut, to the neighbouring farmers; and
I was thus enabled to get some pocket-money which I
could call my own. I started at sixpence a day, and
by the time that I was ten years old I got eighteenpence
a day. When I reached the age of twelve, being a very
strong boy, I 'carried my rig' with the men. I sheared
with the sickle, and kept time and pace with the full-
grown shearers. For this I earned two shillings a day,
with my food. This was considered unequalled for a
boy of my age to accomplish."

There were several customs peculiar to Cumberland
and Westmoreland which were then always observed in
harvest-time. At the finishing of the corn-cutting, the
great object of each man was to shear the last shock of

corn, as it was thought lucky to do so. Therefore each
tried to hide beneath his feet or at "dyke back" a little
shock of corn, so as to get the last cut. He who succeeded, plaited it at night and hung it up on the beams
of the house, where it remained until Christmas morning,
when it was given to the best milk cow. Before leaving
the field, the shearers all clustered together, and one of
them said :—

> "*Blessed be that day that our Saviour was born ;*
> *Our maister's got his hay housed and all his*
> *corn shorn !*"

Then all shouted together "A Kurn! A Kurn!
Halloo!" That night the Kurn-supper was provided,
of which butter-sops formed the principal part. This
was composed of wheaten flour baked on a girdle, like
oatcakes. It was broken up into small fragments, and
mixed with butter, sugar, and rum, and afterwards with
half-churned cream. After the supper, songs were sung ;
and country-dances and reels were danced to a neighbour's fiddle. Sometimes even measure was kept to a
tune given by a good singer, or, better still, by the best
whistler of the party.

To return to George Moore's early education. After
leaving Blackbird Wilson's school at Boltongate, for
which his father paid six shillings and sixpence a
quarter, he was sent to Pedler Thommy's school at
Crookdake, near Leegate. Thommy had been a pedler,
as his name indicated. Though he had broken down as
a pedler, he was thought good enough to be a schoolmaster. He was not a good teacher, though he was
much less cruel and drunken than the Blackbird.

About this time George Moore formed an acquaintance with the Daniels of Newland's Row, Mealsgate.
One of the boys was a good wrestler, and George had
many a hard struggle with him on the Leesrig pasture.

In the evenings, he used to go into their house, and there he learnt to knit—Joseph Daniels seated at one end of the fender, and George Moore at the other,—the girls sitting by at their wheels. They all went to learn dancing together at the Apple-tree public-house at Mealsgate.

By this time George had reached the age of twelve. His father sent him to a finishing school at Blenner-hasset. He remained there for only a quarter : the cost was eight shillings. " The master," he says, " was a good writer and a superior man—indeed a sort of genius. For the first time I felt that there was some use in learning, and then I began to feel how ignorant I was. However, I never swerved from my resolve to go away from home. I had no tastes in common with my brother. I felt that I could not hang about half idle, with no better prospect before me than that of being a farm-servant. So I determined that I would leave home at thirteen and fight the battle of life for myself."

CHAPTER III.

APPRENTICESHIP.

BUT how was the battle of life to be fought? How was George Moore to enter upon the struggle? Where was he to begin? In a very small way, as with all beginnings. A draper in Wigton, called Messenger, having intimated to Daniel Wilkinson that he wanted an active boy, Wilkinson immediately answered, "I know the very boy for you!" The boy was George Moore.

Wilkinson, being a friend of the Moores, told them that Messenger would come out some day and see his proposed apprentice. John Moore did not welcome the suggestion. He did not wish his boy to be a draper, or anything of the sort. Why should he not "stick by the land," as his fathers had done before him? He thought it rather humiliating that either of his sons should enter trade.

Nevertheless Messenger came out to Mealsgate to see the boy. Old Moore would not hear of George going to Wigton. "If you want a boy take Thomas, but leave me George; he's far the better worker." Thomas, however, would not go. He was the eldest son, and was heir to the property. If any one was to go, it must be George and not Thomas.

Mrs. Moore, George's stepmother, wished him to go. He was a favourite of hers, and seeing his eagerness, she strongly advised his father to let him go to Wigton. She did not think he could be of much use at Mealsgate. He would hang on to the estate; and after all he could never rise much above the rank of farm-servant. Besides, George reiterated his determination to leave home. He could not get even the wages that he earned on the farm. He wanted to do something for himself. He *would* go to Wigton.

In the meantime Messenger had been looking into the lad's face. " I like the look of him very much," said he to his father. " He is strong and active. He's just the boy for me. You must let me have him." At last John Moore, who was an easy, good-natured man, and perhaps somewhat under the control of his wife, gave way. " Well," said he, " I fear I maun part wi' him ; God bless thee, my lad." It was at length arranged that George Moore should be bound apprentice to Messenger for four years.

George made the necessary arrangements to leave Mealsgate. He had to part with his donkey, his dearly beloved companion. He sold him to John Dobbins for sixteen shillings, though he had to wait long for the money. Then his clothes and his linen had to be arranged. After everything was ready, they were packed in the hair trunk bequeathed to him by his great-uncle, and sent on to Wigton by the cart. George and his stepmother rode thither on horseback, she clinging to him on the packsaddle behind. There were many things to be arranged at Wigton as to the boy's feeding and lodging.

Wigton is a small country town, about eleven miles west of Carlisle. It used to be celebrated for its handloom weaving and calico-printing; though these trades have now left the place and become absorbed in the great manufacturing centres. It is now principally known for its weekly markets, and its horse and cattle fairs. Its population is nearly stationary.

Mrs. Moore arranged that George should sleep in his master's house and get his meals in the adjoining public-house—the Half-Moon Inn. It was a very bad arrangement for a boy brought from home, without a friend in the place, to have to go to a public-house and get his meals. It brought him into contact with the drinking part of the population, and put him in the way of joining in their drinking habits. He himself says, "My apprenticeship will not bear reflection. My master was more thoughtless than myself. He gave way to drinking, and set before me a bad example. Unfortunately I lodged in the public-house nearly all the time, and saw nothing but wickedness and drinking."

So far as the shop was concerned, George got on very well. He was civil, attentive, and hard-working. He soon made friends with the customers. They preferred to be served by him rather than by his master or fellow-apprentice. He gives the following account of his work:—"I had to make the fire, clean the windows, groom my master's horse, and do many things that boys from our ragged schools nowadays think they are 'too good for.' I should have been happy enough, but for the relentless persecution and oppression of my fellow-apprentice, who was some years older than myself. He lost no opportunity of being cruel to me. He once nearly throttled me. He tried to damage my character by spreading false reports about me, and telling untruths to my master. Even now, after so many years have passed, I can still feel the burden under which my life groaned from the wrongs and misrepresentations of that time.

"After about two years this tyrant left, and I became head apprentice. I had now to keep the books, serve the good customers, and borrow money to pay my master's debts; for by this time he had become very unsteady. The only marvel was that in God's good providence I did not become a victim to drink myself, as I saw nothing else before me. I slept at the shop, but got my food at the Half-Moon public-house. Then I had to give a glass of spirits and water to all the good customers, even if a parcel was bought as small as a five-shilling waistcoat.

"I now considered myself of some importance, having an apprentice under me! He had lots of pocket-money, and I had none. We therefore played at cards, and I won his money. I did it in fair play, having always luck at cards. This gave me a taste for play. I kept a pack of cards in my pocket. I played at cards almost every night. I went to the public-houses and played with men for high stakes. I frequently lost all that I had, but I often gained a great deal. I sometimes played the whole night through. Gambling was my passion, and it might have been my ruin. I was, however, saved by the following circumstance :—

"I had arranged an easy method for getting into my master's house at night, after my gambling bouts. I left a lower window unfastened ; and by lifting the sash and pushing the shutters back, I climbed in, and went silently up to my bed in the attic. But my master having heard some strange reports as to my winnings and losings at cards, and fearing that it might at last end in some disaster to himself, he determined to put a stop to my gambling. One night, after I had gone out with my cards, he nailed down the window through which I usually got entrance to the house, and when I returned, and wished to get in, lo ! the window was firmly closed against me.

"It was five o'clock in the morning of Christmas Eve. That morning proved the turning-point in my life ! After vainly trying to open the window, I went up the lane alongside the house. About a hundred yards up, I climbed to the ridge of the lowest house in the row

From thence I clambered my way up to the next highest house, and then managed to creep along the ridges of the intervening houses, until I reached the top of my master's dwelling—the highest house of all. I slid down the slates until I reached the waterspout. I got hold of it, and hung suspended over the street. I managed to get my feet on to the window sill, and pushed up the window with my left foot. This was no danger or difficulty to me, as I had often been let down by bigger boys than myself with a rope round my waist, into the old square tower at Whitehall, that I might rob the jackdaws of their nests and eggs.

"I dropt quietly into my room, and went to bed. Soon after, Messenger came up to look after me, and found me apparently asleep. I managed to keep up the appearance so long as he remained there. I heard him murmuring and threatening that the moment I got up he would turn me out of the place. This only served to harden me. But in the morning the waits came round, playing the Christmas carols. Strangely enough, better thoughts came over me with the sweet music. I awoke to the sense of my wrongdoing. I felt overwhelmed with remorse and penitence. I thought of my dear father, and feared that I might break his heart, and bring his grey hairs with sorrow to the grave.

"I lay in bed, almost without moving, for twenty-four hours—for it was Christmas Day. No one came near me. I was without food or drink. I thought of what I should do when I got up. If my master turned me off, I would go straightway to America. I resolved, in any case, to give up card-playing and gambling,—which, by God's grace, I am thankful to say, I have firmly carried out.

"I got up next morning, and the good woman at the Half-Moon Inn, where I took my meals, received me with tears; as my master had been telling several persons that he would turn me away, and have nothing more to do with me. She at once sent for two of my master's intimate friends to intercede for me. They came, and after a good deal of persuasion, Messenger consented to give me another trial. From this moment my resolution kept firm as a rock. I gave up all card-playing and gambling. I was very regular in all my habits. I went constantly to a night-school to improve my education ; and I thus proved to all the sincerity of my repentance.

"It was well for me, and perhaps for many others, that all this had occurred. It has caused me, on many occasions, since I have had hundreds of young men in my employment, to forgive what I have seen wrong in their conduct, and give them another chance. Probably I might not have done this had I not remembered the down-falling course that I had entered on during my apprenticeship at Wigton."

The rest of George Moore's apprenticeship may be briefly told. He won the affection and trust of his master, who reposed the utmost confidence in him. When the travellers came round for their money George had to find it for them. Indeed the business would have gone to ruin but for his industry and management. Messenger was drinking harder than ever. When on the rampage, his apprentice had to do all that was necessary to keep the business in order. George had often to borrow money from other tradesmen, giving merely his word that it would be paid back. At his own request he removed his lodgings from Messenger's to Nanny Graves's,[1] in Church Street. He took his meals there instead of at the public-house. He was thus removed out of the way of temptation.

George knew everybody in Wigton. He was a

---

[1] Nanny Graves was the mother of John Woodcock Graves, the author of *D'ye ken John Peel*.

general favourite. He used to be seen scampering about the place without his cap; first running into one house and then into another, asking about the inmates —"How Betty was?" "How Nanny was," and "How all the bairns were?" He met his young friends on "snap-nights," and played games with them. In the long summer evenings, after the shop was shut, he met them on the nearest green. There they played at "set-caps"—that is, daring each other to do the most venturesome things—such as jumping highest, running fastest, or throwing the biggest boy. George kept his hand in at wrestling, and by the time he left Wigton he was considered the best wrestler in the place.

He had, however, ventured too much. He got wet, took cold, and was laid up with rheumatic fever. Then Mrs. Smith took him to her house, and nursed him carefully. He was ill for about thirteen weeks, and when he was able to go about, he was so spent that scarcely anybody knew him. George never forgot the kindness of Mrs. Smith and her servant Susan.

He was accustomed, at the end of the week, to walk home to Mealsgate to see his relatives. Being of a sociable disposition, he had a great wish to extend his hospitality to his friends, and he often took one or other of them with him. They were not always welcome at Mealsgate. The stepmother thought they were in the way, or Thomas thought it extravagant to entertain "fremd folks." On such occasions, George took his friends to Aunt Dinah's at Bolton Hall, where they were always made welcome. They were allowed to run about the farm, to ride the horses, to bathe in the Ellen, and do whatever they liked.

One day George brought with him a friend from Wigton accoutred in boots. Boots were not so common in those days as they are now; clogs being more generally worn. The two lads walked about the fields all day, and, the grass being wet, the boots became thoroughly sodden. When night arrived, and they prepared to go to bed, the boots had to be got off. First one tried, and then another. The whole family tried in turn to pull them off, but they would not budge. So George's friend had at last to go to bed in his boots, tied about in cloths to save the bedding.

When George slept at Bolton Hall he usually occupied the Parlour. There were strange rumours about that room. It was thought to be haunted. Ghostly tappings were heard inside the wall. The little dog of the house would tremble all over on hearing the strange noises. George was in great dread of the bogle, though he himself never heard the tappings.[1] Yet, with the strong love of sleep—for he always slept well—he at last went off, heard no more, and was up, bright and joyous, in the early morning.

To show the confidence with which George Moore was regarded at Wigton, the following anecdote may be related. Mr. Todd, a banker at Wigton, who had often advanced money to enable George to meet the claims of the travellers as they came round, one day asked Messenger to spare his apprentice for a few days, as he wished to send him on a special errand of trust. It appeared that a cattle-dealer of the neighbourhood had a considerable sum of money in Todd's bank ; that he had bought a quantity of cattle in Scotland, and desired the banker to send him the necessary money to

---

[1] The supposed cause of the tappings was ascertained long after George had left Bolton. His uncle, when "sair fresh" one night (that is, pretty full of drink), heard the noises, and getting up, vowed that he would stand it no longer. He got a pick and broke into the wall. A hollow space was found, and a skeleton hand fell out. This terrified the discoverer so much, that he immediately had the wall built up. How the skeleton hand got in was never discovered. But a legend had been preserved which stated that a stranger was once seen to go into Bolton Hall, and that he never came out again.

pay for them. It was for this purpose that Mr. Todd desired the help of George Moore.

The boy, always ready for adventure, was quite willing to give his services, especially to a gentleman who had proved so kind to him as Mr. Todd had been. A horse was provided, and the boy rode away northward with several hundred pounds in his pocket. He crossed the border at Gretna, and made his way westward to Dumfries. There he met the cattle-dealer, and handed him the money. It was all right. His mission had now ended, and he proposed returning to Wigton by the same road that he had come. The cattle-dealer, however, interposed. "What do you say," he asked, "to help me to drive the cattle home?" "Oh," said George, "I have no objections." It was only a little addition to the adventure.

The two remained together all day. They drove the cattle by unfrequented routes in the direction of Annan. At length they reached the shores of the Solway Firth. The proper route into England was by Gretna, though the road by that way was much longer. But the cattle-dealer declared his intention of driving his cattle across the Solway Sands. Here was an opportunity for George to give up his charge, and return home by the ordinary road. But no! if the cattle-dealer could cross the sands, he could cross. And so he remained to see the upshot of the story.

The tide was then at low ebb. The waste of sand stretched as far as the eye could reach. It was gloaming by this time, and the line of English coast—about five miles distant—looked like a fog-bank. Night came on. It was too dark to cross then. They must wait till the moon rose. It was midnight before its glitter shone upon the placid bosom of the Firth. The cattle-dealer then rose, drew his beasts together, and drove them in upon the sands.

They had proceeded but a short way when they observed that the tide had turned. They pushed the beasts on with as much speed as they could. The sands were becoming softer. They crossed numberless pools of water. They they saw the sea-waves coming upon them. On, on! It was too late. The waves, which sometimes rush up the Solway three feet abreast, were driving in amongst the cattle. They were carried off their feet, and took to swimming. The horses, upon which George Moore and his companion were mounted, also took to swimming. They found it difficult to keep the cattle together—one at one side, and one at the other. Yet they pushed on as well as they could. It was a swim for life. The cattle became separated, and were seen in the moonlight swimming in all directions. At last they reached firmer ground, pushed on, and landed near Bowness. But many of the cattle had been swept away, and were never afterwards heard of. Shortly after, George Moore reached Wigton in safety.

Not long after this event George's apprenticeship drew to an end. He remained with Messenger a little while longer. Messenger was rapidly going to the bad. George Moore could learn little more of his business in Wigton. He therefore determined to leave the place and look out for employment elsewhere. Where should he go? He could not think of Carlisle. He must go to London : that only would satisfy him. He had not said much of his intentions at home; but when he at length announced his determination, it came with a shock upon his father and his sister Mary. Mary was his favourite sister. She was about two years younger than himself. When she went into Wigton on market days, she always tried to get a sight of George. One day she lingered about Messenger's shop, passing and repassing the door, but George was busy with his customers and did not see her. She went home greatly distressed. So, when George announced his intention of going to London, she joined with her father in endeavouring to dissuade him from his purpose; but it was of no use. He had made up his mind, for even in boyhood he never swerved from his purpose.'

At length, after many heart-burnings, it was arranged that George should go to London to see whether he could find any suitable employment there. Before he left Wigton, his father came in to take his final leave of him. He brought thirty pounds with him to pay the boy's expenses. He thought it would be enough, but if George wanted more he must let him know. The parting was very touching. The father grat and the son grat, one against the other. At last Nanny Graves could stand it no longer—"What gars ye greet that way?" she said to John Moore; "depend upon't, yer son 'll either be a great nowt or a great soomat!"[1]

At length they parted, George's sister Mary going part of the road with him to carry his bundle. The hair trunk, packed with his clothes, was already on its way to Carlisle. On arriving there, he put up at the "Grey Goat" Inn, the usual place of resort for the Wigton folk; and next morning, at five o'clock, he started by coach for London.

And here ended George Moore's early life in Cumberland. It was a good thing for him that he was born and brought up in the country. Though his education had been small, his knowledge of men was great. He was already able to distinguish character, which can never be learnt from books. The individuality of the country boy is much greater than that of the town boy. His early life is not poisoned by pleasure. He is in active and sympathetic contact with those about

---

[1] A great nothing, or a great something.

him. He knows every person by name and is acquainted with their conditions and circumstances. He lives in a sort of family feeling of community with those about him.

The country boy, in his earliest years, belongs entirely to that which surrounds him. He feels a special attraction towards animals, by reason of the individuality of their lives. He is acquainted with birds, with the places in which they build, and all their signs, and sounds, and habits. He keeps his eyes open, and learns many things of deep interest and instruction, which colour all his future life. He walks amongst wonders, and gathers new knowledge in the life of every day. At length he takes part in the work and pleasures of man. He ploughs, or sows, or reaps in the fields of the home farm. Or he enjoys country sports—running, wrestling, or hunting—the rougher the better,—and he becomes healthy and robust. In the winter evenings he hears the stories of border life, and thus learns the lessons of his race. He also will be bold and valiant, as his fathers were.

What old Stilling said to his grandson on leaving home, John Moore might well have said to his son on leaving Cumberland for London : " Your forefathers were good and honourable people, and there are very few princes who can say that. You must consider it the greatest honour you can have, that your grandfather and great-grandfather, and their fathers, were men who were beloved and honoured by everybody, although they had nothing to rule over but their own households. Not one of them ever married disgracefully, or acted dishonourably towards a woman. Not one of them coveted what did not belong to him ; and they all died full of days and honour."

CHAPTER IV.

IN LONDON.

FIFTY years ago, it took two days and two nights to
make the journey from Carlisle to London by coach.
It was a long, tedious, and wearisome journey. We
complain of railways now, but what should we say if
we were driven back to the old stage-coaches? The
passenger was poked up in a little box inside, scarcely
able to move or get breath. If he went outside, it was
delightful by day, but wearisome by night, especially
when the weather was bad. He had to sleep sitting,
with his back to the luggage and the edge of a box
for his pillow. At a lurch of the coach he woke up
with a start, finding himself leaning forward or in-
clining backward, or likely to fall side-long from the
coach.

Railway travellers now consider themselves very much
aggrieved if they are half an hour late; yet good-
natured people of the olden times were quite satisfied
if they were only half a day late. Though it then took
two days and two nights between Carlisle and London,
the journey is now performed, all the way inside, in
seven hours and a half, with almost unvarying regularity.
Yet we are not satisfied.

And yet there was a great deal of pleasure in travelling by coach fifty years ago. The beauties of the
country were never out of sight. You passed through

shady lanes and hedgerows ; by gentlemen's seats, with
the old halls standing out amidst the clumps of trees;
along quiet villages, where the people, springing up at
the sound of the horn, came to their doors to see the
coach pass.   There was the walk up-hill, or along green
pastures or bye-lanes, to ease the horses as they crept
along.   There was the change at the post-town, the
occasional meal, and sometimes the beginnings of friendship.   All this was very enjoyable, especially to young
fellows on their way to London for the first time, to see
the great city and its wonders.

The coach by which George Moore travelled went
through Lancaster, with its castle perched on the top of
the hill.   Then, by a pleasant drive through moors and
dales, and by many a pleasant town, though now
blurred with the smoke of a thousand chimneys, the
coach proceeded to Manchester.   The town did not
then contain one-third of the population that it does
now.   From thence the coach drove on through the
midland shires to London.   It was fine spring weather.
The buds were bursting, and many of the trees were
already green.   The journey was still interesting,
though towards the end it became monotonous.
At last, on the morning of the third day, the coach
reached Highgate Hill, from which George Moore
looked down on the city of London, the scene of his
future labours.

The end of the journey was approaching, and again
it became more than usually interesting.   Hamlets were
passed ; then cottages and villas.   Then rows of streets ;
although green fields were still dotted about here and
there.   The enormous magnitude of the place already
surprised the young traveller.   The coach went through
street after street, down Old St. Pancras Road, down
Gray's Inn Lane, along Holborn and Newgate Street,
until at last it stopped at the " Swan with Two Necks,"

in Lad Lane, Wood Street. After paying the coachman, Moore was recommended to go to the "Magpie
and Pewter Platter," for the purpose of obtaining accommodation. He succeeded; and went there, hair trunk
and all.

George Moore arrived in London on the day before
Good Friday, 1825. He was too much fatigued to look
after a situation on that day. On the following morning all the shops were shut. He had therefore to wait
until Saturday before he could begin to look for a place.
What was he to do on Good Friday? He knew that all
the Cumberland men in London were accustomed to
have their annual wrestling-match on that day, and he
accordingly went to Chelsea to observe the sports.

When he arrived at the place, he found the wrestling-
green crowded with north-country people,—big, brawny
men, of great girth, noted wrestlers, and amateur wrestlers, mingled with sporting and slightly "horsey" people.
There were many life-guardsmen and foot-guardsmen;
for it must be known that the Border-land, by reason
of the big men it contains, is the favourite recruiting-
ground for Her Majesty's body-guards. More life-
guardsmen have come from Longtown, and from the
Westmoreland and Yorkshire moors, than from any
similar localities in the kingdom.

George Moore found amongst the crowd a young
Quaker from Torpenhow, who had won the belt at
Keswick a few years before. They had known each
other before, and now renewed their acquaintance.
George, inspired by the event, entered his name as a
wrestler. He was described by some who were present
on the occasion, as "very strong-looking, middle-sized,
with a broad chest and strongly developed muscles."
His hair was dark and curly, almost black. His eyes
were brown, and glowed under excitement to a deeper
brown. His face glowed with health. His bearing was

free and open ; it might be called abrupt. But he was civil to everybody.

To those who do not know the rules of Cumberland wrestling, it may be mentioned that though it is an athletic sport, it is conducted in perfect good humour, the loser always taking his fall as a joke. It is practised by boys and men on the village greens in the north, and is not in any way mixed up with betting or drinking,—though it is somewhat different in London. The wrestlers stand up chest to chest, each placing his chin on the other's right shoulder, and his left arm above the right of his opponent. Then they grasp each other round the body. There is often a difficulty in *takin' hod*. Each tries to get an advantage in getting the under-grip. When both men have got hold, the play begins, and they endeavour to throw each other on to the ground. The one who touches the ground first and is undermost, is the loser. Though force goes for much, skill is also indispensable. The " chips," or dexterous strokes, are numerous—including the hype, the swinging-hype, the buttock, the cross-buttock, the back-heel, the click inside, and the outside stroke. These would afford ample subjects for the illustration of a beautiful athletic art.[1]

When George Moore's name was called, he "peeled " and stepped into the ring. The first man he came against was a little bigger than himself, but George threw him so cleverly that the question was asked on every side—" Who's that ? Where does he come frae ? What's his name ? " His name was soon known, and as he again wrestled and threw his man, he was hailed with the cries of " Weel done, George Moore." The

---

[1] English sculptors have been imitating the Greek to death. Why not give us some English art ? Nothing can be seen more lithe, vigorous, and muscular than the wrestlers on an English village-green in the north of England.

difficulties of the wrestlers increase as the sport goes forward. All the weak men have been thrown; now come the strong against the strong. Observe how careful they are in *takin' hod*. Each strives to gain some advantage over his antagonist. They give and take, and bob and dodge round the ring. Then the cry rises, "They've haud!" What an excitement! The men are locked as in a vice! Every muscle is straining and quivering. Then great strokes are played; but it is done so quickly that the "chip" can scarcely be seen; and down goes one of the men, with the other over him.

As the game proceeded, George Moore had a difficult fellow to meet. He was a man of great weight—a well-known champion wrestler, called Byers. He had already settled a "vast o' men;" and now he had to settle this youth of nineteen from Wigton. George worked his way round about him until he got a good grip. Byers tried to grass him by the right leg hype. Then George, taking Byers firmly in his arms, threw him bodily *over his head!* Byers touched the ground first, and George was victor. "Weel done, George Moore!" was again re-echoed round the ring.

At length he met a man who was "ower kittle for him"—a noted champion wrestler, also from Cumberland. He was famous for his left-leg striking, and clicking inside the heel. After a long struggle George went down under his opponent's favourite chip. Nevertheless he came out of the ring winner of the third prize. After the sports were over, the young fellows came and spoke to him. They knew that he was one of their county-men. His strong Cumberland accent could not belie that. Some of them came from his own neighbourhood. They insisted upon his going with them to the neighbouring public-house, where they treated him to drink.

The whole incidents of the day must have elated the lad. Though he had always taken pride in his mode of wrestling, his achievements that day constituted him a hero. Acquaintances crowded about him. They wished him at once to arrange for a meeting, to be held in the course of a few days. Betting began for and against him, and he observed that some of the lads were taking more drink than was good for them. He was at once reminded of his card-playing at Wigton, of his father at home, and of the many reasons why he should keep himself out of this environment of mischief. He accordingly summoned the resolution to tell his new acquaintances that he could not attend the appointment, for it was his determination not to wrestle at the proposed match. He accordingly left them, much to their indignation.

He retraced his way to the city alone. In the course of the afternoon he was told that the inn,—indeed the very bed in which he had slept,—had become notorious; for Thurtell, the murderer, had frequented the inn some time before. This gave him such a horror, that he felt he could not sleep there again. He accordingly looked out for a lodging in the neighbourhood. He was fortunate in finding one near Wood Street. The lodging-house was kept by a motherly body from the north; and her great kindness to the stranger lad helped to give him a lasting belief in the goodness of woman.

On the next morning—the Saturday between Good Friday and Easter Sunday—he set out, full of spirits, to find a situation. The result of his day's work was very disappointing. He was not only discouraged, but provoked. Wherever he went, he was laughed at because of his country-cut clothes and his broad Cumberland dialect.

But he consoled himself. He did not expect to find a

E

situation at once.   He must try again.   He would
begin on Monday morning, and persevere until he succeeded.   There must be plenty of persons in that enormous city wanting a draper's assistant.   He accordingly
went out early in the morning, and returned late at
night.   The result was the same—utter disappointment.
Not a person would have him.   Some pretended they
could not understand his northern dialect.   Was such a
lad likely to serve customers?   After his first inquiry
he was generally shown to the door.

"The keenest cut of all I got," he says, "was from
Charles Meeking of Holborn.   He asked me if I wanted
a *porter's* situation.   This almost broke my heart."

He himself, however, admits that he was rather
"green" and uncultivated; and that there was little
wonder that the West-end shopkeepers did not give
him a place behind their counters.   When afterwards
referring to this early part of his career he said, "I had
no one to take me by the hand.   My very appearance
was against me, for the Wigton tailors were not so
expert as they are now; and when I applied for a
situation it was difficult to convince them that it was a
place behind the counter that I wanted, and not some
meaner situation.   My dialect too was against me; for
though it is pretty broad now, it was much broader
then.   After beating about London for an entire week,
I began to think myself a not very marketable commodity in the great city."[1]

Still he persevered.   He went nearly all over London.
He entered as many as thirty drapers' shops in one day,
always with the same result.   It was the same in the
east as in the west.   There was no employment for
him—none whatever.   He passed amid the roar and
clatter of the streets—pushing his way amongst the keen

---

[1] Speech to the boys of the Commercial Travellers' School.

eager faces of the city, or amidst the careworn crowds of people like himself, wanting work and unable to obtain it.

The second Sunday in London came round. He began to realise the solitariness and the solitude of London. Every house looked black at him. Every door was closed against him. He felt himself an utter stranger. No one knew anything of his troubles and sorrows. And if they knew, they would not have cared. What was he among so many? He thought it almost heartless that these multitudes should be going about on their errands of enjoyment and worship, without taking any notice of him. But his was only the case of thousands. To those who are friendless, London is the most solitary place in the world.

He must, however, send home his promised letter, to tell his father how he was getting on. But when he had written his letter, it was so blotted with tears that he could not send it. He would wait for another week. Early next morning he was at it again. He tried shop after shop : "No vacancy !" "At last," he says, " I was in despair. I now determined, as I could not find an opening in London, to go out to America.

" I called at Swan and Edgar's in Piccadilly, and told a young man there, of the name of Wood, that I was going to take my passage. He then informed me that Mr. Ray, of Flint, Ray, and Co., Grafton House, Newport Market, had sent to inquire if any one knew where I was. Mr. Ray was born in Cumberland himself. His brother owned Lesson Hall, near Wigton. He knew about my father's family, and wished to befriend me. I went at once to see him, and he engaged me, more from pity than from any likelihood of mine to shine in his service. My salary was to be £30 a year; and I joyfully accepted his offer."

Thus, while George Moore, in his despair, was lament-

ing that he had not a friend in London, his friend was
waiting for him and even searching for him. Mr. Ray
had been informed that the son of his old friend had
left Wigton for London ; and not seeing him nor hearing of him, he had sent round to Swan and Edgar's to
make inquiry about him. Cumberland men are generally
ready to help each other in time of need. Hence
the timely assistance which Mr. Ray rendered to George
Moore—a kindness which the latter never forgot.

On the Monday morning after he had been engaged,
George Moore set out to enter upon his situation. He
must also get his ancestral hair trunk removed to his
new quarters. It contained his clothes, his money, and
all that he possessed. He hired a man from the street,
the owner of a pony-cart, to carry his hair trunk westward. After taking leave of the kind landlady, his first
friend in the great city, he and the man with the cart
started for Newport Market. At some turn of the
street—perhaps while he was looking about him—he
missed the man, the pony-cart, and the hair trunk.
Surely never was a poor fellow so unfortunate !

He scanned the passing crowd. He tried to see over
the heads of the people ; but there was no pony, and
no hair trunk in sight. Again he felt his utter loneliness.
He sat down on a doorstep almost broken-hearted. No
one spoke to him ; no one came near him. What was
he to the bustling crowd that passed him by ?—only a
shivering atom on a doorstep ! In his despair, he
thought that the man had robbed him, and carried off
his all

He rested on the doorstep for about two hours. What
an interminable torture it seemed to be ! He continued
to watch the passing crowd. A pony-cart came up ; he
looked, and lo ! it was the identical man, and the identical hair trunk ! The carrier had called on his way
upon some other errand, and was amazed to miss his

customer. When he came up, he not only laughed at
the lad, but rated him soundly for his "greenness" in
having lost sight of him, and trusted a stranger with all
his things.

George was full of delight, and in his exuberance of
gratitude, he offered the man all the money he had in
his pocket, which amounted to nine shillings. But the
costermonger was an honest man. "No, no!" said he;
"it's very kind of you, but the five shillings that we
agreed upon will be quite enough." He then handed
him back the four shillings. George Moore never forgot
the lesson of that costermonger's honesty.

His eyes were still full of tears when he entered the
warehouse. One who was employed there at the
time remembers his first appearance. "On incident-
ally looking over to the haberdashery counter I saw an
uncouth, thickset country lad standing crying. In a
minute or two a large deal chest—such as the Scotch
servant-lasses use for their clothes—was brought in by
a man, and set down on the floor. After the lad had
dried up his tears, the box was carried up stairs to the
bedroom where he was to sleep. After he had come
down stairs he began working, and he continued to be
the hardest worker in the house until he left. Such,"
says our informant, "was the veritable *début* of George
Moore in London. Had you seen him then, you would
have said that he was the most unlikely lad in England
to have made the great future that he did."

Everything was strange to him at first—the shop,
the work, the people, the habits, the life. But he was
willing and eager to learn. He had to begin at the
lowest rung of the ladder. First he did the drudgery
of the house; then he was moved upwards. He was
always ready to do anything. He became a favourite
with his companions. Among the young men at
Grafton House, with whom he became most intimate,

were three Cumberland lads, two Scotchmen, and one
Cockney. Those from the midland and southern
counties thought the Cumbrians generally a rather
rough race. They spoke of them as "the rude
barbarians of the north." That was, however, half a
century ago.

One of George Moore's companions at Grafton House
gives us the following recollections of his life at that
time :—"He slept in the same small apartment with
myself and two others. The room could scarcely be
considered up to the modern sanitary conditions of
life and health ; yet we got on very well. He was very
fond of going to the Serpentine to take an early bathe.
Many a tussle we had. He called me a 'lazy old
Scotchman' for not getting up and going out with him in
the mornings. But I was no swimmer, and did not like
to be made the butt of my companion's ridicule. I was
born at the Lowther Hills, in Lanarkshire, where there
was scarcely a burn in which we could bathe. There
was not a good swimmer in the parish."

"Next to George's integrity and generosity of character, was his love of country and patriotism. He was
always 'deaving' us about his native Cumberland. It
was the finest country, with the noblest scenery, and the
best, strongest, and most vigorous of men. Cumberland
men are very clannish. They stick to each other through
weal or woe. How is it that the natives of a moun-
tainous region are more patriotic than those of a cham-
pagne country ? Perhaps this may arise from their
seeing fewer objects to divide their attention, as well as
from those objects being of a much grander character,
and more likely to take a permanent hold upon their
mind. Be this as it may, I uniformly noticed, during
my three years' residence in London, that young men
from Wales, Scotland, and Cumberland pined after
their native hills and dales ; whereas young men from

the midland and southern counties of England, fell in like a gin-horse to their daily work. They were as much at home in twenty-four hours as a veritable cockney himself. This may probably be a pretty correct solution of the common adage that an Englishman is made by Act of Parliament; that is, that he has no local attachments; and, provided he is protected by the law of the country, and gets enough to eat and drink, all places are alike to him."

And now let us give George Moore's account of himself. "On arriving in London, I obtained a situation in a house of business. I soon found that, coming green from the country, I laboured under many disadvantages. Compared with the young men with whom I was associated, I found my education very deficient; and my speech betrayed that I had not lived in London all my life. Indeed it smacked strongly of Cumberland and Cumberland folks. The first thing I did to remedy my defects was to put myself to school at night, after the hours of employment were over; and many an hour have I borrowed from sleep in order to employ it on the improvement of my mind. At the end of eighteen months I had acquired a considerable addition to my previous knowledge, and felt myself able to take my stand side by side with my competitors. Let no one rely in such cases on what is termed Luck. Depend upon it, that the only luck is merit, and that no young man will make his way unless he possesses knowledge, and exerts all his powers in the accomplishment of his objects."

When George Moore had been about six months at Grafton House, he one day observed a bright little girl come tripping into the warehouse, accompanied by her mother. "Who are they?" he asked of one of those standing near. "Why, don't you know?" said he; "that's the guv'nor's wife and daughter!" "Well," said George, "if ever I marry, that girl shall be my wife!" It was a wild and ridiculous speech. "What? marry your master's daughter? You must be mad to talk of such a thing." The report went round. The other lads laughed at George as another Dick Whittington.

Yet it was no wild nor improbable speech. It was the foreshadowing of his fate. The idea took possession of his mind. It was his motive power in after-life. It restrained and purified him. He became more industrious, diligent, and persevering. After many years of hard work the dream of his youth was fulfilled, and the girl *did* become his wife. Not, however, before he had passed through many trials and difficulties. One of these was of a most serious character, and threatened to cost him his liberty—perhaps his life. He has told the story in his own words :—

"At that time it was the duty of the assistants to carry out goods on approbation to the best customers. It was my lot one day to do this, and I sold some articles to a lady of title at her house. I made out my own note of the articles, and then copied out the bill for her, which I receipted. But I had unfortunately made an error, and in copying out her bill made it £1 more than the amount I had received. The lady, on looking over it afterwards, found out the mistake in the addition, and, thinking that she had paid me the extra sovereign, hastened to Grafton House with the bill. On reference being made to my cheque-book, it was found that the amount entered was £1 less than the bill which I had receipted, on which the lady pronounced me to be a thief.

"At this Mr. Ray was very indignant, and told the lady that he did not keep thieves in his house. He kindly told me to try and recollect the circumstances, and endeavour to clear up the matter. Unfortunately, the more I tried, the more I got bewildered. In despair, I suddenly asked the lady the amount of money which she had in her possession when she began to pay me. She said she was astonished at my impertinence. ‘And yet,’ she added, ‘I can furnish you with the information which you require. Lord Conyngham gave me £20 this morning. I paid so much to the baker, so much to the grocer, and so much to you, and I have so much left.’ I noted down the figures, added them up, and found that they made £21, or a pound more than she had received from her husband.

“I immediately called my employer, and got her to repeat the figures. He was satisfied with their correctness. Providentially, I all at once recollected that I had taken down a memorandum of the articles sold. I produced this, and found that I had received the money according to this memorandum, and not according to the receipted bill which I had left with the lady. Knowing my innocence, I boldly asserted the fact. My employer was satisfied. Nevertheless, the lady left the place in a rage, loudly declaring that ‘the boy was a thief!’

“But when her temper had cooled down, and she had time to recollect all the circumstances of the case, she relented. In the course of the evening, Lady Conyngham sent a polite letter to Mr. Ray, stating that she was thoroughly convinced that the young man’s statement was true, and that she hoped the unfortunate occurrence would not in any way militate against him. And thus,” says Mr. Moore, “ended my escape from Newgate.” The laws were then most severe. Forging, stealing, and shoplifting were punishable with death. Only a short time before, a young shopman at Compton House, in the same neighbourhood, had been hanged for an offence similar to that of which George Moore had been accused.

When the lady had left, George at once expressed
his determination to leave the house. But Mr. Ray
told him to go behind the counter, to show that he
was innocent and that not a breath of suspicion was
raised against him. George took his master's advice.
The moral courage which he had shown raised him
in Mr. Ray's estimation. And when the lady's letter
arrived, showing that she had been wrong in her suspicions, and that George Moore was innocent, his character was also raised in the estimation of his companions.
At the same time he was determined to leave as soon as
possible. He had got a thorough dislike for the retail
trade. He was unwilling to incur the risk of being sub-
jected to a similar charge. In answer to the remonstrance of some of his companions, he said that "he
would rather break stones upon the road than remain
behind a counter."

A companion of Moore's, on being applied to respecting the circumstance above referred to, says that he has
forgotten all about it ; but he adds that "arithmetical
blunders were so common in a large retail establishment
like Grafton House that it would be looked upon as a
very small event. George Moore would have been the
very last man to have committed such an act. Indeed
stern, truthful integrity was the brightest gem in his
character. I often think of him, when I contrast the
humble *début* he made in London with the brilliant
future which he afterwards attained, by reason of his
own unaided, energetic, and persevering efforts."

Although about to leave Flint, Ray, and Co.'s service,
Mr. Ray kindly volunteered to go into the city and
endeavour to procure a situation for his young friend
in a wholesale house. He went to Mr. Fisher, a Cumberland man like himself, and after giving George Moore
an excellent character, he induced him to engage the
young man at a small salary. The firm of Fisher,

Stroud, and Robinson, Watling Street, was then the first Lace house in the city. George entered it at the beginning of 1826, at the salary of £40 a year. In a letter to his father, he says he now feels himself to be "a made man."

Before leaving this part of the subject it may be mentioned that, while he was still at Grafton House, Moore was reminded of the cattle-dealer with whom he had crossed the Solway some two years before. The reason of the unusual crossing was now apparent. The border cattle-dealer, with the usual weakness of his class, was not unwilling to find a stray beast amongst his herd. Perhaps he picked them up as he came along. Now, however, he had been convicted of sheep-stealing. He had more than once been to Falkirk fair and bought a few sheep. But it was curious to notice how they increased from day to day as they proceeded southwards. By the help of his clever dog, he contrived to add a sheep now and then to his flock. The sheep-farmers were however on the alert. They noticed the loss of their sheep. They followed the cattle-dealer ; found their sheep amongst his flock ; apprehended him, and had him convicted of sheep-stealing. The sentence passed upon him was transportation for life.

Transportation was a very different thing then from what it is now. Men sentenced were *really* transported. They were not let out with a ticket-of-leave to plunder people again. Our cattle-dealer desired very much to evade the punishment. He could think of nothing better than to write to the young man who had crossed the Solway with him two years before. His letter to George Moore reached him in a roundabout way. But immediately on receiving it, he proceeded to see the condemned cattle-dealer. He found the criminal in the hulks, chained hand and foot, and amongst the most horrible riffraff that he had ever seen. The

convict was waiting in the Thames for the next ship for
Botany Bay. What should this young man do, but get
up a memorial to the Secretary of State to have the
sentence mitigated. He sent it down to Cumberland,
had numerous influential signatures attached to it, presented the memorial, and actually had the sentence
mitigated from transportation for life to fourteen years
banishment.

During the man's absence, his wife maintained her
family respectably. She had even saved some money.
After the lapse of the fourteen years, the cattle-dealer
returned to Cumberland worse than before. He took
possession of his wife's money, treated her cruelly, and
turned her out of her house. Mr. Moore afterwards
admitted that it would have been better if he had
allowed the law to take its course. " It was," he said,
"the worst-spent philanthropic act that I was ever
guilty of." The man himself died only a few months
ago.

CHAPTER V.

WHEN George Moore entered the employment of Fisher, Stroud, and Robinson, in 1826, he found that he had still many things to learn. He was but a raw Cumberland lad. He had learnt little of manners. He was considered slow. His intelligence had not been awakened. At school, he was considered dull. He was much fonder of bathing than of reading, of hunting than of learning. He had a good deal of country conceit, which Mr. Fisher soon took out of him by incessant ridicule.

" From the fact," Moore says, "of my being engaged unseen (a practice I have always avoided) I suppose I did not come up to Mr. Ray's recommendations. After I had been in the house some weeks, Mr. Fisher began to blame my stupidity. He said he had had many a stupid blockhead from Cumberland, but that I was the worst of them all. He went on repeating something of this sort two or three times a week for several months; until I believed that every word he said was true. The conceit was thus entirely taken out of me."

There were two or three things that George had to study carefully. The first was Accuracy. It was through his want of accuracy that the disagreeable circumstance with Lady Conyngham had occurred.

His adding up the account wrong by a pound might,
with a less forgiving master, have got him into gaol:
it might, in fact, have cost him his life. An inaccurate
man is utterly unfit for business. He gets himself and
everybody else into trouble. He cannot be trusted.
The business man must, above all things, be accurate
in figures. The inaccurate balance-sheet is worthless.
The account must balance, even to a penny. If it does
not, the work must be done over again. Thus trouble
is caused, business is delayed, and everybody is put into
a state of annoyance.

George Moore also wanted Quickness and Promptitude. Country-bred boys are slow, whilst town-bred
boys are quick. Time is of little consequence in the
village ; whilst time is of every consequence in the
city. In the country you may saunter along half
asleep ; whereas in the town you must push along wide
awake. You see the rapidity of London life in the
streets, where everybody is walking with rapidity, bent
on some purpose or another.

It is the same in places of business. Everything is
concentrated into a few working hours. During that
time, everybody is working at the top of his bent.
Hence the rapid movements of the town-bred lad.
He may be shallow and frivolous ; he may know next to
nothing out of his own groove ; but he must be sharp,
smart, and clever. The city boy scarcely grows up ;
he is rushed up. He lives amid a constant succession of excitements, one obliterating another. In fact,
his reflective powers have scarcely time to grow and
expand.

It is very different with the country boy. He is
much slower in arriving at his maturity than the town
boy ; but he is greater when he reaches it. He is hard
and unpolished at first ; whereas the town boy is worn
smooth by perpetual friction, like the pebbles in a run-

ning stream.   The country boy learns a great deal,
though he may seem to be unlearned.   He knows a
great deal about nature, and a great deal about men.
He has had time to grow.   His brain-power is latent.

Hence the curious fact that in course of time the
country-bred boy passes the city-bred boy, and rises
to the highest positions in London life.   Look at all
the great firms, and you will find that the greater
number of the leading partners are those who originally
were country-bred boys.   The young man bred in the
country never forgets his origin.   "There is," says La
Rochefoucauld, "a country accent not in his speech
only, but in his thought, conduct, character, and manner
of existing, which never forsakes him."

George Moore found that he was still without education, at least of that kind of education which enabled
him to keep pace with his fellows.   He therefore continued faithfully to attend his night-school, where he
endeavoured to learn as much as he could.   "I found
in this house," said he, speaking of Fisher's, "a first-rate
class of young men, principally well-to-do people's sons,
well-educated, well-mannered, and well-conducted.   I
soon found out my lamentable deficiency in education.
I had never cost my father more than 6s. 6d. a quarter
for schooling, except the last quarter, which cost 8s.
As our hours were shorter than in the retail trade, I
went to a night-school, being so much ashamed of my
ignorance.   I frequently sat up studying my lessons
until the small hours in the morning.   I often think of
those nights as the most usefully spent hours of my
life.   I learnt more during the eighteen months that
I frequented the night-school than I had ever learnt
before.   If I had not availed myself of that opportunity
I should never have had the chance again.   From the
part in life which I was destined to take, I must
often have blushed for my ignorance, and evoked the

sneers of others, which would have very much galled my sensitive nature."

In after days, Mr. Moore used to say that he had two strong reasons for bearing cheerfully and resolutely the trials of that time. One was, that he knew the fact of his ignorance, and was conscious of how much he had to learn; hence his laborious nightly studies, sometimes until two and three o'clock in the morning. But the other and more powerful reason was his love for Eliza Ray. He had never forgotten his boyish resolution when he first saw her. "If I ever marry," said he, "that girl shall be my wife!" This resolution had settled down into a firm and steady purpose. Eliza Ray was his guiding star. He would be faithful, honest, and true for her. He would work night and day for her. He knew that if, through any ignorance or neglect, he was expelled from his situation at Fisher's, he would have to relinquish his fondly cherished hopes. Hence his settled determination to cultivate his mind, to improve his business education, and to win the approval of his superiors.

In the meantime George had been writing to his father at Mealsgate, strongly urging him to give his younger brother William the best education that could be got in the neighbourhood. "It is the best thing you could furnish him with in setting out in the world. It is better than money. Education will enable him to start fair in the world and to push his own way." William was accordingly sent to the best schools. He was a far apter learner than George had been. He had read extensively, and was well versed in literature. But he wanted that in which his brother George was supreme—intense perseverance. He knew much, but did little. He could think, but could not work.

Nevertheless, George had much confidence in his brother William, because of his superior education and his extensive knowledge. He called upon Mr. Ray and interceded with him to take his brother as an apprentice. Mr. Ray agreed to his wish. William came up from Mealsgate to London, and settled down at Grafton House. The boy was rather delicate, and did not like the confinement. Nor could he stand the roughnesses of the place so well as George had done. It was part of William's work to carry out and deliver the parcels of goods which had been bought by customers during the day.

William found this work very fatiguing and very difficult, because of his want of knowledge of the streets of London. His brother at once went to his help. As the hours of the wholesale houses are much shorter than those of the retail shops, George, when his day's work was over, put on an old coat, and went from the city to the west end to deliver his brother's parcels. Many a winter's night did he walk through wind and rain, with heavy parcels on his shoulders, to deliver them to the customers,—thus literally bearing his brother's burdens.

Mr. Crampton, afterwards his partner, says of him at this time : " My friendship with George Moore commenced at the beginning of January, 1827, when I found him at Fisher's. We became close companions. His friends were my friends ; and so intimate were we that I seemed to merge into a Cumberland lad. George was very patriotic. All our friends were Cumberlanders, and though I was a Yorkshireman, I was almost induced to feign that I was Cumberland too. I was gayer than he, and he never failed to tell me of my faults. He was a strong, round-shouldered young fellow. He was very cheerful, and very willing. He worked hard, and seemed to be bent on improvement. But in other respects he did not strike me as anything remarkable. Among the amusements which we attended together were the wrestling-matches at St. John's Wood. The principal match was held on Good Friday. One day we went to the wrestling-field, and George entered his name. The competitors drew lots. George's antagonist was a life-guardsman, over six feet high. I think I see Moore's smile now as he stood opposite to the giant. The giant smiled too. Then they went at it, *gat hod*, and George was soon gently laid upon his back. By this time he was out of practice, and I do not think he ever wrestled again. Besides, he was soon so full of work as to have little time for amusement."

Among the remarkable incidents of George Moore's early life was an adventurous visit which he made to the House of Commons. The following account was written by himself, at the age of sixty-seven, after he had been invited to stand for the County of Middlesex in conjunction with Lord Enfield :—

"On looking back upon my past eventful life, many strange circumstances crowd upon my mind. After I had been about two years in London, I had a great and anxious desire to see the House of Commons. I got a half holiday for the purpose. I did not think of getting an order from an M.P. Indeed I had not the slightest doubt of getting into the House. I first tried to get into the strangers' gallery, but failed. I then hung about the entrance, to see whether I could find some opportunity. I saw three or four members hurrying in, and I hurried in with them. The door-keepers did not notice me. I walked into the middle of the House. When I got in, I almost fainted with fear lest I should be discovered. I first got into a seat with the name of 'Canning' written upon it. I then proceeded to a seat behind, and sat there all the evening. I heard Mr. Canning bring forward his motion to reduce the duty on corn. He made a brilliant speech. He was followed by many other speakers. I sat out the whole debate. Had I been discovered, I might have been taken up for breach of privilege. Some men are born great; others have greatness thrust upon them. Little did I then dream that I should at a future period have the offer made to me of becoming member for the City of London, and afterwards for the County of Middlesex." [1]

To return to George Moore's position in the firm of Fisher, Stroud, and Robinson. He had now been for some time in the house. He had gained the respect of everybody in it. He was attentive, careful, accurate, hardworking. All the conceit had been taken out of him. Mr. Fisher no longer called him a dunderhead or a Cumberland blockhead. On the contrary, he began to like the smartness, cleverness, and willingness of the lad. At the end of the year, he promoted him to be town traveller for the firm. "Then," says Mr. Crampton, "the character of the man came out. At first his great abilities did not strike me; but when he got scope he burst out, and displayed that energy and perseverance which always distinguished him. He distanced all competitors, and sold more goods than any traveller had done before. He gained confidence in himself (for he had been tamed by Mr. Fisher), he became open and free in his manner, and devoted himself to his duties with immense zeal. Mr. Fisher became proud of his traveller, and George became proud of his firm, declaring it to be the first house in the trade."

A gentleman still living remembers George's visits to his employer. He then held a situation in one of the first west-end houses. "My principal," he says, "who had the purchasing of the lace goods—being fond of good living, and not being blest with much

---

[1] Mr. Moore's visit to the House of Commons must have been made in June, 1827. Mr. Canning's speech on the Corn Bill was one of the last he delivered : he died on the 8th of August following.

modesty—had no objection to an occasional 'high lunch.' When Moore called for orders, he welcomed him cordially, and suggested, 'We must have a lunch to-day!' The traveller promptly responded, on which the principal, turning to the chief shopman, would say, 'You know what we want; look through Mr. Moore's stock, and don't be afraid of making a good parcel.' The lunch was eaten, the drink was drunk, and a good parcel was invariably made. Thus at the commencement of George Moore's career he did not shrink from expense, provided he could do a large business." This was not a very elevating life; still it was the life that George Moore had been trained for, and which he had to follow faithfully and zealously.

He was found to be too good for town travelling. After about eighteen months, his employer sent him on the Liverpool and Manchester circuit. He was then only twenty-three. Indeed, he had scarcely reached manhood. Yet he was selected to occupy this important position. The Liverpool and Manchester district had been badly worked, and the business had fallen off. He had now to take the necessary means to revive and restore it.

There was only one method—Work! Work! Nor did he spare himself. He worked early in the morning, and late at night. Sometimes he "worked" a town before breakfast; making early appointments with the drapers beforehand. After breakfast he packed up his goods, drove off to another place (for there were no railways in those days), and finished his work at a third town within the day.

By this means he soon established a large business. That he increased the returns of his employers did not surprise them so much, as the shortness of the time during which he performed his journeys. This arose from his never losing a moment. He had nothing of the dawdler about him. When he had finished his work in one town, he was immediately ready to start for another.

He used afterwards to say that the position he occupied was very trying, but that it tested the stuff of which a man was made. With him " it was a constant struggle between pride and sensitiveness," though in later years he always considered it to be the best testing work for a young man, before his promotion to places of greater trust.

George Moore was modest in his success. He claimed credit for nothing but his perseverance. His account of the matter always was, " The drapers cannot do without Fisher's goods ; " but his contemporary travellers attributed his success more to his powers of persuasion and his capacity for work, than to the qualities of his wares.

At the inns which he frequented, he was regarded as a sort of hero. The other travellers used to pack up his goods, and thus help him on his way. They took pride in his success and boasted of his greatness. A young traveller who had just entered the northern circuit arrived at the " Star " Hotel, Manchester, while about a dozen travellers were helping George to pack up his goods. " Who's that young fellow they are making such a fuss about ? " " Oh ! It's George ! " " And who's George ? " " What ? Don't you know the NAPOLEON OF WATLING STREET ? Let me introduce you ! "

One of his fellow-warehousemen at Fisher's having been compelled to leave London on account of bad health, accidentally met George Moore at Manchester. The young man had by this time recovered from his illness, and was again ready for work. George immediately interested himself in his behalf. He introduced him to a thriving Manchester firm, by whom he was employed ; and there he settled down and prospered.

The gentleman is still alive, and is proud to record his recollections of George Moore. "Whenever he came to Manchester," he says, "I assisted him with his stock in the evenings. Through his geniality he drew around him a large circle of business friends. These helped him to pack up his stock when he was about to set out upon his journeys. It was no uncommon thing to see at the " Star" Hotel a dozen or twenty of them with him in an evening.

"On one occasion, when he was passing along the corridor by the bar, an order came from the head-waiter's room for 'Two brandies and cold water for No. 47.' 'Why,' said George Moore, 'that's my number! What's the meaning of this?' The explanation given was, that a friend had called upon the waiter, and had ordered the brandies to be put to Mr. Moore's account, thinking that this might easily be done where the account was so large and so difficult to check. After ample apologies and promises from the waiter to book no more fictitious orders for No. 47, Mr. Moore overlooked the offence, and continued to use the 'Star' as his hotel while in Manchester."

To show the energy with which he carried on his business, it may be mentioned that on one occasion he arrived in Manchester, and after unpacking his goods, he called upon his first customer. He was informed that one of his opponents had reached the town the day before, and would remain there for a day or two more. "Then," said Moore, "it's of no use wasting my time here, with my competitor before me." He returned to his hotel, called some of his friends about him to help him to repack his stock, drove off to Liverpool, commenced business next day, and secured the greater part of the orders before the arrival of his opponent.

His extraordinary success surprised his employers.

They had never had such a traveller before. His quickness, his shrewdness, his integrity, his honourable dealings, his knowledge of character, were the subject of their constant admiration. He had secured their perfect confidence, and they gave him full scope. After about six months they began to think whether they might not be able to turn his services to further account. The business in Ireland had fallen off. It had become small by degrees. In fact there was scarcely any of it left. The trade had been carried off by an active traveller named Groucock, partner in a firm which had been recently established. Fisher and Robinson accordingly determined to send their young traveller to Ireland to bring back their trade, and if possible to extend it.

The order was accordingly sent to George Moore to start for Ireland. Before doing so, he took a short holiday in Cumberland. It will be observed that he always had a hearty interest in his native county, and now that he had a little time to spare, he would enjoy himself for a few days amongst his friends. He went from Carlisle to Wigton. He was amazed at the littleness of the place. When he first saw it he thought it a large town ; and so it was, compared with the hamlet of Mealsgate. But now that he had been in London, walking through miles upon miles of streets to deliver his brother's parcels, or taking orders for his employer, Wigton seemed to have shrunk into the smallest possible dimensions. He could walk from one end of the town to the other in a few minutes. He called upon all his old friends. They received him with enthusiasm. His old master, Messenger, had disappeared. He could not maintain his business after his apprentice had left. Like the bees, he had winged his way southward.

But George did not stay long at Wigton. His principal object was to see his father, his brothers, and his sisters at Mealsgate. There he found the old house, the old brook, the old stables, the old trees, the old fields. While everything had been changing with him, nothing had changed there. Age had told upon his father; he was only able to sit in the inglenuik, leaving the entire management of the farm to his eldest son, Thomas.

The old man received George with the warmest affection. "Weel, George, how art thou getting on?" "Oh, bravely! bravely! I am just on my way to Ireland to work up the business there." He looked at George's face. It was the same face, but yet it was different. George had left the old place a boy; he had returned to it a man. Time had written its lines upon his youthful features. They were keen and eager, and yet they were joyous. His manner was quicker and more active. His London life had evidently sharpened him up. He was strong, healthy, and resolute.

George spent part of his brief holiday in wandering over the scenes of his boyhood. He lingered by the edge of the stream where he had caught his first fish. He wandered along the hedges where he had discovered his first bird's nest. He went up to Bolton School, where he had been thrashed by Blackbird Wilson. He went up and down the banks of the Ellen. He saw the fields on which he had shorn. In the evenings at sunset he would lean upon his father's field-gate, and listen to the faint far-off sounds that came to him across the tranquil country. How different from the whirl and bustle of London!

He visited the burying-place of his fathers at Torpenhow, and called upon his relatives at Overgates and Kirkland. But his favourite spots were the old towers at Whitehall and Harbybrow, where he had been let down when a boy to harry the rooks' nests. The towers were still in a state of ruin. He dreamt—it was then

only a dream—that these towers might yet become his
own. And yet his dream was fulfilled.

After a few days of delighful recreation, full of
reminiscences of the past—old thoughts and impressions
rising up and meeting him at every step—he at length
prepared to start for Ireland. He was accompanied on
his way by some of his old friends. They went with
him to Allonby, where they dined together; and then
they saw him set sail for Ireland.

Arrived in Dublin, he set to work in right good
earnest to bring back his masters' business. He had
now, as he said, a "grand confidence in himself," and he
was determined to make Fisher's name carry all before
him. He worked very hard, from morn till night. He
was up in the morning early, called upon his customers
during the day, packed up his goods in the evening,
and set off by the night coach for the next town upon
his route. For weeks together the only sleep he secured
was on the outside of a coach; but he slept soundly. In
the intervals of his work, when he felt unrested, he
would throw himself on a sofa and fall sound asleep.

To sleep well is one of the greatest blessings of life.
" Sleep," says Sancho Panza, "wraps one all round like
a blanket." George Moore had the gift, which is common in strong men and great natures, of sleeping almost
at will. When he was worried or overworked he would
say : " Let me have an hour or two's sleep." A resting
space was thus put between the pressure of the past and
the work of the future ; and he came out of his sleep
again strong, cheerful, and vigorous.

Whilst travelling over Ireland he frequently met his
competitor, Groucock, the traveller who had so greatly
interfered with Fisher's Irish business. He was a young
man, though some years older than Moore. He is
described by those who knew him as "of delicate appearance, but very clever and shrewd." Before Moore's

appearance in Ireland, he had taken the lion's share of the lace trade ; but now he had a foeman worthy of his steel.

Moore met Groucock frequently in the course of his journeys. Moore worked with greater celerity, and very soon divided the trade with Groucock. The competition between them became keen. Moore worked harder than ever, and at last he succeeded in getting back all the best customers for Fisher's. " I represented," said Moore, " the best house in the world, and, with all the buoyancy and ambition of youth, I worked hard, and gradually succeeded in taking the largest share of the business."

George once met Groucock at a town in the north of Ireland. Groucock invited him to sup with a friend after the day's work was over. The invitation was accepted. In the course of the evening their plans were discussed. George openly mentioned the town to which he was next due, and at what hour he would start. He afterwards found that Groucock had started the day before him, reached Belfast, and taken up all the orders for lace in the place. This caused some bitterness of feeling between the two travellers. But George, not to be outdone, immediately left Ireland for Liverpool. He worked the place thoroughly, then started for Manchester, and travelled through the great northern towns, working night and day, until he had gone over the whole of the ground, and returned to London full of orders. This in its turn greatly chagrined Groucock, who had intended to take Lancashire on his way home.

In fact Groucock found it necessary to come to terms with his indefatigable competitor. Through a mutual friend, he made overtures to him. He offered him what Moore called " the incredible salary of £500 a year," if he would travel for his house instead of for Fisher's. It was a very tempting offer, for Moore's salary was only

£150 a year—a sum out of which he could barely contrive to live. The wonder is that Fisher and Robinson had not voluntarily increased his salary, considering the enormous business that he had brought to their firm.

But in answer to Groucock's overture, Moore's answer was firm and direct. He at once refused the offer. " I will be a servant for no other house than Fisher's. The only condition upon which I will leave him is a partnership." At length, in self-defence, Groucock yielded to his terms, and in June, 1830, at the age of twenty-four, George Moore entered as partner into the firm of Groucock and Copestake, long afterwards known as that of Groucock, Copestake, and Moore.

Before he left Fisher's he finished one of his most successful journeys. He did not say a word to the customers about his intended change. He returned to London to give up his accounts, and then he made the important announcement to his employers of his altered position in the trade.

CHAPTER VI.

THE firm of Groucock and Copestake was established in 1825. The partners started on a very small scale. Their first place of business was over a trunk-shop at No. 7, Cheapside. One little room contained their little stock of goods. There was small space for clerks or warehousemen. Mr. Copestake was the principal clerk and warehouseman, while Mr. Groucock was employed in travelling for orders.

The business grew by degrees. Mr. Groucock was an active traveller. He largely increased the orders, and at length the room over the trunkmaker's shop became too small: The firm was crowded out by the increasing stock. They looked about for more suitable premises. They found them at No. 62, Friday Street, and took possession of them in 1829; believing that the accommodation would be sufficient for doing a larger business. George Moore was taken in as a partner in the following year; and a removal to more capacious premises was soon found necessary. The firm removed to Bow Churchyard in 1834, and the premises there, with successive alterations and enlargements, still continue the headquarters of the house.

Though the firm had been doing a considerable business throughout the country, their capital in stock,

fixtures, and cash amounted to only £4,650.   To this
George Moore added £670, which, he says, "my ever-
to-be-revered father supplied me with."[1]   The partnership was to be for three years, during which the junior
partner was to receive one-fourth of the profits.   But at
the end of that period, if his partners were not satisfied,
he was to be paid out his share of the capital, and the
engagement was to cease.

Behold now our young hero of twenty-four travelling
partner for the firm of Groucock, Copestake, and Moore.
His power of work at that time must have been extraordinary.   His perfect health, his iron constitution, and
his power of will and perseverance, enabled him to get
through an enormous amount of labour and fatigue.
Some of his fellow-travellers compared him to a lion,
others to an eagle.   He had the power and endurance
of both.

He worked with a will.   He was now working for
himself.   He had still his great hope before him.   He
was ever faithful to his first love ; and now, he thought,
she was coming nearer to him.   " I believe," he afterwards said, " that I never could have surmounted the
difficulties and hardships which I had to encounter, but
for the thought of her.   I thought of her while going
my rounds by day, and I thought of her while travelling
by coach at night.   The thought of her was my greatest
stimulus to exertion."

It has been well said that this episode in Mr. Moore's
busy career shows that the romance of life is not confined to Belgravia, and that it supplies another to the
thousand proofs that a pure and honourable attachment arms a young man against the siren attractions of

---

[1] His father raised 500*l.* by mortgaging his estate.   The remaining 170*l.*
was the money (with accumulated interest) which his great-uncle George
had left him, together with the hair trunk.

idleness, and the "pleasures turned to pain," with which our crowded cities abound.

Mr. Moore selected for his travelling ground the districts in which he had before been so successful while travelling for Fisher—Liverpool, Manchester, Dublin, Belfast, Glasgow, and Edinburgh. Mr. Groucock, who had few equals as a traveller, selected the midland districts, including Nottingham, where he purchased the greater part of the lace sold by the firm. There was another traveller for the southern districts, and a town traveller. This constituted the whole of the travelling staff.

The first year's returns were comparatively small. Trade was very bad. It was a perilous time. A commercial panic existed throughout the country. The political excitement arising from the Reform Bill agitation was very great. There was severe pressure for money; and many of the weaker houses went to the wall. Distress prevailed in Lancashire. Glasgow was almost bankrupt. There were disturbances in Spitalfields and riots at Barnsley. In the midst of these difficulties, trade in lace (a thing that could easily be done without) was one of the first to suffer.

Nevertheless George Moore continued his journeys. Whatever could be done, he did. His usual day's work occupied about sixteen hours. It must also be observed that he worked on Sundays as well as Saturdays. Like many other commercial travellers, he occupied his Sunday mornings in preparing his accounts and looking over his stock. As a rule he was up two nights a week. He would merely throw himself on a sofa for a few hours' sleep before resuming his journey. The thought of resting to take a few hours' pleasure never entered his mind. He was occupied with business, and with business only. It was work, work, from morning till night.

Yet he was of a cheerful and social disposition, and continued to make many friends. He was popular everywhere. Though he outstripped others in the race of commerce, he never made an enemy. At night, when he was making up his accounts, his volunteer friends came round him and helped him to pack up his goods for his next journey. They were always eager to speed him on his way. Even the servants at the various inns which he frequented ran to help him.

Mr. Crampton, who was with him at Fisher's, and afterwards became his partner at Bow Churchyard, says of him at that time—" He made personal friends wherever he went, and he kept them. George Moore's name was a household word all over the country. His friends used to keep their christenings and festive days till he came round ; and he had god-children enough to found a colony."

Mr. Felix Brown, afterwards one of his branch managers, has given the following account of his first introduction to George Moore :—" The first time I saw him was at the Union Hotel, Birmingham, at eleven o'clock at night, in the year 1832, when I assisted him and his partner to take their stock. I was struck with his quickness and kindness ; and as I was constantly taking models for my own action in life, I shelved him as one. I suppose the good impressions then made were mutual ; for in a few days I was engaged to represent the firm, when I took the senior partner's journey. In my efforts to succeed, I was greatly stimulated by the indomitable perseverance of Mr. Moore, and by his generous, frank manner of doing business. I soon discovered that he could do with a moiety of most men's hours of rest ; for though his body might be reposing, his mind was at work.

" On my second introduction to him at Dublin, where I was summoned to assist him, we occupied a double-bedded room. My usual habit was, when I laid my head upon my pillow, to forget the world and its cares, and go to sleep. But on this occasion my companion kept talking to me, I trying hard to keep awake and listen. But when I dropped into the stupor of slumber I was suddenly wakened up with a voice—'Brown! Brown! what a fellow you are to sleep!' At this time I was a little timid in my new life, and to shake this out of me he sent me to call upon his most important customers, quietly enjoying his practical though useful jokes upon me.

"Success covers many shortcomings. This being the case with myself, I established a confidence with him which was never shaken, but strengthened and grew until his death. During my forty-five years connection with him I observed this consistent attachment to those who had worked for him and with him in his early life; and when he had attained to eminence, none were ever more welcome at his hospitable board than the honest, upright companions of his youth. My opportunities of meeting him in the early career of the house were few, but when we came within a few miles of each other in the course of our respective journeys, we always embraced the opportunity of meeting. His custom was to invite all our customers to dine at my hotel, when he made me the star of the evening.

"During the first ten years I took no holiday. This rather surprised him. Being popular on my journey, I was unwilling to give it up to any one who might be sent thither to relieve me. I told him so. The prompt answer was, 'Will you take a holiday if *I* take your journey?' I accepted his offer. He took my place, and greatly exceeded the returns over the corresponding month of the preceding year. He told all my friends that I had gone to France, and that on my return they would hardly know me because of my French accent and manners. I was often surprised at his memory. He remembered the smallest incident, whether in business or philanthropy. Indeed I shall never forget his kindness to myself and to all connected with me."

Mr. Moore had, of course, many rebuffs to encounter in the course of his journeys as a commercial traveller. With sufficient confidence in his own abilities, he had no personal pride. Though rebuffed a dozen times, though bowed out of a shop again and again without an order, he would call again with his "Good morning," as brisk and cheerful as ever. He used to say that it was a bad plan to fall out with a customer, however rude he might be. He talked with them, he joked with them, he amused them, and finally he brought them round to his side,— which was to order a good parcel.

Many are the stories still told by commercial travellers about George Moore's determination to get orders. He would not be denied. If refused at first, he resorted to all sorts of expedients until he succeeded. On one occasion he sold the clothes off his back to get an order. A tenacious draper in a Lancashire town refused to deal with him. The draper was quite satisfied with the firm that supplied him, and he would make no change. This became known amongst the commercial travellers at the hotel, and one of them wagered with George Moore that he would not obtain an order.

George set out to try. The draper saw him entering the shop, and cried out, "All full! all full, Mr. Moore! I told you so before!" "Never mind," said George, "you won't object to a crack." "Oh, no!" said the draper. They cracked about many things, and then George Moore, calling the draper's attention to a new coat which he wore, asked "What he thought of it?" "It's a capital coat," said the draper. "Yes, first rate; made in the best style by a first-rate London tailor." The draper looked at it again, and again admired it.

"Why," said George, "You are exactly my size; it's quite new, I'll sell it you." "What's the price?" "Twenty-five shillings." "What? that's very cheap." "Yes, it's a great bargain." "Then I'll buy it," said the draper.

George went back to his hotel, donned another suit, and sent the "great bargain," to the draper. George calling again, the draper offered to pay him. "No, no," said George, "I'll book it; you've opened an account." The draper afterwards became one of his best customers.

On another occasion a draper at Newcastle-upon-Tyne was called upon many times without any result. He was always "full." In fact he had no intention of opening an account with the new firm. Mr. Moore got to know that he was fond of a particular kind of snuff —rappee, with a touch of beggar's brown in it. He provided himself with a box in London, and had it filled with the snuff. When at Newcastle, he called upon the draper, but was met as usual with the remark, "Quite full, quite full, sir." "Well," said Mr. Moore, "I scarcely expected an order, but I called upon you for a reference." "Oh, by all means."

In the course of conversation George took out his snuff-box, took a pinch, and put it in his pocket. After a short interval he took it out again, took another pinch, and said, "I suppose you are not guilty of this bad habit?" "Sometimes," said the draper. George handed him the box. He took a pinch with zest, and said, through the snuff, "Well, that's very fine!" George had him now. He said, "Let me present you with the box; I have plenty more." The draper accepted the box. No order was asked; but the next time George called upon him he got his first order, and numerous others followed.

With George Moore's energy and laboriousness the

business rapidly increased. At the end of the three years' partnership, he had made himself so necessary to the firm, that his services could not be dispensed with. He was accordingly made equal partner with the others, taking his third share of the profits. "Groucock and I," he says, "extended the business so rapidly that poor Copestake was often very hard up to pay the accounts for lace. I did almost double the business of any other traveller on the road. Had it pleased God to lay me up for three months, I believe it might have placed the house in difficulty ; but I was as strong as a lion, and worked generally sixteen or eighteen hours a day."

At this time, and for nine years after, Moore had no place to call his own,—not even a lodging. He was travelling about during the whole year, not sleeping more than two or three nights in one place. He arranged his plans, however, so as to reach London the week before Christmas. He looked forward to this day as the great event of the year. A large company of friends was invited to meet him. The enjoyment and hospitality of those days, though it might be of a rough and simple character, lived long in the recollection of many besides himself. Some have said, "There have been no Christmases like them since." The gatherings took place in one of the rooms of the warehouse in Friday Street, and afterwards in Bow Church Yard. Moore always slept in a bed made up for him in the house. This was his only holiday during the year.

There were other things to be talked about by the partners during these annual meetings. There was the position of the house amidst the failures that were constantly occurring—the breakings of banks, the scarcity of money, the knowing whom to trust and whom not to trust. It was indeed a time of great difficulty, and one of peril for so young a house, with so small a capital at its command. Mr. Moore says of this period, "Although Mr. Copestake never went through the hardships that I did, he must have had a great deal of mental anxiety to provide money. I laboured day and night. Our business increased every year. It was my duty to initiate the new travellers and drill them into their work, and to open out to them fresh journeys. In the course of my peregrinations I visited every market-town in England, Scotland, Ireland, and Wales, with very few exceptions. I also visited the Nottingham market, where we had to thank the manufacturers for their always unbounded confidence. Groucock and I also travelled through most of the towns of Belgium and France to buy lace, and to open out operations for the future. Independently of this, I worked my own journey single-handed. For twelve years I never missed, excepting once, starting for Ireland on the first Monday of every month."

George Moore looked upon the Irish voyages as his *rest* for the month. So soon as he got on board he went to his berth, and slept soundly until the ship was in sight of port. It was not, however, always so easy to get on board. His voyage was usually undertaken from Liverpool; but sometimes from other ports. The passenger-boats forty-five years ago were very different from what they are now. There were few steamers at that time. Most of the voyages were made by sailing-ships. Hence the occasional slowness of the voyages from England to Ireland. It sometimes took sixteen hours to get across; though we have heard of a case in which it took six weeks to bring a regiment of militia from Cork to Yarmouth.

On one occasion George Moore embarked at Plymouth for Dublin. The vessel by which he was to sail lay at anchor some distance from the shore. It was a wild winter's night, and the sea was running high. The captain at first refused to weigh anchor, but at Moore's urgent request he consented to take him on board. His next difficulty was to induce the sailors to face the sea in an open boat ; but at length he hired a sufficient number of men to row him out to the ship. The boxes containing his stock of lace were brought down to the shore and hoisted into the boat, lying high and dry upon the beach. Moore had a servant with him, much older than himself, to look after the boxes. This man's fears so far overcame him that he lost all self-command, and entreated his master not to endanger his life and his lace in that open boat. "Stop behind then," said Moore, "for I am determined to go." He then sprang into the boat and signalled to the sailors to start. It was, however, thought necessary to lash them together with ropes to prevent them being washed into the sea.

The boat was then launched through the surf, and for some moments it was hidden from sight by the waves. It was more than an hour before the boatmen fought their way to the vessel through one of the wildest storms that broke along that rocky coast. Eager and friendly eyes watched them until they reached the ship at anchor. The lace boxes were hoisted in ; Moore followed last ; and at length, when the storm had somewhat abated, the ship sailed for Dublin and reached the port in safety.

At another time Mr. Moore had a narrow escape from drowning while crossing Morecambe Sands. He had been travelling in Cumberland, by Carlisle, Maryport, and Whitehaven. He had arrived at Cartmel, in Lancashire, near the head of Morecambe Bay. He was driving his own two-horse conveyance, containing a large quantity of valuable lace. Being unwilling to lose a moment, he determined to make a short cut across the sands to Lancaster, where he was next due. But he seems not to have known the dangers of the journey.

When the tide at that part of the coast is low, the sea runs very far out. Only a little strip of blue is seen in the distance. A large extent of sand and mud is laid bare at the head of the bay. From Cartmel to Poulton-le-Sands, is about nine miles across. If the journey can be accomplished in that way, it saves a distance of about fifty miles round the rivers Kent and Leven. The sands had long been used as a sort of desert highway. It was the custom to have a chartered guide, called the Carter, to attend and conduct strangers across the sands, which were constantly shifting. The registers of the parish of Cartmel show that not fewer than a hundred persons have been buried in the church-yard who were drowned in attempting to cross the sands. This was independent of the numerous burials in the churchyards of adjacent parishes on both sides of the bay. As late as the spring of 1857 a party of ten or twelve young men and women, who were proceeding to the hiring market at Lancaster, were overtaken by the tide, and the whole of them were drowned.

George Moore reached Cartmel towards evening. He did not take time to inquire as to the state of the tide, but drove off at once towards the sands. It was a reckless undertaking, as he soon found out. He drove along with speed. But he was scarcely half way across the sands before he saw that the tide was turning. The man who was with him in the carriage, jumped out and went back. But George, believing that he was on the right track, drove on. The water was now approaching. It was coming on like a mill race. He flogged his horses as he had never flogged them before. The sand shifted under the horses' feet. Then he turned them to one side, and drove them where their feet held. A mirage rose before him, and he seemed to see the land. But it disappeared and reap-peared again and again. The situation became terrible.

The water was now upon him, and the boxes behind him were swimming. He drove first this way, and then that. The firm ground failed him. He was driving towards destruction, for he was driving towards the open sea!

At length he heard a loud shout. It proceeded from some person to the left. He looked round and discerned through the haze a man on horseback shouting and waving his hands. It was one of the mounted guides stationed on the shore to watch the dangerous tracks. The man spurred his horse into the water, suddenly turned round, and waved to the man in the carriage to come onward in that direction. Moore understood his position at once. His horses were now swimming. He pulled them round by sheer force in the direction of the land. By dint of flogging and struggling the horses at length touched the ground. They dragged the carriage up the bank, and Moore's life was saved.

To return to the results of the partnership. At the end of the second year, George Moore's share of the profits amounted to £695. His capital invested in the concern was now £848. The income he had made by his year's hard work did not amount to much, but he was laying the foundations of a large business. For some time it doubled itself yearly. All the partners had their hearts in the work. They lived economically. They put all their spare capital into the concern. Like Moore, Groucock was constantly on the road. When not travelling in England he was travelling abroad, buying lace to supply the constantly-increasing demand. Copestake confined himself to the house. He managed the finances of the firm. He was an excellent warehouseman. He never spent a day out of the office. Mr. Moore says of him : " For half the time that I have been a partner with him he never took a day's holiday. I never took a day for the first thirteen years during all all the time that I travelled."

With all these heads and hands at work, the firm could not but thrive. The business increased from year to year, and yet it was carried on with a comparatively small capital. At the beginning of 1832 the firm owed £14,133, whilst the stock on hand was valued only at £8,435, though the book-debts and cash in hand amounted to £14,406. In fact the firm was trading close upon its means, and it could only keep alive by turning over its capital again and again in the course of the year. Then there were the bad debts, and in such a time of mercantile distress they must have been considerable.

The position of the firm began to be talked about amongst men in the lace trade. One of their special rivals made no secret of the matter. He told his friends that Groucock, Copestake, and Moore were trading beyond their capital, and would soon be unable to meet their liabilities. The credit of merchants is a vital point. Their virtue, like that of Cæsar's wife, must be beyond suspicion. Stories like these, whispered about, soon affect the credit of the merchant. They cease to be able to buy on like terms with others. It was therefore found necessary to put a stop to these rumours in a summary manner. An action was commenced against a particular slanderer in the Court of Common Pleas. The case was tried before Lord Abinger and a special jury. The counsel for the firm was Mr. Thesiger, afterwards Lord Chelmsford; and the counsel for the defendant were the Attorney-General (Sir J. Campbell) and Sir F. Pollock.

In the course of the evidence it came out that the defendant had gone to the London agent of Messrs. Heathcoat, and Co., the large lace manufacturers at Nottingham, and informed him that there was a great deal of talk in the trade about a lace house in a Church-yard. "Do you mean Groucock and Company?" asked

the agent. "Yes, it was Groucock and Company." He
went on to tell the agent that the house could not get
over the 4th of March, having made a bad debt of
£2,000 in Sheffield; and besides, that the great expense to which they had gone in travellers and clerks,
and the many losses they had suffered, rendered it
certain that they must stop! The defendant went down
to Nottingham and propagated the same statements;
the result of which was that Groucock and Co.'s traveller
was prevented buying goods at the ordinary price.

It was a wily and deep-laid scheme for the ruin of the
firm. "It is impossible," said Mr. Thesiger, "to estimate what injury may have been done to the plaintiffs
by the course which has been pursued. Private credit,
like public, depends entirely upon opinion. The plaintiffs
are persons of great respectability; their trade has
flourished: but however deeply their roots may have
struck, and however widely their branches may have
been spread, still their whole business may be over-
thrown by the breath of suspicion."

After a careful summing-up by Lord Abinger, the jury
gave a unanimous verdict for the plaintiffs—damages,
three hundred pounds. They did not place the amount
to the credit of the firm, but divided it amongst the London charities. The honour and reputation of the house
were thus vindicated. The fact of their having been
assailed in such a public manner by their rival, brought
many new friends to their help. They were even offered
numerous sums of money on loan; but they declined
to accept these proffered kindnesses. The trial gave
them an additional start, and they carried on their
increasing trade more successfully than ever.

Mr. Moore had in the meantime continued his friendship with Mr. Ray, his former employer. He saw his
little rosebud growing up into womanly grace and beauty.
At length he told his secret. He was refused. After

this, an interval of five years passed. Five years is a long time in a man's life. It makes ties and breaks them. Still he went on remembering her. Like all true lovers, he always had doubts as to his success in winning her. As he expresses it—"he had served for her with an aching heart longer than Jacob served for Rachel."

At length he heard that some favoured suitor had many chances of being with her, which were quite unattainable for him. Mr. Ray was still most friendly, and George continued his visits to the family, when in town. With his usual perseverance he at last succeeded. On the 12th of August, 1840, he led his first love, Eliza Flint Ray, to the altar. And thus his boyish resolution was at last fulfilled.

CHAPTER VII.

TRIP TO AMERICA—HUNTING.

MR. MOORE'S marriage did not greatly interfere with his business pursuits. His honeymoon tour lasted only a week. He went back to his journeys again. His first house in London was at 17, Canterbury Villas, Maida Hill, but he was rarely at home. He set out for Ireland on the first of every month; and he continued to make his ordinary rounds in the northern towns of England during the rest of the month.

At length, in 1841, after the business of the firm had become well established, he partially gave up travelling. They had now three town travellers and ten country travellers. Mr. Moore confined himself to drilling the new men, and introducing them to his customers. When a journey was not working well he took it in hand himself, in order to give it another push.

When a traveller was laid up, or went on his holiday, Mr. Moore took his journey until he returned. It was difficult work for the traveller to do any business on that road for some time after. On one occasion Mr. Moore took the journey into Wales, and sold so many goods that the traveller who followed him had almost nothing to do during his next journey.

The business had by this time so much increased, that the premises in Bow Churchyard were again enlarged.

Houses in Bread Street were bought and included in the warehouse. Amongst these was the house erected in place of that in which John Milton was born. A bust of John Milton stands on the site of his birthplace. The house itself was destroyed in the Great Fire of 1666.

When George Moore gave up travelling, and took to office work, the change of occupation soon told upon his health. During his journeys he had lived for the most part out of doors. He had breathed fresh air, taken plenty of exercise, and enjoyed the best of health. But now that he had become a warehouseman, and sat at a desk in a stuffy part of the warehouse, breathing impure air and taking little exercise, his health gave way. He began to be hasty and irritable. From being cheerful, he became sombre and melancholy. He had an excruciating pain in his head. He could not sleep at night. He took his business to bed with him, and rose up with it again in the morning. Bow Churchyard was his nightmare. Everything else was prospering with him. Life was the same as before, and yet he could not enjoy it. In short, he was ill; and then he thought of the doctor.

He consulted Surgeon Lawrence,[1] of Whitehall Place, one of the most distinguished men of his day. After stating his case, Mr. Lawrence said, " I see how it is. You have got the City Disease. You are working your brain too much and your body too little." " But what am I to do?" asked Mr. Moore. " Well, I'll tell you. Physic is of no use in a case such as yours. Your medicine must be the open air. You may spend part of your time in gardening; or you may fish, or shoot, or hunt!" " I cannot garden," replied the patient; " I never fired a gun in my life; fishing would drive me mad; and I think that I must take to hunting." " Can you ride?" asked Mr. Lawrence. " Not much! I rode my father's blind horse barebacked when a boy; but I

---

[1] Afterwards Sir William Lawrence, Bart.

have not ridden since." "Well," said Mr. Lawrence, "You had better go down to Brighton and ride over the downs there; but you must take care not to break your neck in hunting."

In the meantime Mr. Lawrence recommended George Moore to go to Mr. Deville, the phrenologist in the Strand, to have his head examined. Phrenology was very much talked about in those days. George Combe and James Simpson were its great apostles, and many medical men believed in it. Mr. Moore says that Mr. Lawrence was not a strong believer, but that he was curious to compare the report of Mr. Deville with his own impressions as to his patient's brain. Mr. Moore walked directly from Mr. Lawrence's surgery to Mr. Deville's office, so that there could be no concert between them. To those who do not believe in phrenology, the report, given below,[1] will be considered a remarkably good "guess" as to Mr. Moore's general character.

[1] "This is a large brain, with a good deal of power. If called fairly into action and fairly exercised, must take a good station in society, but being subject to act with great energy, more particularly under excitement, it will require some care not to overwork it. The moral sentiments, the feelings and propensities, being nearly equally balanced, everything that is likely to excite the latter should be avoided.

"The intellectual regions being large, you should, with but little effort, possess a highly useful general knowledge, and be well fitted for the law, the bar, a scientific, mechanical, mercantile, or physiological occupation. Kind to the young, and warm and zealous in friendship, it may require a little exertion occasionally to hold in check the lower feelings. Anger, a little smart if offended, but soon over upon a kindly feeling being shown.

"Firmness and determination are strong points in the character. The views taken and opinions put forward not readily given up; and if a little excited, strongly expressing the views taken, having the power, by a command of words, to put forward and advocate the same; but a slight modification of the feelings manifested at times might be very useful.

"Those powers fit you to act as a delegate to represent the views of a body, or others; being sensitive to proper positions in society, a motive for some of the actions, but not stooping to servile means to obtain them. A strong sense of honour and justice; not bigoted upon religion.

"Not at a loss for words to express your views and language easily. History, science, mathematics, mechanics, and philosophy may be readily applied to highly useful purposes. Here is power for mirth, humour, and imitation, drawing, or something in the arts, though colouring will require attention, if not some difficulty. Fond of system and method, with a dis-

Mr. Moore proceeded to Brighton with his wife. He hired a horse and hunted with the harriers across the Downs. He managed to keep his seat. The horse he rode was not frisky, nor were there any fences to leap. He hunted two or three times a week, during the month, while he remained at Brighton. He now thought that he was a sufficiently good rider to follow the hounds across country.

Shortly after his return to London he went to his first fox-hunt. The meet was at Chipping Ongar, about thirty miles from town. He sent his horse overnight to meet Colonel Conyer's foxhounds; and he himself started next morning at six, with two friends. He wore white cords, and was rather smartly got up for the occasion. The day was fine; the meet at the cover was most in-spiriting—men, dogs, and horses—sky, sun, and land-scape—were splendid. A fox was found. Tally-ho! Tally-ho! and away they went. Moore's first jump was over a rotten bank fence. The horse, not getting sufficiently forward, tumbled back into a stagnant ditch, with Moore under. After great difficulty, man and horse were at length got out, the rider covered with mud, and his white cords blackened. But his pluck was up, and determined to go straight, he remounted, and set the horse again at the fence. He got over and went on at a gallop.

He had some difficulty in sticking on. The horse did not care for jumping. When he came to a hedge, he preferred rushing through it, to jumping over it. But there were ditches and walls that *must* be jumped. On

---

like to gaudy colours in dress or furniture. Some feeling for poetry and music if cultivated.

"In conclusion, it is difficult to say what such a brain, with perseverance, could not do, than what it is capable of doing."

"Signed,   JAMES DEVILLE.

"*January* 10, 1841."

such occasions Moore usually went over the horse's head, and picked himself together on the other side. He mounted again and pushed on, nothing daunted. If others could follow the hounds, why should not he? Wherever a jump was to be taken, he would try it. Over he went. Another tumble! No matter. After a desperate run, he got seven tumbles. Sometimes he was down; sometimes the horse was down; and sometimes both were down together.

At the end of the run the horse was blown, and thoroughly done up. Old Colonel Conyers—Master of the hounds—seeing George Moore's bloody face, his smashed hat, his ragged and dirty clothes—came up to him and said, "Young man, you have much more pluck than prudence. If you don't take care you will be getting your neck broken some day; I advise you to go home." Of course the Colonel had no idea that the young man was merely following his doctor's prescription. At all events Moore went away, for the fox was killed and the hunt was over. He concludes his first day's hunting experience with these words: "I was nothing the worse. On returning to the inn, I changed my clothes, and drove home the same night, having driven sixty miles that day, besides the run."

He adds a few words about bold riding. "Whatever other people may say about riding to hounds, I have always contended that no man ever rides bold unless he has had a few good tumbles. This, my first day, took away all fear; and ever after, if I rode a really good horse that I had confidence in, I was generally in the right place in the run, and at the end. I always contend that more accidents take place with timid riders than with bold ones."

On his next visit to his doctor he was recommended to take a long rest, and to try a change of scene if possible. Lawrence advised him to go to Australia, or

America, or the Cape of Good Hope—anywhere for a long rest. Mr. Moore had not had a real holiday for about nineteen years—not since he had entered Flint, Ray, and Co.'s in 1825. While he travelled for Fisher's, his life was full of hard work. He had now been travelling eleven years for his own house. During that time he never had a holiday. He had been burning the candle at both ends, and now he was suffering for it.

He at length made up his mind to set out upon his first holiday. His partners were rejoiced at his proposal, for they had observed how much his health had been failing of late. The journey must be done at once. One evening he went home to his wife and said, " You must get my things ready: I am going to America to-morrow!" She was of course surprised. " Why did you not tell me before?" " Well, it was of no use unsettling your mind beforehand. Now I am ready to go." His preparations were easily made. Commercial travellers are ready to start in any direction on a moment's notice. His baggage was accordingly got ready, and by cockcrow the following morning he was off on his journey to America.

He sailed from Liverpool for New York on the 17th of August, 1844, by the *Great Western* steamship. No subject of interest occurred during the voyage. His principal business was tramping the deck, smoking cigars, and consuming meals at the ordinary intervals. " I laid down," said Mr. Moore, " the following rules, which I hope to be able to keep :—Rise at half-past seven, walk on deck till breakfast, read at least six chapters in the Bible the first thing after breakfast, then walk on deck for an hour till lunch, afterwards write for an hour, then walk on deck for another hour, then read any books I have till dinner, between dinner and tea walk and talk, and take stock of the passengers, of whom there are all sorts, then whist until ten, and turn in."

After a pleasant voyage, which extended for about

fourteen days, the *Great Western* reached New York on the 31st of August. Mr. Moore, during his holiday, combined business with pleasure. Though he went to churches and theatres during his travels, his principal visits were to the importers of lace. He had obtained letters of introduction from Barings, Overend and Gurney, and others, which opened all doors to him. A few notes may be given from his journal. He first mastered the geography of the City of New York, and then went the round of his calls :—

"A long day. Observed with regret the loose mode of doing business. All busy. They appear to think good times will last for ever. Nearly all have failed at one time or another. Bankers discounting liberally at present, and all appear to be trying who can sell cheapest. . . . Took a turn among the retail shops to see their system. Mr. T. A. Stewart, Broadway, and a few others, are done upon the London style, but the lower class take any prices they can get.

"Had a long consultation with my old friend and fellow-apprentice, Joseph Blanc, who is in prosperity, esteemed by all who know him, and in possession of the best information about the standing of the different parties in the dry-goods trade. Had interviews with Brown Brothers (the Rothschilds of America), from whom I received marked kindness and most liberal offers to transact our money operations. . . . Dined with Joseph Blanc at his house in Broadway. This was one of the pleasantest days I spent since I left my own fireside. It brought old recollections to my memory that had long since been buried—scenes of my boyhood, when Blanc and I were serving our apprenticeship in Wigton."

During the course of Mr. Moore's visit to New York he saw many of the public institutions, more particularly the New York Infant Orphan Asylum, with which he was very much interested,—being himself a subscriber to the London Orphan Asylum. He also inspected the New York Hospital or Bloomsbury Asylum for the Insane, the Tombs, one of the New York prisons, and some public places of resort. "One morning," he says, " I bought three splendid racoon skins, one of them for Mr. J——, of Liverpool, who, when I was about to leave my native shore, put a magnificent diamond ring upon my finger, as a mark of gratitude, he said, for a disinterested act on my part towards him long, long ago, and which he considered had been the ground-work of his fortune."

After remaining about six weeks in New York, Mr. Moore journeyed southward to Philadelphia. He there called upon the commercial people whom he wished to see. He found, however, that they were mostly supplied from New York. He was delighted with the Fairmount Waterworks, which bountifully provided the inhabitants of Philadelphia with fresh water; the site on which they stand commanding a magnificent view of the city. He also visited the grave of the immortal Franklin, the splendid Gerard College for the education and maintenance of orphans, the Pennsylvanian Hospital founded by William Penn, and the Eastern Penitentiary, where he saw the solitary system in full operation.

"The solitary system," he says, "is abominable. I could not walk a happy man beneath the open sky by day, or lay me down upon my bed at night, with the consciousness that one human creature was suffering this awful punishment, and I the cause of it, or consenting to it in any degree. . . . I was much interested with one prisoner, who had nearly completed his seven years. He stated that he had been guilty of stealing one hundred dollars, and that, his conscience upbraiding him, he took them back previous to being found out; and still he was sentenced to this frightful punishment. I left the place labouring under a feeling of melancholy.

I next visited the Blind Asylum, where we saw the system of reading by raised letters beautifully carried out. They take thirty boys and thirty girls upon the charity, and educate them so that they can get a living in after life. Strange to say, they sometimes get married. I bought some of their work, contributed to the charity, and left much pleased."

His next visit was to Baltimore, the capital of Maryland—"the first *Slave* State that I had ever been in. A shudder involuntarily came over me. Having worked up my imagination, I fancied every black I saw was a slave. Many of them, however, are free. The women here, as in Philadelphia, are very handsome, though they look rather delicate." He then went to the Capitol at Washington, and from thence again to New York. After receiving his letters from home and replying to them, he set out for a short journey in Canada. He sailed up the river Hudson, and describes the magnificent scenery as he passed along. He visited Albany, Troy, and the Shaker village of Watervleit. Of the Shakers he says, "All the possessions and revenues of the settlement are thrown into a common stock, which is managed by the elders. They are capital farmers, and good breeders of cattle ; honest and just in all their transactions ; the only class of people, gentle or simple, who can resist thievish tendencies in horse-dealing."

Mr. Moore's next route was along the Champlain Canal. The boats had been taken off Lake George for the winter. "This fifty miles of road," he says, "was the most frightful travelling I ever had. Great black bears prowl here. Trees and planks were laid across the road to fill up the holes. There were frequent openings in the bridges that a horse might have gone slap into. After going two or three feet into holes, and after many, as I supposed, hairbreadth escapes, we at length arrived at White Hall, at the junction of the canal and lake navigation." Mr. Moore then steamed along Lake Champlain—one of the most beautiful lakes in America—surrounded by majestic scenery. He reached St. John's, within the frontier of Canada. From thence he proceeded to Montreal by railway and steamer. At Montreal he called upon his customers, and "found them all most civil and polite : indeed I cannot speak too highly of them."

From Montreal he went to Quebec. There was little business to be done there. His voyage was for the most part one of pleasure. And yet the weather was cold and muggy ; winter was fast drawing on. The sail down the St. Lawrence was nevertheless most agreeable. He went over the most notable sights in Quebec—the Plains of Abraham, where Wolfe fell, and where a paltry monument had been erected ; and over the fortifications, where the ingenuity of military skill had been exhausted to produce another Gibraltar.

He next proceeded westward, to Kingston, Toronto, Hamilton, and Niagara. His visit to the Falls was one of the great events of his life. It is not necessary to give his description. Indeed no one has yet been able to describe the impression which Niagara makes upon the mind. " It is wonderful to think," says Mr. Moore, "that the outpourings of the lakes—Superior, Huron, Erie, Michigan, and St. Clare—covering a surface of 150,000 square miles, all roll down the 157 feet fall,— with sixteen times the force of all the water-power of Great Britain."

From Niagara Mr. Moore went by Buffalo, Rochester, and Albany to New York. There he took leave of all his friends and customers, and went on to Boston, to visit it on his way homeward. The weather was wet and dirty ; a cold east wind was blowing ; and he did not see the town to advantage. " The houses," he says, "are bright, and have a gay appearance. The sign-boards are painted in gaudy colours. The gilded letters are so *very* gilded ; the bricks are so *very* red ; the blinds and area-railings are so *very* green. The plates upon the street-doors are marvellously bright and twinkling ; yet all looks so slight and unsubstantial in appearance. The suburbs are, if possible, still more unsubstantial-looking. Nevertheless, the city is a beautiful one, and cannot fail to impress all strangers favourably."

Mr. Moore called upon the representative of his house in Boston,—Mr. Schofield, of Henry and Co.'s, Manchester,—" the most decided man of business I had met with for many a long day." He was much impressed by the Boston merchants. " They are first-rate business men," he says ; " no auctions, which I detest ; no over-stocks, which will be the ruin of New York ; everything is well assorted, and in good condition. In fact I felt as if I had been in an English town ; for the men of business here are more English-like than the Americans generally." Mr. Moore was pleased with his visit to Boston ; the more especially as it opened up a large new business connection for his firm.

He had now done his work ; and he was ready to leave by the next steamer for England. Before he left he made this entry in his notebook : " I am bound to add that, during my visit to America, I have met with the most open, frank, and communicative people that I ever came in contact with ; and also that I frequently had occasion to blush for my own ignorance both about Europe and America. To use a common expression, the Americans are a wide-awake people. Their schools, their cheap publications, their thirst for knowledge, and their naturally quick perceptions, place them above the usual level in society. America must rise, and that it will become a great country is my earnest wish and belief."

Mr. Moore left Boston by the *Acadia* on the 1st of

November, 1844, and reached Liverpool in fourteen days,—after an absence of about three months. He came home like a giant refreshed. His health was restored. He had recovered his brightness of spirit, and was ready again to enter upon his labours with renewed zest and vigour.

One of the first results of Mr. Moore's visit to America was the establishment of a branch of the firm at Nottingham. They also erected a lace-factory in the town. It was begun in January, 1845, and finished at the end of the same year. The lace manufactured was of various kinds and qualities,—from twopence per dozen yards to fifteen shillings per yard. They also manufactured lace edgings, silk and cotton nets, and lace curtains—a very important article in the trade. About three hundred and sixty women were employed in the factory, and about thirty men in the warehouse.

While working at his business, Moore again resumed his fox-hunting. In the memoir he has left behind him, he says that he was urged to do so by Dr. Lawrence on his return from America. His first day's hunting with Colonel Conyers had been very disastrous. On that day he had ridden a hired horse. Now he would ride a horse of his own. He bought a brown mare, six years old, for thirty pounds. He sent her down to Brick Wall, near Welwyn, Herts, where he hunted with Mr. Brand's (afterwards Lord Dacre's) hounds, for five or six seasons. There being no railway at that time, Mr. Moore drove down to Finchley to breakfast. He arrived there punctually at seven. He was never five minutes out of time. The servants were so confident of his appearance that as the clock struck seven they opened the door, expecting to see him descend from his trap. From thence he drove to the meet. Sometimes it was twenty or twenty-five miles off. After the hunt he returned to Finchley, dined, and got home the same night.

Mr. Moore could not but enjoy this exhilarating and health-giving exercise. He enjoyed the fresh air, the open country, and the rapid movement. There was the find by the covert-side, the hunt across country, and the brush at the finish. Hunting is a thoroughly English sport. It is a sort of mental tonic. It makes men active and spirited. It gives presence of mind; and though it may be a sort of self-indulgence, it is constantly teaching all sorts of self-denial.[1] " The Englishman," says Emerson, " associates well with dogs and horses. This attachment to the horse arises from the courage and address required to manage it. The horse finds out who is afraid of it, and does not disguise its opinion."

Hunting is one of the outcomes of the national character. It brings together, on terms of equality, all classes of society. Foreigners can never understand how English gentlemen find amusement in riding after foxes at the risk of breaking their necks. When the late Prince Consort and his brother, Duke Ernest, first came to England, they were taken to see everything,

---

[1] Mr. Moore cut from a newspaper the following paragraph, and inserted it in his case-book :—

" When a series of ' concerts for the people ' was begun in Edinburgh, Dr. Guthrie, of the Scotch Free Church, was present to give his countenance and support to the undertaking. He said, ' I have come here to lend my countenance as a minister to innocent amusement. I remember when I was a boy at college, and that was not yesterday, I used to go to Duddingston Loch on Saturday afternoon, in winter, and there I saw a reverend and grave divine playing at—what do you call it ?—Curling. My great ancestor, Guthrie, one of those who were martyrs in the old days for Scotland's right and truth, was one of the first curlers in the county of Ayr. He was a first-rate fisher, but I could try him at that. He was a famous fox-hunter : I have more respect for my neck than to try that. I have no sympathy, I have no patience, with that sickly, distempered religion that frowns upon innocent amusement. All my life I have had a liking for amusement. In that Gospel which I have the honour to preach, I find nothing forbidding such amusement. I maintain here—and though all the bigots in the world were here, I would still maintain it—that there is nothing in the glorious Gospel antagonistic to human nature. Amusement is not corruption. Every creature has its love of amusement. I have come here as a minister for the purpose of giving my sanction to this amusement.' "

and amongst other sights they were taken to the hunt-ing-field. They thought that every one, as at court, would go according to rank,—first a prince, then a duke, then a marquis, and so on ; but they were greatly disconcerted at seeing a butcher's boy riding up to the fence and going straight over it before them.

"I sincerely believe," says Mr. Moore, "that Dr. Law-rence was right in the advice he gave me. Nothing could have tended so much to restore me to health as active outdoor exercise. Before the season was over I felt wonderfully recovered. It was also a great pleasure to me to meet the country gentlemen who belonged to the hunt. They were kind, outspoken, and hospit-able. My companion, Joshua Wimbush, having given up hunting about this time, I presented him with a portrait of himself in hunting costume, as a mark of my sincere esteem for him and his valued father, my intimate friend, and in gratitude for their invariable kindness and hospitality.

" Lord Lonsdale had now started two packs of hounds, and the kennels being at Tring, I resolved to join his hunt. I may state that I was the first man that ap-peared with his foxhounds in scarlet. I was there the first day that he hunted. For some time we had very bad sport, as the country had not been hunted for some years, and our huntsman did not understand his busi-ness. But after another season we got old Morgan, who had hunted for Mr. Conyers. From that time we gra-dually improved. I now kept two horses, and could ride as well as any of them. My friend Mr. J. P. Foster,[1] having joined me, we took a leading position in the hunt, and great consideration was always shown to us by Lord Lonsdale, Mr. Brown, the deputy-master, the huntsmen whips, and all the gentlemen of the hunt.

" In the autumn of 1853 Mr. Howard, of Greystoke

[1] Of Foster, Porter, and Co.

Castle, whose hunting-seat was at Thornbury Castle, Gloucestershire, invited me to send my horses there, and to hunt with Lord Fitzhardinge's hounds. Whatever may be said of my lord's character, I amazingly enjoyed his hounds, as well as Mr. Howard's hospitality. One of the most extraordinary runs we had was over what they term the Rhein country. We had a run of about an hour and a quarter, during which we had to cross about twenty rheins, or water jumps, from ten to twenty feet wide.

"I rode my old chestnut, one of the best brook-jumpers in the world, though he was an awful puller. He was sure to get over them far enough. Out of a field of upwards of a hundred, there were only six of them up at the kill. Indeed I was not up, for at the very last jump a farmer got into one of those deep rheins, and in pity I stopped to assist in getting him out. He thanked me much, and told Mr. Howard that I had saved his life. Mr. Howard himself got into one of the rheins just at the start, and if help had not been at hand he would certainly have been drowned or killed, for he got wedged in with his horse, and could not easily be extricated. One of the rheins which I jumped across was 18 feet 4 inches wide. I believe I jumped some wider. On the following day many people came to see the old chestnut that had made the Great Jump. The consequence was that he and myself got into some notoriety. A long account of the run appeared in *Bell's Life* of the following week.

"I returned to London, and resumed my hunting with Lord Lonsdale's hounds. I spent many pleasant days in this hunt, never failing to meet my valued friend Mr. Foster. As there were four packs of hounds within twenty miles of Tring, we occasionally varied our experience, and sometimes hunted with Baron Rothschild's hounds, as well as with Lord Southampton's. Indeed I may say that I have hunted with nearly all the packs of hounds within sixty miles of London.

"I could relate many good runs that I have taken a good place in, but one will suffice. In 1857 I was out with Lord Southampton in his best country. There was a field of about two hundred. As I had distinguished myself in a run with the same hounds three years before, upon my old chestnut, by simply following Jem Mason, I determined again to follow this excellent leader. We had a run of an hour and twenty minutes, and out of all this large field there were only Jem Mason (the first whip), myself, and Peter Rolt, up at the kill. All the rest were a long way behind.

"Hunting is considered by some to be a low sort of pastime. But this is a great mistake. You meet with some of the most polished and refined gentlemen in the land. I do believe that a man who thoroughly understands hunting, and can get across country, can do most things well. It is one of the best of our national sports ; and who would do away with these ? It has influenced our character ; and produced a race of hardy and daring soldiers.

"Without egotism, I may say that I did some good in Lord Lonsdale's hunt. They all knew that I hated lying, swearing, and loose conversation, and my presence had perhaps some influence in checking these things. I was instrumental in getting up a large subscription for the Herts and Beds Infirmary, and another for the agricultural societies of all the districts through which we hunted.

"In my conscience I do not believe that there is any wickedness in hunting. But I must in candour acknowledge that hunting on Saturdays makes one think, when sitting in church on the following day, of the meet and the run, rather than of the service and the sermon. I have always considered hunting was necessary for my health, and I think so now. If I could have kept my health without resorting to it, I might have employed my time more valuably in doing good to my fellow-creatures. But it is in this as in so many other things: '*Honi soit qui mal y pense:*' Evil to him that evil thinks."

CHAPTER VIII.

SAFETY-VALVES.

BUSINESS and hunting did not altogether absorb the energies of George Moore. He had opportunities of engaging in other work. He hunted two days a week in winter. But what was he to do with his surplus energy in summer? There were a thousand things to be done in London, by those who would take the trouble and pains to do them. When Mr. Moore's partners found him entering upon some new work, they would say: "He has got another safety-valve."

One of the first things which he did, after giving up travelling and settling down in London, was to become the director of a life assurance society, of which he afterwards became the trustee. He did not accept the office without giving his fair equivalent of services. He was not a mere honorary director. He did not think that he had done his duty by eating his lunch and drinking his sherry. He did his best to increase the business of the office. He besought his friends to insure their lives. When customers came up from the country he took them to the office to get them to make their proposals.

He had many conversations with the young men employed in his warehouse. "Is your life insured?" he would say. "No!" "Then you must do it at once."

If they were married, he urged it upon them as an indispensable duty. "You must insure for the benefit of
your wife and children. Remember it is one of the
most self-denying acts you can ever have it in your
power to perform."

The insurance society with which Mr. Moore was
connected, was the National Mercantile Association.[1]
He requested the travellers for his house to act as
agents for it. The travellers, being constantly on the
move, and paying their periodical visits to all the large
towns in the kingdom, succeeded in bringing a large
amount of new business to the society. This was certainly doing a good work ; for the man who succeeds
in inducing another to insure his life, to a certain extent
secures his widow and children from want in the event
of the insurer's death. In order to induce the travellers
to work for the office, Mr. Moore and his colleagues
introduced a clause into the articles of the association
providing that a certain share of the profits should be
appropriated to the support of the Commercial Travellers' Schools, with which Mr. Moore had already
become intimately associated.

Another of George Moore's Safety-valves was the
Cumberland Benevolent Society. This was the first
charitable association with which he was connected.
When he first came to London, and while he was in
receipt of a very small salary, he subscribed to it his
first guinea ; and he continued ever after to be a member of the association. The origin of the society is
scarcely known. It appears, from the old minute-books,
to have been formed about the year 1734, by a number
of gentlemen from Cumberland, who met for the purpose of talking over the scenes and reminiscences of
their early life.

From a social meeting, it gradually became converted

---

[1] It has since been amalgamated with another company.

into a benevolent institution. In the year 1812 it was resolved that a fund should be formed for the relief of distressed persons of Cumberland and their families who were resident in the metropolis. Such was its position when George Moore gave his first guinea to the institution. This, his first act of benevolence, was like a grain of good seed cast into the ground. It sprang up afterwards into a tree of goodly fruit.

As Mr. Moore prospered, he increased his subscriptions. He became prominent in the society, not only for his liberality, but for the active part which he took in the annual festivals given in support of the institution. At the dinner of 1850, when he officiated as steward, his health was proposed. His speech, in answer to the toast thanking him for his services, is worth giving :—

" He said it was ungenerous to call upon him for a reply, as he had distinctly and emphatically declined to appear to-night to take any part in the oratory. He could not, however, but appreciate the intended compliment, looking at the multifarious positions he held,— perpetual steward for the anniversary dinners for the last twelve years, committee-man, trustee to their funds, and occasionally master of the ceremonies at their balls. Although he had on the present occasion mustered a dozen friends to indulge in the cup of unalloyed charity —that peculiar beverage, which, the more it is indulged in, the more healthy does the appetite for it become— yet he could not be expected on many more occasions to have such a force of benevolent spirits to rally round him. He had been favoured by Providence to assume a commercial position, which enabled him to assist, and generally to succeed, in placing Cumberland youths in comfortable situations. To those aspirants for commercial honours in the city of London, his first advice, on procuring situations for them, was—' When you can

afford it, give a guinea to the Cumberland Benevolent
Institution ; it will mark your position ; it will make
you feel that you have taken your stand as a philanthropist.   It will raise your own moral power of action,
in feeling that you have a stake in the well-being of
your once prosperous, but now fallen and unfortunate
fellow-countrymen.'   The more they were blessed with
success in this world, the greater was their responsibility.
Property has its duties as well as its rights.   Take from
me," he concluded, " one kind word of gentle reproof—
although at this late hour it may not be considered in
good taste—that we have each and all of us this duty
to perform towards our less fortunate fellow-creatures.
And mark my parting admonition.   It is better for you
to become bankrupt by charitable contributions here,
than to become bankrupt by ill deeds hereafter."

The funds of the institution did not, however, increase
so rapidly as Mr. Moore desired.   The number of indi-
gent Cumberland men receiving pensions was increased
to forty-five ; but there were many deserving applicants
who were turned away year after year.   Mr. Moore tried
to put his rich Cumberland friends to shame.   He said
at one of the dinners, that there were four firms in one
street in London—chiefly composed of Cumberland men
—whose returns amounted to between two and three
millions sterling a year ; and yet some of them had not
sent them a farthing towards the benevolent fund.   They
seemed to have found it easier to make money by trade
than to spend it on charity.   He regretted to say that
he knew many a Cumberland man in London who was
literally " rolling in wealth," and had more money than
he knew what to do with, who had never favoured them
with his presence, nor even allowed his name to appear
in their list of subscribers.

Mr. Moore accordingly found it necessary to do something to replenish the funds of the institution.   He called

a meeting of his countymen at his office,—the scene of so many works of benevolence,—and urged them to assist him in restoring the efficiency of the society. Mr. Ferguson, M.P., afterwards referring to this meeting, says : " There was not much talking, but a good deal of action. Mr. Moore headed a subscription list with a donation extending to three figures, and a strong barrier was thus erected against the threatened danger of decline." The tide was turned ; the institution was saved ; and Mr. Moore to the end of his life continued one of its most indefatigable supporters.

But a still more important Safety-valve was George Moore's connection with the Commercial Travellers' Schools. He could not but take a deep interest in this institution. He himself had won his spurs as a commercial traveller. His extraordinary success in that capacity had been the foundation of his fortune. In one of his notes he says : " As a body, I entertain the highest regard for the commercial travellers. They were the companions of my early struggles. I have always sympathised with them. I know the risks which they run, the temptations to which they are exposed, and the sufferings which they have to undergo. They spend most of their time away from their homes and their families. They are exposed to every change of weather, from the heat of summer to the storms of winter. They are liable to be cut off by bronchitis and lung diseases. When they die in the service of their employers, what is to become of their children ? They have been able to save but little money, for they are for the most part badly paid. Here, then, is a fine opportunity for charity to step in and help to save the little ones deprived of their father's care."

Such was Mr. Moore's idea of the necessity of a charity for the maintenance and education of the children of Commercial Travellers. The subject had for some time been talked about. The idea of forming an institution originated with John Robert Cuffley, a commercial traveller well known "on the road." He was warmly supported by Mr. George Stockdale, Mr. Roberts, and a few other travellers. They called upon Mr. Moore and placed the matter before him. He at first doubted whether commercial travellers would be induced to combine to support such an institution. But he said to the deputation, "Go on ; try what you can do to raise money and collect subscriptions, and call upon me again."

They went on. They collected in a few months about £2,000, and they then called upon Mr. Moore. He was now ready to go heartily with them, and to give to the society the full influence of the firm in which he was a partner. A public meeting was held at the London Tavern on the 30th December, 1845, with George Moore in the chair. The meeting was highly successful. Mr. Moore undertook to be the Treasurer of the institution, and Mr. J. Masterman, M.P. for the City of London, consented to be chairman. From that time, the success of the project became assured. Mr. Moore devoted himself heartily to the work; and it was mainly by his energy and widespread influence that the institution took root, grew, and flourished, with a rapidity unexampled in the history of any other Orphan charity.

The rules of the institution were drawn up and passed at a general meeting of the subscribers held in the following year. The first election of twenty children (boys and girls) took place in June, 1847. Premises had already been secured at Wanstead for their accommodation. During the next year, thirty more children were elected ; and in the first annual report, published about the autumn of 1848, the names of these children were published. At the second annual examination of the children, held at the London Tavern, it was stated that

I

within a period of two years from the opening of the schools, sixty children were provided for within the establishment, which number will be increased by twelve more. It was also urged that from the rapidly increasing claims upon the bounty of the charity it was necessary to obtain larger premises than the institution at present possessed, and an earnest appeal was made to the commercial body, urging them to co-operate in the raising of a building fund that should be sufficient to provide the requisite accommodation.

Mr. Moore at once set to work to raise the requisite money for the purpose of building the new institution. To use his own words : " I made the institution a part of my business. I canvassed the various houses in London for funds. I travelled to Bristol, Manchester, and Liverpool to summon meetings of the commercial men, and appeal to them in favour of the charity."

At the annual examination of the pupils in 1849, Mr. Moore stated that at least fifteen thousand pounds would be required to proceed with the erection of the new buildings. At the anniversary festival in December, 1850, Mr. Moore, in forwarding his subscription (for his doctor had prevented him attending the meeting), addressed a letter to the Lord Mayor, who was in the chair, in which he said : " I hoped, as treasurer, that I should have had the pleasure of reporting that we had raised the whole of the building fund, whereas we have only raised one-third of it. Will you, with your usual eloquence, stimulate your guests to form deputations for the purpose of canvassing Liverpool, Leeds, Bradford, and the other large towns, where, I have no doubt, the merchants and travellers will respond to the call in the generous and noble manner that Manchester, Bristol, and Glasgow have already done. Thus we should soon have a building without a farthing of debt, which, as treasurer, I have a great ambition to achieve. Will you tell the

commercial men of the United Kingdom that only a
tenth of their number have subscribed, and tell those
also who have not yet subscribed, that their treasurer,
as an old traveller, feels humiliated that every commercial traveller in England cannot afford to give his
guinea a year. A very little economy (three farthings a
day) would enable the institution to educate, maintain,
and clothe the orphan children of every deceased brother,
and to make the widow's heart rejoice."

In this way he urged onward the progress of the
institution. He would not be resisted. He had taken
the thing in hand, and it *must* succeed. He bore down
every opposition. He encouraged some and shamed
others into generosity. He told the commercial travellers that, no matter what their salary, they ought to
subscribe to the schools ; if not, they were very poor-
hearted creatures indeed. He told their employers that
they did not pay their travellers with sufficient liberality,
for the calling of a commercial traveller was a very hard
one, especially when they travelled on commission. At
a public dinner at Manchester he said that he knew of
several melancholy instances of destitution which were
not the result of improvidence or prodigality, but from
the most inadequate payment to meet the expenses of
the road.[1]

At length sufficient money was obtained to enable the
schools to be built. Mr. Moore at first dreaded setting
the architects to work. He was in favour of purchasing
some old mansion, which might be turned into suitable

---

[1] A commercial traveller, referring to this statement in a letter to the
Sun, said—" Mr. Moore, I am sure, will receive the best thanks of all
travellers for his kind consideration ; the more so from the fact of his being
himself a principal, and for many years a traveller, and, to his credit, the
architect of his fortune by indomitable application and industry. I have
known him many years. Ofttimes do I recollect him leaving his bed
before sunrise in the spring of the year, continuing hard at work until the
cock announced early morn again ; so that he is the very best authority for
everything that a traveller requires and desires."

premises. But, fortunately for the institution, the London
and North-Western Company were desirous of selling
a piece of land at Pinner for the purpose of encouraging
building in the neighbourhood. This piece of land, consisting of twenty-five acres, proved to be an excellent
investment; as it might afterwards have been sold for
twice the money. The original estimate of the building
was £15,000, but to suit the limited means of the
institution, the architects reduced it to £10,000.

The foundation-stone was laid on the 20th of July,
1853. It was intended that Prince Albert should have
laid the first stone, but he was prevented from being
present by indisposition. This greatly marred the
enjoyment of the day. John Masterman, Esq., M.P.
for the City, performed the duty in place of his Royal
Highness. Mr. Moore deposited the coins, the chairman
laid the first stone, and Dr. Vaughan, then Head Master
of Harrow, delivered an impressive prayer.

At the *déjeuner* which followed, the health of Mr.
Cuffley was proposed, and in replying, he said that
though he congratulated himself on the fact of having
been one of the original founders of the school, and
one of the first list of 230 who made up 2,300 guineas
to begin with, the institution would never have reached
its present prosperous condition had it not been for the
unremitting exertions of George Moore, the treasurer.

Renewed exertions had still to be made to increase
the funds of the institution. Mr. Moore continued to
be the head and front of the movement. He made
special journeys into the country to collect money. He
trusted a good deal to the anniversary dinners of the
institution. He invited all his friends to attend them.
He called upon them beforehand, and set down the
sums they were to give. He was declared to be "an
indefatigable beggar;" but he did not mind the nick-
name, provided he could get the necessary subscriptions.

For the purpose of inducing his friends to attend the anniversary dinners, he endeavoured to secure the best and most popular chairman. He had a great friendship for Charles Dickens, and on two occasions Mr. Dickens consented to act as chairman at the anniversary dinner. He also succeeded in securing Lord Lytton, Mr. Thackeray, the Duke of Cambridge, and successive Lord Mayors of London.

Mr. Forster, in his *Life of Dickens*, says that "of all the societies, charitable or self-assisting, which his tact and eloquence in the chair so often helped, none had interested him by the character of its service to its members and the perfection of its management so much as that of the Commercial Travellers. His admiration of their schools introduced him to one who acted as their treasurer, and whom, of all the men he had known, I think he rated highest,—for the union of business qualities in an incomparable measure, to a nature comprehensive enough to deal with masses of men, however differing in creed or opinion, humanely and justly. Mr. Dickens never afterwards wanted support for any good work that he did not first think of Mr. George Moore: and his appeals were never made to him in vain."[1] It is singular, also, that Mr. Dickens should have adopted his title of "The Uncommercial Traveller" from his visits to the Commercial Schools, and from his taking the chair at the anniversary dinners of the institution.

[1] Mr. Forster adds in a note,—"If space were available, Mr. Dickens's letters would supply many proofs of his interest in Mr. George Moore's admirable projects; but I can only make exception to his characteristic allusion to an incident that tickled his fancy very much at the time. 'I hope,' he says, (25th of August, 1853,) 'you have been as much amused as I am by the account of the Bishop of ———'s visit to my very particular friend Mr. George Moore's schools. It strikes me as the funniest thing I ever saw—his addressing those unfortunate children concerning Colenso. I cannot get over the ridiculous image I have erected in my mind of the shovel-hat and apron holding forth, at that safe distance, to that sage audience. There is nothing so extravagant in Rabelais, or so satirically humorous in Swift or Voltaire.'"

The first of the dinners at which Mr. Dickens presided was given in commemoration of the foundation of the schools at Pinner. Mr. Dickens delivered one of his best speeches. He described the old travelling and the new—the travelling by coach and the travelling by railway—and the imperfect domestic relations of the commercial traveller. "It is to support the school for their orphans," he said, "founded with such high and friendly objects, so very honourable to your calling, and so useful in its solid and practical results, that we are here assembled. It is to roof that building which is to shelter the children of your deceased friends with one crowning ornament—the best that any building can have—namely, a receipt-stamp for the full amount of the cost. It is for this that your active sympathy is appealed to for the completion of your own good work."

It may be mentioned that during the previous weeks, Mr. Moore had been engaged in making strenuous efforts to raise the requisite sum of money to complete the building, and pay for it in cash. He had visited the principal commercial towns. On the night before the anniversary dinner, he had been at Manchester. This will explain the reference made by Mr. Dickens, when proposing the health of Mr. Moore,—"A name," he said, "which is a synonym for integrity, enterprise, public spirit, and benevolence. He is one of the most zealous officers whom I have ever seen in my life. He appears to me to have been doing nothing during the last week but rushing into and out of railway carriages, and making eloquent speeches at all sorts of public dinners in favour of this charity. Last evening he was at Manchester, and this evening he comes here sacrificing his time and convenience, and exhausting in the meantime the contents of two vast leaden inkstands, and no end of pens, with the energy of fifty

banker's clerks rolled into one. But I clearly foresee
that the treasurer will have so much to do to-night,
such gratifying sums to acknowledge, and such large
lines of figures to write in his books, that I feel the
greatest consideration that I can show him is to propose
his health without further observation, leaving him to
address you in his own behalf."

Mr. Moore briefly referred to the results of his
operations in the provinces, and more particularly at
Manchester. "It was a remarkable fact," he said, "that
a charitable dinner had never before taken place at the
town of Manchester. He supposed that many gentlemen would expect that, having been on a perigrination
to Manchester, he would have to report the accession of
something like 1,500 new members and £12,000 subscriptions. But he could assure them that he had no
such results to announce. He had only obtained 158
annual subscribers, and £1,150 in donations. He hoped
that people in the country were not jealous of them,—
looking upon their schools as a piece of metropolitan
centralisation. On the contrary, he should feel much
obliged by their provincial friends taking the whole
thing into their own hands. This was not a London
school, but a National school, established for the benefit
of commercial travellers all over the country. It was
therefore the bounden duty of every commercial traveller
to support it. He wished the gentlemen from the
provinces to know that on this occasion they had not
rejected one child ; and he could tell them another
thing, which repaid him for all his anxiety, and that
was, that the children, after they had been boarded and
educated, had all been provided with situations. It had
fallen to his lot to provide for a good many. He had
spoken of the gloom that was hanging over commercial
circles. He hoped it would soon pass away ; but it
must be remembered that the rapid transit by railway

was calculated to alter the prospects of commercial travellers. His opinion was, that although these gentlemen might be styled the 'ambassadors of commerce,' and were the means of filling the warehouses with customers, many of the commercial houses were not sufficiently grateful for that result."

The Schools were opened on the 27th of October, 1855. Prince Albert was present on the occasion. The children, a hundred and forty-two in number, were ranged at the entrance of the Schools to receive His Royal Highness. The band of the Coldstream Guards played the National Anthem. An address was read by Mr. Roberts (of Longmans and Co.), to which the Prince returned a suitable answer. The children sang the Old Hundredth Psalm. Dr. Vaughan, Head Master of Harrow, offered prayer. The children then sang "God save the Queen"; after which the Prince, amidst great cheering, declared "the building opened."

After the presentation of purses, the Prince carefully examined the building. No place escaped his notice. He expressed himself greatly satisfied with the arrangements, and said that he had received some valuable hints for the Wellington College, then in course of erection. After consenting to become patron of the schools, and presenting 100 guineas to the building fund, His Royal Highness left Pinner amidst enthusiastic cheering.

The day was considered a red-letter day in the history of the institution. In commemoration of the event of the Prince's visit, the last Wednesday in October of each year is called "The Orphans' Day," when a collection in aid of the funds of the Schools is made in the commercial-room of almost every hotel in the kingdom.[1]

---

[1] At a meeting held on the 27th December, 1857, at which Mr. Thackeray was in the chair, Mr. Moore said, "Some had objected to the contributions arising from the Orphans' Day; but these subscriptions were really obtained from those who did not subscribe regularly to the funds of the institution. These simultaneous calls, as some gentlemen were pleased

The Schools were built at a cost of about £25,000. Two hundred children (boys and girls) were fed, clothed, and educated in the institution. The education was for the most part of a practical character; but where a boy showed particular merit he was enabled, by the scholarships that were afterwards established, to proceed to the City of London School, and ultimately to Cambridge or Oxford. It was Mr. Moore's great pleasure, in future years, to go down to Pinner on the examination days, and to exhort the boys who were about to leave school as to their conduct in after life. They stood up before him, and he gave them their farewell address :—

"Do not," he said on one occasion, "let your want of success depress you ; but struggle on. Labour hard and continuously, and you will win in the end. Do not allow a rebuff or a comparative failure to check your exertions towards the attainment of ultimate success. When I came up to London, a poor lad, without a friend in the world, people's hearts did not seem to be so large as they are now. Instead of having situations found (as I am happy to say is the case with most of you), boys in those days had often to beg in vain for employment. After beating about London for an entire week, I began to think myself a not very marketable commodity in the great city. At length I got employment. I had to submit to many rebuffs. The artificial estimate I had formed of myself completely vanished. All nonsense was effectually taken out of me. To persevere and conquer all difficulties appeared to me a duty. I determined that no one should henceforth justly call me stupid ; and ultimately I had my reward, for I was appointed to one of the best situations in the firm I had

to call them, were not from those who paid their guinea a year, but from the grumblers on the road,—those who never subscribed : and he believed that about eight out of every ten of the children who had been recipients of the benefits of the institution were the orphans of those who had never subscribed to it at all."

entered—a commercial traveller to the principal northern towns. This formed the first stepping-stone to my present position. I therefore advise you, young men just entering into life, never to be daunted by difficulties. Persevere! persevere! and you will be sure to conquer in the end."

On another occasion, remembering how he had once been nearly ruined when at Flint, Ray, and Co.'s, through his want of knowledge of arithmetic, he said: "Book-keeping is the very key of your position. The records of the Bankruptcy Court show how many colossal fortunes are wrecked; how many growing prospects are blasted, through ignorance of this vital part of commercial knowledge." He urged the boys to observe the strictest integrity in all their dealings; to think not merely of their earthly master, but of the Divine Being from whom nothing could be concealed. He also urged them to recollect that in any moment of temptation, not merely their own character, but the reputation of the institution that had done so much for them, was at stake. He advised those who had received prizes not to be too much elated at their success, and not to be led away by the idea that knowledge by itself could command success without thorough honesty and perseverance. At the same time he assured those who had not got prizes that they ought not to be discouraged; but that they might rest assured that integrity and earnest perseverance would be sure to command success, whatever station of life they might be called upon to fill.

On another occasion he said: "You are about to enter upon the battle of life, in which perhaps the competition has never been so severe as at present. Whatever abilities you may have, you may be assured that you never will succeed unless you are in earnest." He recommended them to study the value of time, and to remember that time was money, not only for themselves, but for all with whom they might have dealings ; and he assured them that perseverance and punctuality would ever bring success and reward, even though great abilities were wanting. "Don't," he said, "depend upon your relatives and friends. There is nothing like individual responsibility. If you have self-respect, and trust to your own resources, by God's strength you will succeed. ' God helps those who help themselves.'"

After the institution had been in existence for about twenty years, it was a proud thing for George Moore to say that, "with a single exception, no child educated in that school had turned out badly. They had gone out into the world and maintained the character of the institution. He hoped that that would be the case for many long years to come."

CHAPTER IX.

In the midst of his prosperity, George Moore never forgot "auld Cummerland." His mind was always turning back to the home of his birth, and to the scenes of his boyhood. The very name of Cumberland had a charm for him. When any Cumberland lad called upon him at his office, he welcomed him cheerfully, asked him to his house, and often got him a situation.

We find amongst his letters an invitation to a young man near Wigton to come up to London. Mr. Moore had been devoting a good deal of his time to find out for him a situation. " Come up," he says, " by the first cheap train. You can see the Great Exhibition, as it closes on Saturday week ;[1] and if either of your sisters wished, they might accompany you. Mr. ——, late of the Wigton bank, whom I am trying to get a situation for, lives at a boarding-house near by. You can dine with me every day till I get you placed ; and your sisters also, if they accompany you. . . . Assure your mother from me that I will always take an interest in you so long as you deserve it, but no longer. I have found out from experience that I cannot assist those who will not assist themselves. I need not say that

[1] The letter was written in September, 1851

when you come to London I hope that you will attend a place of worship twice every Sunday, and read at least one chapter of your Bible daily. Always act unto others as you would expect them to act towards you. I must say, however, that I have great hopes of you, or I would not have taken so much time and used so much influence in endeavouring to place you in a good house."

George Moore never forgot any of his early friends. If he could do anything for them, or for their children, he would spare no efforts. His old master, Messenger, for whom, notwithstanding his failings, he had a great respect, failed in business after his apprentice had left for London. His breakdown was one of the numerous instances of the effects of drink. Messenger came up to London, where he obtained a situation. Then his health failed, and he was obliged to give up work. He applied to George Moore, who maintained him while he lived, and paid his funeral expenses at his death. He helped in the same manner the fellow-apprentice who so often thrashed him, and once nearly choked him, while serving his apprenticeship at Messenger's. The man broke down in the world, and appealed to his fellow-apprentice. George Moore had long ago forgiven him, and was only too glad to help him in his time of need.

When a new building was erected at Wigton for the accommodation of the Mechanics' Institute, George Moore did not forget the place in which he had spent so many years. At the first meeting held in the new building, a letter was read from him to the Secretary, in which he said: "I think I cannot commence the new year (1851) better than by sending you a cheque for ten guineas for the Wigton Mechanics' Institute. The reminiscences of my boyhood, and all that concerns the town where I made my entrance into commercial life, are dear to me. I am not insensible to my many deficiencies and

imperfections caused in some degree by my lack of opportunity for learning during my school days and apprenticeship.   Impress upon the minds of the apprentices
how valuable they may make their hours of recreation,
and how they may make them useful in influencing
their future destiny in life.   To those who have spent
part of their time in public-houses, in frivolous amusement, and in idle gossip, I would say, let them endeavour
to cultivate learning and science ; and, above all, the sub-
lime truths of the Gospel.   God speed your meeting !"

George Moore was induced to pay his visits to Cumberland when harassed with his violent headaches.
Indoor life did not agree with him.   He must have
plenty of exercise, and breathe the fresh air of the
mountains.   A favourite place of his was Shap Wells,
in Westmoreland.   The Wells, which have strong medicinal properties, are in the very middle of Shap Fells.
The hotel stands alone near the Spa, many miles from
the nearest villages.   The moorland country is here
seen in perfection.   Nothing but heather and rocks,
and mountain streams forcing their way in many interrupted channels amongst them.   There is not a tree
visible, except the few stunted fir-trees near the hotel.
The change of seasons in the landscape is observed only
by the varying beauty of the mosses in spring time, and
by the purple carpet of heather in the autumn.   Some
consider the place a wilderness of heath and rocks ; but
to Moore it was a paradise.   He delighted in the strong
wind blowing fresh over the mountains.   The complete
change, perhaps, more than the waters of the Spa, did
him a world of good.

Mrs. Moore usually accompanied him on those occasions ; for she had relatives to visit near Wigton.   Mr.
Moore sometimes took the Cockbridge Inn, at Mealsgate, and filled it with friends whom he had invited from
London.   On one occasion his partners, Mr. Copestake

and Mr. Groucock, accompanied him. They were taken over Mr. Moore's favourite haunts,—to the Peel Towers at Whitehall and Harbybrow, to Torpenhow, to Bassenthwaite Water, and to Skiddaw.

His brother Thomas, the Statesman, was working on at Mealsgate in the old way. He was cultivating his bit of land ; and sometimes found it hard to make the ends meet. Thomas was amazed at his brother's " extravagance,"—bringing these Londoners in post-chaises from Carlisle, and giving them such feed and drink for nothing at the Inn. It could only end in one way. " George," he said, " is sure to brek !" Thomas could not believe that the profits of any trade could bear such a terrible outlay. " Yes," he said, " George is sure to brek, and then he maun come on the parish !"

But a great event was in store for Cumberland ; no less than a visit from the Lord Mayor of London ! In 1854, when Alderman Sydney was Lord Mayor, Mr. Moore induced him and the Lady Mayoress to accompany himself and Mrs. Moore on a visit to Cumberland. The affair caused quite a sensation throughout the county, as the inhabitants had never seen a " real live Lord Mayor" before ! The party first arrived at Low Wood Inn, Windermere. They spent a few days there. " We drove," says Mr. Moore, " in an open carriage and four to Patterdale Hall, the seat of William Marshall, M.P. From thence we were rowed on the lake to Lyulph's Tower, the romantic resort of Henry Howard of Greystoke Castle. On the following day we went to see some Cumberland wrestling on the island near Low Wood. The people were wonderfully astonished to see the London Lord Mayor looking just like other people and taking such an interest in their proceedings.

" At St. Bees I invited the West Cumberland magistrates and gentry to meet him at dinner. On

the following day, the Cumberland and Westmoreland
Agricultural Society held their meeting at Whitehaven;
and there we went, the Lord Mayor and Lady Mayoress
being the observed of all observers.   I introduced hundreds of all ranks and grades to them.   The agricultural
dinner took place in the evening, Sir James Graham in
the chair.   When the health of the latter was drunk, he
replied with his usual spirit.   But he said one thing,
which made me very nervous.   After eulogising the
beauties of the county and the qualities of the people,
he said that his friend Mr. Irton, M.P., by his side, had
told him that the people of Cumberland 'were very fond
of drink!'   This caused an uncomfortable sensation.
Although the statement was true, yet this was not perhaps the best time for uttering it.   However, Sir James
Graham with his good tact turned it off with a jest, and
all ended well.

"We next proceeded to Sir Wilfrid Lawson's, Brayton, where we received every hospitality.   They are the
kindest people in the world, and I shall never forget the
consideration shown to me by each member of their
family.   Sir Wilfrid Lawson and most of his family are
teetotallers, but the Lord Mayor pronounced his wine
the best he had ever drunk.   Next day we rode to
Allonby, a delightful watering-place.   We proceeded
from thence to Wigton, the town where I served my
apprenticeship."

A deputation from Wigton had waited on the Lord
Mayor at St. Bees, to request his presence at a public
dinner to be given to himself and to his friend Mr.
George Moore.   His Lordship could not attend the
public dinner; but he agreed to spend a few hours with
the townsmen of Wigton.   The dinner therefore assumed
the form of a banquet.   The two guests, on approaching
the railway station from Brayton, found an immense
concourse of people assembled.   A carriage and four

awaited them. The streets were lined with people, who cheered them as they passed. On arriving at the inn, Mr. Moore introduced his distinguished guest to all the notabilities of Wigton.

The proceedings went off well. The health of Mr. Moore was proposed by Mr. Reed, an old friend. In reply, George told the old story—one of which he was never tired—the story of his own life. A few extracts from his speech may be given :—

" I assure you that I scarcely expected or wished that any honour of this demonstration should be paid to me, but to my worthy friend the Lord Mayor of London. This evening carries my mind back to the time when I first migrated to the metropolis from this town. It is just thirty years ago, for I am now forty-seven. If you knew the troubles, difficulties, and anxieties that I have gone through, you would be convinced that a great deal depends upon one's own efforts. It is often said with reference to a man who has improved his position, 'What a *lucky* fellow he is!' But depend upon it, if you were to rely upon luck, you would in the end find yourself very much mistaken. I may say that I attribute much of my success to having had proper ideas instilled into me by my parents. My father was known to many in this company ; he was a man of probity, an honest Cumberland statesman, who always spoke the truth and despised what was not straightforward. * * * I left London to visit you with as much buoyancy of spirits as ever a schoolboy left school. And if Providence spares me, I shall always be glad to meet you in my native county at least once a year."

Mr. Rigg, in responding for " The Town and Trade of Wigton," expressed the hope that more of the apprentices would achieve the distinction that Mr. Moore had done—or, as he was going to say, GEORGE Moore, for that was the name by which he was best known in

K

Cumberland." To which Mr. Moore replied, "Ay, always call me that if you please."

The next day the Lord Mayor went to Mealsgate. "There," said George Moore, "is the place where I was born." It was a fine feature in his character to maintain his early attachments—to venerate his father, to love his relations, and to do all that he could to help the people of his neighbourhood. How many self-raised rich snobs are there who deny their birth-place, forget their relations, and, looking down upon their early life as a thing to be forgotten, aspire to rank amongst the higher classes of what is called "society."

On a future occasion Mr. Moore paid a hunting visit to his friend Sir Wilfrid Lawson, whose son (the present baronet) was master of the Cumberland foxhounds. He went down in November, and had some memorable hunts. The meet was at the Brayton kennels. The master "held hard" until the arrival of the officers of the Carlisle garrison. The field consisted of thirty-five riders, well mounted and ready for the fray. A neighbouring fox cover was beat, and signs were heard of the game being afoot. A deep chorus was wafted from the further side. The inspiring "tally-ho!" was sounded, and Reynard stole away, the hounds crashing after him through the whins. After crossing Aspatria Road, the fox made for the plantations round Brayton, crossed the lawn before the Hall, where Sir Wilfrid Lawson, on his favourite chestnut, showed in front. The huntsmen in pursuit took the heavy dropleap into the park. The fox sped away to Crookdale Mill, over the Leesrigg pasture, and on to Bolton Common. He crossed to the right by Well-rash and the How to Bolton Gate; thence on to the ridge of the hill to Sandale, Fauld's Brow, and the mountains thereabout. He took refuge in a quarry in Rush Fell, but was speedily dislodged, when, after a very short view, he was pulled down, after an hour and fifty minutes of very hard running.

Mr. Moore says :—" I greatly enjoyed this visit. I had never hunted in Cumberland since I rode my father's old horse, bare-backed, after John Peel's harriers. Wilfrid Lawson is an excellent master, civil and obliging to all ; not what I would call a bold rider, but he always knows his way, works his hounds well, and shows excellent sport. We had an excellent run, that appeared in *Bell's Life*. What added much to my pleasure was that I had trodden every yard of the ground in my boyhood, and had not seen many parts of it since then. It was a real delight to me to be well up all through the run, and when the *Who-hoop !* came, I got the brush."

George Moore was already a great favourite in Cumberland. He was proud of his county, and his county was proud of him. Wigton had welcomed him with enthusiasm. The country gentry invited him to their houses. Men of both sides of politics showed him marked courtesy and kindness. " I have not forgotten," he said, "my own position. I have sprung from the people and I hope I have done them no dishonour. I also trust that with all my worldly prosperity I have never forgotten the poor relations surrounding the place of my birth."

On one occasion he was invited by Lord Carlisle to visit him at Naworth Castle, one of the hoary places of antiquity in the north. The Castle is a characteristic specimen of a great border fortress, when war was the normal condition of the northern counties. Here " Belted Will "—of whom Lord Carlisle was so proud—kept his garrison of a hundred and forty men, and held the border, while he reigned in a state of peace. He was the terror of the moss-troopers and the scourge of the Scotch freebooters. Fuller, the Church historian, says of him,

K 2

that "he sent many of them to that place where the officer always does his work by daylight."

On the present occasion, however, the entertainment was of a more peaceful character. A number of the neighbouring gentry had been invited to Naworth to witness the sports at Talkin Tarn. A regatta took place on the lake. There was afterwards a bout at wrestling, which Mr. Moore greatly enjoyed. "Lord Carlisle," he says, "in his usual easy, good-humoured way, made everybody happy about him. In the evening we dined at Naworth Castle, about twenty in number. I shall never forget the thoughtful, kindly way in which the Earl introduced me to his mother, the Dowager Countess. At the end of a sumptuous entertainment we were about to retire—I thought to the drawing-room—when Lord Carlisle, putting his arm in mine, took me with him, and from behind a screen we saw the full length of Belted Will's Hall, about eighty feet long. There we saw some fifty or sixty in what seemed curious costumes, dancing at full swing. I had heard the music before, but I thought it was outside, on account of the company staying in the castle. I was surprised at the sight, and could scarcely believe my eyes; the livery of the servants dancing looked like old court-dresses. It seemed like a scene in fairyland. As we walked along the ancient hall and approached the dancers, Lord Carlisle asked me if I would join in. 'Yes,' said I, 'by all means.' He then introduced me to Mary, 'the dairymaid,' and away we went. I had never seen so good a sample of buxom Cumberland lassies before. All the company joined in the dance, his lordship included, and we kept it up till a late hour.

"To see the kindness and courtesy of his lordship to all his domestics did my heart good. How they, one and all, must have loved him! Afterwards, when Lord Carlisle was appointed Lord-Lieutenant of Ireland, I

spent a delightful morning with him in Phœnix Park.
I joined him at a distinguished dinner, which he gave
the same evening. Each gentleman present must have
felt that Lord Carlisle paid a special attention to himself,
for he was kind, cheerful, and considerate to every one.
Among the pleasant things he said to me was, that he
was sure his brother Charles would be delighted that
I had dined with him.

"I must say that the Hon. Charles Howard has shown
me unvarying kindness, and I feel a real attachment to
him. Many a happy day have I spent with him at
Greystoke Castle ; and indeed to him and other members
of the Howard family, I can never be grateful enough
for their interest—I may say their friendship."

Such were amongst the pleasant days that George
Moore spent in Cumberland while he was merely a man
of business, and before he had become possessor of a foot
of land in the county.

CHAPTER X.

.

WORK IN CUMBERLAND.

IT must not be supposed that Mr. Moore devoted himself wholly to amusement during his summer holidays in Cumberland. He was a cheerful whole-hearted man, ready to enjoy himself and to take part in the pleasures of both old and young.

During the early part of his career, he had visited Cumberland at irregular intervals. He remained for a few days visiting the lakes and the mountains, and returned again to his business in London. But when he was able to remain for a longer period, and to live for a month or two at Mealsgate, he was able to investigate the moral and social condition of the place where he was born.

In the summer of 1852 Mr. and Mrs. Moore made a considerable stay in Cumberland. Being already interested in the education of the children of commercial travellers, he proceeded to make inquiries as to the education of the children in Mealsgate and the neighbourhood.

He found that education was making no progress. It was no more advanced than when he left Cumberland. There was no desire for better education, and very little for more knowledge. The schools had done well enough for their fathers and grandfathers. Why should not the children be left to learn their A B C in quiet? Why bother them with certificated masters and new methods of instruction?

In fact the country-folks were asleep. They were droning on in the old way. Everything was in a state of stagnation. While the world outside was undergoing rapid movement, the world in this little bit of England was standing stock-still. The schools were there, but nobody looked after them,—neither gentry, clergy, statesmen, nor ratepayers.

Such was the state of things when George Moore came down to Mealsgate to take his holiday. He was one of those men who could not be idle. If there was no work ready at his hand, he made work. He was of an active, persevering, indefatigable temperament. Here was work to be done, and he immediately set to work to do it. He would stir up the indolent stagnation of his neighbourhood, and rouse the people into activity. He would infuse into them some of his own energetic spirit.

His first effort was to secure the erection of a new school-house at Bolton, in lieu of that at Boltongate, where he had received his first instruction from Blackbird Wilson. How he succeeded will be best told in his own words :—

" As I have already confessed, I was ashamed of my education when I first entered the house of Fisher and Co. During my visits to Cumberland I observed with grief and sorrow that no improvement had taken place. The people, though shrewd and intelligent, have great narrowness of thought. Perhaps this is not to be wondered at, as they scarcely ever travel beyond their market town. I had often heard my revered father say that he had never travelled further than to Gilsland Wells, or to Carlisle,—a distance of fifteen miles. I also found the people very suspicious of foreign dictation. They did not like to have their schools, any more than their farms, interfered with. The schools, of course, were very bad. Most of the schoolmasters were composed of men who could not succeed in any other occupation. They were for the most part disabled by accident or demoralised by drink.

"The yeomen and farmers nevertheless liked the schools, partly because they had been educated at them, as well as their fathers before them. People in local districts, far removed from towns, wish their institutions to spring up naturally among themselves, and to be the growth of their own class. It does not matter how bad they are ; they do not wish them to be interfered with. This I found to be my first great obstacle. They shied at my benevolent notions. They kept me at a distance. They did not see why they should subscribe for a new school when they had an old school of their own. They knew the native education which they had received ; but they knew nothing of the national education which I desired to introduce amongst them, under the periodical examination of Her Majesty's Inspectors.[1] I may also observe that the mistresses' schools, or dames' schools,

---

[1] We must here state the opposite view of the case. The writer was an intimate friend of George Moore's. "Although education," he says, "was at that period very low in Cumberland, and is, in its present transition state, not very high now, it was easier, before the Church or the Government undertook the education of the people, for a clever youth to get advanced in a commercial and mathematical education than it is at present. There was free trade in schools, and there was always some schoolmaster in a village, or not far off, who could take a pupil far on in mathematics, and in an English education. One of these noted men, was a predecessor of George Moore's schoolmaster at Boltongate. This man was Robert Elliot. He could teach navigation, and had the character of making 'grand' scholars. When a boy made a mistake in fractions, Robert used to say he was like a butcher at Maryport, who had made a deal of money, but who, like him, did not know much about fractions and decimals. One of a friend asked him if he would take a share in a ship that was building in the harbour. The butcher replied, 'He didn't mind.' 'Would he have a ——teenth?' 'O wounds!' said he, 'it's far too much for me, a third or —— of ——teth ——quite enough!'" Notwithstanding this defence of the old ——, it must be observed that these grand teachers, such as Robert E——, D——n, were quite exceptional. It should be remembered that Robert Elliot was succeeded by Blackbird Wilson, a bad teacher as well as a drunker.

were no better than those of the masters'. They were
even worse.[1]

"The old masters saw that my new system would re-
volutionise theirs. The trustees of the endowed schools
knew very well that they had never taken the slightest
interest in their management. And the clergymen,
whose duty it was closely to superintend them, scarcely,
if ever, entered the buildings. The masters were engaged without any testimonials. They only took to a
schoolmaster's life when they could do nothing else.
So that a want of capacity seemed to be the only qualification necessary for a schoolmaster. I found that those
who ought to have taken the lead and management of
the schools—the landowners, the farmers, the clergymen
—were all alike. They either could not or would not
find time to enter into the depths of the subject of education. Nor could they examine the claims of those
who made application for the office of teacher. They
knew less about education than about any other subject.

"In my native parish, that of Bolton, containing
1,100 inhabitants, there were three schools. Two of the
masters were addicted to drink. They had no books,
and had no proper method of teaching. The third was a
poor fellow, a collier who had fallen down a coal-pit. His
leg was badly broken, and had to be cut off. This accident was his only qualification for the office of schoolmaster! I must always express my gratitude for the
way he behaved when he found out what I was striving
at. He said to me, 'Mr. Moore, I know I'm not fit to
be a schoolmaster, but how am I to live?' I said, 'If
you will come to London I will get you a situation ; and
if you do your best, I promise you I will never let you

---

[1] One of these dames is still remembered by many now living in the
parish of Torpenhow. The book used in the school, after the spelling
book, was the New Testament. When a child came to a word the mistress
did not know, she would say, "Spell it, call it summ'at, and go on."

want.' He trusted my word, and with great perseverance on my part, I succeeded in getting him a situation.
He has got on step by step entirely by industry and good
conduct, and for many years he has been a trusted and
valuable clerk of the Great Eastern Railway Company.
I really feel a great pride in his success, and am always
pleased to welcome him to my house.[1]

"I may here observe that I would have built the new
school at Bolton myself. But I have always found that
if I can induce other people to subscribe, I enlist them
in my favour to some extent, or at all events avoid their
opposition. Accordingly, I personally canvassed all the
parish. I did not despise a shilling subscription, provided I could make a friend or neutralise an opponent.
The best freeholders in the parish consented to become
trustees. An excellent school, with a schoolmaster's
house, was erected at a cost of about £650. I selected
a good teacher from the National Society's Training
School. I fixed the fees at about half the rate of the
old schools, and relied upon an annual subscription to
make up the deficiency.

"It is scarcely necessary to speak of the vexatious
opposition which I experienced in getting the school
built and set to work. After it was opened, the poor
master and his wife were perplexed and worried by the
parents, who would not have their children taught in
classes, but separately and individually, as under the
old system. Many took their children away on this
account. But we held on. With God's blessing and

---

[1] A friend of Mr. Moore's gives the following recollection:—"It was a
treat to hear George Moore's tales of the past, in striving to polish the
crude habits and customs of his native countrymen by introducing a better
system of education, and his constant stirrings-up of the old conservative
do-nothing parsons. There are many who will recollect how he would tell
of a wooden-legged schoolmaster of the olden type, for whom he was
compelled to procure a more mechanical limb, the thumping-spoke of a
cart-wheel being a hindrance to the man's getting profitable employment in
London."

the master's Christian spirit, all opposition was eventually overcome. I shall ever respect this good man, John Moorby, for the difficulties which he encountered, the prejudices which he reconciled, and the admirable manner in which he performed the duties of his calling as teacher of the young."

Mr. Moore was by no means satisfied with what he had done at Bolton. He had only begun his work, and was determined to go forward with it. He was very much in favour of doing one thing at a time, and doing it thoroughly. He proceeded to visit all the schools in the neighbourhood, for the purpose of ascertaining their condition. He went more particularly on examination days, when he took a number of prize books with him, which he gave to the most proficient scholars as rewards for their past labours, and as stimulants to their future perseverance. In this way he visited the grammar-school at Uldale, and the free school at Bothel, in the parish of Torpenhow. On these occasions he addressed the children, impressing upon them the necessity of constantly attending school and of strict attention to their duties ; for there the foundations of their future destiny were to be laid.

It was always a joyful day for the children when George Moore attended the school, for, after the examination, he provided the scholars with an abundant tea-feast. After tea he would take the children into some adjoining field, where he "scrambled" nuts and sweet-meats among them, and gave small prizes for races and other gymnastic amusements, in which the children, boys and girls, eagerly contended.

About the year 1853 Mr. Moore was appointed trustee of Plumbland School, and with the determination to be thoroughly posted up in the details of every institution with which he was connected, he made frequent visits to the school to ascertain its actual condition. Plumbland had always been considered the best school in the district. Its endowment amounted to about £87 a year. The master was Andrew Bell, the "father of Cumberland schoolmasters." Mr. Moore, at his first visit, was pleased with the smartness of the scholars, and requested permission to have a public examination of the school. This took place in August, 1854, the Rev. W. M. Gunson, of Bagrow, officiating as inspector. The examination was eminently satisfactory. Mr. Moore made a distribution of prizes, and promised to revisit the school for a similar purpose in the following year. It has been stated that "the idea thus dropped into his fertile brain soon developed, until, what was at first but the natural gratification of a desire to make himself acquainted with his new responsibility, ended in the Competitive Scheme, which gave so great a stimulus to education in the district."

Another school was wanted at Allhallows, adjoining Bolton. The parish was very small, containing only about 250 inhabitants. The Rev. W. M. Gunson informs us that it was he who first suggested the building of this school. He began to solicit subscriptions from the landowners and farmers towards the erection. There were of course many objectors. They said, "We shall never get thirty children to the school, and then how can we pay the master?" Nevertheless, the subscription was set on foot. On Mr. Gunson's mentioning the scheme to Mr. Moore, he at once took it up warmly. He offered to pay half the deficiency in the money that was required, and, as a matter of fact, Mr. Gunson and Mr. Moore paid, in equal shares, about four-fifths of the cost of the building.

Like most good efforts, the scheme met with success. The people of the neighbourhood had seen what an ornament Bolton school and schoolmaster's house were to the parish, and they knew how much good the new schoolmaster was doing. When Allhallows school was built and opened, it was soon filled with children. There were about two acres of ground in connection with the school, which were worked by the scholars themselves. It was laid out in small plots ; and the master had a portion for his own use. John Green was a certificated teacher, and he proved an excellent schoolmaster. His wife, to the astonishment of the parish, taught the girls sewing. Such a thing had never been known in the neighbourhood. The number of pupils grew to between sixty and seventy ; for the excellence of the teaching attracted scholars from the neighbouring parishes.[1]

Among the other schools in which Mr. Moore took a special interest, were Bothel school and Bromfield school. These were both endowed. When Mr. Moore first examined Uldale school, above referred to, he found that it was ill-contrived, badly ventilated, and without conveniences of any sort. "After a great deal of perseverance," he says, "I got the Committee of Council on Education to confirm a plan for enlarging and improving the school. They had seen, by the report of Her Majesty's inspector, that I was in earnest about improving the education of Cumberland. They showed me a great deal of consideration and gave a good grant of money. The school was thus greatly improved, and the teacher was stimulated to new efforts by the regular annual inspection. Since then, the improvement in this school has been quite marvellous.

"Bothel school was the worst of the lot,—miserably small for so large a parish, badly ventilated, and filthy in the extreme. The deed of the London property— the rental of which formed the endowment of £50—

---

[1] It may be remarked, that within the ground attached to the building, there stands a stone pillar with an inscription, stating that there had passed the famous military road connecting Ellenborough (Maryport) with Old Carlisle, two of the fortified sites on Adrian's Wall from sea to sea, A.D. cxx.

had been lost. It had not been seen within the memory of man. This was a formidable opposition to any alterations or improvements. After three or four years' perseverance and hard work, we have got the school greatly enlarged, and an excellent master's house built. We have received a new deed through the Charity Commission and the Committee of Council on Education. The school is now under regular inspection, and is doing a great deal of good. The education given in it is a credit to the county." As for Bromfield school, Mr. Moore adds : "I have tried hard to get this school renovated, but up to this time I have not achieved anything, except to get the school placed under Government inspection." This, however, was accomplishing a great deal

We must now interrupt this record of Mr. Moore's educational achievements, by referring to the movement which he initiated for carrying on the education of boys and girls after they had left school. Every one knows that only the beginnings of education are learnt at school. In the country, boys and girls leave at about twelve years old, just as they are beginning to acquire the first outlines of knowledge. And unless they continue their education after they have left school, they continue children intellectually throughout life. If they have not the power or the means of forwarding their own education, they must be helped. George Moore was one of those who helped them liberally : by libraries, reading-rooms, and evening-classes. He founded the Perambulating Library,—a simple, cheap, and efficient method of maintaining adult education in the country districts, and of keeping reading people in contact with the pure and healthy literature of the time.

The idea of the perambulating library was not new. But George Moore did not mind whether it was new or not. He found it suited for his purpose, and he adopted it. It may be mentioned that the system of itinerating libraries was founded in 1817 by Samuel Brown, of Haddington. He was a man of pure mind, of great perseverance, and worked zealously throughout his life for the good of his fellow-creatures. He began his system with a library of 200 volumes. These were increased from time to time until they reached 3,850 volumes. The number of branch libraries throughout the County of East Lothian was gradually increased, until there was not a village and scarcely a hamlet in the county that was not supplied with a stock of valuable books. Thus the invaluable habit of reading was not only developed, but fostered and kept alive. The writer of these lines remembers with thanks the good effects of the library upon himself. When a boy, labouring under ill-health, he rummaged and read the books of nearly the whole library, and thus laid the foundations of a considerable amount of useful knowledge. But to return to George Moore's operations.

In the year 1851 he resolved to establish his perambulating library. He did so in conjunction with Mr. Richard Abbatt and Mr. J. P. Foster. He made a journey from London to Cumberland for the purpose of starting the scheme. He called a meeting of the clergymen and laymen likely to take part in the work. The rules were adopted, the books were bought, and the library was set in operation. It embraced nine villages, situated somewhat circularly. These were selected as the Stations. A librarian was appointed in each of them, to give out the books to the subscribers, who paid a penny a month, or a shilling a year. The names of the villages or stations were—Ireby, Torpenhow, Bothel, Mealsgate, Crookdake, Bolton Low Houses, Boltongate, Sandale, and Uldale. A neat case of new or fresh books was delivered to each station every six weeks by a paid messenger.[1]

The perambulating library proved a great success. The books were nearly always out. The country people were thus induced to read good books. At the end of the first year's operations, in 1852, a grand *fête* was held at Kilhow, while Dr. Cowan was president of the association. About six or seven hundred people were present. After several speeches had been made, the company danced on the lawn, and the evening finished with fireworks. Another entertainment of a similar character was given at Grange, High Ireby, in the following year. This also was attended by a great number of people. There were the usual speeches, tea, dancing, and fireworks.

But the most important *fête* was held in August, 1856, when Mr. Moore became president of the institution. On this occasion the new president determined to outshine all previous efforts to entertain the people Dr. Cowan kindly permitted him to use the grounds of Kilhow for the purpose.

The magnificent scenery by which Kilhow is surrounded,—the hills and valleys, with Skiddaw in the distance,—rendered the day one of great delight. There seemed to be a general holiday in the neighbourhood. People came from all the villages where the perambulating library had its stations. But many came from greater distances. The road to Kilhow was crowded with omnibuses, carriages, phaetons, cabs, and other vehicles. The mayor of Carlisle was there, and many of the neighbouring gentry; with

---

[1] This messenger was John Sanderson, a noted walker. In 1822 he performed the feat of walking 150 miles in 48 successive hours. He accomplished it two hours within the time, and did the last four miles within an hour. John Sanderson was long seen on the roads, with a case of books in a light vehicle, running them to the next station, dressed in a scarlet button coat of George Moore's.

pedestrians almost innumerable. The Warwick Bridge brass band attended, and played to the dancers on the lawn. Some fifteen hundred persons took tea in the marquee which Mr. Moore had caused to be erected, and refreshments for about two hundred persons were provided in the house.

Several speeches were delivered; Mr. Moore, as president of the library, taking the first place. After referring to his election as president, and to the fact that the society emanated from himself and one or two others, he said that if he had lived in the county he should have attended to the duties of the office with more zeal and ardour. " However, having been elected your president this fine summer's day, I shall feel happy to do my duty to the best of my power. I wish to remind you that you are assembled here as working men in particular. Nobody works harder than I do. Some of you may think it very pleasant for me to come here and make speeches. Perhaps you may think that I have got into my present position by accident. There you are very much mistaken. I can assure you that it required a great deal of hard work, anxiety, determination, and wear and tear of brain. All have the same chance and opportunity that I had when I left this part of the county. Many of you, indeed, have been far better educated than I was; and if I had received a better education I might have been able to do more good and have effected much greater improvements. But since I left my native county I have used every means to improve myself; and yet I have not done half enough. There is nothing more calculated to improve the mind than reading good books; and I hope that each gentleman here, and especially the clergy, will use their best exertions to induce their neighbours to become subscribers. I can only say that unless you are anxious to improve your minds, you will do nothing. God only helps those who help themselves; and unless you assist yourselves, and help yourselves, no other person can possibly help you. Such has been the result of my long experience in the commercial world."

Mr. Moore stated in the course of his speech that he expected that the Bishop of Carlisle (Villiers) would have been present on the occasion; but that he would certainly preach at Bolton parish church on the following Sunday. Mr. Moore had invited the Bishop to come over to Bolton during his visit to Cumberland, and his Lordship gladly complied with the request. The event caused a great excitement in the neighbourhood. A bishop had never preached in Bolton church before. Most of the parishioners had never even seen a bishop. Hence the concourse of people that crowded Bolton Church on that wet Sunday morning. The Bishop preached a sermon which made a great impression. Mr. Moore says, "His powers of preaching are great. He is most persuasive. He shows the greatest firmness with the greatest kindness. I think him the most large-hearted Christian gentleman I ever knew. He is also very honest and straightforward in his opinions. I think it the greatest blessing, that he is sent to my native county to regenerate it; and with God's blessing he will."

A mutual friendship sprang up between the Bishop of Carlisle and George Moore. The Bishop visited him in London, and in the following year George Moore visited the Bishop at his residence at Rose Castle. He was greatly pleased at the open-hearted reception—at the free and easy manner of the family towards him, and at the "impressive family worship." George Moore had, however, a little business to do on this occasion. He wished his lordship to preach at Bothel, in aid of the school funds, and to accom-

pany him on his journey.   They started early on
Sunday.

"It was a lovely morning," says Mr. Moore.   "We
had a pleasant drive of sixteen miles.   Whilst going
along, the Bishop (as I thought jokingly) asked me
what he was to say in his sermon, as he always
preached extempore.   I said he was to tell them that
the school was a disgrace to the country, that it was
without ventilation or any conveniences, that it was
enough to engender not only disease but all sorts of
immorality—that the sin of the neighbourhood was
illegitimacy and drunkenness.   We reached Bothel,
and he preached to a crowded congregation.   To my
utter astonishment, he told them exactly what I had
suggested.   But he put it most judiciously, honestly,
and forcibly.   He made a great impression.   I acted
as pew-opener, and wedged every seat full.   After the
sermon there was a good collection.

"After dining at Mealsgate we proceeded to Allhallows Church.   His Lordship was to preach there
in aid of the Church of England Education Society,—
a society in London, which had given several grants to
both Allhallows school and Bolton school, and in
which both the Bishop and myself were deeply interested.   Allhallows Church is perhaps the smallest in the
county.   On our arrival I found the churchyard was
crammed.   I inquired why the doors of the church
had not been opened.   The reply was that the church
was full!   I was delighted, because I had calculated upon
this; and the Bishop and I had come to an understanding, that if the people were too numerous to get
admission to the church he would turn out and preach
to them in the churchyard.   On inquiring of him
what I could do, he said, 'Bring a table and a chair,
and put them in a situation out of the glare of the
sunshine.'

"I got all arranged, and looked round. I think it was the grandest sight I ever saw. There must have been from eight to nine hundred people sitting on the gravestones, or on the grass plats in the open air,—with the hills of Cumberland and the woodland scenery in the distance. The bishop preached a most powerful and forcible sermon, and made a deep impression on the people. He was as much pleased as I was. It was the first sermon he had preached in the open air."

George Moore long continued to take the same interest in the Cumberland schools. He visited them yearly. He gave prizes, addressed the children, and treated them to tea and sports after the examinations. At length he resolved to extend the principle, and not only to make the children of one school compete with each other, but to bring the various schools together and make them compete with every other school. "In August, 1857," he says, "I suggested to Her Majesty's inspector that we should have a monster examination of all the schools in the immediate neighbourhood of Allhallows. When the examination took place, the schools were nine in number. More than thirty boys and girls from each school underwent examination. Prizes of books were awarded to all the successful candidates. The examination passed off with great *éclat*. Many of the surrounding gentry were present, as well as the neighbouring clergymen. After the examination, I gave a luncheon at Mealsgate to between seventy and eighty of the gentry and clergy of the district. I gave tea to about five hundred children and their parents, and supper to seventy or eighty trustees and their families, and to others who took an interest in education.

"It is extraordinary how much good results from bringing all these people together. Parents and children take the greatest interest in the proceedings. Education is thus popularised among the people. The success of this meeting induced me to suggest to the Rev. G. R. Moncrieff, Her Majesty's inspector, that he should issue a circular in anticipation of a similar examination in August, 1858."

The circular was issued by Mr. Moncrieff. It began :—" The success of the examination recently held at Allhallows school has induced Mr. George Moore of London to propose to me to hold a similar examination next year. The undermentioned are the regulations." Ten children were to be sent from each school certificated by the master. The subjects for examination were the Book of Genesis and the Gospel of St. Mark ; reading, arithmetic, mental arithmetic, writing from dictation, writing from copy, geography, English grammar, and (for girls) needlework. The prizes were to be ten shillings to each successful candidate, and gift-books were to be distributed amongst the whole body of children.

The competitive examination of 1858 greatly outshone its predecessor. The Bishop of Carlisle, Her Majesty's inspector, the clergymen of the district, and about three thousand people of the neighbourhood, were present. The pupils of the various schools mustered about 800 strong. Without regard to the spacious marquee, brought by Mr. Moore from London, and to the banners and mottoes with which it was ornamented, we proceed to the examination of the scholars themselves. The actual examinations had occupied several days of hard work. Then came the closing day, when the pupils had to be finally examined and the prizes had to be awarded. The preliminary *vivâ voce* examination had begun at an early hour in the morning. During the whole of the day, the schoolroom was crowded. The zeal and care of the inspectors were only equalled by the attention and assiduity of the scholars. Then came the final reward, when the whole party proceeded to the Green, where the Bishop of the diocese called the successful candidates before him.

Some time previously, amidst an immense crowd of spectators of all ranks and classes, the names of the successful scholars, and of the specially successful schools, were read out, and a list of the prizes that were to be awarded. The latter consisted of everything that could be thought of; and it was no slight task, as time passed on, to find prizes that would differ and be attractive from year to year. Watches, sewing-machines, china tea-services, teapots, desks, and books were the favourites for the masters. It was much easier to provide a variety for the scholars.

After the Bishop had distributed the prizes to the successful candidates, the Old Hundredth was sung by the assembled multitude; the Bishop addressed the audience, and also, in a special manner, the children. A few more addresses were delivered, and the meeting separated.[1]

George Moore had now given a fair start to the school education of Cumberland. The Bishop called it "a revival." He had generously assisted in the building and enlargement of the schools. He had instituted a system of competitive examination. He now desired that the Diocesan Education Society should take up the work and carry it on throughout the county. Accordingly, at the meeting of the society, held at Carlisle a few days after the examination at All-hallows, Mr. Moore offered an annual subscription of

---

[1] A few years later, the number of schools competing (they were called in Cumberland "Moore's Lot") had become so great that the Lords in Council on Education decided that the Government inspectors must no longer be allowed to go on with this examination unless they chose to do so during their holiday.

a hundred pounds, and such further help as might be necessary, to encourage improvement in the schools of Cumberland. The offer was accepted, Mr. Moore stating that, "as long as he was spared the Allhallows examination should be kept up. It was the most decided way of stimulating all parties—scholars, parents, friends, squires, clergymen, and above all schoolmasters. They could have no conception how it would act upon the parents of the children. In fact that was the pivot upon which the success of the whole scheme depended."

There can be no doubt as to the great benefit that was conferred upon the rising generation by the energetic action of George Moore. There were few resident landowners in the neighbourhood ; the clergy had before taken little interest in education ; and the farmers rested strong in the conservative notion that "what had satisfied their fathers would do well enough for them !" George Moore returned to his native county after a life of hard work, and roused them all up. The clergy were induced to take an interest in the schools, and the farmers were at length compelled to look after the education of their children. Not only were the schools properly built and inspected, but Sunday-schools were also established in many parishes. Sunday-schools had not existed there before. The attendance at church was greatly increased. A new life was infused into the district. Boys and girls found a new interest in life, and these boys and girls were yet to be the men and women of Cumberland.

"There is no work," says George Moore, "that I have ever undertaken that has given me greater satisfaction than the result of my design to raise and better the schools, by giving them a higher standard to aim at. The schoolmaster has been reached through the medium of the pupils ; for the success of the latter at the examinations, proved the very best advertisement for the teacher. His energies were awakened, and he set to work to improve and raise the character of his scholars. The experiment proved the motto of 'helping others to help themselves.' The parents observed the schools which had succeeded best at the examinations; and they could not be content with a lower means of instruction when a better was within their reach."

Such was the work in Cumberland on which George Moore spent his holidays. We return again to his beneficent work in London.

CHAPTER XI.

THE work done by George Moore in Cumberland was only holiday-work. The greater part of his time was spent in London. His business required a great deal of attention. When he gave up travelling in 1841, the firm employed ten country travellers and three town travellers. But now, in 1852, it employed seventeen country travellers and ten town travellers. The premises had again been considerably enlarged, and an entrance made into Cheapside. It was found necessary to open branches in the larger towns of the kingdom. The expense of conveying a huge bulk of stock from one town to another, runs away with profits. Hence warehouses were taken in Manchester, Liverpool, Edinburgh, Birmingham, Plymouth, Bristol, Brighton, Norwich, and Portsea. Warehouses had been established in Glasgow, Dublin, and Paris, about six years before.

In carrying on a large business of this kind, knowledge of character is essentially necessary. The most successful merchant is not the man who personally works the hardest but the man who possesses the greatest powers of organisation,—whose experience and knowledge, combined with common sense, enable him to discern character and select the men best fitted

to carry out his operations. George Moore was great
in these respects. His insight into character seemed
almost to be the result of instinct. He had a rapid
power of judging whom he could trust. And he rarely
made a mistake, either in the heads of departments,
or in the partners who from time to time were introduced into the firm.

One would have supposed that with such a large
and rapidly-increasing business, George Moore would
have had little time to attend to the organising of
charitable institutions. But it was with him as it is
with many other hard-working business men. If you
wish to have any good work well done, go to the busy
man, not to the idle man. The former can find time
for everything. The latter can find time for nothing.
Will, power, perseverance, and industry enable a man
not only to promote his own interests, but at the same
time to help others less prosperous than himself.

In the midst of his many labours Mr. Moore was
"pricked" by the Lord Mayor, in June, 1852, as Sheriff
of London. Mr. Grissell, the well-known contractor,
was "pricked" with him. Mr. Moore was then so
much occupied with the benevolent institutions which
he had started, as well as with his own business, that
he could not indulge in the luxury of holding the office
of sheriff. It would have involved him in many civic
dinners. It might have led to a knighthood. It might
have led to the office of Lord Mayor. But he could
not give up the works of benevolence which he had
undertaken to prosecute, nor could he give up the
additional time from his business, which holding the
office of sheriff would have involved. He accordingly
declined the offer. Mr. Grissell did the same; and
the fines of £400 each, or £800 in all, were levied
from the recusants, and paid into the funds of the
Corporation.

More honours were offered to him, which for the same reasons he refused to accept. He was unanimously elected alderman by the liverymen of Cordwainers' ward, and a second time by those of Bread Street ward. He refused to serve in both cases. "I once thought," he says, "that to be Sheriff of London, or Lord Mayor, would have been the height of my ambition. But now I have neither the ambition nor the inclination to serve in either office. To men who have not gained a mercantile position, corporation honours are much sought after; but to those who have acquired a prominent place in commerce, such honours are not appreciated. At the same time I am bound in gratitude to say that I have always received the most marked courtesy and consideration from the corporation, even although I did not feel disposed to join it."

In the same year that he was "pricked" sheriff, Mr. Moore was nominated by the Lord Mayor, at the request of Lord Palmerston, and appointed to the Lieutenancy of London. He accepted the office, which involved no extra labour ; but " up to this day," he says (February 10, 1858), " I have not got my regimentals nor my court-dress." He was also invited to represent the electors of Nottingham in Parliament. He had many opportunities of being sent to Parliament unopposed. But he invariably refused. He was of opinion that Parliament should be composed of the best, wisest, and most highly educated men in the country. He always averred that he was not one of such men.

He was not a bigoted politician. He never took an extreme side. He did not like sudden changes of any sort. He was a moderate Liberal. He wished rather to repair the breaches in the constitution which time had made, than to pull it down by radical changes, and endeavour to reconstruct it upon no very certain foundation. He thought that the best of all things to adopt was to educate the people up to the highest standard ; so that they might be fitted for whatever privileges Parliament might think proper to confer upon them. Such was the course which he himself adopted in his endeavours to improve the education of the rising generation.

Mr. Moore was however a strong friend of free trade. As early as 1845, when Mr. Cobden was agitating the country in favour of the county registration movement, and urging people to buy freehold qualifications, so that they might vote for county members of Parliament, Mr. Moore and five others bought a small freehold in Middlesex, and during twenty years and upwards they all voted for free-trade candidates. Mr. Moore stuck to the free-trade movement, and when the corn laws were repealed the firm of Copestake, Moore and Co., were amongst the largest subscribers to the Cobden Fund.

Besides the repeated invitations to stand for Nottingham, where he could have commanded a large amount of support, he was also invited to stand for West Cumberland. "On this occasion," he says, "had I even felt the inclination to accept it, I believe that I could not have succeeded, as in that quarter they think more of landowners than of rag-merchants. However, I never could get my own consent to go into the House of Commons. First, because if I had gone there, I could not have rested satisfied with being a silent member. It is my nature to make myself master of all that I have to do with. Then the business of the House of Commons would have occupied much of my time. It would have acted detrimentally to me in taking me from my own business, to which I was in a measure bound, and in which I have so large a share. Not to 'have done my share of work, would have been dishonest in principle. And secondly, because I knew my value to the many charitable institutions to which I am so warmly attached. Apart from my business pursuits, I considered this to be my proper sphere of usefulness."

Mr. Moore, however, warmly assisted in canvassing for his political friends. Thus he took an active interest in the return of Lord John Russell and the other Liberal candidates for the City of London in 1852. He also canvassed the Cumberland voters in London, and took down with him forty-four East Cumberland freeholders to vote for Mr. C. Howard and Mr. William Marshall. This he did without a shilling of expense to the candidates. "This hard work," he says, "almost knocked me up. We won the election by a large majority. At the dinner given by the members I felt so ill that I was obliged to leave the table, and therefore could not make the two speeches that were assigned to me. I returned with Mr. Howard to Greystock Castle, and the quiet soon restored me. I afterwards went to Shap Wells to meet Mrs. Moore. The waters there always benefit me.

"What was my surprise, when at Shap Wells, to receive a visit from Lord Lonsdale. He invited me to stay with him at Lowther Castle. I had been determinedly opposed to his candidates. I had come down from London expressly to assist in returning the Liberal members. I was so much surprised, that I declined the invitation. 'No,' said he, 'I have come over expressly on purpose to invite you.' 'If that be the case,' said I, 'I shall do myself the honour of visiting you.' On my arrival at the castle I found it was filled with the opposite party in politics. They could not make out how it was that I should be there, and I must confess that at first I did not feel quite at home. But his Lordship's and Colonel Lowther's kindness, and indeed that of all the party, soon made me feel as easy as a glove. I felt myself a little in the way when politics were the topic of conversation. But to Lord Lonsdale's credit be it said, that he never, either directly or indirectly, hinted at making me a convert. I have since felt that it was a most friendly act to invite me to his house, when the heat of the party contest had scarcely subsided."

At the General Election of 1857, Lord John Russell again stood for the City. He had become somewhat unpopular at the time, for what reason he did not know. At first he thought of giving up the seat, and trying another constituency ; but, on second thoughts, he determined to stand. He sent his nephew, Mr. Russell, to Mr. Moore, to ask if he would be deputy-chairman of his committee. By all means ! George Moore threw himself heart and soul into the contest. A large meeting of voters was held at the London Tavern, when Lord John made a magnificent speech, and created a deep impression on the electors. Mr. Moore seconded a vote of confidence in him, which was agreed to. Mr. Moore also seconded his nomination, and worked hard for him until he was returned. " I entertained," says Mr. Moore, " his Lordship and Lady Russell, and his friends, at Bow Churchyard. The large crowd that followed him excited a great sensation. He was decidedly the popular candidate. Owing to his old friends and colleagues turning against him, he got a great deal of sympathy ; as Englishmen do not like to see a man victimised. I have always been an ardent admirer of Lord John, and he was pleased to think that on this occasion I had been instrumental in securing his return.

" On the same night," he continues, " I started for

Brayton to assist Wilfrid Lawson in his contest for West Cumberland. I never had such a hard week's work in my life. On the first day, Monday, William Lawson and I were at Crookdake at half-past six in the morning. We had two excellent hunters under us, and went straight across Leesrigg pasture, jumping all the fences to Allhallows and Torpenhow. After canvassing with energy, we finished the night by arriving at Brayton at 10 o'clock P.M. The following day was the nomination day. Wilfrid drove me to Cockermouth. He was the popular candidate, though not the candidate to win. There I had a *rencontre* with my friend George Bentinck. He told me that I had no business to make such a dead stand against their party. However, after a paper war we got reconciled again, and were as good friends as ever.

"I found that all the farmers voted with the landlords. They were not allowed to think and act for themselves. The screw was put on in every shape. Out of a large constituency, Wilfrid Lawson was beat by about 250 votes. I took charge of the polling booth at Bolton, my native place. I did not throw a chance away. But there is no satisfaction in elections. They cause strife, heartburnings, and all sorts of evil.

"The election was over on the Friday. We had an excellent day's fox-hunting on Saturday. I started for London the same night, very much tired with my hard week's work. I paid the entire expenses of the London canvass, and the expenses of such voters to Cumberland and back as could not themselves pay the cost of the double journey, and I got a great deal of abuse from the yellow [1] papers; and thus ended the West Cumberland election."

In the year 1854, Mr. Moore removed his residence

---

[1] *Yellow* papers. In most counties *yellow* is Whig; but in Cumberland it is Conservative.

from Oxford Terrace to a mansion in Kensington
Palace Gardens. He always regarded this as an
extravagant step. He had lived very happily in a
small house. Why should he remove to a larger one?
Nevertheless, the site was bought and the building was begun. The house cost him about double
the estimate. "Although," he says, "I had built
the house at the solicitation of Mrs. Moore, I was
mortified at my extravagance, and thought it both
wicked and aggrandizing—mere ostentation and vain
show—to build such a house. It was long before
I felt at home in it, nor did it at all add to our happiness. I felt that I had acted foolishly. But, strange
to say, a gentleman offered to take the house off my
hands and to give me three thousand guineas profit.
I made up my mind to accept this offer; but my dear
wife had taken such an interest in the house that we
could not decide to sell it. I accordingly declined the
offer.

"As our young men and women at Bow Churchyard
had been instrumental in helping me to gain the wealth
for building such a house, I determined that they
should be the first to visit us. We gave a ball to
about 300 of our own people, and allowed the young
men to invite their female friends, to equalise the sexes.
After the dancing there was a grand supper. We gave
a second ball to all the porters and their wives, the
drivers, and the female servants. There were about
two hundred in all. We employed omnibuses to
bring them to the house and send them away. They
got abundant refreshment, and danced to their hearts'
content.

"After this we kept a great deal of company. The
house was looked upon as a work of art. All our
friends expected to be invited to see it and partake of
our hospitality. We accordingly gave a large dinner

weekly, until we had exhausted our numerous friends
and acquaintances. My wife kept an account of above
eight hundred who dined with us. But happiness does
not flow in such a channel. Promiscuous company takes
one's mind away from God and His dealings with men;
and there is no lasting pleasure in the excitement."

We return to Mr. Moore's philanthropic work, which
was really the crown and glory of his life. It will
be remembered that he was fined £400 for refusing
to accept the position of sheriff.

Notwithstanding this act of injustice, he thought it
right to perform some of the duties which are supposed
to belong to the office. "Although," he says, "I did
not eat any of the civic dinners, I determined to visit
every prison in London." He first visited the new
City prison at Holloway. He was received by the
Rev. Mr. Cohen, the chaplain, who took him over the
gaol. Mr. Cohen says, "He took the most intense
interest in the whole place, and in the inmates thereof.
He was making a tour of the prisons and reformatories all
over London. His practical view of things led him to
suggest the establishment of a reformatory for discharged
prisoners."

Mr. Moore says that he was struck with the fact, that
when he inquired of the chaplains what became of the
poor fellows after the expiration of their term of imprisonment. their answer was, "They can do nothing but
return to stealing, as nobody will employ them." "I at
once determined," says Mr. Moore, "with God's help, to
establish a Reformatory for young men. I enlisted my
valued friend, James Cunliffe, banker, in the cause; and
we immediately took large premises and grounds at
Grove House, Brixton Hill.

"I called upon Lord Shaftesbury to consult him on
the subject. I was much pleased with my visit and the

M

great encouragement which I received. Experience has
convinced me that Lord Shaftesbury is the most zealous
and persevering philanthropist of the day. He is
always ready for every good work, and I never knew
any man who could get through so much. He never
tires of doing good. He has extraordinary tact and
ability as a chairman ; and he has perhaps had more
experience in that position than any living man. His
kind and courteous manner, his large-heartedness, and
his zeal in every good movement, will give him an im-
perishable renown, and an everlasting inheritance with
his Heavenly Master.

"Lord Shaftesbury consented to be our president.
We engaged Mr. —— as governor. And now my
anxieties and troubles began. This person had been
in the City Mission, and was inspector of Ragged
Schools. But, in my opinion, he was the worst man of
business I ever knew. With all our endeavours, we
could not get the establishment to work satisfactorily.
We certainly got it filled with young men, but the
governor had not the slightest moral influence over them.
They caballed ; they became insubordinate ; and the
whole affair got into disorder. In fact we found that
Mr. —— was a hypocrite in disguise, and we got rid of
him, pretty well sickened with the work.

"But I am not in the habit of giving up things in
this way. *Persevere* has always been my motto ; and I
determined to try again. We had a long lease of the
premises, and I felt that we must do something to
establish the work on some firmer foundation. I felt
however that I had undertaken a job that I could not
manage by myself. I lost my excellent friend James
Cunliffe by sudden death ; and my other colleagues
rarely came to my help. The whole burthen was thus
thrown upon me.

"But Providence very often steps in at the right time

to help us. On looking about, I found that Mr. C. T. Jenkinson and Mr. Joseph Moore lived close to the reformatory, and that they were willing to join me. Mr. Bowker also rendered me the greatest assistance, giving up much time to it; and to their invaluable superintendence I am indebted for the increased success which for some time attended the work. We have been fortunate in our new governor. He was young and inexperienced at first, but he improves every year. I may now say (November 9th, 1857) that this has been the most interesting work that I have ever been engaged in. You can observe the good you are doing. You have ocular demonstration of it. When the men come in, they look like fiends, sunk in sin and degradation; but when we train them to work and send them out, they are altogether changed in outward appearance, and also, I trust, in soul and in spirit."[1]

One of the most remarkable and almost unique forms in which George Moore displayed his benevolence, was in marrying people who were not, but who ought to have been, married. The City Missionaries, with whom he was in constant communication, found multitudes of men and women living together without the ceremony of marriage having been performed. The women were in a disreputable social position. The children were growing up illegitimate. In order, therefore, to protect the women and give them a tie upon their husbands, as well as to give their future children a legitimate start in society, he paid the marriage fees of

---

[1] This passage was written in 1857. The reformatory was then flourishing, and, it was hoped, doing good. Mr. Moore was the soul of the work so long as it lasted. He visited it often, and gave freely. He also exerted his influence to induce others to help him. It existed for about ten years. But the second manager proved no better than the first; and his maladministration eventually wrecked the institution. Besides, the lease of the premises was up. The buildings were falling to pieces, and the Reformatory was at length closed. Mr. Moore used to say in later years "that this was the only work he had begun and given up."

thousands of persons. He did this for about twenty years. It was all done privately. The clergymen who performed the ceremony knew nothing of the donor of the marriage fees. The people who had been married never knew their benefactor. The whole of the work was done through the City Missionaries, who kept the matter secret.

We have before us a letter to George Moore, dated August 4th, 1854, in which the missionary says:—"I find on inquiry that we have £7 or £8 yet in hand of the wedding fund. Constant demands are being made upon it; but I have found it needful to check inconsiderate applications. Glad should I be if all were married who are living together in an unmarried state. But I am wishful that the means we still have should be applied to the assistance and relief of those who see and feel that they have done wrong, and who had not the means of doing right." Mr. Moore continued to help these people to get married, to the close of his life. We find from his accounts that he paid more than five hundred pounds for marriage fees.

His connection with this undertaking revealed to him one of those dreadful things in cities that lie almost unheeded about us,—the demoralisation of multitudes of women who, in their right position, should be the safeguards of society. He cordially concurred with his friend Mr. Robert Hanbury, M.P., in endeavouring to establish a refuge for fallen women. The work was full of difficulties. It could only be done through the medium of women themselves. And yet how few respectable women are there who will condescend to come into communication with the lowest of their sex! Mr. Moore, at one of the meetings of the Reformatory and Refuge Union, offered to give a hundred pounds annually for the first two female missionaries who would work amongst the fallen. "With

God's help," he says, " I am determined to persevere
in this good cause. But it is more difficult to grapple
with than any matter I have ever undertaken. Mr.
Hanbury is as zealous as myself. We *may* do some
good. At all events we can place those whom we reclaim in homes and refuges. They are to be pitied and
cared for. The rascality of man is cruel, disgraceful,
and abominable. How many men are there who make
the destruction of poor unsuspecting girls their study.
If there be men who are to experience the curse of God,
it is they."

One who knew Mr. Moore at this time says of him :
—" It must have been soon after the Reformatory and
Refuge Union was established that I first knew George
Moore. His brusque business-like way of discussing
the questions which were proposed at the committee
marked him in my mind as an exceptional character.
When the introduction merged into an acquaintance,
and afterwards into a friendship, I was increasingly impressed by the downright thoroughness with which he
carried out whatever he put his hand to. No half-and-
half measure met with his support. Like a sturdy
blacksmith, he struck with the sledge-hammer of his
honest opinion, caring little how the sparks of his
bluntly-expressed views might fall on those around
him.

" George Moore's desire to be useful in his day and
generation was greatly strengthened by his pecuniary
resources. He gave ungrudgingly, but never without
satisfying himself that it was for a sound and well-
matured object. Such a plan must have often involved
him in great trouble ; but if it were more generally
adopted by other rich philanthropists, it would to a
great extent prevent much mischievous almsgiving."

One of George Moore's next objects was to endeavour,
in conjunction with others, to establish a home for

Incurables. "The same year," he says, "in which I resolved to do some good to my fellow-creatures, I visited the hospitals, and found that many patients were turned out as Incurable,—hospitals being for the cure of diseases, and not for the accommodation of those who could not be cured. These destitute creatures had no prospect before them but starvation or the workhouse. To persons brought up in respectability, this was almost equal to death. I was glad to join with James Peek in assisting Dr. Reed in his project for founding a hospital for incurables. I was made a trustee of the institution. As the candidates for election were all visited by the committee, I had the opportunity of seeing many cases of woeful misery ; men and women who had been well brought up, prostrated and broken down by incurable diseases ; in many cases starving from want of the common necessaries of life ; strangers to everything like comfort or luxury ; and with no prospect before them but protracted dying and the grave. My dear friend Charles Dickens has given a vivid account of these poor neglected suffering creatures ; and he has called all benevolent spirits to assist in establishing a home for the help of the incurables."[1]

The institution was not however established until some years later. When Dr. Reed called upon Mr. James Peek on behalf of the Asylum for Idiots, the latter suggested that the establishment of an asylum for incurables would be a noble wind-up to his life ; and

[1] From an article published in *Household Words*, August 24th, 1850, Mr. Dickens say—

"It is an extraordinary fact that among the innumerable medical charities with which this country abounds there is not one for the help of those who of all others most require succour, and who must die, and do die, in thousands, unaided. It is indeed a marvellous oversight of benevolence that aid of any should have been so long withheld from precisely the sufferers who most need it. Hopeless pain allied to hopeless poverty is a condition of existence not to be thought of without a shudder. It is a slow journey towards the Valley of the Shadow of Death, from which we save even the condemned criminal."

he offered five hundred pounds as a beginning. At a second visit Mr. Peck offered to double his donation. At the same time Mr. Moore was ready, with several others, to aid Dr. Reed in his benevolent efforts. A small meeting was held in the Egyptian Hall, Mansion House, when a few friends of Dr. Reed formed themselves into a committee. Funds were gradually collected, and the institution was started. The first home was at Carshalton, and the next at Putney House, Upper Richmond Road. Every bed was full. The applicants for admission continued to increase. Dr. Reed worked to his utmost on behalf of the institution, and its success at his death crowned the self-sacrificing and philanthropic labours of his life.

Another institution in which George Moore took a special interest,—an institution which, in fact, originated with himself,—was the London General Porters' Benevolent Association. He called the porters of his own establishment together and laid the matter before them. The object of the institution was to relieve disabled porters, and their wives and families in event of their death. He said that he had been as much obliged to porters during his long commercial life as they had been to him. He had never been defrauded by them ; they had conscientiously adhered to their trust ; and they were well worthy of their reward. They had seen many benevolent institutions started for affording relief and assistance to necessitous widows and education and maintenance to their orphan children. Why should they not have a similar institution for the benefit of Porters ? Would they help him to establish this institution ? Their universal reply was, " Yes ! "

"Then," said he, "you must immediately set to work ; you must collect subscriptions ; you must invite your fellow porters to join you ; and when I see that you are in earnest, come to me again, and we shall launch the Porters' Benevolent Association at a public meeting!" The porters found many persons willing to help them—merchants, travellers, and porters themselves. The first public meeting was held at the Shaftesbury Hall, Aldersgate Street, on the 9th December, 1857. Upwards of seven hundred porters were present. A committee was elected to frame rules for the government of the Association.

The Association was fairly launched at a public meeting held in the London Tavern, on the 16th February, 1858. George Moore took the chair. He had summoned all his friends to be present, and there was a goodly array of London merchants and warehousemen on the platform. About twelve hundred porters were present. "A more gratifying scene," says Mr. Moore, " I never beheld. I made a speech to my mind, which I seldom do. I inaugurated and launched the institution to my own satisfaction, and to that of all present. I have a great regard for this class of men, and no one can know them better than I do, from my long experience of their value. We ought to bear one another's burdens, and so fulfil the law of Christ. I have now resolved to work this institution well, and to start no other. I think that I have now my work fairly laid out."

The resolution " to start no other institution " soon broke down. He could not be idle. It was like Sir Walter Scott saying, " Kettle, kettle, don't boil!" The kettle will boil, notwithstanding all resolutions to the contrary. Mr. Moore did not stop here. His help was never wanting where ignorance had to be educated or fallen humanity reclaimed. His large heart and liberal hand were always ready to help on every good and noble work.

"The riches which God has given me," he says, "may, if rightly used, be a blessing to many ; but, if otherwise, they may only prove a curse and a snare." He did not take so much pleasure in giving as in doing. What he gave, he gave with fellow-feeling and sympathy. One of his maxims was, "Sympathy is the great secret of life." At Kilhow he said, "If the world only knew half the happiness that a man has in doing good, he would do a great deal more. We are only here for a time, and ought to live as we would wish to die."

George Moore had discovered what many people never find out, that man's duty in the world is not merely to "get on" without regard for others, or to spend his accumulated money on mere selfish gratifications ; but to help those who want help, to instruct those who want instruction, and to endeavour to lift them up into the higher light of civilization and Christianity. Every year he wrote the following words in his pocket-book. They became ingrained in his soul, and to a certain extent, formed his creed :

> " What I spent I had :
> What I saved I lost :
> What I gave I have."

CHAPTER XII.

Mr. Moore left amongst his papers many passages relating to his religious life. In the early part of his history he thought very little about religion. He was satisfied to do the work of the time without thinking much of the life to come. To him, as to many others, the words might be applied, " Rejoice, O young man, in thy youth ; and let thy heart cheer thee in the days of thy youth, and walk in the ways of thine heart, and in the sight of thine eyes ; but know thou, that for all these things God will bring thee into judgment."

The philanthropic efforts in which he had been engaged arose for the most part from the promptings of a benevolent heart. This was especially the case with the Commercial Travellers' Schools, to which he devoted so much of his time and attention, and also with the Cumberland Benevolent Institution, to which he gave his first spare guinea. His life had been one of prosperity. He had suffered no great sorrow. The societies with which he was connected prospered like himself. He had " troops of friends." He was solicited to occupy the highest offices. Everything went well with him.

And yet much suffering awaited him. Dear friends fell away from him one by one. He began to think of the uncertainties of human life, and then he thought of the future.

In 1850, he spent three months at Shap Wells and St. Bees. His nervous system was at that time much shattered. He said he felt as if his brain were worn out. He could not bear the sight of a book or of a letter. The very moaning of the ocean oppressed him. The pain in his head was intense. Once he could sleep at will; now he could not sleep at all. He was greatly depressed in his mind. He thought upon his past life, and felt how much better his life might have been. The following passages from his papers will illustrate this point :—

"I have always been obliged to act from sudden impulse, never having had time to think or mature my thoughts. I have always been obliged to act *as I thought*, or my poor brain would have been overwhelmed with the variety of subjects I had to deal with.

"In looking back upon my past life, I have a great deal to deplore and repent of. In my struggling days, when I travelled and worked on Sunday and Saturday, and sometimes all night, I scarcely ever heard the Word of God. I did not understand the scheme of salvation ; yet, strange to say, I had a sincere belief in the efficacy of prayer.

"I was a popular traveller, and was much courted both by customers and brother travellers. At that time of day, the dinner hour was one, and the mischievous pint of wine was the daily allowance, with hot suppers and grog at nights. I often thank God that I did not become a drunkard. My temptations were very great. All customers that came to see my stock of goods were invited to drink, no matter at what hour.

"During my travelling days I had no time to think.

At night I tumbled into bed without asking God's blessing, and I was generally so tired that I fell asleep in a few minutes.

"It was not until I gave up travelling that I regularly went to any church, and then I attended the ministry of the Rev. Daniel Moore. For the first time I felt my conscience pricked. About this period my brother-in-law, the Rev. Mr. Ray, died suddenly. This was a great blow. I felt that in the midst of life we are in death. But the Spirit of God was not in me. I had no peace of conscience. God wrestled with me, and sorely afflicted me. When I was at St. Bees, in 1850, I gave up all hopes of ever being well again, and I then for the first time felt my real danger.

"It pleased God gradually to restore me to health. For a long time afterwards I felt my brain giving way if I worked too hard. I never hoped to be able to attend to business again. I have always had a great pleasure in business; and felt that it might have shortened my days if I gave it up. So, on my recovery I continued to take part in my business as before."

Mr. Moore's next great blow arose through his business connection. He says, "I had no sooner recovered my health so as to be able to attend to business than my worthy partner Mr. Groucock broke down. His illness gave me great concern. His complaint was ossification of the artery near the brain. The Rev. J. O. Jackson, and afterwards Mr. Bowker, travelled with him; and changes of scene of all sorts were tried both at home and abroad, but with no avail. His health gradually declined, and he died in 1853."

Mr. Moore had many religious conversations with Mr. Groucock, whose thoughts had latterly almost entirely dwelt on religious subjects. Their mutual friend, Mr. Hitchcock, of St. Paul's Churchyard, had taken many occasions to speak with Mr. Moore as to the importance of not neglecting his soul's interests while occupied with the cares of this life and the anxieties of a great business.

Mr. Moore says, after one of these interviews, " How I long to realise the forgiveness of sins, as promised in the words, ' He that spared not His own Son, but delivered him up for us all, how shall He not with Him also freely give us all things ? '—and ' This is a faithful saying, and worthy of all acceptation, that Christ Jesus came into the world to save sinners.' " His thoughts were thus strongly directed to the state of his mind and heart.

Among his most intimate friends, to whom he opened up his anxieties and conflict of soul, were the Rev. Daniel Moore and Mr. Bowker, of Christ's Hospital. He was much helped by both of them. He also had letters and conversations on sacred subjects with Mr. Moggridge (Old Humphrey). Of the latter he says, " How I envied his mind and heart! Yet he lives on only a scanty pittance. He called upon me once when I was in a desponding mood. How he comforted and supported me! He was one of the most lovable old men I ever knew. His mind was as pure as the snowdrop."

Mr. Moore continued greatly depressed. He suffered almost as much as Mr. Groucock had done. He afterwards thanked God that he had not been left to die in that state of melancholy. Nor did he as yet see his way clearly. The world was too much with him. To use his own words, " I only enjoyed a moderate share of worldly religion. My works were greater than my faith, and I had no peace, and little happiness, save in excitement. I had never felt any gratitude to God for my prosperity, nor for my many worldly blessings." He regretted also " his irritable temper, his quickness at retort, and his inconsiderateness for other people's feelings." He desired to throw these things off like a garment. His spirit was willing, but his flesh was weak.

"I trust," he says in another passage, "that I am beginning to see and feel the folly and vanity of the world and its pleasures. Oh that I could feel that I had at length entered the strait gate, and was travelling the narrow road that leadeth to eternal life! As Newton says, I know what the world can do and what it cannot do. It cannot give or take away that peace of God which passeth all understanding. It cannot soothe a wounded conscience like mine, nor enable me to feel that I could meet death with comfort. I feel a constant conflict of conscience with inclination, of the desire to do right against the promptings of evil. I feel that I am unstable as water—poor, weak, and simple. If I could realise faith in Jesus, I should be wiser and stronger, and abound in grace."

In this way did George Moore strive and struggle for peace to shine on his inner life. He regretted deeply that he had never been instructed in the knowledge of the Bible in his youth ; and that for many years he had paid little attention to religious matters. The only thing he realised was the "knowledge of his depraved heart." He prayed for the new birth ; he longed to be converted ; he hoped for some special signal of his change. He expected that after this, he would be no longer a prey to doubts, fears, or temptations. He says, "I have been earnestly praying for the last two years for God to give me some *sudden* change of heart, but no sudden change comes. I read and hear of some whose wills are given up to God, and that they have communion with Him. I do not experience this, and sometimes think that it is no use trying or praying."

Sometimes he could not sleep at night from anxiety,

but would rise and pray for help from above. He
vexed himself about difficult and perplexing questions
of doctrine, such as election and predestination! He
invited his friends to tell him what they meant, but he
could get no insight. " I do not understand the doctrine," he says ; " it is a mystery. But this I know, that
" Christ died for all men.' " He sometimes thought
that God had hidden His face from him. He sought
repentance with tears. God did not appear to answer
his prayers. " If He hears my prayers," said he, " He
does not answer them. He has said, ' Come unto Me,
all ye that labour and are heavy laden, and I will give
you rest.' But I get no rest—no peace of soul. Yet I
must persevere, for God is the same yesterday, to-day,
and for ever."

At length comfort came to him. Light began to dawn
on his soul. " I am determined," he says, " for the future,
not to perplex my mind with seeking for some extraordinary impressions, signs, or tokens of the new birth.
I believe the Gospel. I love the Lord Jesus Christ. I
receive with confidence the promise that ' He that
heareth My word, and believeth on Him that sent Me,
hath everlasting life, and shall not come into condemna-
tion, but is passed from death unto life.' "

And again, " The new birth must be a change of
mind, from ungodliness to belief in and worship of God,
through our blessed Mediator. This is expressed in
the Old Testament by the promise of God : ' A new
heart also will I give you, and a new spirit will I put
within you ; and I will take away the stony heart out of
your flesh, and I will give you an heart of flesh. * * *
And cause you to walk in my statutes, and ye shall
keep my judgments, and do them * * * ; and ye shall
be my people, and I will be your God.' "

Without further analysing his self-revelations, we may
return to Mr. Moore's works of benevolence and mercy,

which were, in fact, the actual outcome of his struggling faith and his believing soul. He had often thought of improving the spiritual condition of the young men in his employment. He remembered the time when he himself had served in London, with no one to care for him. He had no guidance, no direction, no home influences to guard him against evil courses. Provided he did his day's work, it was enough ; he might do as he liked with the rest of his time.

It was the same in most warehouses at that period. The young men were allowed to take their own course. They went to theatres and other night resorts. They amused themselves in the evenings as they best could. At the premises in Bow Churchyard, the young men got up a stage and scenery, and performed plays.

To raise the character and improve the spiritual condition of the persons employed by the firm, Mr. Moore proposed to establish family worship at a quarter to eight every morning. His first difficulty was to obtain a suitable room for the purpose, as every portion of space in the warehouse was fully occupied. He spoke to his partners on the subject ; and though they thought it would not work well, they willingly agreed to everything that he proposed. At last he resolved to turn four or five beds out of a room, and begin family worship there.

It was sometime before there seemed to be any prospect of success in the movement. " A failure on this subject," says Mr. Moore, " would have been very unsatisfactory to all parties concerned. To attempt to *force* young men to be religious would probably have had a diametrically opposite effect. I knew that if I had asked our old hands to attend, and they had refused, it would have placed us mutually in a wrong position. I therefore consulted some of those that I thought were well disposed, and they readily agreed.

For some time a good many attended, one of the older men doing the duty. The numbers fluctuated. At times there were very few; at other times none at all; and at last the meeting for morning prayers almost expired.

"As I was determined with God's blessing to continue them, and as one of our young men had studied at St. Bees for the ministry—the Rev. Mr. Richardson—[1] and as I had got him a curacy at St. Andrew's, Blackfriars Road, I engaged him to attend to the morning prayers at fifty guineas a year. I now considered it my duty to insist upon all the apprentices regularly attending family worship."

The Rev. Mr. Richardson commenced his duties as chaplain on the 28th of January, 1856. It was announced that he had been one of the young men employed on the establishment, as it was supposed that this would have less the appearance of interference. The attendance was voluntary, with the exception of the apprentices. The service was at first commenced in a small room, but it was soon found necessary to enlarge the accommodation. The service consisted in reading the Word of God, with a short exposition, and prayers,—all within a quarter of an hour.

That the service was successful, the following petition of the *employés* will show:—"The young men who habitually attend morning prayer in the establishment are desirous to see their numbers increased; and in order to secure this desirable object they beg to suggest

---

[1] Mr. Richardson says, "My note of introduction to Mr. George Moore, in January, 1850, at once secured me an appointment in the establishment at Bow Churchyard. When I afterwards left and went to St. Bees, I wrote to Mr. Moore in reference to an address made by Mr. Groucock to the young men. Mr. Moore replied, 'I am glad to hear from you at St. Bees, more particularly as it is to be hoped the Spirit of God has moved you to a calling so sacred and responsible. . . I shall with great pleasure take upon myself to present you with Dr. A. Clarke's *Commentary on the Bible*, in Mr. Groucock's name.' " The Rev. Mr. Richardson is now vicar of St. Benet's in the East.

N

most respectfully to the firm that the hour of attendance
should be altered to eight o'clock, thereby affording an
opportunity to those who live out of the house, and
others who would find it more convenient to attend at
that time than at a quarter to eight."

The privilege was at once conceded by the partners.
The attendance rapidly increased. The young men
began to take a special interest in the undertaking.
Many of them helped Mr. Richardson in his Ragged
and Sunday-schools. A young men's mutual improvement society was started, as well as a Sunday-morning
Bible-class. The moral atmosphere of the place improved, and yet Mr. Moore was not satisfied. "I may
here acknowledge," he says, in 1857, "that notwithstanding all my anxiety to benefit them, I do not appear
to be able to do all the good that other people do. I
suppose it is a false delicacy on my part,—perhaps a
want of moral courage. Yet, when I take the chair at
a lecture, which takes place as often as they like, I
generally take the opportunity of urging the young men
to pursue a godly, moral, and straightforward course in
life; and they invariably receive my advice and admo-
nitions with the greatest kindness."

Besides the young men of the house, there were the
young women to be attended to. Mr. Moore had
great difficulty in getting them to attend family worship; but with the same perseverance, he induced them
to attend Mr. Richardson's service. He also got the
City Missionary whom he had by this time appointed,
to conduct family worship to the workwomen in Milton
Street. Notwithstanding all his efforts, Mr. Moore
says : "I am ill at ease with what I have done. I have
fallen far short of my endeavours. I feel the great
responsibility that rests upon me. I wish them all to
feel that they have souls to be saved. We have great
mutual respect one for another. I always recollect that

I was a young man myself, and I might have been a servant yet, but for God's help."

Referring afterwards to the progress made in the attendance at family worship at Bow Churchyard, he says, "The chaplain now reports most favourably of the large attendance at prayers. He says that the seed he is sowing will in due time produce good fruits. I find that I have not got on so well with the young women at our house in St. Andrew's Hill. Although I have made many vigorous efforts to increase the number of attendants, I must still persevere. If I cannot drive them, I will do all in my power to lead them.

" I can say without egotism that all the people in our employ are perhaps better cared for in these respects, than in any other establishment. There is a mutual regard between the employers and the employed, which, I think, is an example to the commercial world. We seldom have a case of dishonesty or drunkenness. They all attend places of worship, and I believe that a high tone of morality prevails throughout the house."

At the same time that Mr. Moore was attending to the spiritual improvement of the young men and women in his employment in London, he was deeply impressed with the idea of raising the spiritual standard of his native county-people in Cumberland. Besides the schools which he had built, and the competitive examinations which he had provided for the benefit of the rising generation, he felt that much had yet to be done for the elevation of the adult population. As far back as 1850 he had thought and felt much about the ignorance prevailing in the districts near which he was born. Many of the inhabitants never went to church, and the clergymen were seldom seen within their doors. Pastoral duty was almost unknown. There were some exceptions, especially where the clergymen had been appointed

during recent years; but as several of the parishes had
non-resident rectors, there were few to whom the parishioners could turn for spiritual help. Much had been done
to awaken an interest in religion by Sir Wilfrid Lawson
of Brayton, who had organised evangelistic services in
his own neighbourhood.

Mr. Moore resolved at his own expense to appoint
a lay missionary for his native village of Mealsgate.
The County-town's Mission found an excellent man for
his purpose in John Heritage. George Moore thus
speaks of him and his labours :—

"The people were so ignorant that it was to be expected he would meet with many rebuffs and even insults ;
but he was armed with the power of the Holy Spirit, and
visited them house by house. Had the people known
that I had been the means of sending him, they would
have abused me as they did him. Many wondered who
had sent him, and for a long time they believed that he
had come to get money out of them. At first no one
showed the poor man any sympathy except my brother.
Indeed he had not the countenance or support of a single
individual of standing. But in spite of many discouragements, he laboured away faithfully, zealously, and honestly,
and some seeds that have been sown will doubtless bear
fruit. It filled my heart with gratitude to God to see
the Sunday-school at Quarryhill filled with children. In
the case of many of them, this was the only education
they received. Until this good man went amongst them,
they had never heard of a Saviour's name. Who can
tell the good that these poor children may do to their
ignorant parents? I have always thought that a child
with knowledge is the best of missionaries in a poor
man's home.

"I was so much pleased at the success attending the
first missionary, that I next thought of Wigton, where I
had served my apprenticeship. The place was then in

a dark state. I asked help and advice from friends in Carlisle, but they gave me little encouragement. My partner, Mr. Groucock, had just died and left the Town Mission Society £500. They therefore made me a grant of £20 for three years ; and with some further help from Cumberland men residing in London I got another missionary appointed.

" Emboldened by this success, I held a meeting of three or four friends in Carlisle, and proposed that we should establish a Scripture Reader in every market town in the county. They thought I had gone mad ; especially after hearing of the difficulties I had encountered at Mealsgate and Wigton. Some promises of help were made at that meeting, but they were never fulfilled. Still my motto, then and always, has been ' Never despair.' I got the County-town's Mission to promise me £20 the first year, provided I could get four more missions established in as many places. The first kind friend who came forward to my help was Thomas Scott of Brent House, Penrith. The next was Mr. Wilson of Broughton Grange, who in like manner promised to raise the means for establishing a missionary at Maryport and the collieries in the neighbourhood. The next was Mr. Fisher of Woodhall, for Cockermouth. And the last was Mr. Wilson, who promised the means for establishing a missionary at Whitehaven. My friend John Grey also established a Scripture Reader at Workington.

" Some time after, Peter James Dixon established a missionary at Longtown. Thus we went forward until I had got eight men at work. The Hesket Caldbeck mining district was next thought of, and through the help of Mr. Howard of Greystoke Castle, a missionary was appointed. The excellent Bishop of Carlisle, Montague Villiers, gave me his cordial sympathy and help.

" I must acknowledge," says Mr. Moore, "that God raised up men to assist me in a marvellous manner. I never saw the direct working of God so manifest in any work I ever undertook; and I never knew a mission more blessed in its result. The great point is to get the right men in the right places, for unless a Scripture Reader is *steeled* with the Spirit of God, he can be of little use in his sacred calling. I have always kept them well supplied with Mr. Ryle's and other tracts, and monthly periodicals. I sent as many as twenty pounds' worth of tracts at a time. I had the *Band of Hope Almanacs* framed, and given to poor people, conditional on their putting them up in place of the filthy and abominable prints which hung about their rooms. Each mission was supplied with a good library. The books were lent very largely, and were instrumental in doing a great deal of good."

Again, he says, with reference to the opposition which he encountered—" I am bound to say, although I do it with sincere and heartfelt regret, that in establishing these missionaries they were in many instances strenuously opposed by the clergy. This was to me incomprehensible. In business we like to get men to do our work well. If we be servants, we like to see our master's work done well. Is not expounding the Word and prayer doing the work of our Master; and why should not clergymen help Christ's servants in doing this work? I believe in my conscience that missionary work is the best way of getting at the poor, the degraded, the outcast, and the drunkard. The missionary easily gets at the people, face to face. The clergyman often only preaches to them. He is not able to elicit their opinions, or to get at their hearts. It is a melancholy fact, but true, that the poor in this country are not a Church-going people."

To return to Mr. Moore's personal affairs. Though his house in Kensington Palace Gardens was finished and occupied, it took a long time to furnish it properly. At this time Mrs. Moore who had been long ailing, was now very ill. She suffered greatly during her journey from Shap Wells to London. She then took to bed, and remained there for many months.

"Her dreams of happiness in her new house," says Mr. Moore, "have been sadly marred by her severe affliction. The great anxiety she went through during its building and furnishing have not been repaid; she has ceased to enjoy these splendid rooms. Now it appears like a wilderness. During my melancholy forebodings of God's providence to us, I wonder what is ordained for the future. What a blessing it is that the future is unknown to us poor mortals! . . . I have never seen the use of hoarding up money. We may gather riches, but can never know who is to spend them. God preserve me against the sin of covetousness. It is a curse that eats out the heart and dries up the soul of a man."

Everything was done for the restoration of Mrs. Moore's health. The best physicians and surgeons were called in and consulted. They declared her to be seriously ill. The anguish of her husband cannot be described. He had served for her twice the length of time that Jacob had served for Rachel, and now the great sorrow of the world was to come upon him. She was to be taken away, and he was to be left desolate. Mr. Moore says :—

"A few days after Sir Benjamin Brodie's opinion of the helplessness of her state, my dear wife began to settle her worldly affairs. She gave away all her jewellery as keepsakes to her valued friends. Their letters of thanks nearly broke my heart. She gave away every article of her dress. She gave me a list of poor pensioners that are to have quarterly allowances so long as they live. She dictated and signed twenty letters that are to be sent to some of my valued friends, with a copy

of my portrait.[1] She wrote down the names of friends
that are to receive a letter after she is gone to her rest.
She arranged the mourning and presents for our servants.
She had the names written down of the gentlemen who
are to attend her funeral. She left a book full of memoranda to be carried out after her death. In fact, it is
more difficult to say what she has not arranged, than
what she has. One thing, however, she has not *told*
me, but it is written down for my guidance. It is that
I must place her remains where I wish my own to be
placed; as it is her earnest wish that we should lie
together."

It so happened that Mr. Moore had just completed
the purchase of the Whitehall Estate in Cumberland.
It occupies the greater part of the parish of Allhallows,
Mealsgate, where Mr. Moore was born, is very near the
parish church. He had long desired to buy the estate,
and so soon as it was offered for sale, he purchased it.
He had now the place he most desired to possess in
Cumberland. Amongst other pleasant things in prospect, he wished it to be the summer residence of his
wife; but, alas! it was now to be her tomb. A private
mausoleum in Allhallows Church belonged to the
estate; and there the burial-place was prepared.

Mrs. Moore died on the 4th December, 1858. Her
remains were conveyed to Cumberland. On arrival at

---

[1] This is Mrs. Moore's last letter:—"DEAR SIR,—Some time ago a
number of gentlemen formed themselves into a committee and subscribed
a large sum, unknown to Mr. Moore, for the purpose of having his minia-
ture taken by the distinguished Cumberland artist Carrick, and presenting
it to me. It was very much against Mr. Moore's wishes, but having been
urgently solicited by myself and by the subscribers, he at last reluctantly consented. The subscribers afterwards kindly presented me with several impressions, and knowing the respect you bear to my husband, I have great
pleasure in presenting you with his portrait. With kind regards, believe

"Dear Sir, yours truly,

"E. F. MOORE.

"To the Rev. Thomas Richardson."

Carlisle, Mr. Moore slept in the Station Hotel. It seemed strange to him, that while in his comfortable bed, his dead wife should be laying cold in the railway truck outside, within sight of the hotel windows. The funeral party set out on the following morning, and arrived at Leegate Station on the 11th December.

When the body was lowered into its place at All-hallows churchyard, Mr. Moore fairly broke down. "The thought struck me," he afterwards said, "that my poor corruptible body would be the next to lie in the same place ; and I ejaculated a prayer that our spirits might be again found in the region of bliss, where the wicked cease from troubling and the weary are at rest."

Mrs. Moore was long remembered in the neighbourhood by those who had experienced the blessings of her bounty. She used to say that she took more pleasure in administering to the wants of the poor than in visiting the affluent and the wealthy. A splendid monument was afterwards erected by Mr. Moore to her memory at Wigton, in the shape of a memorial fountain. Mr. Woolner was the sculptor, and Mr. Knowles the architect. The general design is that of an obelisk, imposed upon a massive pedestal of polished granite. The height of the whole is about thirty-two feet. The four bas-reliefs, executed by Mr. Woolner, are in his finest style. They are inscribed on each side of the square block of granite, eight tons in weight, forming the die of the pedestal. The subjects are, Feeding the Hungry, Clothing the Naked, Comforting the Afflicted, and Instructing the Ignorant. The water fountain which forms part of the monument, is skilfully worked into the design. The architecture of the memorial almost puts to shame the humble shops and dwellings by which it is surrounded. It is situated at the end of the street in which Messenger's shop is situated, where George Moore served his apprenticeship.

In the month following Mrs. Moore's death, Mr. Moore presented an organ to the parish church of Wigton. It was opened on the 26th of January by the organist of Carlisle Cathedral. The full cathedral choir assisted on the occasion. The Bishop of Carlisle preached in the morning, and the Rev. Mr. Simpson of Carlisle in the evening. The shops and places of business were closed as a compliment to Mr. Moore, and the church was crowded at both services. The organ bears the following inscription :—

" In gratitude to Almighty God, and in remembrance of early days, this organ is presented to the parish church of Wigton (the town where he served his apprenticeship) by George Moore, A.D. 1859."

CHAPTER XIII.

ITALY—PHILANTHROPIC WORK IN LONDON.

GEORGE MOORE had lost what was dearest to him on earth. He had lost her who had been his helper in youth and his companion in riper years,—who had watched over his success and enjoyed his prosperity. His first thought was, that he was left solitary and alone in the world. He felt as if he could have no further joy in life. He prayed for spiritual help and spiritual comfort. A fortnight after Mrs. Moore's death he writes in his diary :—"I feel that God's grace is giving me more power daily to sustain my drooping spirits. I do not wish to refrain from sorrow, or hide realities from myself. I do not wish tribulation to work insensibility, but I want patience and patience — not forgetfulness, but experience — not unconcern, but hope."

His old malady, sleeplessness, came back. He got up in the morning between four and five, lit his own fire (not wishing to disturb the servants), and read and wrote. This threatened again to injure his health. His medical advisers ordered him to leave home and business for a time, and take recreation in a foreign tour. At length he determined to visit Italy in company with Alderman Sidney and young Mr. Copestake. The last thing he did before leaving London was to visit the Royal Free Hospital, in Gray's Inn Lane. He was then the chairman of the board of management.

The party started on the 30th of December, and reached Paris on the following day. . . "I could have wept," says Mr. Moore, "at my lonely position." But time works wonders. New sights and new scenes, day by day, occupied his attention. At Lyons, he called upon Mr. Milsom, silk merchant, a gentleman who had for many years devoted himself to the maintenance of the Vaudois churches, more particularly those situated in the high Alps of Dauphiny. After an interesting conversation with Mr. Milsom, during which Mr. Moore gave him some help for the poor Vaudois, the party left for Avignon, Arles, and Marseilles, where they first saw the Mediterranean, sleeping under its deep blue sky. Touching at Cannes, Mr. Moore called upon his old friend Lord Brougham, who gave him a hearty welcome. Lord Brougham riveted him by his conversation for an hour; asked about the progress of the competitive examinations — at one of which he had delivered the prizes — and sent him off full of encouragement.

At Nice he visited Count Guichiardini, who explained to him the improvements which he had made in the reading of the Scriptures at Florence, and the great progress which Italian Protestantism was making throughout Italy. Mr. Moore afterwards called upon his customers at Nice, and found them "a seedy lot." By way of Spezzia and Carrara, he reached Florence, and there he had "a delightful conversation" with the Rev. W. Gordon as to the progress of the Italian and Vaudois churches.

The party reached Siena. There they heard that the brigands were out. They had attempted a robbery during the previous night. "We may thank our stars,"

says Mr. Moore, "that we have escaped. We started
early and ascended a steep hill. At the top we had
a splendid view. Shortly after descending the hill on
the other side, we entered the Campagna of Rome.
When we first saw St. Peter's we gave three cheers.
We reached the long-wished-for Rome late in the
evening."

Rome is a city past description. The very word of
Rome is a mighty name. What processions of nations
it has seen! Consuls, emperors, and popes have
governed it. Generation after generation have left
their marks there—triumphal arches, palaces, baths,
forums, theatres, and above all the Coliseum. "I was
quite amazed, bewildered, and astonished with Rome,"
says Mr. Moore, "it is an almost incredible city. I
was reminded of the early apostolic times. In one
place I saw where St. Paul's hand had been chopped
off; in another where he had been suspended and
tortured, head downwards; and in another where his
body lay."

> " Ah ! little thought I, when in school I sat,
> A schoolboy on his bench at early dawn,
> Glowing with Roman story, I should live
> To tread the Appian. . . or to turn
> Tow'rds Tiber. . . or to climb the Palatine."

So says Rogers. Mr. Moore was wholly absorbed
by the sight of the Roman remains. He had the
honour of being accompanied through the city by
Monseigneur Howard, one of the handsomest and
courtliest of men. He pointed out the most wonderful things in Rome, and gave him an *entrée* to the
best society. Mr. Moore visited the Pope's gardens;
ascended the dome of St. Peter's; attended St. Peter's
at the Festival of the Purification of the Virgin; saw
High Mass at the Church of the Jesuits, when all the
Cardinals in Rome were present; witnessed the Car-

nival; saw St. Peter's and the Vatican by torchlight, and the Coliseum by moonlight—the Coliseum, the monarch of all views, desolate within, but glorious without.

The tour included a journey to Naples by the Pontine Marshes, the ascent of Mount Vesuvius, a visit to Pompeii and Herculaneum, and a voyage to Capri. After returning to Rome the party separated. Mr. Moore set sail for Marseilles and arrived in London on the 25th of March, having been absent for about three months. His health was greatly improved, and he was again ready for work.

On his return to London George Moore found two letters and a telegram inviting him to stand for Nottingham. Mr. Walter intended to retire and offer himself for Berks. The Liberal electors of Nottingham accordingly met to arrange for their next representative. Four gentlemen were put to the meeting, and on a show of hands being taken for each, the choice fell upon George Moore. His name was again put to the meeting, and he was unanimously selected. On the message reaching him, he was greatly disconcerted. He had many other things to attend to, which had been neglected during his absence. We give his own words:—

"I am sorely perplexed about Nottingham. Every one urges me to accept it. If I am to be a member of Parliament, this appears to be the time and the opportunity. But I feel that my abilities are not equal to the task. My education is deficient." At length he enters these words:—"I decline standing for Nottingham, though I am almost certain of being returned. My objections are:—

"1. That my education is not equal to the position; and I have a great dislike of public speaking.

"2. That I can do much more good in other ways than by representing Nottingham in Parliament.

"3. That it would keep me more and more from serving God and reading my Bible."

In his letter to the Nottingham committee he advised them to decide upon electing Mr. Samuel Morley. On the day after his refusal he enters in his diary, " I have been severely condemned to-day about Nottingham. Certainly such a chance will never occur again. But I have a higher motive than mere ambition. Worldly honours are golden fetters for the soul."

Mr. Moore returned to his labours of love. He was at this time Treasurer to the Cumberland Benevolent Society, Treasurer to the Commercial Travellers' Schools, Trustee to the Warehousemen's and Clerks' Schools, Trustee to the Cordwainers' and Bread Street Ward Schools, Trustee to Nicholson's Charity, Governor and Almoner of Christ's Hospital, Trustee to the Penny Bank in Milton Street, Chairman and Trustee of the Young Men's Christian Association in Marlborough Street, Chairman of the General Committee of the Royal Free Hospital, Trustee of the Metropolitan Commercial Travellers' and Warehousemen's Association, Member of the Board of Management of the Royal Hospital for Incurables, Trustee of St. Matthew's Church, St. George's in the East ; and also trustee or chairman of the various institutions in Cumberland to which we have already referred.

On the same day in which Mr. Moore declined to stand for Nottingham, he attended a dinner of the Royal Hospital for Incurables,—an institution in which he had taken a great interest. His position as member of the board was not without some disagreeable results. On the 30th of July, 1859, he writes in his diary, " I attended a meeting of the board, and prevented a quarrel about the proposed site for the building." The site was afterwards a source of great discord. The founder of the institution desired that the permanent building should be erected at Coulsden, on the side of a bleak hill. Mr. Moore went to see the place, and was not at all satisfied with it. It was not, he thought, fitted for the residence of incurable patients.

He also found that the estate was without water. He sent his private secretary to the place to bring him two bottles of water, one from the valley underneath the estate, and another from the opposite hill, for the purpose of being analysed. The result of his inquiries was, that Coulsden was not the site for an hospital for incurables. He stated his opinion without reserve at the board. A majority of the directors were of the same opinion. The minority determined to appeal to the subscribers ; and a meeting was held at the London Tavern for determining the site. The following is from Mr. Moore's diary :—

"A most exciting meeting at the London Tavern. The room was packed with two hundred ten-and-sixpenny votes, just purchased. They swamped the majority of the board. They will now build at Coulsden.[1] As I have conscientious objections to that place, I retired from the Royal Hospital."

Mr. James Peek, Lord Raynham, and others left with him. They were not, however, disposed to relax in their efforts to provide a permanent home for the incurables. They took immediate steps to raise another home, for which there was abundant room. After canvassing their friends for subscriptions, they held a meeting at the Mansion House. The following is again from Moore's diary, 20th July, 1861 :—

"I have exercised the talent God has given me at the

---

[1] After all, the Royal Home was not built at Coulsden. After Dr. Peek's death, Melrose Hall, Putney Heath, was purchased, and has since been largely extended. It is a most valuable institution. At his death Mr. Moore left it a legacy of two thousand pounds, and the directors have named a portion of the building as "George Moore's Ward."

Mansion House to-day. I made a forcible speech in seconding a resolution to form the British Home for Incurables. I felt in earnest, and God gave me words. I hope He will prosper this undertaking."

A large sum of money was collected, and numerous annual subscribers were obtained. The British Home for Incurables was then started at Clapham Rise. Mr. Moore was appointed treasurer. Mr. Peck says of his efforts :—"He took a very active part in the institution, and adhered firmly to it to the end of his days, lending both his purse and his personal efforts to its success." Thus two homes for incurables were established, both of which continue to help the sick and unfortunate, and to extend the blessings of mercy and charity to those who cannot in any respect help themselves.[1]

Mr. Moore was fully occupied with many other things after his return from the Continent. He worked for others more than for himself. He rose early, and after a ride on his favourite horse Zouave, he frequently went to Bow Churchyard to join his young men at family worship. It did his heart good, he often says, to see the numbers that were present. The young people were cheered by his attendance. They saw that he was in earnest. In the forenoon he had his business to attend to, letters to write, and orders to give. But he was often drawn away from his business by other things. His partners, he often says, were the best of men, and

---

[1] The secretary to the institution informs us that the British Home for Incurables has been a great success. "Since November, 1861, there have been elected to the benefit of the Home 124 in-patients ; and 270 pensioners of £20 a year have also been elected. I remember on one occasion, a few years ago, when Mr. Moore was in Cumberland, I wrote to him asking him to accept the office of steward at the festival dinner. By return of post I received one of his characteristically concise notes, which usually came to the point at once, saying that if I would persuade nine other gentlemen to give a hundred pounds, he would give the tenth. I am happy to say that the work was accomplished, though without such an incentive I should never have got together in the short space of six weeks so large a sum from so limited a number of gentlemen."

never interfered with his doings. He could easily add an hour or two to his day's work.

Whether in town or country, whether in sorrow or in joy, he was perpetually at work. When a society or institution was getting short of funds, the promoters endeavoured to enlist him. He was not so much interested in the affairs of the institutions that were thriving, as about the institutions that were failing and going down for want of funds. Everybody concerned in charitable institutions in London knew that Mr. Moore was one of the most indefatigable of beggars.

Yes, a great deal of the charitable work of London is done by begging. The bulk of men are so busily engaged in money-making that they have no time to think of anything or anybody else. They enter the City in the morning ; they are engaged in business all day ; and they leave it in the evening for their pleasant home in the country,—little thinking of the wretched, forlorn, neglected thousands, who suffer the blackest bitterness of poverty in the richest city in the world.

For nearly twenty years of his life, George Moore went round amongst his friends, and amongst many who were not his friends, and implored them for money on behalf of the charitable institutions of London. With his friends he was often very abrupt. When he entered their offices they knew what he was about. They saw it in his face. "What is it now, Mr. Moore?" "Well, I am on a begging expedition." "Oh, I know that very well. What is it?" "It's for the Royal Free Hospital—an hospital free to all, without any letters of recommendation. I want twenty guineas." "It's a large sum." Well, it's the sum I have set down for you to give. You must help me. Look sharp!" The cheque was got, and away he started on a fresh expedition.

But he often visited those who were not his friends,—

men rolling in wealth, but who had never subscribed a
farthing to any charitable institution—men of a single
idea, Money, and how to make the most of it,—men
bound up in selfishness and utterly regardless of the
misery of their fellow-creatures. On such occasions
George Moore was met with rebuff after rebuff. This
sickened him for the day ; and he went home tired of
his work. But he returned to his begging next day,
until he had made up the sum that he wanted. " I
must not be discouraged," he said ; " I am doing Christ's
work."

The Royal Free Hospital, to which attention has been
called, was founded in this way. In the winter of 1827
a wretched girl, under eighteen years of age, was seen
lying on the steps of St. Andrew's Churchyard, Holborn
Hill, after midnight, actually perishing from disease and
famine. All the hospitals were closed against her,
because at that time letters of recommendation were
required before patients could be admitted to the public
hospitals, and then only on certain specified days. The
girl died two days after, unrecognised by any human
being. This distressing event being witnessed by the
late Mr. W. Marsden, surgeon, he at once set about
founding a medical charity, in which destitution and
disease should alone be the passport for obtaining free
and instant relief. On this principle the Free Hospital
was established in 1828. *Look at me: I am sick, I
am poor, I am helpless, I am forlorn!* Such were the
patient's credentials.

When the cholera broke out in 1832, the Free
Hospital threw open its doors to all persons afflicted
with that dreadful malady, notwithstanding that the
other hospitals had closed their doors against them. Her
Majesty the Queen became its patron, and commanded
that in future it should be called the Royal Free
Hospital. It struggled on from year to year. It had

great difficulties to contend with, the greatest of which was its want of funds. It was in this state when George Moore took it up.

" I joined it," he says, "at the urgent request of my late dear friend Dr. Rice of Christ's Hospital, simply because it was in difficulties. I have continued to stick to it because it is free to all who are poor and destitute, without any order of admittance. I am sure that this hospital is less abused than any other in London,—as every applicant undergoes a strict ordeal of inquiry into his circumstances and position ; whereas at other hospitals the orders from governors get sadly abused, and many people who are able to pay get their medical attendance for nothing ; the tendency of this arrangement being to pauperise the population.

" The Royal Free has struggled hard, and yet has done immense good. On Christmas Day, 1856, I resolved, after going over it, to raise a thousand guineas for the hospital on the following conditions : That I would give a hundred guineas, and my partner, Mr. Copestake, another, provided the committee would find the remainder. The proposition failed. The committee could not find the eight hundred guineas. I then determined in June that I would raise the money myself. I made my subscription two hundred, and I personally begged for the remainder. With Mr. Copestake's subscription, it made eleven hundred guineas. I have often said that faith without works is dead. If the Royal Free is to remain ready with eight beds unoccupied for want of funds, it is an everlasting disgrace to this wealthy London. I cannot conceive any excuse that the most niggardly miser can have for not giving his money to an hospital like this."

This, however, was only the beginning of Mr. Moore's work for the hospital. It was the last institution that he had visited before setting out for the Continent. It was one of the first that he took up on his return. A few days after, he took the chair at the quarterly meeting. He writes in his diary on the 18th April, 1859,—" Had a hard day's begging for the Royal Free Hospital, with Mr. Nicholson " (the secretary). In the following May, Lord Carlisle, at his request, took the chair at the annual dinner, when a large sum was obtained. He induced the Fishmongers' Company to vote a grant of a hundred pounds, and ten pounds annually to the hospital. Indeed the Fishmongers' Company bled very considerably in support of the charities with which Mr. Moore was connected during the time that he was on the court.

To pass on to the close of Mr. Moore's connection with the hospital. In 1863 he resolved that the freehold of the land should be purchased; for the large ground rent, as well as the interest on the mortgage, were a heavy annual charge upon the funds. A special appeal was made, and George Moore set to work to beg the requisite money. In working for the purchase, he used to say that he wore off the soles of a pair of boots. On the 7th of April he says, " I am persevering to get the money to buy the freehold of the Royal Free. Morrisons have sent me a hundred pounds. If I did not think it Christ's work, I should not submit to the unpleasant duty of begging." And again, on the 17th, he says, " Had a long day canvassing for money for the Royal Free. I think that few men would take the trouble and unpleasant office of begging money that I do." On the 24th he says, " Canvassed the west-end bankers for the Royal Free. I am worrying myself every day about it." On the 1st of May he says, " I have collected myself £4,300 for buying the freehold of the hospital, and obtained about four hundred annual subscribers." On the 6th of May Charles Dickens took the chair, when the result of the appeal was made known, and an additional large subscription was obtained. After this the Royal Free Hospital got into comparatively easy circumstances, and it is now one of the most valuable institutions in the metropolis.[1]

Mr. Moore's usual practice in helping any institution that was in difficulties, was to set out with his own liberal subscription, and then to ask others to give the same amount ; or he would offer a subscription towards raising a certain sum, provided the remaining subscriptions could be obtained from others. For instance, when he heard that the British Orphan Asylum was languishing, and that there were fifty or sixty orphan children wanting admission—of whom the governors could only elect four—he wrote to an energetic friend on the committee, proposing to give a hundred guineas, provided nine others would do the same. The members were thus roused to exertion. They did not like to lose Mr. Moore's offer, and they set to work to raise the remaining sum. At the end of four months Mr. Moore's energetic friend called upon him with his list made up. "Thus," he says, "by making a hard bargain, a thousand guineas was raised for the institution."

[1] In the report of the hospital for 1877 it is stated :—" In the year 1863, many through the zealous exertions and personal influence of the late George Moore, Esq. (then chairman of the committee), the freehold of the hospital was purchased from the Right Hon. Lord Calthorpe, at a cost, inclusive of incidental charges, of £5,265 10s. 7d., the whole of which sum having been raised by a special appeal, the property of the hospital, disencumbered of interest on mortgage, and of annual rental, was vested in trustees." In another passage, the following words occur :—"Mr. Moore for many years filled the office of chairman of the general committee, and he was an active member of the committee and of the weekly board, as well as one of the trustees of the hospital. It was whilst filling the office of chairman of the committee, in 1863, that Mr. Moore suggested the expediency of raising funds for the purchase of the freehold of the hospital ; and, as many of the governors of the hospital are aware, it was mainly owing to his zealous exertions and personal influence that this important work was accomplished. Mr. Moore's liberality towards the charity did not cease with his life ; for he bequeathed a legacy of £3,000 to the hospital, which is directed by his will to be applied in some way that may yield a permanent benefit to the institution."

In this way he induced others to take part in his begging for money. There were, however, many cases in which he alone could do the work. For instance, the London Porters' Benevolent Institution had for the most part originated through his influence ; and after he had taken the chair at the London Tavern to inaugurate it, he felt bound in honour to see it established and free from its difficulties. Thus we find him, shortly after his return from the Continent, canvassing the large houses for the Porters' Benevolent Association. He got about £600. A few days later he says, " I canvassed the city for the Porters' Benevolent Association. Got Mr. Walker and Mr. Morley to finish the wholesale houses ; " and two days afterwards, he adds, " I concluded the canvass for the porters."

Mr. Moore also took a great interest in the Warehousemen's and Clerks' Schools. In fact, this institution, like the Porters' Benevolent, was started in his warehouse. The subject was mooted by Mr. Richard White as early as December, 1853. His object was to have a school for the orphan children of the warehousemen and clerks, such as the Commercial Travellers had at Pinner. Mr. White enlisted the sympathies of the young men in the house, and the influence thus created extended to the other houses in the city. Funds were gradually collected. Some of the wholesale houses gave handsome subscriptions. Mr. White was made deputy-chairman of the board. In 1854 six children were selected for maintenance and education. The number gradually increased as the funds increased, until now it supports about 250 children yearly.

Although Mr. Moore helped the institution liberally, and cheered it on through every difficulty,—when he found that it had got into safe hands—into those of Mr. Leaf and Mr. Morley—he abstained from the active management of its affairs. He let well alone. He visited and examined the schools. He attended the private and public meetings of the institution, and helped in it in all ways, by speeches and contributions. On the 30th November, 1859, he enters in his diary, "I attended the Warehousemen's and Clerks' Schools for five and a half hours. Made a speech which prevented me from sleeping. The money announced for the building is £6,000. He refused to take the chair at one of the annual dinners, "because," he said, "if I accept the invitation, I shall be called upon to take the chair at all sorts of charitable institutions. I am not fit to undergo the speaking, or to endure the sleepless nights that follow the dinners."

Of all the orphan schools with which he was connected, the Commercial Travellers' was his first love, as it continued to be his last. Whenever he had an afternoon to spare, he went down to Pinner to visit the boys and girls. He took with him many distinguished friends: the Bishops of Carlisle, Durham, Ripon, and London, amongst others. Charles Dickens took great interest in them. He was twice the chairman of the anniversary dinners—once in 1853, and again in 1859.[1] Mr. Dickens was an excellent chairman. His speeches were graphic and eloquent, and they were always well reported. This tended to give a considerable impetus to the institution. All the influences which Mr. Moore could exercise were employed for the benefit of the Commercial Travellers' orphans.

[1] On this occasion Mr. Moore sent out four hundred letters, signed by himself, urging his friends to attend and support the institution by their subscriptions. The following is Mr. Dickens's letter in answer to Mr. [Moore's invitation] to take the chair:—"MY DEAR MR. MOORE,—My [...] engagement are too numerous, and I am so much occupied, that I [...] less than your note would have induced me to undertake a chairmanship. But I have a great respect for you, and I know what a good and [...] order society that is in whose behalf you exert yourself. So I am [at] [and] your disposal for the next dinner; but I have to stipulate that it [shall] not take place on the 23rd December or on the 1st of January. I am faithfully your, CHARLES DICKENS."

A circumstance may be mentioned in proof of this. He had at one time been a director of the National Mercantile Assurance Company. As it required too much of his time, without any corresponding beneficial result, he gave up the directorship, but afterwards became a trustee. At an early period in the history of the company, it had been arranged in the trust deed that, on account of the large amount of business brought in by the commercial travellers, one-sixteenth of the profits should be given over to the Commercial Travellers' Schools. Mr. Jenkin Jones, the manager, finding that, in course of time, this sixteenth might amount to a very large sum, insisted (after Mr. Moore had given up his directorship) upon its being converted into a subscription of a hundred guineas annually. This was agreed to.

Shortly after, the manager made arrangements to transfer the business of the office to the Eagle Insurance Company. Mr. Jones made very good terms for himself, but not for others. It was found that he had not informed the Eagle of the hundred guineas annual subscription to the Commercial Travellers' Schools. On ascertaining this, Mr. Moore at once called upon Mr. Jellicoe, the manager of the Eagle, and informed him, that as trustee, he would, unless the subscription were continued, "stop the amalgamation." Mr. Jellicoe at once saw the justice of the arrangement, and the annual subscription was continued.

It would be impossible to give an account, in detail, of the enormous amount of work that Mr. Moore accomplished during this part of his life. Scarcely a day passed during which his time was not fully occupied, with business, with correspondence, with interviews, with beggings for charities. He went from one meeting to another; from an orphan charity school

to an hospital; from a bible society meeting to a
ragged school tea; from a young men's Christian
association to a working man's institute.

He attended to the wants of the poor in his own
locality. There was a very wretched district at that
time in Kensington, since swept away to make room
for Baron Grant's house and grounds, to which he
devoted a good deal of his attention. Mrs. Bayley,
the author of *Ragged Homes, and How to Mend Them*,
had established day and Sunday-schools and mothers'
meetings in this poor neighbourhood, and she worked
hard to improve the people. Mr. Moore was always
ready to help her with his pen, his presence, and his
purse. He often took the chair at the tea-meetings of
the Ragged School, and spoke to the poor people from
his heart.

Mr. Moore also supported the Working Men's Institute at Kensington, started by Mrs. Bayley. He
took the chair at the first meeting, and made a long
speech. The institution still thrives. Though it was
"a pill to take the chair" on any occasion, he was
repeatedly called upon to preside at Bible-Society meetings, at Ragged-school meetings, and at meetings of
young men's Christian associations in Exeter Hall and
at Marlborough Street.

From these works he was occasionally called away
by political or social movements. On the 27th of June
he seconded Lord John Russell's nomination for the
City; after which Lord John, the Lord Mayor, and
a large party lunched with him at Bow Churchyard.
His connection with politics induced his friends to
urge upon him to represent some constituency in parliament. His friend Mr. Hanbury asked him, in 1861,
if he would stand for Marylebone? "No," he replied,
"I can make better use of my time than that. There
are many abler persons than myself willing and

anxious to enter parliament ; but how few there are
who are willing to help the ragged and orphan children ?
That is my work. No, no, let me remain as I am."

But again he was requested to represent a constituency in parliament, and this time it was the highest
constituency in England—the City of London. His
answer was the same as before. He declined the honour
with much respect. " I do not think," he says, " that
I have either the brains or the education required to
represent the City. Indeed, I had no idea that I
should be considered strong enough for the place."

Another characteristic of George Moore may here
be mentioned. He was the constant resort of young
men wanting situations. If he could not provide for
them in his own warehouse, he endeavoured to find
situations for them amongst his friends. He took no
end of trouble about this business. After his young
friends had obtained situations, he continued to look
after them. He took down their names and addresses
in a special red book, kept for the purpose, and repeatedly asked them to dine with him on Sunday
afternoons. He usually requested that they should
go to some church or chapel in the evening. We
find repeated entries in his diary to the following
effect :—

" Dined twenty-two of the boys that I had got
situations for ; besides the people that were staying
in the house. I never forget that I had no one to
invite me to their homes when I first came to London."

He used to give these young men good advice. He
told them that he would never forget them. And he
held out to them the importance of conducting themselves well in the situations that he had obtained for
them. They must do it, he said, for their own honour
as well as for his.

It was, no doubt, well for these young fellows to know that they were not left alone in London; but that there was a good man at their back, who was ready to justify them and encourage them in all that was right and excellent.

The following letter represents George Moore's kindly disposition towards young men. It came to the author of this book quite unsolicited. The writer of the letter had heard that a memoir was in course of preparation, and he desired to bear his testimony to the goodness of George Moore.

"When I went to London, I had some difficulty in obtaining a situation. I then applied to Mr. Moore, who had already received a letter as to my character. He told me that there were more hands in his own place than he had work for; 'but,' said he, 'keep up your spirits, and I'll get you a place.' Accordingly he wrote for me a letter of recommendation to a draper at Blackheath. He said, on giving it to me, 'If you do not succeed, come to me again, and I will give you a letter until you get a place.' He asked me how much money I had. I told him I had just received a post-office order for three pounds. He said, 'You can have the loan of two or three pounds now, or come to me when you have finished your three pounds.' He next asked if I had dined. I answered 'Yes.' 'Well,' said he, 'Cumberland lads can always take *two* dinners; follow me.' He led the way through the warehouse to a private room, where I dined again. When leaving me, he said, 'Any time you are passing, come in and dine with the young men, lots of whom I am sure you must know.' I remember his words well, for they were the only kind words spoken to me while I was seeking for a situation in London."

It may be added that the letter of recommendation

which Mr. Moore wrote to the draper at Blackheath immediately secured an appointment for the young man. Many years have passed since then, and the writer of the above letter is now a prosperous man in the city of Carlisle.

CHAPTER XIV.

LONDONERS OVER THE BORDER.

In the beginning of 1856, Mr. Dickens called attention in his *Household Words* to the rapidly increasing population in the neighbourhood of the Victoria Docks, situated at the easternmost end of London. The district being separated from London itself by the East India Docks and the River Lea, Mr. Dickens designated the district as " London over the Border."

The population consisted of an agglomeration of the refuse of London. They were the sediment or dregs of the great city. They had been pushed eastward by the vast mass of struggling life in London, across the River Lea, into the Essex marshes. The navvies and labourers went first, to excavate the docks and build the quay walls. Warehouses and manufactories followed, with a teeming mass of miserable people, willing to work at anything, so that they could but earn a scanty pittance to live upon. They lived by the manufacture of vitriol, of patent manure, and of other foul-smelling productions, which the health-loving city had driven away by nuisance-laws beyond the Lea to the untenanted Essex marshes.

When the docks and warehouses had been finished houses were erected for the occupation of the inhabitant. Everybody knows what London contract cottages

are. They are erected by the hundred, of the worst
and cheapest materials,—of mud scraped from the
streets and burnt into brick, of half-rotten wood put
together in the most slovenly manner,—offering a very
poor protection against the winds and storms of winter.
The ground on which these miserable dwellings stood
had only recently been reclaimed from the Essex
marshes. Some of them appeared to be built on
islands of liquid filth; and in wet weather the roads
were literally impassable. All the diseases arising
from malarious exhalations—ague, fever, rheumatism
—were constantly present in the district.

The Victoria Dock constituted the centre of the
population. The people who lived in the contract
cottages, endeavoured to obtain some of the irregular
employment which docks always furnish. None but
the very poor lived there,—except, perhaps, the keepers
of ginshops and beerhouses. There was no church,
no chapel, no school, no workmen's institute—nothing
that was in any way calculated to improve or uphold
the moral and physical condition of the population.

In 1857 the Bishop of London appointed a clergyman to take charge of the place. An iron church was
built and fitted up, and the clergyman, Mr. Douglas,
began his operations under the greatest difficulties.
He could scarcely find a house fit to live in ; but at
length he settled down next door to a labourer. Well-
to-do workmen would not live in the district. When
they had done their day's work, they fled into some
healthier place to sleep in. When there was no work
at the docks, there was nothing but poverty in the
district.

There being no such thing as resident gentlemen in
the neighbourhood, and no parochial charities to fall
back upon, the clergyman, in one of his direst extre-
mities, determined to appeal to public opinion. In the

course of one of the constantly recurring periods of
destitution, when the cry for food and fire was frightful,
Mr. Douglas inserted a letter in the *Times* appealing for
help.[1] The editor supported the appeal in a leading
article. Nothing could have better helped Mr. Douglas
in his merciful intentions. The public responded heartily.
Some sent money for food ; some for clothing ; some
for a school for young females ; some for the building of
a new church. People of all classes and orders contributed—men, women, and children. Two touching little
notes were received from West Wickham. One of them,
in a child's round hand, reads thus : *Ada and her brother
send a small gift for the distressed around the Victoria
Decks.*

Mr. Douglas did the best that he could for the immediate relief and employment of the poor. He gave
coals, food, clothing, and money to the most destitute.

---

[1] *Times*, 23rd December, 1859. In the leading article which supported
Mr. Douglas's appeal, the following passages occur :—"Probably never in
this world and, if Dr. Whewell's theory is to be believed, never in the
universe—was there, far and wide, such prosperity, comfort, and happiness
as are brought by this Christmas to some hundred thousand homes. There
are blazing fires, abundant cheer, brothers and cousins, youthful prizemen,
dancing girls, games and forfeits, contented servants, and everything that
love and money can bring together in this happy isle. . . . Read Mr.
Douglas's account of his *Londoners over the Border*—poor fellow-townsmen
passing, or rather pushed by the glacier-like pressure of this vast mass of
struggling life out into the Essex marshes. Compare the scenes be pictures,
with those we started with ; and then answer whether progressing prosperity has not a poor cousin of its own in the form of progressive misery.
. . . There is a battle with the marsh ; it is the oldest fight of all—with
c— r—self. . . . A tone of distress pervades the narrative, and saddens
the very flow of the words. One may perceive the restlessness of fever, the
burning of the scene, consumptive weakness, and mental prostration invading
the very mind of the man who witnesses and describes these sad scenes.
No doubt the faithful pastor must suffer this martyrdom. The hopeful
clergy's expectant knows the danger, and looks for the rough and rash
c— at the utter want, and stand the infection of misery. . . . Clergy,
whether curate, Scripture readers, the light infantry and riflemen of the
host, are wanted for this work. The press, too, must help them ; for
how else shall they be heard? . . . But for the present, industrious
people are there, sick, famished, and dying, even at this Christmas. We
we are confident that Mr. Douglas will soon be able to do something
for these."

He employed a number of young women to make gloves, and others to make shirts. He employed boys to cut firewood and split laths. The boys were enrolled as cadet volunteers, and were drilled by a sergeant thrice a week. Without some such provision, hundreds of them must inevitably have become thieves and vagabonds. An industrial kitchen was started, in which women were taught to cook food properly; and a soup kitchen was also established for the relief of the very poorest.

By the end of 1860 as much as £14,000 had been received by Mr. Douglas. His most sanguine hopes had never reached one-tenth of this magnificent bounty; and yet it had been realised and greatly exceeded. "The distribution of charity since last winter," he said, in another letter to the *Times*, "has relieved much distress, and probably averted great evils; but it has not, to my certain knowledge, pauperised a single individual. The best proof of this is the eagerness with which my poor people avail themselves of every opportunity for work which is afforded them."

And now began the voice of detraction and envy. Here was a clergyman with £14,000 in his possession, doing what he liked with it; using so much for a parish church; so much for a school; so much for a parsonage. Was this to be allowed to go on? Certainly not. Let us see how much money he has received, how he has expended it, and what balance remains. Perhaps he has spent the money for his own purposes. At all events, let us know; let his accounts be examined and audited. Such was the tone of the letters which appeared in the newspapers.

Mr. Douglas then appealed to Dr. Tait, Bishop of London, to institute an inquiry into his accounts, and to ascertain the actual disposal of the money intrusted to him by the public. The Bishop requested Mr. Moore to undertake the inquiry by himself. Mr. Moore hesitated to undertake this responsibility single-handed ; but at the same time he expressed his readiness to enter upon the inquiry in the interest of the public, provided he was associated with some gentleman of acknowledged repute. The following occurs in his diary :—" The Bishop of London has prevailed upon me to undertake the investigation of the charges made against the Rev. Mr. Douglas. I have chosen Alderman Dakin as my colleague. The affair is exciting great interest. God give me wisdom to come to a right decision !"

The inquiry began and lasted for about a fortnight. Mr. Moore started at nine in the morning for the Victoria Docks, and worked for about twelve hours daily at the accounts. " It is a most trying inquiry," he says in his diary : " there is a great deal of bad blood ; and the accounts are complicated. My task is appalling. But with God's assistance, I shall get through."

The accounts were very complicated for this reason : Mr. Douglas had done the whole of the work himself. He had no committee, no secretary, no bookkeeper to help him. He had received hundreds of letters with contributions, and had entered them anyhow. He was one of those clergymen, of whom there are many, who know little about business. He was afraid to pay a large sum for a professional bookkeeper, thinking it would be spending money that was intended for the poor. Hence the complication of the accounts.

The commissioners had accordingly to go over the whole of the affairs in detail, the moneys that had been received and the moneys that had been expended. Mr. Moore's private secretary attended to take down the minutes of the commissioners. Everything that had been done since the appearance of Mr. Douglas's letter in the *Times* was taken into consideration. The person who had publicly challenged the appropriation of the money was present, attended by his solicitor; so that nothing was left unattended to. The contributions in cash, and the letters accompanying them—nine hundred in number—were read and considered. Mr. Douglas also submitted his statements of receipts and expenditure.

Numerous witnesses crowded the doors, anxious to give evidence in favour of their pastor; and many of them were examined and cross-examined. The accounts for coal, provisions, glove-making, wood-cutting, soup-kitchens, needlewomen, and clothing, were gone into in detail. The memoranda of minutes taken at the several meetings, and the statement of accounts, amount to about a hundred closely-written pages, so that it is impossible to give any sufficient abstract of them. The whole interest centred in the balance-sheet; and to the astonishment of those present, and of the public, they balanced to a shilling.

A report was prepared and sent to the Bishop of London, containing the result of the commissioners' examination.[1] While entirely acquitting Mr. Douglas of the malversation of funds with which his enemies had charged him, the commissioners added :—" We deem it our duty to express a feeling of regret that Mr. Douglas, who seems to have been actuated by the best motives in all that he did, and to have displayed great energy, labour, and self-denial, should not have thought it necessary to associate himself at the outset with some well-known men of business to share his responsibility.

" It is our decided opinion that no single individual should alone undertake the office of almoner for the public; and the great use of the present inquiry may be to show the danger and anxiety to which any one may be subject who unwisely undertakes such an office.

---

[1] The report appeared in the *Times*, 4th February, 1861, and was followed by a leading article on the following day.

We are accordingly glad to observe in Mr. Douglas's letter, published before his administration had been challenged, that 'as soon as possible all these branches will be placed in the hands of a committee of management.'

"We would estimate character more by the amount and activity of its virtues, than by its freedom from defects. We have felt it right, in the impartial discharge of the anxious duty committed to us, to point out some defects of administration—which indeed Mr. Douglas has himself admitted to us—but we unhesitatingly affirm our belief in the purity of his motives and in the honesty of his conduct ; and we trust he may be spared for many years to labour in a district where so much requires to be done, and for the accomplishment of which he seems to be peculiarly fitted."

Mr. Moore returned to his City work, to his Reformatory and Refuge Union, to his meetings for fallen women, to his Bible societies, to his milliners' dressmakers' and needlewomen's meetings,[1] to his Royal Free Hospital, and to his various orphan and ward-schools. He did not mind the particular class of men with whom he worked, provided they were good Christian men. He worked with Churchmen, Dissenters, Methodists, Catholics. "I often thank God," he said, writing to his sister in April, 1860, "that I am not a bigot in religion, as I have really little choice between the Church of England and the Dissenting bodies. But as I have been brought up a Churchman, I stick to it. Many of the Bishops and clergymen are my most intimate friends, yet I have the greatest respect and affection for the Rev. Samuel Martin, Independent ; Dr. Brock and Baptist Noel, Baptists ; and Mr. Arthur and Dr. Punshon, Wesleyans.

[1] On the 1st of June, 1858, he say , "I attended the meeting of the poor milliner , dressmaker , and needlewomen. I must work in this c   ."

As long as men preach Christ, I am with them, heart
and hand."

George Moore took a particular interest in the Home
Mission Societies. He held that clergymen and ministers were not enough for the work there was to be done'
in London. The ignorant, he said, must be excavated
from the mass of sin and wickedness. He held that city
missionaries, who could see the people face to face in
their unexplored dens, were the best of all men to do
the work. Here Churchgoers, who paid for a pew, and,
did their fashionable weekly Churchgoing, were not the
people whom he respected, so much as those who came
out of the regular ruts, and helped the uncivilised by their
sympathy, by their good advice, and by their good works.

He continued to take the deepest interest in the spiritual condition of the young men in Bow Churchyard.
He obtained the best of lecturers. On one occasion
Miss Marsh addressed a crowded meeting in the dining-
hall at Bow Churchyard. The attendance at morning
prayers increased after that event; but shortly after it
slackened. Then he called in Dr. Brock to consult with
him as to what should be done to improve the attendance. Next morning Mr. Moore attended family worship, and found only thirty out of about three hundred
young men in the house present. "We must make much
greater efforts," he said, "but refrain altogether from
making the young people hypocrites. Everything must
be done voluntarily."

The whole affair was under a cloud. It was sleepy,
lingering, and becoming useless. He then called in the
Rev. Mr. Rodgers, and had a long discussion with him
and the Rev. Mr. Richardson as to the reorganisation
of the scheme. A few nights later, the Rev. H. Stowell
Brown addressed a crowded meeting. Mr. Moore took
the chair, and informed the audience that he had arranged with Mr. Rodgers to assist Mr. Richardson in

the discharge of the spiritual duties. He afterwards spoke to all the fresh young men, and told them that he expected they would attend family worship. He writes in his diary: "I am deeply anxious to get the service at Bow Churchyard arranged before I leave for Cumberland"; and on the following day he enters: "To Bow Churchyard at 8 A.M. Mr. Rodgers prayed and exhorted. I am now determined to have him." From this time the attendance gradually improved, until at length, as we shall find later on, the institution became firmly rooted and established.

Among the numerous charities, hospitals, orphanages, schools, and missions, which Mr. Moore helped with his mind, and hand, and purse, may be mentioned the National Orphan Home. He first became connected with it in the year 1861. We find him writing in his diary on the 24th of April: "Went to the National Orphan Home, Ham, to finally organise and set in motion all the improvements. I never worked more earnestly for any institution than I have done for this." The object of the charity was to receive orphan girls, without distinction as to religion, into a home where they could obtain a plain English education and practical instruction in the kitchen, house, and laundry, so as to fit them for domestic service.

Mr. Moore stuck to this institution throughout his life. He was a member of the committee and helped forward every means for promoting the objects of the Orphan Home. He used to supplement the funds on the occasion of the anniversary dinner. He often begged for the institution. There was in his word " My friend," —which all who remember him will recognise—an appeal which could not be refused. His last munificent act for the Home was to head a list with a thousand guineas, provided four thousand more could be obtained. He begged for the rest, and filled up the list.

The secretary of the institution informs us "That it was not only in the institution itself that he took an interest, but in the welfare of the officers connected with it. It was his annual custom to invite the different secretaries of the societies with which he was connected (and they were large in number) to his hospitable board; and take the opportunity of showing the interest he took, not only in their temporal but their spiritual welfare."

After the death of Mrs. Moore, he felt very lonely in his magnificent mansion. "I feel very desolate," he says in his diary, "and have no one to care for me but Christ." Again he says, "I retired to rest, depressed with my lonely condition. Here I have no continuing city. Let me seek one that is to come. What matters about my lonely condition? It cannot be for many years, for life is fleeting." Sleeplessness again beset him. He enters these words, after one of his sleepless nights :— "The sound of cock-crow, heard in the early morning, serves to remind us of many profitable reflections, associated with the example of those who have gone before us, as well as with the duties that devolve upon ourselves."

At length he again began to entertain company. The first friends that he invited to his house, after the death of his wife, were his old Cumberland chums in London. Some of them had risen in the world, whilst others had made very little progress. Yet they spent a pleasant evening together, talking of old times, and canny Cumberland ways. Perhaps they compared, some with gratitude, others with regret, their different social positions. Many subsequent dinners succeeded. The house was often full of company. Sometimes Mr. Moore gave up his bed, and had to sleep in a neighbour's house.

He curiously mixed up his guests—Bishops, Business men, Dissenters, Methodists, and poor friends from

Cumberland.   On one occasion we find him entertaining
the Bishop of Carlisle, Dr. Brock (Baptist), the Provost
of Queen's, the Rev. Mr. Martin (Independent), Professor Cope, the Rev. Mr. Wilkinson, and others.   The
number usually entertained was twenty-four.   He had
often five dinner parties of this number within a fortnight.
He followed up with a dinner to " nineteen of the boys
that I have got situations for."

His house was used for many purposes.   He had
Bible-readings and expositions every alternate Monday.
He took the greatest and most characteristic interest in
these simple gatherings of fifteen or twenty persons,
principally men, for the study of the Bible.   His friend
Mr. Bowker, of Christ's Hospital, presided over them,
and George Moore often says in his diary, "these meetings are the happiest evenings of my life."

The Kensington Auxiliary Bible Society, the Pure
Literature Society, the Book-hawking Society, the Open
Air Mission, the Diocesan Home Mission, and the Theatre
Preaching Committee, frequently held their meetings at
George Moore's house in Kensington Palace Gardens.

The Diocesan Home Mission was established in the
summer of 1857, chiefly through the instrumentality of
Dr. Tait, then Bishop of London.   The object of the
Diocesan Home Mission was to provide the means
of the Gospel for thousands of persons in London
who could not be reached by the ordinary parochial
machinery.   Amidst the spread of buildings in the
neighbourhood of London, whole masses of people became congregated together, without a school, without a
church—with nothing but a gin-shop.   The Licensed
Victualler is very watchful of these new settlements.
He i there long before the school and the church.   His
bright gas-lit gin-shop is the best-frequented place in
the neighbourhood ; and he often makes a fortune and
retire , before the church has made its appearance.

It was, as we have said, to supply the defects in the parochial system that the Home Mission was established. Its object was to infuse a missionary character into the Church, and to bring the people under the influence of religious ministrations. In connection with the objects of the Home Mission, were open-air preaching in summer, and theatre preaching in winter. If the people, said the clergy, can't come to us, we must go to the people; we must find them in their popular resorts, and endeavour to make them listen to the Gospel.

The first open-air service was begun in Covent Garden, and conducted by Lord Wriothesley Russell. It was followed by other services, conducted by clergymen and members of the mission. Thus multitudes of people were enabled to hear the Gospel who had never heard it before. Churches, in the opinion of many of the lower-class Londoners, are for the well-to-do, or for those who have got Sunday clothes. Indeed, few know much of the ignorance, the recklessness, the thriftlessness and the degradation of the neglected classes of London. During winter, preaching in the open air is scarcely possible. The cold and biting weather drives everybody within doors. It was accordingly determined to hire the theatres for Sunday preaching.

Mr. Moore threw himself into this movement with all the energy of his nature. He was present at the first committee. He attended one theatre after another on Sunday afternoons, took the chair, and gave out the hymns. He appeared on all sorts of stages, mostly in the poorest parts of London—at the Pavilion Theatre, the Victoria Theatre, the Garrick Theatre, the Sadler's Wells Theatre, the Standard Theatre, and others. The best preachers in London took part in the work, and on many occasions from three to four thousand persons were present at the services.

Mr. Moore not only used his own house for the promo-

tion of these and other efforts, he also used the dining-
room at Bow Churchyard. We find him, while the
theatre preaching was going on, inviting a large party,
about a hundred in all, to dine there. Among them were
Lord Shaftesbury, Lord Ebury, the Honourable A. Kinnaird, Robert Hanbury, Esq., R. C. L. Bevan, Esq.,
Samuel Morley, Esq., and about seventy of the most
eminent ministers and clergymen of all denominations.
The Earl of Shaftesbury, in returning thanks for his
health, which had been proposed by Mr. Moore, said that
"with regard to the amount of good which their excellent host had so kindly represented him as doing, the
fact was, that Mr. Moore himself was doing a much
greater amount of good, though his modesty would not
permit him to allude to his efforts for the social and
spiritual welfare of his fellow-men. Mr. Moore was
doing incalculable good, unseen and unknown, except
by those who were the subjects of it, whilst the good
that he himself was doing was on the surface, and was
consequently seen and known to all men."

One of the most singular things in Mr. Moore's life,
was his Diary. No matter how busy he was—whether
in the warehouse, or at charities, or at meetings for
various purposes—he found time to write down a short
account of his day's work, and often of his thoughts and
experiences of life. He continued to do this for about
twenty years, whether well or ill, whether at home or
abroad. We are thus enabled to ascertain his everyday
life, and his everyday thoughts. Some of the extracts
from his diary have already been given, but a few dis-
connected thoughts may also be added.

"I wish," he says, "that my faith was as strong as
my works ; and I also wish that the works of many of
those with whom I have to do were as strong as their
faith. With some faith is everything, and works
nothing."

"The trouble we expect scarcely ever comes. How much pain the evils cost us that have never happened."

"How often clouds and darkness overshadow our minds. They clear away like an uplifted fog, and you see the clear blue sky above them."

"All sorrows, follies, errors, committed towards us by other have their edges wonderfully softened off by retrospection."

"When a man is faithful and true in small things, depend upon it that he will be faithful and true in great things. Great principles depend upon small details."

"'Godliness is God-likeness.' It is seated in the heart. Godliness makes a man content with his circumstances. Godliness is not carelessness. No one is so rich as to be at liberty to be extravagant. Godliness does not remove the curse of labour, but dignifies it."

"A man has just as much Christianity as he has Humility. Oh, God! give me more humility. Enable me to keep myself in the background. But I must live for others as well as for myself."

"Better be wrong in the effort to do right, than be indifferent."

"There is no greater mistake than in investing religion with gloom. Wisdom's ways are ways of pleasantness, and all her paths are peace."

"The enchantments of the world are dangerous to the spiritual health, as tending to stupefy the soul, and bring it into captivity and spiritual lethargy."

"The grand interpreter of the Word of God is common sense."

"How often have I found that apparent adversity has worked far greater happiness than the greatest prosperity. He that sows in tears shall reap in joy."

"That which is wanted to hold together the bursting bonds of society, is not so much kindness, as *sympathy*."

"In the present life we can only judge a man by his works. Hereafter, when the councils of the heart are made manifest, works will be judged by the man himself. 'A man's life consisteth not in the abundance of things he possesseth.'"

"I am convinced that profuse charity to the poor, given indiscriminately and without inquiry, does no real good. It fosters idleness. It rears up a class of professional mendicants. It promotes dissolute habits amongst beggars, and enormously increases the evil it is meant to relieve. Like Lord Brougham, I think that Drink is the mother of Want and the nurse of Crime."

It may be stated that Mr. Moore makes frequent mention in his diary of the benefits which he received from attending the ministrations of the Rev. J. W. Reeve, of Portman Chapel. "He makes the scheme of salvation," he says, "much plainer to me than any one else." In another place he says, "He is one of the best companions one can have. He makes the house bright by staying in it." And so on, all through the diary.

CHAPTER XV.

WHITEHALL is an old Border tower in the parish of Allhallows, about six miles south-west of Wigton. It is situated in a green valley on the banks of the Dowbeck, a little burn which runs into the River Ellen about a mile further on. Within sight of Whitehall is another old border tower, Harbybrow, a very picturesque object in the scenery of the neighbourhood. These towers were erected about the end of the fifteenth century, as strongholds against the inroads of the Scots.

Whitehall in early times belonged to the Border Percys. The Salkeld family next occupied it, and from them it descended to the Northumberland Charltons. Its proprietors had always been Roman Catholics. They were strong Jacobites, and sympathised with, if they did not actually take part in, the risings in favour of "The King over the Water" in 1715. Any one who has read *Redgauntlet* will remember the incident of young Alan Fairford being confined in "Fairladies," where he had an adventure with Father Buonaventure. There is reason to believe that Whitehall is the "Fairladies"[1] described by Sir Walter Scott.

[1] "They had not," says Sir W. Scott, "proceeded a pistol-shot from the place where they parted, when a short turning brought them in front of

After the union, when the Borderers had no further need for strongholds, a house connected with the tower was erected, most probably by the Salkelds, for the purposes of residence. Their arms are still to be found on the building, and their initials are carved on almost every doorhead. But in course of time, the place fell to decay. The owners went to live on their estates in Northumberland. The house and tower remained in their partially ruined state until quite recently. The old hall of the building was used as a cow-shed and granary. Another part of the building, which forms three sides of a square, was occupied as a residence by the steward of the Charltons.

Whitehall is close to Mealsgate, where George Moore was born. It was his pleasure, as a boy, to fish in the Ellen, and wander about the valley in which Whitehall and Harbybrow are situated. It will be remembered that he climbed the Peel towers, and harried the jackdaws' nests in the old chimneys, or in the hollow places of the walls. Every spot of the ground was known to him. His forefathers had lived in the neighbourhood from time immemorial, and their descendants—the statesmen—still farmed their own small estates at Overgates, at Kirkland, and at Mealsgate. George Moore was much attached to the place. When he became a prosperous man he often thought of buying the Whitehall property, especially after he

---

an old mouldering gateway, whose heavy pinnacles were decorated in the style of the seventeenth century, with clumsy architectural ornaments, several of which had fallen to decay and lay scattered about, no further care having been taken than just to remove them out of the direct approach to the avenue." After the men proceeded up the avenue, Fairford found that they were "traversing the front of a tolerably large mansion-house." "At last, by ascending some stone steps, decorated on the side with griffins or some such heraldic animals, he attained a terrace in front of the place of Fairladies; an old-fashioned gentleman's house of some consequence, which it rather, of notched gable-ends and narrow windows, relieved here and there by an old turret about the size of a pepper-box."—*Redgauntlet*, Ch. xx.

had made it his custom to pay an annual visit to
Cumberland, to look after the schools he had built or
helped to build, and to preside at the competitive
examinations which he had established.

At length, in 1858, the Whitehall estate, which now
included Harbybrow,[1] was offered for sale. He had
now the opportunity of having a "stake in the hedge,"
in his dear Cumberland. He could thus realise the
words of Wordsworth—

> " When wishes formed
> In youth, and sanctioned by the riper mind,
> Restored him to his native valley, here
> To end his days."

"On the 7th October," he says, "I arranged about
purchasing the Whitehall estate. I hope I shall not
put my trust in land, yet I think I am justified in
buying it. I have worked very hard for all that I have
gained." At length he bought the Cumberland Border
Tower and the estate over which he had shorn when
a boy.

But a great deal had to be done before he could enter
into possession of his Northern Home. Mr. Moore was
under great obligation to his friend, Henry Howard, of
Greystoke, during the rebuilding of Whitehall.

Mr. Howard had advised that the best architect, and
the most famed for the restoration of old places, should
be employed. Mr. Salvin was accordingly persuaded
to undertake the work. During the next three or four
years Mr. Howard not only saw the plans, but constantly went over to Whitehall to judge about the
alterations. George Moore speaks of him as my " head
clerk of the works ;" and at another time, "I owe
everything to Mr. Howard. What anxiety he has

---

[1] The Border tower of Harbybrow, about half a mile from Whitehall,
was formerly in the possession of the Highmores. It is the scene of one
of the later Border Ballads.

spared me about this building! This is another proof
of the many services I have received from him during
seventeen years."

Two hundred navvies were employed to remake the
terrace and replace the bowling-green. The ruined
buildings were repaired. The cows were turned out of
their byres; and the old hall restored to its former
uses. The old rooms and the old rafters were carefully
preserved. New rooms were built on the old foundations. The outline of the whole was preserved, as far
as possible,—so that the entrance by the forecourt, the
square tower to the east, the gables to the west front,
and the bastions of the terrace wall, should look as
they had done to the possessors of Whitehall for
centuries past.

All this occupied several years. But in the mean-
while George Moore continued his annual visit to
Cumberland to carry on the competitive examinations.
This usually occurred in July or August.

When he began school examinations, he had no wish
to keep the direction of them in his own hands. His
object was to influence opinion, and to get them established, extended, and taken up by the Diocesan Education Society. He accordingly rejoiced when they took
up the religious part of the scheme, and extended them
to all Cumberland.

Another movement that Mr. Moore started at this
time, was Book-hawking by *colporteurs*. The Perambulating Library was doing good work, but Mr. Moore
desired to see the benefit of reading good books more
widely extended. This could only be done by sending
men about the country with books for sale. They
might also in some sense be made missionaries, as
was the case with the colporteurs who kept Protestantism alive in France during its long period of
persecution under the Bourbons.

Mr. Moore gives the following account of his connection with the book-hawkers. "I was on the committee of the Pure Literature Society, and one of its principal working supporters. This circumstance brought under my notice the great good that was to be done by book-hawking societies. I resolved to start two book-hawkers for Cumberland, giving them £25 each for the first year. Cumberland people are very slow to adopt or support any new projects. Numerous objections were raised to the scheme. Many thought that books were of no use to working people. They said that a rural population was better off without education and information. Others feared the dangers of the book-hawkers as missionaries."

Nevertheless, a book-hawking society was started in Cumberland. It was supported chiefly through the influence of Mr. Moore. From the report of 1858, we find that 635 Bibles, Testaments, and Prayer-books, had been sold during the year, and 1,598 copies of other books. The Bishop of Carlisle took the chair at the first meeting, which was held at Carlisle. After some discussion, Mr. Moore observed that so far from seeing any necessity to relax their efforts, he saw great cause for encouragement in the number and character of the books sold. They could not expect great success all at once. They must walk before they could run. Almost every county in England supported a book-hawking society, and it would be a disgrace to Cumberland not to do the same. As for talking about withdrawing one of the hawkers, he should be ashamed of the county which gave him birth were he to do so. He urged that instead of reducing the number, the society should go on increasing them. Instead of withdrawing one, he moved that *three* others be appointed, which was done accordingly.

We quote this, merely to show the thoroughness

with which he proceeded with his work. If a scheme
was good, and worthy of support, why not urge it
on by every possible effort? He stirred up the people
about him. He called them into activity, and made
them work with himself. In the same way he
urged on the County Town Mission in Cumberland,
which he had instituted. The local clergy were indifferent to it at first. "Some of them," he said at
Wigton, "are like dogs in the manger; they will not
work themselves, nor let others work." But he called
in his friend the Bishop of Carlisle (Villiers) and the
Dean (Dr. Close). They helped him to establish the
Country Towns Mission; and the local clergy then
followed their example.

The Bible Society was one of his most cherished
objects. For about twenty-one years he invariably
took the chair at the local meetings held in Allhallows
School. He summoned friends from a distance to
attend it—Bishops, Deans, and Clergymen, with ministers of other denominations. The meetings were very
successful.

He was made justice of the peace, and attended the
sittings of the magistrates at Wigton. He was present
at the meeting of the Archæological Institute at Carlisle,
and contributed various objects of antiquarian interest.
He was made chairman of the Wigton Agricultural
Society, though there he was not in his proper element.
One day he accompanied Mr. Howard of Greystoke
Castle to the Penrith Cattle Show. At the dinner
which followed the exhibition, he was called on to make
a speech. "I could not speak about cattle," he says,
"but I brought in my favourite subject, Education, and
worked it well. At least, so the speech reads in the
local papers."

It was a good time for the school-children when
Mr. Moore went down to Whitehall. Indeed it was

a good time for everybody, rich and poor. He stirred
everybody up. The first thing he did was to look
after the schools. He came down about the time of
the competitive examinations. Indeed he never missed
them. Crowds of children came to Allhallows School
to be examined. He had the Bishop and Dean of
Carlisle, Lord Brougham, and others to distribute the
prizes. There was luncheon, tea, and supper for all,
numbering often 1,500 or more.

There was no end to the hospitality at Whitehall.
One day he received the Rifle Volunteers. "They
came along the road playing a lively tune. They and
the farmers, about four hundred in all, got a good hot
dinner. I carved for all." Every time he was at
Mealsgate, while the reconstruction of the house was
going on, he gave the workmen an entertainment before
he left for London. He also provided for their religious
instruction, and sent the missionary whom he had appointed, with interesting books and periodicals likely to
be of use to them.

Mr. Moore returned to his old amusement—hunting.
He had sold his horses some years before, when he
was in great sorrow; but now he could resume his
wonted exercise. "Mr. Howard," he says, "tempted
me this morning to ride one of his horses. I felt
as much at home in the saddle as ever; but I got
a good tumble to remind me of olden times. I
really enjoy the hunting. It does my health so much
good."

He also hunted with his friend Sir Wilfrid Lawson,
master of the West Cumberland foxhounds. "I rode
my bay mare to-day. She nearly pulled my arms off.
Yet we had a splendid run—an hour without a check.
I kept a good place."

The estate also had to be shot over; but though Mr.
Moore could hunt, he was not much of a shot. He

invited his friends down from London to shoot over the grounds. Sometimes he went out by himself. He says in his diary (13th August):—"Rose at 5 A.M. and ascended the mountain; I came to a village called Watendlath, the most primitive place I ever saw in Cumberland. I entered one of the houses. There was no fire-place, but only logs of wood and turf burning on the floor. I ascended the moors. The birds were very wild, and I only got a brace and a half. Drove back to Mealsgate very tired." On the 1st of September partridge-shooting began.

One day, when he was accompanying his friend Colonel Henderson through the Waver wood, on a partridge-shooting expedition, a curious ramshackle object appeared before them. It seemed to be a sort of big drosky with a long broad trunk at the back end. "What is that?" asked the Colonel. "Why," said George Moore, "that is the trap which I have driven into every market town in Great Britain and Ireland!" In fact it was the carriage in which George Moore had travelled through the country while achieving his success as a commercial traveller.

There was one thing that struck Mr. Moore very much during his visits to Cumberland, and that was the low rate of pay of the clergymen. Every one remembers the story of the Rev. Robert Walker, curate of Seathwaite, Cumberland, whose stipend amounted to only seventeen pounds ten shillings yearly. He could not live upon that; so he kept a school, tilled his glebe, and spun yarn for home use. And yet he married and brought up a family of eight children. He maintained one of his sons at Trinity College, Dublin, until he took orders and entered the church.

In the olden times the chapels in the Dales were very small, affording room for about only half a dozen familie. The stipends were so small that they could not maintain a clergyman, and the curacies were often held by unordained persons. These were, however, afterwards admitted to deacon's orders without any preliminary examination. The pay was often not more than three or four pounds a year, and the Reader used to maintain himself by other occupations, such as that of clogger, tailor, or grazier.

The times were very hard for statesmen in those days, and still harder for clergymen. They were subject to poverty and even to actual distress. It is difficult to understand how they contrived to live and bring up a family. There was a gentleman called Marshall, parish priest at Ireby. His stipend was only £35 a year. Yet upon that he married, brought up a family, and gave his children a good education. He and his daughters built their own house. The daughters—tall, handsome girls—led the horses which carried the stones, and Marshall himself did most of the building. The wonder was how they contrived to build it. They called it Puzzle Hall, but no one could solve the puzzle. It remains Puzzle Hall to this day.

The stipends of clergymen were still very low—almost at starvation point—when Mr. Moore began his inquiries as to their temporal condition. He makes the following entry in his diary (Aug. 22, 1859):—

"To my astonishment I find from the Bishop that he has in his diocese eleven livings under £50 a year; nine under £60; sixteen under £70; twenty-six under £80; twenty-one under £90; and thirty-five under £100; that is 118 clergymen with an average income of about £83 a year! Is not this melancholy? It is a satisfaction to me that I have given £500 to augment Allhallows."

George Moore determined to ventilate this question. At a meeting at Allhallows School, he made a speech which was reported in the newspapers, protesting against

the small stipends paid to clergymen. A Mr. Sheehan
of Cork, seeing the report of his speech, wrote a letter
to the *Wigton Journal* in which he said, " I know for a
positive fact that Mr. Moore has upwards of seventy
porters in his establishment, and the half of them are
receiving more pay than seventy curates in England and
Ireland." No doubt this is true. A writer in *Blackwood's Magazine* says, " The secret records of the
Clergy Aid Society could tell many a piteous tale of
dumb and inarticulate suffering of which the world hears
nothing and suspects nothing."

Mr. Moore communicated on the subject with Villiers, Bishop of Carlisle, and sent him sums of money
from time to time in order to relieve the more distressed
clergymen. In the Bishop's answer to his first donation
he says, " In two cases during this present week your
present has enabled me to help poor clergy ; and I do
believe that I have carried essential comfort to homes
which I really could not have done without your kind
assistance. I cannot help letting you share the pleasure. . . . The hiring question is still exciting much
interest. . . . I am hoping to stir up sermons for working classes in Carlisle during Advent." In another note
the Bishop says, " One line to thank you for your prompt
and liberal reply to my note regarding Allhallows. It
is a joy to think that the Lord has not only given you
the power but the *will* also thus to serve Him."

Two years after the date of this letter the Bishop
accepted the see of Durham, and made arrangements
for leaving that of Carlisle. When informing George
Moore of the intended change he said, " Now, my dear
friend, I cannot allow this opportunity to pass without
again and again returning my warmest thanks for the
increasing kindness and noble generosity I have experienced at your hands. I am afraid there are no George
Moores at Durham."

During George Moore's visits to Cumberland he had always received the Bishop's cordial support. The Bishop saw that Moore was in earnest in his efforts to improve the education and advance the spiritual welfare of the people. An earnest man was the delight of his life. A warm friendship had sprung up between them, which death alone severed. To a certain extent the two friends were alike in character—strong, courageous, straightforward, and unflinching in the pursuit of their respective objects. They were alike manly, cordial, and popular. Their intimacy, however, did not last much longer. The Bishop did not hold the see of Durham for more than a year. After a painful and protracted illness he died on the 8th of August, 1861. George Moore's name was among the last words he uttered.

The arrangements for the repair and reconstruction of Whitehall were now proceeding rapidly. The house would soon be ready for George Moore's reception. But he was alone. He had no wife and no children. One day he went to see an intimate friend. "How blessed he is," said he, "amidst his lovely family. I wonder whether he has a coffin in any cupboard."

Mr. Moore felt an increasing sense of loneliness. He could only relieve himself by inviting numerous friends to dinner. "I seem to be afraid," he said, "of being alone." Again he says, "I fear I am bringing more anxiety upon myself by establishing a second house at Whitehall. All my thoughts are centred in Whitehall —the plantations, gardens, fencing, and such like." At his large, beautiful mansion in Kensington Palace Gardens he said, "I feel very lonely, with no one in the house but myself." At length Whitehall was finished, and on the 2nd of October, 1861, he dined in the Hall for the first time.

Some of Mr. Moore's friends hinted to him the necessity of marrying. He was so social and affectionate in his nature, that solitariness at home depressed him very much and was specially unfitted for him. When he entered his house, tired with his day's work, there was no one to cheer him, no one to sympathise with him, no one to lean upon. No matter how faithful the friends were who came and dined with him, they did not light up his home with joy. When they had departed and the last man had left the door, the host was left solitary and joyless. One day at Whitehall he writes in his diary, "All this afternoon and evening I have had time to think. When shall my solitary state be changed?"

One of his intimate friends wrote to him from Brieg in the valley of the Rhone, when on his way to the conference at Geneva, giving Mr. Moore his confidential views on this and other subjects. Indeed, Mr. Moore seems to have asked him for his advice. "I have often thought," said his counsellor, "that you might like a partner for the remainder of your earthly career. If you find one of God's sending, she would no doubt add much to your happiness, share all your cares, and spare you much trouble. . . . Wait for a little till she falls in your way, and do not allow yourself to be *looking out* for one."

Some months after the receipt of this letter, George Moore found one on whom he could firmly set his affections. In his diary he speaks of her as his "castle in the air."

He invited her relations, the Wilkinsons and Dents, who were then in London, to dine at his house. "I like them very much," he said, "but they are awful Tories." He sought the lady out, and took her to the private view of the Royal Academy. He found many opportunities of serving her. His affections were at length deeply engaged. He visited her family in Westmoreland. At last he secured the long-prayed-for and long-hoped-for consent. "I never," he says, "felt so grateful to God in my life."

It would be out of place to enter into the details of this union. It may be sufficient to state that the young lady was Agnes, second daughter of the late Richard Breeks of Warcop in Westmoreland. That she proved a right loyal and noble wife will be found in the course of the following narrative.

The marriage took place in St. Pancras Church on the 28th Nov. 1861, when they were married by the Rev. J. W. Reeve. The newly-wedded pair proceeded on a tour through France and Italy.

While at Rome, Mr. Moore made the acquaintance of Mr. Adams-Acton, the sculptor, which afterwards ripened into a friendship. Mr. Moore made the round of the studios with him, and purchased several works of art. Mr. Adams-Acton looks back to that period with much interest. He says :—

"I well remember my first interview with George Moore at Rome. I was impressed with the sturdy terseness of his manner, and the way that he looked into, and electrically read your character. He had also a fearless way of probing you, and never parted from your company without knowing more about you ; but withal, his talk was always savoured with kindness and good humour. He had a taste for art, and had always a desire to possess the very best works of the best masters. He accompanied me to some of the best studios in Rome, and on each occasion he purchased works of interest and beauty.

"He seemed also to enjoy, as few men do, the society of every class of people ; and he had the quickness and perception to make every one about him quite at ease. He expressed as much interest and pleasure in the society of artists and their works, as he would have done with men with whom he had been engaged in matters of business all his life. I remember on one occasion, in connection with M. Dasulavi, a very celebrated landscape painter in Rome, getting up at one of the old Roman osterias in the Trastevere, a dinner as nearly as possible the same as those enjoyed by the Romans of old. Mr. Moore entered into the spirit of the occasion as few men would have done ; and M. Dasulavi spoke of him afterwards as a man of wonderful elasticity of temperament."

After a tour of about four months, Mr. Moore and his wife returned to London.

CHAPTER XVI.

MR. MOORE immediately recommenced his charitable
work. Mr. Masterman, M.P. for the city, having died
during his absence, he was offered the presidency of
the Commercial Travellers' Schools. But he declined
the honour. "I am very useful now as Treasurer,"
he said, "and I prefer the useful to the ornamental."
He continued to give his utmost support to the institution. He took many of the bishops—of London,
Ripon, Bath and Wells—to Pinner, to examine the
scholars and award the prizes.

At the anniversary dinner of 1863 he had the pleasure of stating that of the two hundred and eighty-
five boys who had left the school, only one had turned
out badly. Those who had gone into business had
done well; and all those who had gone to the Oxford
Middle-class Examinations had passed. When they
considered the number of children who had not been
merely saved from ruin, but who had been fairly
started in life, surely they had a portion of their reward.
It was also pleasant to find that the boys who had left
them did not forget the benefits they had received, for
several were now subscribing five guineas annually for
the benefit of the institution, and some of them had
given ten guineas to be life-governors.

Mr. Moore gave ten pounds annually for the purchase
of books, which were distributed amongst the best

boys and girls of the schools. The "George Moore
Prizes" were usually presented by some distinguished
scholar, or by some dignitary of the Church. The
object of presenting them was to reward general good
conduct and perseverance, as exhibited in the results
of a written examination.

Mr. Moore's substantial help to the institution had
been so great that the subscribers desired him to sit
for his portrait, to be hung up in the hall as a memorial
of his services. The portrait was painted by Sir Daniel
Macnee (now President of the Royal Scottish Academy),
and was presented at the annual examination of the
schools in June, 1864. The honour, Mr. Moore says,
was forced upon him.

In commemoration of the event, Mr. Moore established
a scholarship of £75 a year. The sum was applied
to the support and maintenance of a scholar for at
least three years at a higher class school. His object
was to bridge over the gap between the common schools
and the Universities; and the result showed that he
was correct in his anticipations. Mr. Stockdale, chairman of the committee of management, followed with
another scholarship of the same amount. At one of
the annual meetings, held in 1872, when the Rev. Dr.
Farrar conducted the examination, Dr. Butler, head-
master of Harrow, who was present simply as a visitor,
was so much struck with the singular ability of one
boy, who was about to leave the schools, that he made
a voluntary offer to pay for a third scholarship for three
years, to enable this boy to be sent to a higher class
school. This third scholarship was afterwards continued by Mr. Copestake, George Moore's partner, and
is now called the Copestake Scholarship.[1]

---

[1] George Moore also offered to found a scholarship in connection with
the Warehousemen's and Clerks' Schools. Mr. S. Copestake and Mr.
Copestake J. Leaf proposed to do the same, but for some reason or other the
offers were refused.

At a recent annual dinner of the Commercial Travellers' Schools, the late William Longman, Esq., publisher, occupied the chair. George Moore could not attend, being confined to the house by a bronchial cold. But he wrote a letter to Mr. Longman, which was read to the meeting. He said :—"I have most pleasant recollections of our rides across country some years ago, when you were never behind. I only hope that on this occasion you will be able to ride the Travellers hard, and *kill your fox.*" The chairman explained that by killing your fox Mr. Moore meant that he should get good subscriptions, which he did.

Mr. Hughes, in replying to the toast of " Success to the Commercial Travellers' Schools," spoke of the energetic character of his partner, George Moore. " When he saw a thing that wanted to be done, he endeavoured to do it promptly and efficiently. If Temple Bar had been in Bow Churchyard, he would have had it removed long ago. If Mr. Moore had been an architect, the new Law Courts would have been finished long since. If he had been an engineer, the Straits of Dover would have been tunnelled before now ! "

Mr. Moore went about on his different works of charity and mercy. He went from the east to the west, begging for the charities in which he took an interest. He enlisted others in his service. He made them help him. "No recruiting officer," said one of his friends, " ever had a keener eye for a smart-looking recruit than he had for a lively worker in his charitable objects." Mr. Foster says of him, "Of all the persons I ever knew, he had the greatest power of extracting talents from others. No matter what it was, he would make them either work for him, or work with him. He could never tolerate drones."

As he begged from all, so he was begged of by all.

An open purse is always assailed. Beggars saw his name on the various charity lists, and inundated him with applications for money. " I am worried," he says, " more and more every day with begging letters. To investigate all these cases is entirely out of my power." For it must be stated that he never contributed to any object without thorough investigation beforehand. Even when he went to Cumberland, parcels of begging letters followed him. At Whitehall he says : " In this lovely place I have received packets of all sorts of applications for money. I really feel astonished at some people's assurance."

During one of his rapid visits to Cumberland in 1862, to look after the reconstruction of the buildings on his estates, he invited the sons of his farmers to go up to London and see the Exhibition. He paid their expenses, and entertained them at his house in Kensington Palace Gardens. The young fellows had never had such a treat before. They saw the Exhibition, and went over London, seeing the sights of which they had so often heard. Mr. Moore arrived in London a few days after they had started. " I found," he says, " all my farmers' sons happy and grateful."

He varied his labours in London with journeys on the business of his house. He went down to Liverpool and visited all his customers. He says : " I really feel as well up in business as I ever was in my life. Suppose I came to grief, I could still work up a business, and make it prosper." " I make it an invariable rule in every town I visit to pay my respects to our customers. I have done this to-day, and received everywhere a kind reception. I hope I shall never forget the bridge that carried me over."

Towards the end of 1862 Mr. Moore took cold at one of his city meetings, and was laid up for some time. The cold took the form of inflammation of the

lungs, which was succeeded by pleurisy. Mr. Ray,
his brother-in-law, and Dr. Gull attended him during
his illness.　His life was for some time despaired of.
Mrs. Moore attended him during this trying time with
rare devotion.　She wrote up his diary for him.　" My
mind," he said one day, "wanders over all the world—
to my friends, to Cumberland, back again to London
—to my past sins, to Whitehall, to our rides last
summer, and then to the future."　He uttered these
words with a rapidity truly alarming, probably under
the influence of delirium.　Then he muttered a great
deal about his traveller's life—how he used to be away
the whole year, coming to Bow Churchyard only at
Christmas, constantly travelling, working his brain
night and day, because there was a report that the
house was breaking, and he knew that the blame
would fall upon him, as he had introduced so many
new plans.

Such dreams as these rushed through his mind : just
.as the whole events of one's past life start up before
us in some moment of intense suffering or peril.　By
and by his dreams passed away.　As the bells of old
Kensington Church rung out the old year and rung
in the new, George Moore fell into a profound sleep,
which lasted many hours.　It was the turning-point
from which his convalescence began.　He rapidly grew
better.　His medical attendant called one day and gave
him a strong lecture about the absolute necessity of
giving more rest to his brain and more healthy exercise
to his body.　The advice was listened to, and was
followed to a certain extent.　But so soon as he had
got rid of his weakness, he returned to his old work.
A brain like his could not be idle.

He reflected on his narrow escape.　" I have been,"
he said, "in the valley of the shadow of death.　I
have got up some steps of that ladder which reaches

to the heavens." He went to his senior partner, Copestake, to arrange with him about private affairs, in case God should take either of them, or both. Nevertheless, he continued his old rounds in the city, until sleeplessness again followed him home. One day he notes the following :—

"I attended the British and Foreign Bible Society Committee; then the Fishmongers' Company, on account of the Prince of Wales's reception of the freedom; then the Committee for Theatre Preaching, and the Commercial Travellers' Schools Committee. Had a bad night." No wonder!

To get rid of his city work for a time he went down to Cumberland for a holiday. He went in February. The weather was fine, and he enjoyed the planting and laying out of his grounds. He was not, however, very much satisfied with the people. "I fancy," he says, "that the folks down here do not think they have any souls. The churches are comparatively empty." Before he left, he started another *colporteur*.

He returned to London in time to see the Princess of Denmark, the future Princess of Wales, make her entry into the city. About a thousand persons were at Fishmongers' Hall to see the Princess pass. It was a scene that will never be forgotten in England.

His young men had next to be attended to. He got up one morning at 6.30, and went into the city to prayers, in the midst of fog and darkness. The Rev. Mr. Rodgers was now conducting family worship to about a hundred daily. Several associations had been started for the benefit of the young men and young women. There were Devotional meetings, Bible classes, a Mutual Improvement Association for adults, and a Self Help Association for apprentices. The library contained more than a thousand volumes, and was supplied with upwards of forty daily and weekly newspapers, besides periodicals. Lectures were delivered by men of high position and influence.[1]

We ought also to state, that Mr. Moore took the same pains with his *employés* at Nottingham, as he had done with those at Bow Churchyard and Milton Street, London. The Rev. Francis Morse, vicar of Nottingham, himself undertook the office of chaplain at the factory. He said prayers, and gave a short exposition from scripture every morning. Mr. Moore expressed his gratitude to him for the earnest and loving interest which he showed in the work.

Another feature in Mr. Moore's character was his extensive patronage of religious books. He took edition after edition. He ordered books by the hundred and the thousand, to give to his young men, and to send to the missionaries throughout the country. He bought endless copies of Miss Marsh's books. He sent a copy of Arthur's *Italy* to every library in Cumberland. He ordered thousands of Ryle's *Exposition of St. Luke*, which he distributed all over the country. The *Memoirs and Remains of Dr. M'Cheyne* was a special favourite.

On the death of Mr. Western Wood, M.P., in 1863, Mr. Moore was again invited to offer himself as candidate for the City. A deputation of Liberals waited on him, and urged him to stand. Many others, independent of politics, offered their support. Even the secretary of the Conservative Registration Committee informed him that in the event of his coming forward they would not oppose him. No! he would not stand. He could not leave his charitable work; he could not

---

[1] Among the lecturers at Bow Churchyard, we find the names of the Archbishops of Canterbury and York, the Bishops of London, Winchester, Peterborough, and Carlisle, the Rev. Baptist Noel, Dr. Brock, the Rev. Newman Hall, the Rev. J. C. Ryle, Capt. Trotter, Miss Marsh, Mr. Stevenson Blackwood, the Rev. J. Bowen, Dr. Allon, Dr. Parker, the Rev. Hugh Stowell Brown, the Rev. R. Macguire, the Rev. Mr. Arthur, the Rev. Mr. Braden, the Rev. Mr. Maclagan, Dr. Stoughton, Dr. Cummings, Professor Fowler, and others.

R

have his business. He was still of opinion that he would not be in his right place in Parliament. "Let them get younger men—men educated as statesmen should be." Instead, therefore, of offering himself as a candidate, he went to the Guildhall and spoke in support of Mr. Goschen, who was returned. Mr. Moore writes these words in his diary,—" How strange is the wheel of fortune! Who could ever have thought when I left Wigton, that I should have been asked to represent the City of London in Parliament?"

On the day after the election he visited a number of poor people. He visited fifty-three of the pensioners of the Fishmongers. At 7 P.M. he attended a Bible reading at one of the dormitories of the establishment in Charterhouse Square, and afterwards visited the Porters, a hundred in number, to establish classes for their mental improvement. Besides these classes he took steps to establish a library at 49, Bow Lane, for the use of the porters of London. One day was, however, so like another in his city work, that it would weary the reader to give an account of his labours in detail.

While engaged in these works he entered the following words in his diary : " There are many seasons when I am devising, planning, scheming, and arranging. But I have only been rough-hewing as yet. The mason is not a sculptor. My life contrasts greatly with that of many Christians, whose whole lives are full of perplexity, anxiety, and care. But I am not sufficiently grateful for all my blessings. When I die I shall carry nothing away. My memory will soon be forgotten. The good deeds I have done (and they are but few) will not descend after me. Every day I feel more and more my unworthiness. I have nothing to rest upon but Christ, yet surely that is enough for me."

Mr. Moore was already treasurer of many institutions, and now he was appointed treasurer of Garibaldi's

Fund ! Many will remember the extraordinary sensation produced in London by the reception of Garibaldi in April, 1864. Mr. Moore was somehow drawn into the demonstration. He went to Nine Elms Station, with the self-constituted committee, to receive him. He sat with him in the open carriage in which he proceeded through the streets of London to the Duke of Sutherland's palace. He invited him to dine with the Fishmongers' Company. He contributed a hundred guineas towards buying him an estate in his own country. But Garibaldi was too independent to receive money from his entertainers. Accordingly George Moore divided his intended donation between the Church Missionary Society and the Pastoral Aid Society.

All this occurred amidst much business and many meetings. The day after Garibaldi's reception, Mr. Moore attended the annual dinner of the British Home for Incurables, where the purse collected by him was the heaviest. The day after, he took the chair at the City Mission Meeting at Kensington. He was still attending the Committee of the Royal Free Hospital ; the Boys' Refuge ; the Ragged Schools ; and other societies too numerous to be mentioned in detail.

A few entries may be given from his diary : " I visited all the model lodging houses in London. We can do no good for the souls of the poor until we have got their bodies properly housed. I afterwards attended the first meeting of the Boys' Refuge.

" God often reads us the story of our lives. He sometimes shuts us up in a sick room, and reads it to us there. I shall never forget all that I learnt this time last year [during his attack of pleurisy].

" There is a crook in every lot, and a briar besetting every path of life, from youth to age. Is not life full of trouble ? We exchange only one scene of trial for another. But so long as God directs, we cannot go wrong.

"Called upon the Duke of Cambridge at 12 noon. Posted him well up about the Travellers' Schools. He asked me all about my business in the City, and said he was astonished how it could be so easily managed.

"The Duke of Cambridge [on the following day] took the chair at the Travellers' Schools dinner. He did capitally. I did badly. I told him all I knew. He recollected it, and made my speech." We got £1,170. I made every exertion that man can do.

"Bought 752 of *M'Cheyne's Memoirs*, and 500 of Bonar's *Way of Peace*. Gave them to each of our young people, and to the country town missionaries. I am always watering other people's vineyards. Let me not neglect my own!"

Among the *new* things that he began to support during the years 1865 and 1866, were the Little Boys' Home and the Field Lane Ragged Schools. He began his donations to the former in 1865, and continued his support to the end of his life.[1] He arranged with Mr. Hanbury and others for the purchasing of the land for the Home at Farningham, in Kent. He sent out numerous letters to his friends urging them to subscribe. In one of his letters he says, " There are ten Family Homes at Farningham with their groups of thirty boys in each, making 300 in all. Besides the home training which is given them, they are educated by efficient teachers, and trained to industrial work by which they may earn an honest livelihood.[2]

---

[1] In 1866, Mr. Moore gave £200 towards building the Little Boys' Home, and in 1870 Mr. Moore gave £1,000 to build the last House. In 1876 Mr. Moore left £3,000 to the institution.

[2] The Home has its workshop, in which are carried on the various trades. First, home : second, education : third, industrial training. All boys over ten years of age are half-timers, attending school and work alternately. The trades are superintended by the Fathers of the Houses, and embrace breadmaking, printing, shoemaking, engineering, bookbinding,

I wish you to understand that we take in children that are not eligible for any other institution. They are too young for any of the refuges, and too destitute for any of the orphan asylums. We want about £2,000 a-year to carry on our work, besides our present sub-scriptions." The result of this application was that a considerable additional subscription was obtained.

The institution was principally founded for the pur-pose of affording a home to ragged boys who were in danger of falling into crime. It was founded on the plan of the Müller Orphan Asylum at Bristol. It consisted of a series of houses over each of which a house-father and house-mother presided. One of these houses was provided by Mrs. Moore, and is called the " George Moore Lodge." Several boys were sent by her from Cumberland to this Home.

Mr. Walter has well described the kind of boys who enjoy the advantages of the Home.[1] " They come," he said, " from the highways and byways, the streets and the alleys of this metropolis and other crowded thoroughfares—they come from the hedges and lanes of remotest country districts, from the wilds of Cumberland and the moors of Cornwall—they are what lawyers called in olden times the flotsam from the wrecks which drift past us in the great tide of human existence."

And again, in contrast with the district schools for pauper boys, he said :—" The characteristic of this institution was that it was a Home ; and a home was what no child could afford to be without. In that word rested the whole secret and charm of the institution. They might, perhaps, remember not very long ago that Lord Beaconsfield, on another occasion in which he

tailoring, gardening, painting and glazing, carpentering, farming. The workshops form part of a large central building, which also contains the needle-room, the laundry, the swimming bath, and the superintendent's residence.

[1] At the annual dinner, 1877, Mr. Walter, M.P., in the chair,

was equally interested, described home as *the unit of civilisation*—a very happy expression, as he thought. It was the unit of civilisation, because it was the centre of all those domestic affections which make men, women, and children what they are. In fact, all the ideas and associations which impart joy to youth, rest and comfort to manhood, and peace and consolation to old age, cluster round the word. That was the key of this institution, and certainly it was a most happy name to have selected for it."

Besides attending to the orphan boys of London, Mr. Moore gave a good deal of his time and attention to the outcasts of London. No one knew better than he did, the misery and wretchedness of the lowest dregs of society. He knew the rich and he knew the poor—the luxury and seeming brilliant gaiety of the upper ten thousand, and the misery and wretchedness of the lower ten hundred thousand. He knew the "whited sepulchres, which were beautiful without, but within full of dead men's bones, and of all uncleanness."

He knew London by night as well as by day. He knew it from the East to the West. Many a time he went down to St. George's-in-the-East, and to Wapping, to look after the poor. He accompanied the missionaries into the lowest dens of London. Scarcely a day passed without his being engaged in doing some good work for the destitute ; and yet he grievously complained of the little he could do compared with what he ought to have done.

One day he enters these words : "Again I went out amongst the poor with the missionary, and relieved them. Such dreadful filth, rags, and poverty!" How little could he do to uplift them from their wretchedness and misery. He saw what social neglect had done for these poor creatures,—debased physically and morally. As for religion, they had never heard of it.

The pale cheeks, the stunted bodies, and the weary eyes of the children, haunted him. He could not get rid of the sight. He was summoned, however, to make new efforts on their behalf.

One night he went, accompanied by a superintendent of police, by the permission of his friend Colonel Henderson, through some of the lowest parts of London. What sights he saw! Poor ragged souls searching for somewhere to sleep; drunkards, making night hideous; wretched women plying their unhallowed trade. They passed through casual wards, and saw life in its vilest conditions.[1] He was shocked to find human beings in such degradation. Recklessness and vice lay huddled together. Faces haggard with woe and brazen with iniquity, were turned up for a moment to the solitary light which gleamed dimly in the apartment. The thieves' lodgings were still worse. There he saw festering masses of criminals, gaol-birds and others, living by crime. All this was lying close under the surface of the civilisation of London—the richest city in the world !

To George Moore it seemed that the only true way of teaching these people was to get hold of them when young,—to bring the children of the poor into schools, and thus get them under better influences. Hence his support of ragged schools, and ragged school brigades, in all parts of London. Hence also his support of orphanages, especially for the poorer classes. And as these people would not go to church, he strenuously supported the city missions, so that the poorer classes might be visited at their own houses and brought under religious influences as much as possible.

---

[1] This subject was afterwards referred to by the Lord Mayor at a meeting at the Mansion House. He said Mr. Moore had visited by night the West London Union, at Battle Bridge, and informed him of the result of his visit.

In June 1866, Mr. Moore was requested to become Treasurer of the Field Lane Ragged Schools. Many years before, he had given fifty guineas to start the first ragged school in London. Since then he had generously supported them. Day by day throughout the year he sent (with the consent of his partners) the surplus provisions of his warehouse dinner, which supplied substantial meals to a large number of ragged children—perhaps the poorest to be found in London.

The reason why Mr. Moore consented to become treasurer may shortly be explained. It was found that the number of annual subscribers had fallen off, and that the institution was getting into debt. The Committee proposed to get the help of some leading member of the aristocracy; but one of them said, "No no! let us get the help of some hard-working, practical man: let us go to George Moore!" The suggestion was unanimously approved, and a deputation waited upon him at his counting-house. Though already hard pressed by work, when the circumstances connected with the institution were made known to him, he at once consented to accept the treasurership, and went a-begging accordingly.

We have before us the pass-book in which he entered the names of the new subscribers. He himself started the list with £100 annually. This was an example for others. Barclay and Co., Rothschilds, Mr. S. Morley, followed him. Some houses of great wealth and influence followed very lamely, and many contributed nothing. But the result of the begging was a considerable increase in the funds of the institution.

The objects of the institution may be briefly mentioned. It included baby schools (*crèches*), infant schools, boys' and girls' schools, night schools for girls, and also for men and boys in situations. There was an industrial school for girls, where they learnt to sew and make clothes. There was also a mother's class, to sew and mend clothes. The building was a refuge for the home-less poor,—men and women. Young women were kept there until situations could be obtained for them. The institution contained a penny bank; Bible classes; a ragged church, where as many as from 700 to 900 people attended ; a prayer meeting; a youth's mutual improve-ment institute ; and other excellent arrangements.

To show the depths of society to which the ragged schools descended, it may be mentioned that the parents of the children educated there included beggars, street-singers, street-salesmen, porters, hawkers ; in a word, the migratory and helpless poor of London. The men and women who frequented the Refuge included those who had been overwhelmed by misfortune, but who had never-theless maintained integrity of character ; and who, but for the temporary help of the refuge, must have sunk down in hopeless despair. Bible instruction was given every evening by voluntary teachers, most of whom were engaged in mercantile establishments in different parts of the metropolis, and who therefore had many oppor-tunities of providing destitute persons with employment.

The Refuges were still more useful as regarded young women, reduced by sudden illness, misfortune, or want of employment, to utter destitution. During the first year of George Moore's treasurership, 1,800 respectable young women took refuge in the institution. Over 800 of these found situations, employment, or were restored to their friends. What the fate of these young women might have been but for the refuge, need hardly be sug-gested. It acted as a friend in need to those who, but for it, were never at any time in their lives more in need of a friend.

At one of the meetings held shortly after George Moore became treasurer, he said that there were five free schools, in which twelve hundred boys and girls were educated without charge, and through which, since their

opening, 20,000 children had passed, of whom 4,000 had
been placed in situations, thereby gaining their own
living. Another feature in the report was the class of
young girls of from ten to sixteen, half of whom were
already able to earn their livelihood. Then there was
the mothers' class, in which sewing and mending clothes
were taught, but the main feature of which was religious
instruction—in a word, Bible truth. At the ragged
church, 200,000 souls had already come under the influence of the Gospel. During the previous year, nearly
15,000 persons had benefited by the institution. These
were great facts. Experience was the best test of truth.

The Rev. Dr. Brock followed Mr. Moore, and related
some interesting facts. One was that of a man originally
taken from the "gutter," who after training in a ragged
school, went to South Africa, where he became a respectable member of society, and eventually a Wesleyan
preacher. Another case was that of a young man who
was trained in the schools, and went out to Canada.
Hearing that his sister had become a fallen woman, he
got six weeks' leave of absence, came over to London,
waited in the Haymarket until he met her, and carried
her out with him to Canada. There she married, and,
with the exception of her brother, was the happiest in
the land.

But the institution was still in difficulties. At the
beginning of 1870 it was £2,000 in debt. George Moore
sent round a circular amongst his friends, and followed
it up with a personal visit. "Long experience," he said
in his circular, "teaches us that the most effectual means
of relieving poverty and preventing crime is to educate
the young in the habits of usefulness and industry before
they have become hardened in idleness and crime." He
earnestly requested all his friends to visit the institution,
and make themselves acquainted with the nature and
utility of the works carried on.

He devoted several days to going the rounds of his friends. The result was that by one great effort he cleared off the debt. On the 26th of May he said at the annual meeting that he was happy to be able to inform them that the institution was *entirely out of debt!* He did not like debt as regarded either private or public institutions, and he had determined to wipe it off, and get them out of their difficulties. He had collected more than £2,000, and obtained from four to five hundred new subscribers, many of whom had previously entertained a prejudice against the schools and the refuges.

Thus, whatever George Moore undertook to do, he did thoroughly. He spared no pains and shirked no labour in effecting his object. Many thought it an undignified thing on the part of a rich city merchant to go about amongst ragged and filthy people; amongst thieves, tramps, and vagrants; even though it were to elevate their idea of duty, and lift them up into a higher life. He himself said, he felt that nothing could reach to the depth of human misery, or heal such sorrow as theirs, but the love of Jesus—the Good Shepherd who yearned over them with Infinite Pity, and had given His life for the sheep.

It was not so much the amount of money as the amount of thought that he gave to these afflicted people. The poor and the destitute were constantly in his mind. He could not sleep for thinking about them. The weary eyes of the hungry children haunted him. Lowest of all —beneath the tramps, the beggars, and the helpless— were the miserable women whom he met on his way to the midnight meetings. What could he do to reclaim them? He did what he could, and yet he was often thrown back by the fruitlessness of his work.

But he had many encouragements. His labours did not sink into the ground. He shed a sort of sunshine amongst those he worked for. He diffused blessings

around him.   He had the love of all ; and love is growth.
A little kindliness will produce a great deal of happiness.
Even a friendly grasp of the hand will help a struggling
man upward.   It is sympathy that is so much needed.
This was the maxim under the influence of which George
Moore worked.   And thus he lifted up many of his
poorer fellow-creatures—making them holier, happier,
and better.   " Inasmuch as ye have done it unto one of
the least of these My brethren, ye have done it unto
ME."

CHAPTER XVII.

LIFE IN CUMBERLAND.

GEORGE MOORE'S life was many-coloured. He led a town life and a country life. After tramping the city in search of subscriptions, he went down to Cumberland to ramble over the Fells. When oppressed with brain-work, he started for Brighton, and had a gallop over the downs with the harriers. When wearied with his Committees, he would set out for Tring, hunt with Lord Lonsdale's foxhounds, and be in at the death with the huntsmen.

Among the happiest days in George Moore's life were the days of his arrival at his Border Tower in Cumberland. He was then seen at his best. He enjoyed with almost child-like feelings his north-country home. He was there, in true English phrase, really jolly. Instead of sitting in his London office, oppressed with business, or correspondence, or worry, he was in the midst of the scenes of his boyhood, and amongst the friends whom he loved. Everybody knew of his coming, and all who could, welcomed his arrival.

When George Moore's flag was up, everybody knew that great things were coming. The children of the neighbourhood, more than all, welcomed his arrival ; for were not the competitive examinations coming on, and with them the prizes, the books, the sweetmeats, and the tea-feasts? He had scarcely settled down in his country home, when friends and acquaintances gathered round him: Archbishops, bishops, deans, nobles, artists, squires, clergymen, dissenting ministers, farmers, merchants, city and county missionaries, schoolmasters, great men from London, and small men from everywhere.

There was no end of things to be done at Whitehall. The farmers had to be visited, and the repair of the farmsteadings looked to. His own home farm was inspected, and the state of the shorthorns inquired into. The gardens, the plantations, the fencings, the outbuildings, had to be seen, and various orders given about them.

There were numerous meetings to be attended after his arrival. The Perambulating Library was still on foot, and he presided at the annual meeting. He went to Carlisle and took an active part in the Book-Hawking Society. He attended the schoolmasters' conference at Wigton. He summoned conferences of Scripture-readers to meet at his house. On these occasions, addresses were given in the hall.

The hall is a grand old place. The walls are wainscoted with oak as in border times, and adorned with armour, spears, steel jacks, horned heads, flags, and banners. How different were Mr. Moore's assemblies in the hall from the scenes in the olden times, when the cry of the men-at-arms as they set out on their border forays, was "Snaffle, spur, and spear!"

Although Mr. Moore went down to Whitehall for recreation, he worked almost as hard there as he did in London. He was inundated with letters. One day he says, "The letters I receive are really astonishing, and I have to answer them all myself." After breakfast he retired from the hall into the smoking-room with his bundles of letters. This was his *own* room. It was fitted up with an escritoire, shelves full of books, and

other suitable furniture. Over the quaint old-fashioned
oak fireplace was a piece of metal work, fastened into
the wall, containing the old saying : " How much pain
the evils have cost us which have never happened."
This was the place in which he stored his numerous
books for prizes, for county missionaries, and for distribution amongst people of all classes and ages. Here he
had the photographs of his dearest friends, the pictures
of the Pinner schools, and the sketches of his favourite
horses.

He usually occupied this room in the morning from
ten till two, rarely allowing himself to be disturbed
from his work. Those who wanted him knew they
would find him there, though they could scarcely
reach him because of the numerous letters which he
had answered, and that were strewn about the floor as
thick as snow-flakes. He sometimes wrote from thirty
to forty letters in a day. " Indeed," he said, " I work
harder here than in London." In the same room he
gave audience to his tenants, to his outdoor servants,
to the labourers on the estate, and to the village
missionaries labouring in the surrounding district.

In the smoking-room also hangs an illuminated
tablet, on which is inscribed the address on charity
written by St. Paul to the people of Corinth. At the
head of the tablet, in large bright letters, are the
words, " Charity never faileth ; " and at the end, " Now
abideth faith, hope, and charity, but the greatest of
these is charity." The words were, in fact, a true
illustration of Mr. Moore's character. He took them
to heart, and tried to work them out into fact. To do
good and to communicate was the joy of his life.
" The more I give," he said, " the more I get."

The house was always full. One party succeeded
another. It emptied and filled from week to week.
One day he records : " All the beds and dressing-

rooms are filled. Two bishops, the high sheriff, the
chancellor of Carlisle, and many more. My dear wife
much fatigued." No wonder! Then the partridge-
shooters came, and the house was again "brim full of
guests." He had a long day's shooting with them,
during which he walked for eight hours.

In August, 1864, the competitive examinations were
at their zenith. He owed the suggestion of this particular examination to the Rev. G. T. Moncrieff, Dr.
Simpson of Kirby Stephen and the Rev. Canon Hodgson. The two first arranged all the details, set the
papers, and had all the labour of the examination.
Without their knowledge and assistance the thing could
not have existed ; and Mr. Moore always acknowledged
that these men deserved all the credit of the scheme
and the success of its working. In that year the prizes
were given by Lord Brougham. Though a veteran in
years, his intellect was as unclouded as ever, and his
conversation was remarkable for its satire and keenness
of observation. He gave proof of his powers when
giving an address to the schoolmasters and others after
the prizes were distributed. He made a quotation from
Milton on the blessings of peace, but his memory failed
him at the two last lines. He stood silent, with lips
apart and outstretched hand for what seemed moments
of suspense, and then repeated two lines of metre which
fitly took the place of the right lines.

After dinner that evening, there were many present
who wished to hear Lord Brougham converse ; but he
was tired and reserved. George Moore asked him if he
thought the Empress of the French had much influence
over her husband in Church matters. " She has just the
influence," he replied, "that every woman has on her
husband : she nags, nags, NAGS, till she gets her own way."

In August, 1865, the prizes were presented by the
Archbishop of York. The Bishop of Carlisle, the Lord

Mayor of London (Alderman Hale), Dr. Percival (Master of Clifton College), Sir Wilfrid Lawson, and other distinguished persons were present. Sir Wilfrid, in the course of his speech, said that Mr. Moore, when he came down among them in Cumberland, acted very much the part of a despotic monarch. They lived, while he was present, under what he called a mild despotism. This day, and the ceremonies connected with it, were, as he might say, one of the "time-honoured institutions of the county," and it must be very gratifying to Mr. Moore to observe how popular and how successful that useful and time-honoured institution had become.

The Archbishop, after presenting the prizes, made an excellent practical speech on education, and on the system established by Mr. Moore of competitive examinations. He then proceeded: "The reason why so many parishes in this country have no schools is, that the inhabitants don't take an interest in education. They don't value it ; their minds are not right on the subject. The upper classes are content with a low standard of knowledge, and they allow the lower classes round about them to remain uncultivated and untaught. Now, Mr. Moore has done his best to stir up in the country round about a great interest in education. He knows that as soon as men's minds are directed to the difference between a being thoroughly untaught in everything and a being properly instructed in the knowledge of God and in the knowledge of the world around him, all people with common hearts and with common good feelings will set their minds to work to remove the ignorance, and lead the people out of darkness into light.

"I think it is a beautiful thing that a man immersed in business to an extent hardly any of us can conceive, yet finds time every year to come here. He does not

S

say he is very busy, that he has a headache, or that he
wants to go abroad ; but he comes here every year for
ten years, and busies himself about these poor children
whom we have looked upon with such interest, and to
whom he has given a pleasure that will never be forgotten by them as long as they live. I call that recollection of the home of his childhood, which has often
shone upon him in the hours of business, and given him
the greatest pleasure, a beautiful romance of real life—
a *romance of Cheapside*—as good as any other romance,
and I, for one, feel the greatest interest in it."

Besides examining boys and girls, Mr. Moore examined cattle and sheep. He was beginning his herd
of short-horns. He went to all the cattle-shows. He
gave prizes for horses, donkeys, and shepherds' dogs.
He was asked to take the chair at the dinners following the cattle shows, and on those occasions he made
speeches. In 1865, for instance, he presided at the
dinner following the Cumberland Cattle Show, the
Wigton Farmers' Club, the Wigton Cattle Show, the
Cottage Gardeners' Meeting, and the Cumberland
Agricultural Society. "After four nights of conse-
cutive speaking," he said, " I am entirely *pumpt out!*"
But he was not yet done. The Bible Society's Meet-
ings came round, and he attended them at Wigton,
Allonby, and West Newton.

Nor did he forget his business in the midst of his
speechifying. From Whitehall he started for Glasgow
to look after the branch there. In 1863 he set out for
Aberdeen, where he " found all in an uproar ; an apprentice, a porter and his wife, being in prison for
stealing goods, and another person for receiving them."
Having put matters straight, he returned to Edinburgh,
where he called upon his customers ; after which he
attended the meeting of the Social Science Association
and dined with Lord Brougham. During the time he

stayed in Edinburgh he resided with Mr. Cowan, now member for the city.

Living at Whitehall was a sort of perpetual picnic. Mr. Moore was the soul of every entertainment. He had a happy knack of making all his guests heartily welcome. At breakfast-time he would take no refusal for the specially cured ham, or the little trout taken from the River Ellen, "the best in the world," of which he was justly proud. When Sir Thomas Chambers visited him, George Moore said, when he was helping the guests, " You do not *press* the article. There, I will give anybody a penny who will eat this egg!" By his cheeriness he always made the breakfast one of the pleasantest meals of the day.

Those who had the pleasure of visiting Whitehall will recollect the enthusiasm with which excursions to the surrounding scenery were planned, or the picnic organised on some fell-side or mountain-top. One day a pleasure party would be at Caldbeck, where they climbed the rocks to gather parsley-ferns. Another day they went to Bassenthwaite and rowed on the lake ; or they ascended Skiddaw, from whence they had a glorious panorama of the Cumberland lakes and the Cumberland fells.

Then there was the drive back to Whitehall in the twilight, when George would tell stories of the olden times, when highwaymen were hanged for stealing a leg of mutton, and of the days of his boyhood, his hunts with John Peel's " scratch pack," his schooldays with Blackbird Wilson, and of the Bogles at Bolton Hall. He would rivet the attention of his listeners too while he told his tales, and his cheeriness spread quickly over all about him.

Nor was a walk with him over the farm without interest. He had erected model byres for his short-horns, under the direction of his friend Mr. Foster of

Killhow. He had brought water some distance from the River Ellen, and had at great cost placed a turbine wheel to work all the thrashing and other machinery of the farm. His fields by extra cultivation yielded heavy crops. His herd of shorthorns was improving from year to year, and was becoming well known. He delighted to show his improvements and his failures to his visitors. Or he would take them into some farmhouse to sup curds or have a dish of tea, and would talk to the mistress in pure Cumberland dialect of her lad's prospects,—the lad probably owing his start to Mr. Moore's finding a situation for him.

His considerate care for the wants of his guests, his disposition to consult their wishes, and that perfect freedom which is the great charm of an English house of the higher sort, rendered a visit to Whitehall one of the most delightful of pleasures. It is said that to know a man as he is, you must travel with him or live with him. Those who knew George Moore merely as a man of business or as an attender of charitable committees, did not really know him. It was only at Whitehall, in the midst of his guests, or when " frisking over his own soil," as he called it, that you could know the thorough geniality, joyousness, and hospitality of the man as he really was. None ever left Whitehall—no matter of what class or condition—without carrying away with them some very pleasant and abiding recollections of the welcome which they had received from both host and hostess.

Though he had many dignitaries of the Church to visit him and receive his hospitalities, he did not forget the Dissenting ministers. Every year a party of them dined with him at Whitehall. He was greatly indebted to them for the missionary help which they had given him. He was told that the Wesleyan chapels were very much in debt. He offered to give twenty per cent., provided the people would bestir themselves to pay off the remainder. In numerous instances great efforts were made, and most of the chapels that had been sadly burdened with debt became free.

"Mr. Moore informed me," says a Wesleyan minister, "that he made his gifts towards Wesleyan chapels conditional, that he might stimulate others to deeds of liberality. His generosity in this case encouraged our people to renewed efforts, and many a sinking cause was stimulated into new life. He often sent me parcels of books for the use of our Sunday-schools, and many a suitable volume for our local preachers. George Moore's name will ever be a household word among the Wesleyans of Cumberland."

George Moore was like the good old English gentleman, who, "though he feasted all the rich, he ne'er forgot the poor." The very poor folk and old widowed women were warmly welcomed at Whitehall. There was an annual feast for these old pensioners. At tea he always waited on them with his wife; and gifts of tea, clothes, and money, were distributed to each of them. He received them separately in his smoking-room, where their special circumstances or troubles were listened to, and he frequently refers to it in his diary— "Had our old women's tea-feast—the happiest day my wife and I spend in Cumberland." It was always the last entertainment before he returned to London for the winter.

The servants of the household were not neglected during Mr. Moore's stay at Whitehall. No one was kinder to those of his household than he was. One day he mounted each of his men-servants to go to the hunt at Brayton, but "Geering (the coachman) came to grief." Another day he sent every servant in the house to Keswick to see the lakes and the mountains. The schoolmaster and his mother accompanied them. During their absence, George Moore and the Rev. H. Harris taught the children in the school, and Mrs. Moore and th· visitors cooked the dinner. " I taught the children all day," he says, "and my wife and Louisa Groucock cooked the dinner, and some one else made the beds, and we all were tired to death at night. I shouldn't care for it often ; but I do rejoice in giving pleasure to others."

Among the various persons whom Mr. Moore invited to Whitehall were the city missionaries of London and the county missionaries of Cumberland. He paid their expenses during their holidays. Rooms were appropriated for them at the home farm, and also by Mr. William Lawson, at his farm at Blennerhasset. He treated them as he did his wealthier friends. He cut out many excursions for them. He sent them up the fell-sides ; drove them to Bassenthwaite, and made it a real holiday for them.

They were most thankful for the treat. They felt that "their lines had fallen in pleasant places." On one occasion, when the city missionaries and their wives had returned to their labours in London, they wrote a conjoint letter of thanks to George Moore. They said, " We beg most gratefully to acknowledge our thanks for your great kindness in affording us the means of three weeks' rest in Cumberland. Our observations of nature—of the rivers, lakes, hills, and valleys—especially of Mount Skiddaw and the Bay of Allonby, have greatly tended to enlarge our views of the wisdom and power of God. Our visit to Cumberland has also given us the opportunity of having much intercourse and fellowship with each other, for which we feel truly thankful."

Another of the Cumberland missionaries on his return home wrote as follows :—" Having fairly got to work

again, refreshed and enlightened by our delightful conference at Whitehall, I desire to express my gratitude
to you for affording us such a favourable opportunity
for meeting to confer with one another upon subjects so
important to us as teachers of so many others.   It gives
us the opportunity of knowing our own littleness, which
often becomes an important element in our usefulness.
Altogether, too, it is always a profitable season for us,
though an expensive one for you.   But never, I am
sure, will your princely kindness be bestowed upon men
more grateful in return than the poor Scripture-readers
of Cumberland.   All of us have carried away a feeling
of gratitude to you and your worthy lady for your
kindness and countenance to our gathering; also to
your household servants, who were all so courteous
and polite.   I am sure, sir, you have all our prayers.
God bless you!"

Mr. Moore also invited many of his young men from
Bow Churchyard to Whitehall to share in its enjoy-
ments.   Most of the young Cumberland fellows, for
whom Mr. Moore had got situations in London, called
upon him in the course of their holidays.   One of them,
for some time in his employment, says, "Since a boy I
have known him intimately.   I can yet feel his grasp
of my arm, with 'Well done, Blinraset,'[1] when I took
a prize at his first competitive examination.   To me
he was always the same kind, blunt George Moore of
Whitehall and even of Bow Churchyard.   His first
greeting removed all embarrassment.   His character at
Bow Churchyard was only partially known amongst the
employés, but to those who had the privilege of visiting
him at home in Cumberland he showed the most unbounded kindness.   He has often told me that he
considered it a mark of disrespect if any of the young
men from London neglected to call upon him at White-

---

[1] Blennerhasset, a village in Cumberland.

hall and dine with him,—no matter how many lords, bishops, or commoners were there. All were alike welcome, and once inside his house, he soon made you feel it."

There was often a very mixed assembly at Whitehall, —of Bishops, Scripture-readers, warehousemen, farmers, city missionaries, Sunday-school children, pensioners, and Statesmen. One day, when the children were playing about, Thomas Moore came up the fields, covered with hay, and the hay-rake over his shoulder. George Moore introduced him to the Bishop of Carlisle as his brother Thomas, the distinguished Statesman! And statesman no doubt he was, though not of the Parliamentary order.

Amongst those who were invited to the Hall, were the porters from Bow Churchyard. Some of the elder porters came first, and amongst them John Hill, the oldest in the establishment. During their visit, Mrs. Moore went out one morning, and was crossing the park, when she came upon a venerable person, standing on a rising ground, staring about him with astonishment at the gardens and buildings. "Are you looking for somebody?" asked Mrs. Moore. "No," said he, "I am just looking round about, and thinking what a fine place it i , and how *we* helped to make it ; I have really a great pride in it!" With tears in his eyes, old Hill told how he had worked forty years for the firm ; how they had all worked hard together. "I was the *only* porter then," he said. "All has changed now. We are the biggest firm in the city. And yet," he continued, "those days do not look so far off either." John went up to the top of the Peel Tower, at Harbybrow. He looked along the valley to Whitehall ; and round the surrounding hills. It was a grand estate. "Yes," he said, "WE did it."

Mr Moore sent his invitations far and wide. He offered an old friend and fellow-helper, the branch manager at Bristol, to come and visit him at Whitehall. "No," said Mr. Brown, "trade wants close attention at present, and I can't take a holiday this year." By the next post a letter arrived from Mr. Moore, inviting him and his wife to Whitehall, and inclosing fifty pounds to pay their expenses, "in order," he said, "that you may have no excuse for not coming." Mr. Brown and his wife accordingly went, and, while there, enjoyed the house and estate as if they had been their own. When parting, Mr. Moore presented his friend with a vase which he admired, as a remembrance of the visit.

George Moore was much distressed about the little good that he could do for his native country. "I went," he says, "to the Rev. Mr. —— about his school. I am determined to get one built in his heathen parish." He was amazed to find a clergyman protesting that he "had no time to look after his schools." Another day he says, "I do not appear to be able to do any good in Cumberland. Ignorance prevails; and yet when such clergymen as Lyde of Wigton and Schnibben at Bromfield are doing their utmost, good results must follow. Wigton has privileges that were unknown in my day. The lads won't make use of the reading-rooms and libraries as they should. If they only knew how they will regret this afterwards, they would be wiser."

A great stir was roused in 1865, by a letter addressed by Dr. Percival of Clifton College to George Moore, on the morality, or rather the immorality, of Cumberland and Westmoreland. Dr. Percival was himself a Westmoreland man, and, like George Moore, was an ardent admirer of his native county. Yet here was a blot upon the morality of both counties, revealed by the Registrar-General's returns, which he thought ought to be obliterated. Eleven out of every hundred children born in Cumberland and Westmoreland were illegiti-

mate. The *Times* published the letter and followed it
up with a leading article on the Modern Arcadians of
Cumberland. " How is the matter to be remedied ? "
said the writer. " We know of no agency capable of
reaching it except publicity. Let it be clearly understood and widely made known that the labours of
clergymen, schoolmasters, and scripture readers are
thwarted and defeated by conditions of life in these
counties which ought to be curable."

The following is from George Moore's diary :—" Had
three hour's talk with Mr. H.—— as to illegitimacy. I
find that he does not like my doings. Still he was kind
and sensible. He said I had raised the anger of some
of the upper ten thousand. He believed that if I
persevered, I should lose my political influence. This I
am prepared to lose. *Excelsior !* must be my motto."
In the midst of these inquiries, Mr. Moore went to
Carlisle, to see the hiring fair. " I was shocked," he
says, "to see men and women bought like sheep in a
market, and engaged without knowledge, or references,
or character."

Numerous letters appeared in the local newspapers.
The subject was taken up at the conference of the
Evangelical Union at Keswick. George Moore was
blamed for publishing Dr. Percival's letter, and for
throwing dirt upon Cumberland and Westmoreland.

George Moore himself was doing the best that he
could to remedy the evil. The building of schools in
his native district, the improved education which he
had sedulously fostered, the extension of Sunday
school, the appointment of missionaries who visited the
poorest of the people and ministered to their spiritual
welfare, the establishment of working men's reading
rooms, where pure and wholesome literature was circulated, were among the means which, if rightly carried
out and earnestly persevered in, were calculated to

foster morality and elevate the sons and daughters of toil into a better and purer life.

The Dowager Countess Waldegrave, an old lady of eighty, came to his help. She attended George Moore's competitive examination at Wigton, and addressed the pupils and their mothers on the subject of their social duties, especially upon thrift, carefulness, and simplicity in dress. She had watched through a long life, the increasing tendency of English girls to wear fine and often tawdry dresses. She told the girls that they spent more than they could afford in unnecessary and useless finery, and that they did not look well after all. She had also a word for the mothers, who had so much influence in forming the characters of their children, especially of the girls. Nothing, she said, could be done without the help of the mothers. It was quite true, what Lord Shaftesbury had said : "Give me," said he, "a generation of Christian mothers, and I will undertake to change the whole face of society in twelve months."

Another important subject occupied Mr. Moore's attention while in Cumberland,—the improvement of cottage dwellings. He held that morality begins in the home ; and that if you would have society pure, you must improve the conditions in which people live. You must provide abundant space for sleeping accommodation, plenty of pure air, and good drainage. Unless these are provided, moral and spiritual influences can have but little effect in raising people out of the mire in which they have lived. In a letter to the *Wigton Advertiser*, Mr. Moore said—" The crowded condition of a large number of the labourers' cottages, and the pernicious influences they create, are a scandal to the proprietors, and would sap the morality of any class of people. It is a *moral cancer*, and education itself is of little use while these evils exist."

In attempting to improve the labourers' cottages of

Cumberland, Mr. Moore was beginning at the beginning.
To encourage this object and to give the people a pride
in their homes, he started a competition of cottage
gardeners. Mr. Potter, his head gardener, was one of
the chief judges on these occasions. After receiving
their prizes, the cottagers were entertained in George
Moore's hospitable mansion.

George Moore continued as ardent a hunter as ever.
He had a strong fibre of joyousness in his nature, which
firmly touched the solid earth. His love of athletic
sports showed an amount of animalism in him which
was no bad foundation for a superstructure of practical
morality and virtue. Nor was it inconsistent with religion. His knowledge of men and human nature was
great. He could work with all and sympathise with all.
He was no narrow bigot. He had a heart as wide as
the world.

At the same time he sometimes became jealous of his
love of sport. Was the devil, in this way, trying to draw
him away from better things? Not at all! It was
wholesome, it was healthy. He delighted in taking a
good gallop, because it was good for his constitution,
and worked off his nervous energy.

When he went down to Cumberland he knew the
ground thoroughly, and hunted with more delight than
anywhere else. One morning in October he met the
hounds at Westward Parks; he had them all to himself,
except the huntsman. Three days after he met the
hounds at Brayton. They killed the fox, and George
Moore got the brush. But he did not forget his social
duties. The same evening he went to see his poor
pensioners at Boltongate, visited them, and gave them
relief.

On another day he met the Cumberland hounds at
Waverbridge. "Found a fox in my covers, and ran him
to earth at Brayton. Found again, and ran him back to

my covers to earth.   Bolted him again, and killed him
in the open.   I never rode better."   A few days after
he went to a hunt breakfast at the Honourable P. Wynd-
ham's.   The pack found and killed two foxes.   "I
hunt," he says, "not only for pleasure, but for my
health.   The exercise does me great good.   I really do
not see any harm in a gallop with the hounds, if I did,
I would not go out again."

But again he hesitates about it, and asks, "Is it consistent with my profession?   Taking the chair at a
young men's meeting, attending prayer and Bible readings, and then hunting?"   Again he says, "Had a good
gallop with the hounds; killed two foxes.   Is this my
sin, my besetting sin?   If I thought it were, I should
never hunt again."

One day he goes out to meet the hounds.   "My new
horse, Bold Boy, on seeing the hounds, rose up on his
hind feet.   I threw myself off, thinking he might come
down upon me.   However, I mounted again, and had
a capital gallop."   Again, "I met the hounds at Crofton
Hall; ran three foxes.   I must have ridden nearly fifty
miles.   I make my health my excuse.   The fresh crisp
air does me good.   I am always at home when on
horseback."

In March, 1867, he met with an accident which put
a stop to his hunting for a time.   The meet was at Torpenhow.   From thence they went to the top of Binsey,
a heathery fell to the south of Whitehall.   There they
found a fox, and viewed him away.   Always anxious
to keep up with the hounds, Mr. Moore rode fast down
the hill.   But his bay mare got her foot into a rabbit
hole, and the rider got a regular cropper.   He found
that his shoulder was stiff.   Nevertheless he mounted
again, and galloped away.   The hounds were in full cry.
He kept up pretty well, though his shoulder was severely
hurt.

Next day he entertained a dozen friends, amongst whom was the master of the hunt and Frank Buckland. Nothing was talked about but fox-hunting. "I think," says Mr. Moore, "I must make yesterday my last day's hunting." Shortly after he consulted a celebrated surgeon at Carlisle about his shoulder. The joint was pronounced to be "all right;" though the muscles were found to be strained and hurt. Nothing could be done for the pain but to grin and bear it.

Notwithstanding the intense pain in his shoulder, Mr. Moore hunted once more. The year after his shoulder had been injured, he invited the Cumberland Hunt to meet at Whitehall. About sixty horsemen were present. They breakfasted in the old Hall, and then proceeded to mount. Mr. Moore was in low spirits, because of the pain in his shoulder. At first he did not intend to join his friends. But Geering, his coachman, urged him to go, and Sir Wilfrid Lawson joined in his persuasions. At length Mr. Moore's favourite horse, Zouave, was brought out, and with his arm in a sling, and a cigar in his mouth, he consented to mount. Mrs. Moore and Lady Lawson ascended the tower, and saw the brilliant red-coats ride away through the park.

The array of horsemen passed on to Watch-hill and found a fox. He was viewed away, and went across Whitehall Park, close under the wall of the west-front garden, followed by the hounds and riders. It was a sight not often to be seen. The day was splendid, although it was in November. The sun was shining, and the red-coats, jumping hedges and fences amidst the green fields, brightened up the picture. The fox went up the hill, out of sight of the gazers from the tower, and was lost in Parkhouse cover.

Again the hunt proceeded to Watch-hill, and found another fox. Away it went, almost in the same direction, passing through Whitehall Park, with the hounds

and hunters at its heels.   There was a slight check at
Park-wood.   Then it took straight away for Binsey,
went up the side of the hill and passed on to Snittle-
garth, and was lost at Bewaldeth.

It grew dark.   No more could be done that night.
No fox had been killed, though the hunters had got a
splendid run.   Mr. Moore returned home with his arm
in his sling, though nothing the worse for his day's
exercise.   "It was," he says, "a very enjoyable day.
I do like a day's hunting.   I always feel more light
and buoyant after it."

This was his last hunt!

CHAPTER XVIII.

ON his return to London from Cumberland, Mr. Moore
found plenty of work waiting for him. "I am now a
City man," he says on one occasion; "I find three
drawers full of letters, reports, and applications for
money. I have the best of partners, who let me spend
three or four months in Cumberland at my will."
Indeed Mr. Moore had now been working hard for
the firm for nearly forty years, and was fairly entitled
to an occasional rest.

Nevertheless he stood to his work as usual. His
reappearance at Bow Churchyard was the signal for
bustle and hard work. It seemed to set the whole gear-
ing in quicker motion. The word "George Moore has
arrived!" passed like magic from mouth to mouth. It
found every man at his post, from the smallest errand
boy to the oldest in the firm, at "attention!" When
George Moore was in the house, he was a sort of paternal despot. His influence was great over all who came
in contact with him. His will was never disputed; and
he never abused his power.

One of the young men who served under him—now in
Iowa, America—says of George Moore, "He was the
most particular man in small things that I ever saw, and

no doubt this was a great cause of his success. Few men could find out a flaw in the accounts which he audited, quicker than he did. He was very apt at figures, and his decisions, like his movements, were quick and correct. I may mention an instance. I was engaged in making out the private accounts against the firm— George Moore's account amongst the rest. To show how strict and business-like this merchant prince was, and it marked his character all through, he found that I had debited his account with 3d. for a ''bus to Euston,' for which we had no voucher.

"We had to keep a voucher for every penny paid out; and though hundreds of such items occurred throughout the year, we had no voucher for this. Mr. Moore audited the accounts, and though he went over hundreds of pounds, he stopped at the threepence for the 'bus to Euston. 'Where's the voucher for this?' he asked. 'If the account be threepence wrong, it might as well be three hundred pounds wrong. Find the voucher!' We hunted together—two of us—for three days, without effect. We searched through every letter and voucher for a year back. Every drawer was ransacked; and still no success. The search was at last given up as hopeless. Mr. Moore was told that the voucher for threepence could not be found. He was furious; he refused to pass the accounts; and we couldn't balance.

"I then recollected a circumstance which had occurred some time before. Mr. Moore had sent to Bow Church-yard for a fish, which he requested to be sent to Euston station by a porter. Mr. Moore was in a hurry; he was going down to Whitehall. He hadn't time to give the porter either a ticket or the money; but promised to send it, or give it on his return. The man neglected to ask him for it; and the clerks, knowing the expenditure to be right, had debited it to him without a voucher,

T

t us infringing one of the strictest rules of the firm. On the circumstance being mentioned to him, he at once admitted its correctness ; but at the same time he gave the clerks a sound lecture for their inaccuracy."

Among the *new* objects which he attended to at this time, besides those already mentioned, was the Christian Community, the Haverstock Hill Orphan Asylum, and the Industrial Dwellings Company founded by Alderman Waterlow. He took a particular interest in the latter company, as its object was to erect cheap buildings for the labouring classes. As has already been said, he held that without the solid foundation of a healthy home, all the efforts made to raise the lower classes from their depraved condition, would for the most part be comparatively fruitless.

During the absence of his wife at Ems for the benefit of her health, Mr. Moore visited Charles Dickens at Gadshill, and enjoyed himself there for several days. "I was delighted," he says, "to find that Charles Dickens was sound upon the Gospel. I found him a true Christian without great profession. I have a great liking for him."

Mr. Moore afterwards proceeded to join his wife at Ems. He went by steamer to Antwerp. During the voyage he encountered a distinguished-looking clergyman walking the deck. He soon made up to him, and the two entered into conversation. They first spoke about general topics, and then proceeded to talk about the work of the Church. They found that they held very different views as to Church policy, and yet they were very much pleased with each other. "Who can this b ?" thought George Moore. "I know most of the Low Church divines. This must be one of a different order." At last he took the liberty of asking his fellow-traveller's name, at the same time giving his own.

The stranger proved to be Archdeacon Denison. The latter has kindly furnished the following recollections of the voyage :—

"It was easy to see that we were of very different— I might say of opposite—schools in the matter of the religious life. Such differences there must always be, and there is no larger field that I know of for the exercise of 'charity.' I had much talk with Mr. Moore, and it left a lasting impression upon me,—not more lasting than comforting. I found a man ready and glad to extend to me all the respect and kindliness which I was ready and willing to extend to him,—one who had done great things for himself and for his ; and who had not been content to rest there, but had done great things to his fellow-men wheresoever he came into contact with them. I looked upon him and listened to him, with all our wide difference, with the respect, and I will add with the love, that is always won by a character and life like his. I parted with him with regret, and the day has always lived among my happy memories."

"I never knew a man," said one who knew him well, "whose religion was more thoroughly a part of himself." He was not ashamed of the views which he held, but was ready, on suitable occasions, to speak out his mind. When dining with a friend, one of the guests ventured to ask in general terms, "Surely there is no one here so antiquated as to believe in the inspiration of Scripture ?" "Yes, I do," said George Moore, from the other side of the table, "and I should be very much ashamed of myself if I did not." Silence followed, and the subject was changed.

The ladies went to the drawing-room, and the gentlemen followed. "Can you tell me," asked the non-believer in inspiration, of a lady, "who is the gentleman who so promptly answered my inquiry in the dining-room ?" "Oh, yes! He is my husband." "I am sorry," said he, "you have told me that so soon, for I wished to say that I have never been so struck with the religious sincerity of any one. I shall never forget it."

One thing astonished George Moore, as it did many others,—to see clever men assuming the cast-off garb of Tom Paine, and going about the country teaching atheism under the name of " Science."   " There are many proud philosophers," said he, " strutting about amongst us, telling us that it is of no use to pray to God, as He cannot and will not alter the laws of nature. In my belief, such philosophers are mere blasphemers." And again :—" My theology is utterly untouched by the plague of rationalism.   I have no wavering about the inspiration of the Word—no picking and choosing amid alleged myths—no paring down of the atonement."

Mr. Moore was a great lover of the Bible.   He circulated it far and wide.   He sent thousands of copies to Cumberland, to be distributed amongst the people. He circulated it through the lower parts of London by the hands of the City Missionaries.   He made presents of it to his young men and women, to his porters, and to the poor people whom he entertained.   He tried to introduce it into the bedrooms of every first-class hotel in Paris.   He succeeded in ten cases ; but failed in three.

When the Emperor of Russia was in London in 1867, George Moore, with two members of the British and Foreign Bible Society, waited upon him to present the " Bible of every land," and to express their congratulations upon his Majesty's providential preservation from the wicked attempt made upon his life during his visit to the Paris Exhibition.   To this address, the Emperor said : " I thank you from my heart for the sentiments which you have now expressed to me.   I have been profoundly touched by them, and I beg that you will make this known to all your countrymen.   I sincerely

thank you for waiting upon me with this address."
Laying his hand upon his heart, he again said, " I
have been deeply touched by the sentiments you have
expressed."

Religious principle had been a great power in George
Moore's own life. He wished it to be a great power in
the lives of others, and he did what he could to make
it so. Works distinctively Christian were very dear
to him. Beginning with children and youths, he was
immovably resolute as to the supreme importance of
their religious training. He insisted upon having Scripture reading in every school whose councils he directed.
He cared comparatively little for what is called denominational teaching. He liked the Prayer-book, but he
loved the Bible. The daily Bible-lesson was a *sine quâ
non* of his help. Thus, when the Middle-class schools
were established, Mr. Moore joined hand and heart with
other wealthy merchants of London in furthering the
success of the undertaking.

He was called upon at the end of 1865 and informed
of the intention to start a series of middle-class Schools
in and about London. The scheme was so entirely in
conformity with his views of bridging over the gap between the day-schools and the universities, that it at
once met with his support. He promised to give a
thousand pounds on one condition—that the religious
education was to be conducted in the same manner as
in the City of London School. The same condition was
required by Alderman Hale, then Lord Mayor.

Dr. Abbott, Head Master of the City of London
School, informed him that prayers were read there every
morning and evening, that the Bible was read and the
knowledge of the boys tested by examination in every
class of the school. The sons of Jews and Roman
Catholics who objected to the religious instruction
given, were of course exempted. This was quite satis-

factory to Mr. Moore, and he accordingly attended some of the meetings of the Middle-class Education Committee.

One day he was absent : there had been many proposals made for and against, when the honorary secretary, a clergyman, gave his opinion of the discussions that were going on about "sound religious instruction," by uttering the expressive formula, "Hang theology, let us begin!" "These terrible words," says the *Saturday Review*, "were duly read by Mr. Moore in the *Standard* of next day and his resolution was at once taken. Whether the hanging of theology is or is not sanctioned by the Bishop of London, it is not, it seems, adopted in the City of London School, and accordingly Mr. Moore assumed that the stipulated condition had been disregarded, and that he was therefore freed from his bargain."

A controversy took place between Mr. Tite and Mr. Moore. The former demanded the promised subscription : the latter refused, because the condition on which he had promised the subscription had not been complied with. Besides, Mr. Moore ascertained that religious instruction was altogether disregarded. "I am in a position to state," said one who knew, "that no class in the Middle-class School begins or ends with prayer, nor is the Bible used in any way. There is no approximation existing, or likely to exist (so far as present experiences go) towards religious instruction in that school."

Mr. Moore stuck to his point. It was not a matter of money with him, but a matter of principle. He declined to pay a farthing until the promised condition had been fulfilled. In the course of the correspondence Mr. Moore said that "education, without direct religious teaching, is a mere delusion. It is like launching a ship on a dark night, in a storm, without helm or compass.

It is professing to train immortal beings that they may run the race of life and obtain a happy hereafter, and yet not giving them any rule how to run so as to obtain."

The strong, clear, direct common sense, which had gained him his reputation as a man of business, guided him throughout. He saw that to talk about a good and complete education, from which religion was purposely excluded, was sheer nonsense; that teaching morals without religious practice, was merely building upon a foundation of sand. In his Diary, he says: "The Bishop has given me liberty to publish his letters for my vindication in the case of the middle-class schools. Tite, M.P., has been bullying me for months for the money I promised conditional on their being identical with the City of London School. I hope I am not mistaken in standing out. If I am wrong it is very sad."

The correspondence was published. Mr. Moore was inundated with letters approving of his conduct. The newspapers were full of articles and correspondence on the subject. It was at last found necessary to fall in. with his wish. The Bishop of London visited the schools, and examined the arrangements. He informed Mr. Moore "that the head master now gives religious instruction to each boy whose parents do not claim that he should be exempted. These religious instructions, which occupy the first hour of every day, are commenced by prayer given by a clergyman of the Church of England. This is the arrangement which, I am assured, has been adopted in consequence of, or at least following upon, the correspondence of last summer, and I think they are wise and good."

· This assurance was perfectly satisfactory to Mr. Moore. He went himself to visit the schools. He enters this memorandum on the subject: "May 5th,

1868. I have this morning heard the Rev. Mr. Jowett give two lessons at the Middle-class Schools which lasted an hour and a half. This was my second visit. I am bound to say that I have no longer any hesitation in paying the thousand pounds, which I have done to-day. I thank God that I have fought this fight manfully, and have succeeded in getting the Bible and prayers into these schools. This has been accomplished by perseverance. I felt it was my duty, or I could never have fought the battle single-handed against the Council, composed as it was of the first men in the city."

It may also be mentioned that Mr. Moore supplemented his gift to the Middle-class Schools by investing five hundred pounds in the name of the Corporation for the encouragement of the study of Holy Scripture. There is a half-yearly examination on the subject, and the income arising from the amount is expended in prizes for the boys who distinguish themselves.

While this controversy was going on, Mr. Moore was occupied in erecting a church in the northern part of London. He had, from the first, been on the committee of the Bishop of London's Fund. Something had been accomplished, but a great deal more remained to be done. George Moore modestly says in his Diary: "I spent three hours to-day with the Bishop of London's Fund; but I don't think myself useful." In June, 1866, he invited a distinguished party to his house in Kensington Palace Gardens, to receive statements of the work which had been done, and of the further help that was required. The Bishop of London and Lord Shaftesbury were the principal speakers. In the course of the Bishop's speech, he said of one district:—[1]

"Not one person in a hundred habitually attends a place of worship. Of the 228 shops in the district, 212 are open on Sunday; though about 70 are closed on Saturday, the Jewish Sabbath. Not half the Gentile population can read; half the women cannot ply a needle. One mothers' meeting has seventy members, half of whom, though living with men and having families, are unmarried. Nine families out of ten have but one small room in which to live, eat, and sleep. Not one family in six possesses a blanket, or a change of clothing. Not one in four has any bedding beyond some sacking, which contains a little flock or chopped straw. Not one in twenty has a clock; not one in ten has a book. Many of the houses are in the most wretched condition of filth and dirt. The walls, ceilings, floors, and staircases are broken and rotten. Drunkenness, brawling, blaspheming, and other sins, are fearfully prevalent. Forty-three lodging-houses accommodate two thousand lodgers, who pay from threepence to sixpence a night. Some are occupied by poor hard-working people, gaining an honest livelihood, while others are called 'thieves' kitchens,' the lodgers living by theft, burglary, and other criminal practices."

What a picture of London in the nineteenth century! —London, the richest city in the world—London, with its mercantile wealth—London, with its gaiety, its luxury, and its enormous expenditure; and yet London, with its seething mass of want, wickedness, and crime lurking underneath—a mere whited sepulchre, beautiful outward, but within full of dead men's bones and all uncleanness!

George Moore knew well enough the condition of London in its lowest aspects; but this picture of it by the Bishop moved his heart, and immediately suggested the question—What can I do to remedy this terrible spiritual destitution? An attempt had already been made to erect a new church in Kensington, where the people were rich enough to build any number of churches. But could not something be done for an utterly lost neighbourhood, such as this? His resolve was at once made. "Do you find the site and the place," said George Moore to the Bishop, "and I will find the money."

A place was pointed out. It was at Somers Town, —a poor and long-neglected district. It lies north of the New Road, between Euston and King's Cross Stations. It contained some fifteen thousand people. A walk through the main street in which the Sunday market was held was enough to impress one with the semi-barbarism which prevailed in the neighbourhood. Care and poverty were written on every face. Rags and dirt abounded. The food offered for sale was coarse, and the manner of buyers and sellers was no better.

Into this modern heathendom, the Committee of the Diocesan Home Mission had been urged to introduce the Gospel. Two centres of missionary labour had been established, and some successful work had been done. But it was not enough. The cry still was, "Come over and help us." Such was the state of things when George Moore took the matter up. A few days after the interview at Palace Gardens, he went to Somers Town to examine the district. He says in his Diary:—"I walked over the worst district in London. Fifteen thousand population. No one pays more than £30 rent a year. I decided at once that I would build a church here for the Diocesan Home Mission."

No sooner said than done. Lord Somers provided a freehold site for the church in Charlton Street. An architect (Mr. Newman) was employed, who prepared the design of the building. Contracts were entered into, and the church was finished and ready for opening by the end of 1868. Schools were afterwards added. Accommodation was provided in the church for about a thousand people and in the schools for over a thousand children. The latter received day-school instruction on week days, and Sunday-school instruction on Sundays. Mr. Moore spent £15,000 on the buildings ; and he also subscribed £250 a year to carry on the parish work necessary in so poor and miserable a locality. The Ecclesiastical Commissioners granted an endowment of £300 per annum to the vicar of the new church. The work was a great and a happy one, as the results afterwards proved.

The style of the church is simple, but chaste. It is in the early English decorated style. Mrs. Moore presented the finely-carved pulpit, which bears the following inscription : " The gift of Agnes, the loving wife of George Moore, who built this church for the glory of God." The organ was presented by Mr. Copestake, and the font by Mr. George Stockdale,—both intimate friends of Mr. Moore. The church was opened and con-secrated by the Archbishop of Canterbury-elect, on the 23rd December, 1868. It was his last official act as Bishop of London.

After the morning service, the Archbishop and some sixty or seventy ladies and gentlemen, lunched with Mr. Moore at his house in Kensington Palace Gardens. On that occasion Mr. Moore stated that the church which had been consecrated that day owed its existence to the fund which his Lordship had been instrumental in forming. He had done what he could to supply the spiritual wants of the neglected population of Somers Town. There were hundreds of wealthy men in London who could do the same for other districts. Let them come forward, and take their fair share in the work. The Archbishop-Designate followed Mr. Moore. He said :—

"I do not know that there could be a more appropriate way of ending my connection with the diocese than in consecrating this church. We have been engaged now for a great many years in the very important work of endeavouring to increase the means of spiritual instruction in the destitute parts of London. We have always tried to bring before the consciences of those whom God has blessed with wealth, the duty of assisting their poorer brethren ; and of the many notable instances which, in the course of the last few years, we have had to record of persons who have come forward to assist in this work in destitute places, there is none that is more satisfactory to my own mind than the particular instance which has brought us together here to-day. Here we see a man whom God has blessed with wealth, and whom he has raised to a great post through the influence of commerce, recognising the responsibilities that lie upon him and looking out, not for a place in which he is personally interested, but for a place which has no particular claim upon him except its poverty and destitution ; and that is the very thing we have been endeavouring to force upon men's consciences for a number of years past. I am not going to praise my good friend Mr. Moore, for I know that to do so would be distasteful both to him and to Mrs. Moore. I have known him for many years. Our connection began in Cumberland, where we joined together in good works, especially in regard to education, which was perhaps the first thing that brought us together. During the time I have been in London Mr. Moore has been a great supporter to me in works of this kind, and I trust that for many years to come he will in this great city show forth the example of a man who uses God's gifts for the good purposes for which God has given them."

Mr. Moore followed. He said that "he did not wish to claim any credit for building the church, and that if anybody owed any gratitude to God, he was the man. When he first came to London he never expected to be able to do so much ; and he thought he might honestly say that what he had done he had done disinterestedly."

It may be mentioned that, in connection with the new church, funds were appropriated for the support of national schools, Sunday schools, church choir, maternity society, general missions, district society for visiting the poor, coal club, clothing club, parents' tea, school treats, temperance society, and penny bank.

With regard to the latter institution, it may be mentioned that, in the poorer districts, there is no better
method of checking intemperance, the curse of modern
society, than by inducing young as well as old to save
their spare pennies in a penny bank; for whatever is
deposited there is so much money rescued from the
public-house.

A week after the consecration of the church at Somers
Town, the confirmation of the new Archbishop of Canterbury took place at St. Mary-le-bow, Cheapside, close
to the warehouse of Mr. Moore and his partners. After
the ceremony, the Archbishop of Canterbury, the
Bishops of Oxford, Gloucester, Ely, and the Bishop-elect
of London, with many of their chaplains, lunched with
Mr. Moore and his partners in Bow Churchyard.

Nor did Mr. Moore confine his help to the Church of
England. He was large-minded and heart-whole. "If
any of my fellow-Christians," he said, "live in Church of
England Square, Wesleyan Street, Independent Road,
Baptist Lane or Brethren Row, I am still to love them,
and to seek their welfare."

He took the chair at Mr. Spurgeon's Tabernacle, and
helped the Orphanage by a liberal subscription. "I
went to Mr. Spurgeon's in the evening," he said. "What
a wonderful sight! He sent for me, and I introduced
my friends to him."

When the Rev. Morley Punshon was about to set out
for America, Mr. Moore was requested to take the chair,
and he had the pleasure of presenting him with a purse
of seven hundred guineas, which had been collected
amongst Mr. Punshon's friends.

One of his warmest friends was the Rev. Dr. Stoughton, who took part in his Bible-readings, and often lent
him his schoolrooms at Hornton Street for his Christmas dinners. "Dr. Stoughton," he said in his diary,
"is a living Christian. He speaks well of all denomi-

nations. Thank God there will be no denominations in heaven."

Mr. Moore frequently took the chair at Dr. Stoughton's chapel, at the meetings of the schools, and of the Young Mens' Missionary Association.

On such occasions he had to make a speech. This was a great burden to him, for speaking at public meetings often prevented him from sleeping at night. Yet he cheerfully undertook the work, thinking it to be his duty. "I have often," he says, "made stern resolutions not to overwork myself, and to take more relaxation, but NO is not learnt in a day."

Among the institutions in which he took a great interest was the Christian Community, founded by the Rev. John Wesley in 1772. Its objects were to visit and preach the Gospel in workhouses, lodging-houses, asylums, public rooms, and in the open air. George Moore was attracted by the work. Its object was to find the lost and raise up the fallen. The members of the Community visited the hospitals, the female refuges, and even the lowest threepenny-a-night lodging-houses. George Moore helped them liberally with his purse and with his voice. On one occasion, when the anniversary of the community was held in Shaftesbury Hall, Aldersgate Street, Mr. Moore presided, and made one of his best speeches.

"He was heartily glad that he had fallen in with such a society. He liked their principle: it was aggressive. They did not wait for the people to come to them: they went to the people themselves. The good the Community had done would never be known by the world. He advocated their having a hall of their own. At present they had not a place to put their heads into. He thought it was a great shame to London that such a self-denying society as this should be crippled in its onward progress and good work for want of funds. Why, as to funds, they had not a fourpenny-piece to give to any poor creature who might solicit their alms. He thought all could do something to help so great a cause. Many people thought they could do nothing in consequence of their position being humble, and their means so small. He believed that all could do something, no matter how little it was. He knew many men in the City who seemed to him to do nothing else but work, eat, drink, and sleep. They never thought or cared for anything else; they never cared for anybody but themselves. On the other hand, some men wanted to do too much. They promised to attend to ten or twenty things, but neglected them all. He believed, however, that mere money, unless it was given for the love of Jesus, would be as filthy rags in the sight of God. He looked to the heart, not to the action. The Bishop of London's Fund had become a very fashionable thing, and many persons gave money because it was the fashion; but there their work ended. . . . He was desirous of seeing the gulf that stood between the rich and the poor lessened, and he was of opinion that mutual advantage and benefit would arise to all by their more frequently mingling together."

In 1867 Mr. Moore was appointed justice of the peace for the county of Middlesex. This was done at the instance of Lord Salisbury. He took his seat on the bench, and attended to the administration of justice. He also frequently attended the committee to administer relief to the poor at the Mansion House. This was during the Winter of 1867, when great starvation existed in the east end of London. " The Mansion House distress fund," he says, " occupies a great deal of my time. And yet I like this work. My correspondence constantly increases. All sorts of applications for money and advice."

About this time Philip H—— dined at his house. " He is a Roman Catholic," said he, " but he is safe for heaven." And again he writes, " There is a strange tendency in human nature to take trusts as possessions, and gifts as rights. We see it in everything. We live on the wealth of another : we rest on the work of another."

In July, 1868, he was again asked to represent an important constituency in Parliament. He was requested to contest Mid-Surrey along with Sir Julian Goldsmid. "The only condition," said the letter of invitation addressed to him, "that would be required, would be to support Mr. Gladstone's Irish Church policy." It was stated that if he consented to stand, his return was certain. He declined, not only because his numerous engagements prevented him, but because he did *not* support Mr. Gladstone's Irish Church policy. The party might be trying their hand on the English Church next. He wished the Church to be reformed, not destroyed. He accordingly declined to propose Mr. Crawford for the City, and Lord Enfield for Middlesex. He writes in his Diary : "I am called a turncoat. My Liberal friends assail me. These friends of tolerance are rather intolerant. I must go *their* way, and not mine. I will not vote for any man that wishes to destroy the Irish Church. Thank God, I have a conscience left. My Liberal friends don't see this."

In June, 1868, Mr. Moore became prime warden of the Fishmongers' Company. He had been elected on the court about twelve years before, and regularly attended the meetings of the company. The Fishmongers is one of the oldest guilds in the City of London. Originally its use was to protect the rights of the merchants' ships and boats bringing fruit and fish from the southern seas. It had special rights on the waters of the Thames, and to this day appoints two persons, the company's "meters," who prevent the landing and sale of unwholesome fish within the jurisdiction of London. The company had always been associated with the Whigs and Liberals ; consequently George Moore had become early identified with its interests. When he was elected on the court, he took frequent opportunities of pointing out the good objects to which the funds of the company might be devoted. He regarded it as a source[1] from which money might be obtained for beneficent objects. The court was always most generous in yielding to his applications.

He did not do the work connected with the Fish-mongers' Company in a perfunctory manner. He did it thoroughly, as was his wont. The company had a large number of pensioners. He did not trust to the reports of visitors, but visited them himself. He spent whole days in going about from house to house. One day he visited about sixty poor people, pensioners of the Fishmongers. Then, the company had large estates in Ireland. He determined to look into their condition himself.

During one of his summer visits to Whitehall, he resolved to make his Irish journey. He went by Silloth to Dublin, to visit his branch establishment there. "Many old and living scenes," he says, "were repro-duced in my mind. It was often my resort in olden times." He next went to Killarney, and proceeded northwards by way of Athlone and Enniskillen—taking the opportunity of calling upon his customers in all the towns that he passed through.

[1] Among the subscriptions which Mr. Moore obtained from the Fish-mongers' Company were the following :—

A hundred guineas for the British Home for Incurables.
A hundred guineas for Mr. Spurgeon's Orphanage.
£50 for the Neapolitan Refugees.
£100 and £10 annually for the Royal Free Hospital.
£100 for the Great Northern Hospital.
£500 for the Bishop of London's Fund.
Fifty guineas for Mrs. Meredith's Home for Female Convicts.
£30 for Bread Street Ward Schools.
£50 for the Little Boys' Home.
Fifty guineas for Cabman's Benevolent ; the same for Cabman's Mission.
Twenty-five guineas for Workshops for the blind.
And £1,000 for the Middle Class Schools.

U

He then arrived at Londonderry. From this point he visited the estates held by the Fishmongers. He visited the farms and the farmers; the two dispensaries; the Catholic church, and the two Presbyterian churches. But most of all he visited the schools. He had one of his competitive examinations at Ballykelly school. He gave the children prizes, and entertained them at tea. There were eight schools in all to visit, with the same objects. He was not pleased with the manner in which the schools were conducted. He had come fresh from his own schools in Cumberland. "I am quite convinced," he said, "that we are here upon a rotten system. The examination by the Board is a farce, and also by the Church of England inspectors. I had a long consultation with the Northern Board at Ballykelly. The Rev. Mr. Edwards thereon roughly agreed with me about the system—that it was inefficient."

Mr. Moore next visited the tenantry. At Walworth he walked through five or six hundred acres of wood. He then lunched with George Cuther, one of the best and largest farmers. On Sunday he attended the Ballykelly church, and heard an excellent sermon from the Protestant preacher. After looking over the slot embankment, erected to inclose a hundred acres of land, and visiting all the remaining farmers on the estate, he returned by way of the Giant's Causeway and Belfast, and embarked for Morecambe Bay,—which he reached after an absence from England of about three weeks.

The usual splendid banquets of the Company were given during his Prime Wardenship. There was the Liberal Ministerial Banquet, at which the Prime Minister (Mr. Gladstone), and nearly all the principal ministers were present. On that occasion Mr. Gladstone was presented with the freedom of the Company. Mr. Moore distinguished himself by the vigour of his speeches. In proposing the health of the Army, he said : "There is an old maxim, but experience has not proved its wisdom in practice ; it is, 'if you wish to preserve peace, prepare for war.' I am of a different opinion ; if you wish to preserve peace, prepare for peace. Nations that are constantly arming, adopt the readiest means to promote war, and nations that have made great preparations for war are very apt to test the efficiency of their army." And with a broad hint to certain men very much given to foreign interference, he said : "I hope the day has gone by when Ministers are perpetually discussing the affairs of other nations un-asked, instead of attending to their own."

In the course of his Prime Wardenship, he had one particular banquet, at which the two Archbishops were present, six Bishops, and many leading clergymen and ministers, of whom the Rev. Mr. Binney was one. On the 24th of June, 1869, he says: "I presided over the Fishmongers' banquet for the last time. Thank God, it is over !"

While he was Prime Warden, he was suffering from the intense pain in his shoulder, caused by his accident in the hunting-field in March, 1867. He had consulted the most eminent surgeons. They could find no cure for the pain in his shoulder. Some called it neuralgia, others rheumatism. Some recommended a six months' sea-voyage ; others strapped up his shoulder with plas-ters, and told him to keep his arm in a sling. At length the pain became unbearable. Sometimes the shoulder grew very black. The dislocation forward, which it seems to have been, interrupted the circulation of the blood. On the 7th December, 1868, he writes with difficulty in his diary : "I was struck down with neural-gia at the Middlesex Hospital, when on a committee for selecting a clergyman. I had my shoulder cut open to insert morphia : pain *very* bad !"

He was taken home in a cab by the late Mr. De

U 2

Morgan, surgeon. When he entered his house, he clung by a pillar, as if he were drunk. He could scarcely get up to his bedroom, and there he dozed and rambled; but the pain was somewhat relieved. He called in one of the most eminent surgeons in London, but, as Mr. Moore writes, "he did not understand my shoulder." Another surgeon was called in, and still another; but the result was the same. It was with great difficulty that he could attend the consecration of his church in Somers Town, with his arm in a sling. "The shoulder," he says, "is not so black as formerly, but the pain is more acute." Then the first physician in London was called in, but he could only say, "It is a most painful affection of the shoulder joint." The patient already knew that. But the physician as well as the surgeons could do nothing for him.

He went about, though looking very ill, to the Field Lane Refuge, to the Industrial Dwellings, to Christ's Hospital, to the Court of the Fishmongers. He even travelled down to York to stay for a few days with the Archbishop. On his return to London, he attended a meeting of Christ's Hospital "about a reform in the mode of education in the school." A few days later he says, "the neuralgia came on fearfully all day, and at night I was in torture." Mrs. Moore "rushed off in the brougham to fetch Dr. ——, that he might see my arm at the blackest." Still nothing could be done. Then Mr. —— came, and plastered and bandaged up my arm." The patient could not write; it was with difficulty that he could sign a cheque. His wife then became his amanuensis. At a banquet at the Fishmongers', he was seized with one of his furious paroxysms of neuralgia. A surgeon was sent for, who came and gave him chloroform.

At length he could bear his pain no longer. He had been advised to go to a well-known bone-setter. No!

he would not do that.   He had put himself in the hands
of the first surgeons of the day.   Why should he go to
an irregular practitioner ?   At length, however, he was
persuaded by his friends.   As the surgeons had done
their best, why should he not try the bone-setter ?   He
called upon Mr. Hutton at his house.   He looked at the
shoulder, " Well, he would try and put it in."   This was
new comfort.   Mr. Hutton recommended his patient to
buy some neat's-foot oil, and rub it in as hot as he could
bear it.   "Where can we buy the stuff ?" asked Mrs.
Moore.   "You can take a soda-water bottle and get it
at a tripe shop in Tottenham Court Road."   "We have
not got a soda-water bottle with us."   "You can get
one at the corner, at the public house !   You might get
it at a druggist's," he continued, " but he will charge you
three times as dear."

The neat's-foot oil was at last got ; the shoulder was
duly rubbed with it ; and the bone-setter arrived at
Kensington Palace Gardens to do his best or his worst.
He made Mr. Moore sign a paper before he proceeded
with his operation, in which the former agreed to be
satisfied whether failure or success was the result.
Hutton took the arm in his hand, gave it two or three
turns, and then gave it a tremendous twist in the socket.
The shoulder-joint was got in !   George Moore threw
his arm out with strength, straight before him, and said,
" I could fight," whereas a moment before he could not
raise it two inches.   It had been out for nearly two
years.

Mr. Moore was taken to task by his professional
friends for going to a quack about his shoulder.   "Well,"
said he, " quack or no quack, he cured me, and that was
all I wanted.   'Whereas I was blind, now I see.'"

After presenting a bust of Lord Brougham and a
silver claret-jug to the Fishmongers', in memory of his
prime wardenship, he set out for Cumberland, and in-

vited Mr. Hutton to join him at Whitehall as a friend.
When "his benefactor," as he called him, arrived at
Whitehall, he gave him a hearty welcome, and sent him
away rejoicing.   Mr. Moore was no more troubled with
his shoulder.

Hutton died very soon afterwards, and Mr. Moore
remarks in his diary that he was as much struck by his
unworldliness as by his skill,—for he refused to take any
fee additional to the £5 that was at first asked.   It was
with great pressure that Mr. Moore prevailed upon him
to take £5 more.

During his repeated accessions of pain, he entered, or
made Mrs. Moore enter, many memoranda in his diary,
of which we subjoin a few :—

"We must wait till the day dawns and the shadows
flee away, to know how wise and suitable every dealing
of God is with us."

"I am ashamed to think that I sometimes doubt
whether God hears my prayers,—they are so poor, so
weak, so spiritless.   I thank God my faith is as simple
as a child's."

"I have sorrows to go through, but they will only
prove joy afterwards.   Whom our Master loveth, He
chasteneth.   'No cross, no crown.'   As I suffer, so I
shall enjoy."

"Prayer is the mightiest influence men can use.
Like the dew in summer, it makes no noise.   It is
unseen, but produces immense results."

"Exercise is the secret of a healthy body, and active
working for God is the secret of a healthy soul.   He
that watereth others shall be watered himself."

"This is the last July Sunday I may ever see.   This
wasting frame may sink beneath the sod.   This busy
hand may then be still.   Every day I get warnings ; so
many of my old friends are passing away."

"'Just as I am, without one plea,'—a poor unworthy

sinner. Christ takes me as I am—without money, or price, or works. Oh, my works are nothing!"

"It is a great trial to my faith to reconcile man's liberty with God's sovereignty; and yet no one can read the Bible without seeing both plainly."

"Christ does not uproot human feelings. He only directs and elevates them. It is right for a man to be ambitious of success, to be ambitious of usefulness in His good service."

"What is the unpardonable sin? Is it a clear intellectual knowledge of the Gospel, with a deliberate rejection of it, and a wilful choice of evil?"

CHAPTER XIX.

THE revival of education in Cumberland had so far
succeeded. It had started from a small beginning. At
first it embraced only the neighbourhood of Mealsgate.
From thence it had extended to the neighbouring
parishes. When the Competitive Examinations were
begun, the whole of the adjoining schools were influenced.

But now that the thing had got fairly established,
George Moore desired that it should stand by itself.
He was anxious to get rid of the responsibility of getting
up and undertaking the competitive examinations. He
attended a meeting of the Diocesan Education Society
at Carlisle, where he carried all his resolutions, for the
purpose of organising a competitive examination in
every rural deanery in the diocese.

George Moore took a special interest in the last competitive examination held at Wigton. Two hundred
and eighty prizes were given away to masters and
scholars, who came from all parts of the county to receive them. The Bishop of Carlisle (Waldegrave) examined the scholars in Scripture, and presented the prizes.
The meeting was held in a large marquee, capable of
accommodating a thousand people, yet many could not
find admission, and crowded round the entrance.

The Rev. Dr. Jex-Blake, Master of Rugby, was present, and made an excellent speech. He said,—"He was too happy at school as a boy, and his school recollections were too fresh and pleasant, not to be thoroughly at home with the boys; and his own present work at Rugby was too intensely interesting for him not to be thoroughly in sympathy with the masters. He could particularly sympathise with them when they had to struggle against those who ought to be their best friends, the parents of children, who grudged their children's time, and who would not permit them to receive a good sound education. He knew how hard the mere routine of a teacher's work was, but he must believe in culture for its own sake. He had recently seen a pleasantly-written article in the *Quarterly* on Westmoreland, in which he came across a proverb, which he feared he would spoil in quoting. It was lamentably one-sided, and something like the following:—'*Nobbut gie us a guid skeulmaister, and a varra moderate parson will deu.*' He believed in the good schoolmaster, but not in the moderate parson. He had been told that the increase and progress of education in this county had been very great. He was certain that he who was now at the head of the diocese was most zealously determined to maintain and work up the education to the highest possible standard in God's sight. Still schoolmasters could do a great deal. He instanced Scotland as a country which had been greatly benefited by the common spread of education. What was it that enabled so many Scotchmen to attain far higher positions than those from which they originally came? It was the kirk and schools of the country,—her sturdy faith in a sturdy Protestantism, and a sturdy education."

One of the most interesting events of the meeting was the presentation of a parting address of the schoolmasters of the district to George Moore, which had been beauti-

fully illuminated on vellum for the masters by a lady in
Wigton.   It was as follows:—

"DEAR SIR,—We, the undersigned teachers, whose pupils
attend from time to time your competitive examinations, beg to
fulfil the desire, long cherished in our hearts, of testifying how
highly we appreciate the deep interest which you take in the cause
of education generally, and in our own schools in particular.   The
present occasion being one of more than ordinary interest, has
been thought a fitting time for doing so ; but we assure you that
the address is not presented as a mere matter of form : it is a
spontaneous proof of our heartfelt gratitude for numerous benefits
received at your hands.

" We desire to express to you our sense of the obligations under
which we lie for your uniform kindness, hospitality, consideration,
and sympathy ; and to assure you that to your cordial aid in divers
ways much of the success that has attended our labours for the last
few years is exclusively due.   We feel especially grateful for your
great boon to the cause of education—the Wigton Prize Scheme—
in which such deserved prominence is given to religious instruction,
assuring you that its good effects cannot be over-estimated.   It has
created a spirit of generous rivalry among teachers, and infused a
more lively interest in their studies into the minds of the children
by supplying a stimulus in the shape of emulation, prizes, and
rewards, such as exist in the great public schools.

" Thus a great impulse has been given to the work of education ;
a higher standard has been reached, a higher tone induced, and
greater mental vigour developed ; schools have increased in number, and the evils of irregular attendance have been modified.
Nor are the good effects confined to our schools.   The large number of valuable books which you distribute every year provide the
recipients with the means of carrying on their education after
leaving school, and also supply their parents with a great induce-
ment to employ their leisure hours in reading.

" As schoolmasters we are glad of the privilege of sending
candidates to your competitive examinations, and feel it an honour
to be thus connected with you in a common cause.   The only re-
ciprocal service in our power we now offer—the tribute of our
esteem and respect.   Long may Mrs. Moore and you live to be the
objects of regard and channels of blessing to all around you, continuing to carry on the plans of benevolence supported by your
princely munificence.   That God's richest blessing may rest upon
her and you, and also upon your labours of love, is our fervent
wish and prayer."

The address was signed by fourteen schoolmasters.
Mr. Moore replied to them as follows:—

"I beg to thank you most cordially for your address, and for the
kind mention you make of my wife and myself in it.   The desire

to help forward in some measure, however small, the education of the children of my native county has been very dear to me; and it is very gratifying to have your sympathy and your approbation of my efforts. When I look round on you all, and see what an intelligent and earnest body of men are here as schoolmasters, I feel thankful indeed that it is so.

"Not many years since the idea was somewhat prevalent that any man was good enough for a schoolmaster. I can recall many instances of men who had broken down in other walks of life (perhaps as colliers, having unfitted themselves for a coal-pit life by breaking a leg) being made schoolmasters, assuming the responsibilities of educators of youth, and no one was surprised at the assumption. This state of things, thank God, has now gone to that prison house of the past from which there is no recall.

"For my part, I confess that I hold no man fit for the office who has not something of the missionary in him. He must have a large portion of the spirit of Him who 'went about doing good.' In other words, he must give himself to his vocation as a man who feels that it is one of those works which are to be undertaken with a willing heart and fervent spirit, and for no selfish ends.

"The Bishop of London the other day, in a correspondence on the Middle-class School, gave the following axioms, which he says he inherited from Dr. Arnold, if he did not receive them before he came under the influence of his great authority. First,—That a system of mere secular instruction is not education. Secondly,—That there can be no real education without religious teaching, and that such religious teaching must be based on doctrine in the highest and purest sense of that word. Thirdly,—That when circumstances make people rest satisfied with a system of mere secular instruction in any educational institution, they consent to act under a great disadvantage, to which they ought not to subject those whom they would instruct without a proved necessity, and without taking other means to fill up the deficiency. Fourthly,—That it is quite possible to give a sound Christian education and instruction, based on the great Gospel verities, which shall include the mass of English children, even those who do not belong to the Church.

"I am sure you understand that I do not underrate storing your pupils' minds with all knowledge—this is your work; but I feel that education without religious teaching is a mere delusion, and will have no abiding influence on your scholars.

"I thank you especially for what you say of the good brought about by my prize scheme. When I look back at the twelve years we have now worked together, and at the discouragements I first met with, I must say I am grateful for what you say. Many then said it would end in the masters being mere 'crammers of a few boys to obtain the prizes,' without any solid and honest education. We have lived down this unjust reflection, for I was sure you would always do justice to the work to which you have been called.

"You know I have always spoken the truth to you, sometimes very plainly. Now I wish that such a thing as a drunken schoolmaster was a thing unknown; thank God, there are but very few of them left. Many of you labour in some remote village, where you are almost the centre of intelligence to those you teach, perhaps to their parents also. From you might flow the influence to raise the tone of morality and sobriety around you. The most frequent cry we hear now in the newspapers is of the ignorance which prevails in all our rural agricultural districts; I hope that this cannot be said of this part of Cumberland. You have no doubt many difficulties and trials, and schoolmasters have always had my real sympathy. They seem so often to have to fight their battle singlehanded, and sincere and earnest as they may be, disappointments and failures and sorrows must be a part of their work.

"But *we are apt to dwell too much on the burden of our lot. My own theory of life is, that it would be worth nothing if it were not f r work, and duty, and responsibility;* and surely yours is a noble work. When you consider the numbers of the next generation over whom you have such influence, is it not a noble life-work? You are nearly all young men now before me—many scarcely in your prime; see to it that when you are old your recollections of your school may not be mixed with bitter regrets for opportunities wasted and the good seed *un*sown, as it might have been, on the living souls daily around you. 'He that sleepeth in harvest is a son that causeth shame.' Many of you know and love your Heavenly Father, and desire to work to please Him. Be not then sons that sleep over your work, but labour hard, that when, at the great fore-gathering, you have to give up your account, you may bear many sheaves with you rejoicing.

"And now let me, in conclusion, again thank you for your kind address. The meetings which I have had with you in connection with the prize-scheme have been a source of great interest and pleasure to me from year to year; and though disappointments and anxieties have not been wanting, the results and improvements have been a full reward. I feel that now the competitive scheme has in a great measure *done* its work hereabouts. The new revised code (paying for results) has partly superseded our work, and the little encouragement given to me by My Lords of the Committee of Council on Education, who say:—'H. M. inspector must employ about it no time except such as is left to his own disposal,'—has put a great barrier in the way of its continuance. But, however it may end, be assured individually of my help and sympathy, as much as is in my power, and of my cordial good wishes."

Mr. Moore was not so successful with his farming as with his schools and missionary work. "I am beginning," he said on one occasion, "to understand something about farming. It gives me an object for exercise; for I am constantly going about to see how things are going on. But as for returns, it proves a very poor affair." In 1867 he had a balance-sheet prepared. He found he had *lost £157* on his home farm, besides the interest upon £300 for draining. Certainly a very bad pecuniary result of his farming industry.

While at Whitehall Mr. Moore attended the bench of magistrates at Wigton, and, with Sir Wilfrid Lawson, endeavoured to the best of his power to keep down the licences for public-houses. At first they failed, but at last they succeeded in rejecting most of the new licences. There was much reason for checking drunkenness in the neighbourhood. One day he enters in his diary, "Attended a funeral. The man drowned himself. A sad affair. He is the third given to drinking who has died within three weeks."

Another day he says, "At Wigton on the bench. Had nine cases of 'drunk and disorderly.' Very sad !" And again he says, "Went to see a school. The Rev. Mr. —— was half drunk. He insulted me and hurt my feelings very much." This was enough to make him despair. One day he says, "I had a long discussion with Mr. —— about the immorality of Cumberland. I encouraged him to get the Ritualists to try their hand, as the Evangelicals had failed." Yet he went on appointing Scripture-readers and county-town Missionaries as the best methods of reaching the population.

When he returned to London, he was much occupied in endeavouring to get reforms introduced into the schools of Christ's Hospital. Mr. Moore had become a governor of the institution when a comparatively young man. In September, 1854, he attended the annual sermon delivered in Christ Church, Newgate Street, by Dr. Jacob, the newly-elected head grammar master. The sermon astonished Mr. Moore. He said, "It was the most extraordinary exposure of bad management and supposed grievances that I had ever heard of in any public establishment."

The text of the sermon was, "Through wisdom a house is builded; and by understanding it is established." Dr. Jacob proceeded to give his idea of the "understanding" by means of which this great charity was managed; and he did so with no flattering words nor empty compliments. His whole object, he said, was for the good of the hospital. The governors themselves did not know the facts connected with the education and discipline of the place, and it was therefore necessary for those, like himself, who did know, to tell the whole truth.

The preacher held that the intellectual discipline of Christ's Hospital was behind that of the public schools of the age;—"that a large mass of the boys were found unable to compete with the scholars of a well-conducted national school; that the various subjects which were specially needed for a good modern education, and to fit youths to play their part well in the stir and struggle of commercial life, were not taught at Christ's Hospital; and that modern languages, various branches of practical or applied science, physical and historical geography, English composition, elementary art, were all but absolutely interdicted."[1] The moral and religious condition of the school was also eminently defective. In other schools of a similar character, boys generally resided under a master's roof, and were under his humanising and Christian influence; whereas at Christ's Hospital the boys were entirely removed from the master's sight and charge except during the actual hours of the schoolroom. The masters were not required to have either work, care, or interest in the moral training of the children.

"It must be added," said Dr. Jacob, "that the absence of day-rooms which might be used out of school

---

[1] Sermon preached in Christ's Church, Newgate Street, on St. Matthew's Day, September 21st, 1851, by the Rev. G. A. Jacob, D.D., p. 15.

hours for numberless wholesome purposes,—the absence
of a library, which would encourage a taste for reading
and voluntary improvement, and keep many a boy from
idleness and vice,—the absence of almost everything
which might develop and strengthen the better feelings
and tendencies of boyhood,—help to encourage some of
the worst habits, and to throw boys upon the gratification of their lower appetites as their only source of
pleasure ; than which nothing can be more prejudicial
to all moral good. . . . Earnestly do I hope and pray
that all who are engaged in the government of this great
and noble house may duly feel the sacred responsibility
of their position, and may rise with willing hearts and
hands to encounter all the difficulties which impede the
full development of its great resources, and keep it so
far behind the requirements of the age."

This was a bold and honest sermon. But it was a
dangerous course for Dr. Jacob to adopt at the commencement of his mastership. The sermon acted like
a bombshell thrown in amongst the governors and
almoners. Some were angry, some were indignant,
some thought they had been insulted. "The first thing
I did," says George Moore, "on returning home, was
to write a strong and forcible letter to the treasurer. I
requested that the almoners should publish the sermon
on the following grounds :—First, that if the sermon
was true, the almoners were not worthy of the confidence of the governors ; and, second, that if the
sermon was not true, Dr. Jacob ought to be dismissed."

The treasurer was indignant at George Moore for
writing such a letter, and the almoners were still more
indignant at Dr. Jacob for preaching such a sermon.
The fat was in the fire—all through his doing. The
almoners gave Dr. Jacob notice to quit. Many of the
governors thought this hard treatment. It seemed like
hushing up abuses. They claimed that a full investi-

gation should be made before dismissing the master.
Dr. Jacob published his sermon, so that it might be
carefully examined and considered. George Moore
worked hard amongst his friends to get them to be
present on the day of battle. Dr. Jacob also urged all
the governors, whether in town or not, to be present on
the occasion.

"We had a large meeting on the 21st of November,"
says Mr. Moore, "to determine whether Dr. Jacob
should be dismissed or not, and the almoners were
beaten by a large majority. They would not, however,
resign. They organised their forces, and determined
upon a second trial of strength, not merely for the
dismissal of Dr. Jacob, but also upon the point of
whether the almoners were to be a self-elected body
for the future ; and upon that point they got a majority.
By this time, however, the hospital had got into disorder and confusion. No authority existed. Insubor-
dination prevailed everywhere. It was impossible to
introduce or carry any reforms in the hospital. The
almoners at last voluntarily consented to divide with
the governors the election of the succeeding almoners.
A reconciliation was thus effected. Russell Gurney,
Esq., Alderman Wire, and myself were elected, three
of their most determined opponents during the recent
discussions. I at first declined to accept the office,
being so much occupied with other engagements ; but
my friends anxiously urged me to accept it as a duty,
and I at last consented. I am bound to say that I
have found this a very pleasurable duty. The almoners
are composed of some of the first men in the city ; and
I have ever found them amenable to reason, and
anxious to carry out all legitimate reforms."

Mr. Moore at once proceeded to make himself
acquainted with the duties of his office. He inspected
Christ's Hospital, saw the reforms that were necessary,

and endeavoured to get them introduced. He visited the schools connected with the hospital at Hertford. "I made myself," he says, "thoroughly acquainted with the girls' school; and am determined to have it put upon a better footing." The school certainly wanted looking after. It had been allowed to go to sleep, like many other things connected with the institution. There were only about forty pupils there when Mr. Moore first visited the school; and the education given was comparatively inefficient. But after an increased interest had been taken in the school, the attendance rose to about two hundred, and the education and training given to the girls became greatly better.

At the death of Alderman Thompson, President of Christ's Hospital, it became necessary to elect a new President. It had been usual to elect the Lord Mayor of London, on such a vacancy taking place. On this occasion, however, the majority of the almoners proposed to elect the Duke of Cambridge as president. George Moore was opposed to this. He was of opinion that the officials might get hold of the Duke, Ko-tou to him, and thus obstruct all necessary reforms. He therefore opposed his election. The Duke was nevertheless elected by a large majority; and George Moore was defeated. "I am bound to say," he afterwards observes, "that I am not at all sorry for this. The Duke is a shrewd, clever chairman; he has great authority; he knows the value of time, and prevents unnecessary discussions. At the same time, he encourages improvements and alterations, showing the strictest impartiality. He thinks for himself on all subjects, whereas the presidents of most institutions lean to the powers that be. Such officers are merely nominal; they are not real presidents.

"We have introduced many improvements. Great care is exercised in the admittance of boys; so that none but the children of needy parents are admitted. We have just dealt most rigorously with Mr. —— for offering a presentation for sale. We have deprived him for ever of another presentation." [1]

Mr. Moore regularly attended the almoners' meetings. A discussion arose as to whether the Hospital should not be removed to the country. The Duke of Cambridge took one side ; George Moore took the other. On the 8th December, 1868, the latter says in his diary :—" Attended Christ's Hospital. The Duke in the chair ; he made a long speech. I replied, and did pretty well. The Duke very civil to me, as he always is. We got a majority of one."

The majority of one by no means settled the question. The *fight*, as George Moore always called it, was renewed again and again. He was of opinion that as the school consisted exclusively of boarders, the arguments for its removal to the country were over-whelming. In 1870, the ancient foundation passed under the scrutiny of the Endowed Schools' Commission. Mr. Moore was one of those who proposed that a scheme should at once be drawn up for their approval. In the midst of various other work, the subject was uppermost in his thoughts. He attended thirty-three meetings of the committee of almoners, when eleven members out of thirteen agreed to the draft scheme. It was submitted to the governors on the 5th of April. " I had a desperate fight to-day," he says, " at Christ's Hospital. I never made a better speech. We adjourned the debate about removing the Hospital out of town."

---

[1] Mr. Moore himself made a presentation to one of his warehousemen in Bow Churchyard. He presented himself before the court and was asked, "Can you maintain and educate this boy?" "Yes, I can," frankly answered the warehouseman. "Then we cannot admit him." Thus George Moore's own presentation was rejected by the rigidness of the rules which he himself had laid down. Of course, these rules are very often evaded.

In the meantime George Moore made arrangements for the final struggle. He published a long letter in the *Times* urging the governors to come up to vote on the 27th, when the adjourned debate was to be resumed. He again threw himself into "the fight" with all the intensity of his nature. He made a stirring speech, giving eight good reasons in favour of the removal of the Hospital to the country. He wound up in the following characteristic manner :—

"I beseech you, governors, not to be led away by the prestige of voting with His Royal Highness and the Treasurer. It will be infatuation on your part not to support the eleven who have met thirty-three times, and with much patience and care have produced this excellent scheme."

The confirmation of the report was put to the meeting, and it was rejected by a majority of fourteen votes. Fifty-seven voted for the removal, and seventy-one against it. "I expected," says George Moore, "two to one against us." There seems to have been some feeling of soreness amongst the almoners, as he adds two days afterwards : "We had a meeting at Christ's Hospital. I made a good speech about peace. All were pleased—particularly the Duke of Cambridge. I threw oil on the troubled waters." On the night of the "great fight," Mr. Moore went to Ned Wright's thieves' supper, and was much interested by his address.

He had another interesting day at Christ's Hospital. "I carried my resolution," he says, "which was seconded by Russell Gurney, that Christ's Hospital should be sold when we could get a good price. On the same day, the Duke of Cambridge lunched with Mr. Moore at Bow Churchyard. Sir Hope Grant, Colonel Henderson, the Bishop of Carlisle, and others, were present. "The Duke," he writes in his diary, "has

shown me unvarying kindness, although I have always
been the ringleader of the fights at Christ's Hospital."

Mr. Moore continued to work for Christ's Hospital
during the rest of his life. About three years after the
above contest, he settled £1,000 in new 3 per cent.
annuities, as a conditional endowment for providing
prizes for the boys and girls who exhibited the greatest
proficiency in the knowledge of the Holy Scriptures.
The court, in acknowledging the gift, offered him their
cordial thanks for the liberal gifts of money which he
had on previous occasions entrusted to the head master
for the same purpose. Two years later, he made a gift
to Christ's Hospital of a thousand pounds, to be invested
for the benefit of the Rev. W. Hetherington's excellent
charity to the Blind, which is connected with the institution.

In November, 1870, Mr. Moore was strongly urged
by many of his friends—and amongst others, by the
Right Hon. W. H. Smith, now First Lord of the Admi-
ralty—to offer himself as a candidate for the London
School Board ; but he decided to decline the position.
He was overwhelmed with work of all sorts, educational
and otherwise. "My motto," he said, "is, whatever is
worth doing at all, is worth doing well ; and the duties
at the board will absorb a great deal of my time.
Besides there are numerous candidates in the field, all
declaring for Bible teaching in the schools. I have
already done a good deal of educational work ; let
younger men take their share."

The first Jubilee of the Commercial Travellers'
Schools was held in 1870. George Moore had now been
treasurer for twenty-five years. He had seen with
pride the growth of the institution. He had worked as
hard for it as if it had been his own business, bringing
in a large income. Indeed the labour which he had

voluntarily given, would, if exerted for himself, have produced a fortune.

Mr. Moore distinguished the Jubilee year by establishing his scholarship and prizes of the united value of eighty-five pounds a year. For establishing the scholarship, his objects were—as stated on the tablet erected in the school :—*First*, to stimulate and encourage the children while they remain inmates of the institution, in an earnest and diligent pursuit of religious and secular knowledge ; and, *Secondly*, to provide a means whereby boys possessing great natural ability and energy of character, may, on their leaving, proceed to one of the public schools of a higher grade, and continue their studies for a further period of three years, with the hope of their afterwards obtaining, through means of other scholarships, the highest educational advantages of the country.

He consented to take the chair at the Jubilee dinner held in December. He was then reminded of the deaths of many of his old friends. Old faces had gone, and new faces had come. What could he say now? Only what he had said before. It was a quarter of a century since he had taken the chair to organise the schools. Now their benefits were extended far and wide. They had saved many children from the workhouse ; and they had raised many boys to high positions and influence. Twenty old pupils had become annual subscribers and ten life-governors. "We are all travellers," he said, "and every step we take conveys us nearer and nearer to our journey's end." .

Such was George Moore at the end of 1870.

CHAPTER XX.

AT the beginning of George Moore's diary of 1871, the following words occur:—"My heart is sick at the carnage and death which this war is now causing throughout France. We have not heard from the managers of our Paris house for two months. We do not know whether our people are dead or alive!"

Paris was then besieged by the Germans. The network of iron closed round the city on the 19th of September, 1870, and the citizens were left, in the words of Bismarck, to "stew in their own gravy." The city had been scantily provided with food, and starvation soon began to be felt. Horse-flesh was nearly eaten up. Cats and dogs were scarcely to be had. Rats and mice were eagerly consumed.

A system of rations was provided by the government. Long *queues* of starving women were to be seen waiting at the butchers' doors, for their quarter of a pound of meat. Though the frost was biting, the women would wait for a dozen hours, half-clad and unsheltered, on a cold winter's morning. Sometimes they took up their station the night before, so as to be ready for the first opening of the shop.

Fuel, like everything else, was scarce; and people lay in bed to keep themselves warm. Hence the rapid increase of deaths. The mortality amongst children was fearful. At every step an undertaker was seen carrying a little deal coffin. Adults were conveyed to the cemetery in handcarts, for the horses had mostly been eaten. Starvation had done its work, and Paris at last surrendered.

In the meantime a large subscription had been got up in London, under the presidency of Alderman Dakin, Lord Mayor. The committee consisted of men of all ranks and denominations. London wept for Paris. A fund of about £120,000 was raised to provide for the immediate wants of the people when the gates were opened. George Moore was one of the active members of the committee. " The French distress," he says, " gives me a great deal of work." " Thank God," he says on the 28th of January, " there is an armistice in France. I fear I shall have to go over to distribute the Mansion-House fund. If I go, it is as an act of duty." On the 31st he says : " The Lord Mayor and many others made me promise to go over to Paris. I started at a quarter to 8 A.M. amidst a very severe frost, with snow upon the ground. May God take care of my darling wife in my absence ! "

The party consisted of George Moore and his clerk, Colonel Wortley, and a French lady, Madame M——, who had been separated from her husband during the siege. The commissioners took with them seventy tons of food and £5,000 in money. They travelled by Newhaven and Dieppe. All the other routes to Paris were closed until the terms of peace could be arranged.

On arriving at Dieppe next morning they found no porters ready to receive them. The inhabitants did not know that the blockade of Paris had been raised. The town was held by the Prussians, who had possession of the railway and public offices. The day passed

without any carriages or waggons being provided. At
length the directors of the railway were found. They
promised that a train should start next evening at
eleven. Another day passed. They contrived to start
at night amidst a terrible scuffle. They were anxious
to be first in Paris with the food. As George Moore
afterwards said : " I think I should have died had I not
been first in Paris."

They had, however, many difficulties to encounter.
The rails had been torn asunder, the bridges had been
blown up, and the line was in most cases only tem-
porarily repaired. The waggons with the food from
London were the first to pass. The train arrived at
Amiens at 6 A.M. There had been terrible fighting at
this place. The station was much knocked about. It
was all dirt and confusion. The buffet was closed,
and nothing was to be had to eat or drink.

A speculator in flour had, by some means or other,
got three or four of his waggons placed before the
London waggons. The train was stopped at every
station and referred to the German commandant. He
looked at the credentials and allowed the train to pass.
It reached Creil at two o'clock in the afternoon. After
stopping for two hours it was allowed to pass over the
creaking temporary bridge, scarcely finished. Crawling
along—the engine stopping, watering, and groaning
away—the train at length reached Chantilly at five
in the evening. There it was shunted into a siding
and waited for three hours, until the Grand Duke of
Mecklenburg had passed in a special train. The party
then got through St. Den's, and finally arrived at the
Paris station at eleven at night. They were rejoiced to
find that theirs was *the first train* that had arrived in
Paris with food for the poor beleaguered Frenchmen !

The station of the Northern Railway was deserted.
Not a porter was to be seen. The station was in total

darkness, although the moonlight made the huge balloons standing in the square of the station look quite ghost-like. The streets were empty. The city seemed to be deserted. The party walked on for about three miles to the Boulevard Malesherbes. The lady, who had accompanied them from London to ascertain the fate of her husband, found that he had left that morning for London in search of her!

The commissioners were up early next morning, and presented their credentials to Jules Ferry at the Hotel de Ville. They were accompanied by M. André, Mr. Moore's banker, a deputy-mayor. After a long interview it was decided that the food should be supplied to twenty *arrondissements* in proportion to their population. Up to this time, a little bit of black bread had been distributed, and a piece of horseflesh about the size of a walnut, so that the wants of the inhabitants in the respective districts were well known. It was also decided to open a depot in a central situation; and, to save expense, George Moore threw open the warehouse of Copestake, Moore, and Co., in the Place des Petits Pères.

And now came the difficulty of getting food to the people. Getting the food from London to Paris was nothing compared with this. Fifty thousand horses had been eaten. Those which remained were dry, scraggy, and uneatable. They were only used for dragging about the cannon. George Moore felt vexed, angry, and in a rage with the men in office. He says in his diary, " I felt as if the lives of thousands depended upon our efforts." He went from Jules Ferry to Jules Favre; then to Picard, "a jolly fellow," who seemed more at ease than the others; then to General Trochu, whom he found greatly depressed. At last General Vinoy allowed some of the artillery horses to be employed to drag down the stores to the Warehouse.

Two days after reaching Paris, the food was ready for distribution. Crowds of people assembled in the Place des Petits Pères. "Never," says George Moore, "did I see such an assembly of hollow, lean, hungry faces —such a shrunken, famine-stricken, diseased-looking crowd. They were very quiet. They seemed utterly crushed and hopeless. It is now ten days since the armistice began, and yet there is no food in Paris except what we have brought. There is still the black bread, made of hay and straw and twenty-five per cent. of the coarsest flour. Well may the poor creatures look pale!

"We went about the markets. There was positively nothing to see, except a few dead dogs and cats—no flour, no vegetables. Hundreds, perhaps thousands of old people, little children and ladies, have died of hunger. The sufferings of the little ones will never be forgotten. For four months there was no milk— no fat except at fabulous prices—no fuel, no light. Indeed they have died in vast numbers.

"Paris has been surrendered because of the hunger of the whole city. The words of Nahum seem to be fulfilled, 'She is empty, and void, and waste; and the heart melteth, and the knees smite together, and much pain in the loins, and the faces of them all gather blackness.' There is no fuel for fires in Paris, only here and there a little damp wood can be found, and is burnt. We have telegraphed urgently for fuel; Wortley and I suffer very much from the cold."

George Moore himself made a repast of horse-flesh at the house of his banker. He had expressed great disgust with the food at the time of his arrival; but the banker had nothing better to give him, and it was only after he had dined, that M. André told him what he had eaten!

The distribution at the warehouse was now in full

operation. It was constantly crowded. One evening, after the daily distribution had been made, and the warehouse was closed, George Moore went to look after the arrangements for the following day. He found a long *queue* waiting at the warehouse door. He went in and asked, "If the poor people have not got their food." "Yes! Those at the door are waiting for the distribution to-morrow morning!" He at once had the doors opened, and a distribution was made to all who were present. They were mostly women—some of them ladies with veils—boys for sick parents, and old, haggard people, ghastly with hunger. George Moore never forgot these dreadful scenes.

The food was distributed as follows :—" Each person gets a good ration, enough to last a family of five or six for a week ; cheese, milk, bacon, coffee, Liebig's essence of meat, biscuit, salt, rice, sugar, and Batty's preserved meat." Arrangements were made to issue provisions at the several depots all over Paris. The mayors were elected during the siege, and were a rather low class of men. " Some of them," says George Moore, " are a bad lot. We are a good deal worried by them. We go about from early morning till twelve at night ; but in some cases I don't believe their reports. But now that we see our way, we are keeping the distribution much more in our own hands. We have sent to the Archbishop of Paris, to the chief Rabbi, and to the French pastors, a good deal of food, to be distributed privately by the Sisters of Mercy and other ladies among the better class. We find the small shopkeepers, clerks, and such like, are those who have really suffered the most—*les pauvres honteux*, who are ashamed to beg. We have arranged a special place for them, at 2, Rue de la Bienfaisance."

During his visit to Paris, Mr. Moore went about seeing the ravages made by the siege. He went to Versailles to see Mr. Odo Russell, an old friend. He found great crowds of people at the Bridge of Neuilly. He passed through St. Cloud, which was almost entirely destroyed. He breakfasted with Mr. Russell, in the very room where Wellington and Blücher so often dined. On the same evening he was back at the warehouse.

The elections were then going on, and disturbed the work of distribution. The means of locomotion were very bad. Many of the locomotives of the Northern Railroad had been destroyed. There was still a great lack of horses and waggons. George Moore got a very strong letter from Baron Rothschild to the manager of the Chemin de Fer du Nord, of which he was chairman, to facilitate, as much as he could, the conveyance of food to Paris.

" We had a large meeting this evening (9th February) at Eugene Plon's, the printer and publisher. Twenty gentlemen were present. They all agreed to look after the Mairies, in conjunction with M. Yriarte, and see to the proper distribution of food. M. Plon's son speaks English, and told me of all that was said."

Next day he met the Archbishop of Paris. " He is most grateful. I find him a particularly gentlemanly man. He is to be appointed chairman of the committee we leave behind to carry on our work. Our warehouse is crowded from morning till night. We are doing an enormous amount of good. We have opened a private store for the better class people. I get sometimes fifty letters a day, and send them there to be executed."

On the 11th February, he makes this entry : " Hard at work getting food sent to the private gentlemen we have appointed, who are all in earnest. We sent a ham each to Creton, Dr. Herbert, Marshall, Dr.[1] and Odo

---

[1] Dr. Russell, who was with the German army at Versailles, in returning his thanks, said, " What a glorious pig that must have been! My only difficulty and it is a great one—relates to the cooking of his upper hind leg, for there is not in my kitchen any vessel that will hold half of it.

Russell, Laurence Oliphant, Madame Mallet, Madame André, and one to *Au Bon Marché's* son. We also sent one each to M. Thiers, General Trochu, Jules Favre, and Mr. Wallace. The crowds at our warehouse increase every day. Our visit has been greatly appreciated by all classes, who vie with each other in paying us respect. I cannot speak too highly of our staff of young men at the warehouse!"

On the 12th:—" The crowds at the warehouse increase. This we keep exclusively for women. There is a *queue* of ten or fifteen thousand waiting there to-day; they have waited all through last night. I felt heart-sick when I saw them. It was one of the wildest nights of sleet and fearful wind; and, starved and exhausted and drenched as they were, it was a sight to make a strong man weep. We are straining ourselves and all about us to the utmost. I believe we were just in time; a few days more and the people would have been too far gone ; many were hardly able to walk away with their parcels. After waiting with wonderful patience, when they got the food many of them fairly broke down from over-joy. I have seen more tears shed by men and women than I hope I shall ever see again."

One of the principal depots—the Bon Marché—was selected near the Bourse. The crowd there was quite as great as at Mr. Moore's warehouse. Some ten thousand people bivouacked in the streets during the night, waiting for the opening of the depot in the morning. The *queue* extended, four or five deep, for more than half-a-mile. The people, who were mostly women, had come from all parts of Paris—from Belville, from Vaugirard, from the Faubourg St. Antoine. The pavement was occupied on both sides with recumbent

Thanks for your putting the difficulty in my way. . . . I hope to see you on my return to London, in the good time coming, with peace and healing on its wings."

figures, lying in rows wrapped in blankets. The correspondent of the *Times* visited this scene at midnight. He asked one of the women when she expected to arrive at the door of the warehouse where she would receive her portion. "The day after to-morrow morning," she replied. "What! are you prepared to pass two successive nights in the street?" "*Pourquoi pas?*" she said, "all the others do it." At the head of the column, he found those who were to be first served in the morning. "How long have you been here?" he asked of a lady-like young woman in black, evidently of a superior class to those by whom she was surrounded. "Since nine o'clock yesterday morning," she replied. She had actually been thirty-nine hours in the *queue!*

"We continue," says George Moore in his diary, "to look after people in a good position of life. They will not send for food. We have to find them out. I took food to a countess who lived six stories high, and to Mrs. O'Connor, who lives eight stories high. Her husband has good landed estates, but he cannot get a penny of rent. It tries my wind to get up these stairs, but, thank God, I am equal to my work. Colonel Stuart Wortley is indefatigable in going about alone to people's houses, and giving them food and money. He has been written to by some of the highest class, begging for food to be sent to some relative in great need. We now feel that we have got master of our work. God be praised! I have little time to read the Bible, but I read the 91st Psalm every morning, which is a great support to me."

The Honourable Alan Herbert was often with him. He had remained in Paris during the siege, working with devotion at his profession in the hospital; he knew the needs of the better classes, and how it was able to meet them. Dr. Herbert said of this time,

"What struck me most was Mr. Moore's informal and generous way of doing things ; it was a surprise to the French people, but specially delighted them."

Mr. Moore was inundated with letters from England, from wives asking him to look after their husbands, from fathers to look after their daughters, from exiled French people of all classes inquiring about the safety of their relations. Most of these letters were addressed to Mrs. Moore in London, and forwarded by her to her husband in Paris. One of these letters runs thus : " I am very anxious about one of M. de Bergue's brothers. He belonged to the National Guard. He has a wife and two children—one a very delicate creature, my godchild. I shall be very grateful if Mr. Moore will make inquiries after them, as they must have suffered a great deal." Mr. Moore found them out, and helped them.

Another lady writes from Carlisle inquiring after her husband, also in the National Guard. She had been residing in Normandy on account of her health when the war broke out, and she was unable to return to Paris. She was now in Cumberland with her friends. " I have written to him," she said ; " I have sent money to him, and I have despatched a box of provisions to him, but I can hear nothing of him. I suffer the most horrible fear and anxiety. I am very ill, and know not what to do." After giving her husband's address, and inclosing a note to him, she goes on : " I scruple, dear sir, to ask so much of you ; but in my great misery I must throw myself on your pity and kindness."

The person inquired after was found out and helped. His letter to Mr. Moore was a sort of general hurrah for England. " Vous êtes, vraiment, la Grande Bretagne, et du reste, j'ai parmi vous, gentleman d'Angleterre, des amis de cœur. . . . Vous avez été admirables Anglais dans tous les temps. Mais, avant tout, comme race supérieur, noble et généreux race, permettez à un Français qui vous respecte et qui vous aime, de vous exprimer sa profonde reconnaissance pour vos bontés. Hurrah for England!"

Another lady, who had been relieved, writes as follows to her friend in Switzerland:—"I went on Monday, but there was no possibility of approaching Mr. Moore's bureau; so I came back and wrote a short note, inclosing yours. An answer arrived, telling me to be there at 7.30 next morning; for I was really starved to death. Off I went with a bag, not knowing what I should get, accompanied by Désiré (her husband) to help me. When I got admittance I was greatly recompensed for my trouble; for not only did your good benevolent friend provide me with good provisions, but gave me 25 francs into the bargain. He really must be, as you say, one of the best of men—a real Christian, able to feel the pains and sorrows of others. You must know that all this was done in the twinkling of an eye, for thousands of people were waiting to be supplied. You cannot tell what misery we have endured night and day. We have seen nothing but cannon balls and shells flying through the air. We have been reduced to utter destitution, being nearly always without fire, though the winter has been so severe." Another lady, residing in Paris, writes as follows:—"I have lost my husband here, and am without funds to return, which I am anxious to do immediately. Will you kindly, on receipt of this, send me some money to the inclosed address."

About sixty thousand pounds' worth of food had been got into Paris, and it was distributed as fast as possible in forty different depots. One of the effects of the distribution was, that the health of the city rapidly improved. Fever and small-pox were less fatal in their attacks. Food was now coming into Paris, but the prices were still high. On the 12th, Mr. Moore gave instructions to issue double rations. The crowds round the depots continued as great as ever ; but the destitution and starvation were disappearing. More food was exposed for sale in the markets, and the people began to look more cheerful.

The crowds were still great at the Bon Marché and Grand Condé—two of the largest shops in Paris. On the 17th February some 8,000 people were seen crowding round the entrance of the latter place—packed like sardines in a box—all struggling to reach the door. A detachment of the National Guards was there ; but they proved of little use. The scene was fearful,—women were screaming and fainting, and had to be handed over the heads of the people without their portion of food ! Thus all their labour had been in vain.

"I had with me," says Mr. Moore, "Colonel Wortley, Mr. Mallet, Oliphant of the *Times*, Mr. Landells Marshall of the *Telegraph*, and the Honourable Alan Herbert. We vainly tried to keep the people back. We loudly supplicated them to stand still, as all should be served ; but it was of no use. The surging mass grew still denser. At last we were forced to pull the front ranks through the door to save them from being crushed to death. Five unconscious women were borne in upon our arms. We brought them to life again with aromatic vinegar and stimulants. It was a regular fight for food. If they had not been in extreme want, such a fight could never have taken place."

"On the 18th," Mr. Moore says, "the food is still coming in. The convoys report themselves. We have had Lieutenant Wood, son of Lord Halifax, Captain Green, of the Hussars, Harry Bourke, brother of Lord Mayo, and Mr. Louis Davidson, a cousin of the Rothschilds. They have all stuck to their waggons, and brought them right through. I must confess that the

Y

military officers, who had volunteered as convoys, were
very successful in getting their waggons on rapidly.
Two others (of the civilians) came to me and complained
that 'they could not get through.' One had left his
provisions in charge of some one at Amiens; and
another, rather nearer Paris. I ordered them back with
a very few words, and told them not to come to me
again till they had got their waggons *into* Paris, and
could report so." [1]

On the 19th he writes : "Now that we have mastered
the details of our operations I feel greatly more at ease.
I can never sufficiently thank God for all His blessings
to me—preserving my health, and giving me clear judgment. I rise early, go to bed late, and sleep soundly.
Madame Mallet's, in the Boulevard Malesherbes (where

[1] Since the publication of the first edition, Mr. Louis Davidson has sent
me the following account of his services in respect of the conveyance of food
to Paris :—

"I left London at midnight on the Saturday, arrived at Folkestone
early on Sunday morning, was detained there until the afternoon, during
the delay of the ship with the provisions, and arrived at Boulogne after
a rough journey passage on Sunday night. On the following day, I had the
greatest trouble to procure the necessary labourers to fill the trucks with
the provisions, although they were lying alongside the vessel in the harbour,
the truck men were told the food was most urgently needed in Paris. I, at
length, with the help of the agent of the South Eastern and Northern of
France Railways, succeeded in hiring a number of men to do the work (by
extra pay) — I left with my convoy on Monday night. I was in the
train until the Wednesday night, and, on arriving at the goods depot,
found that all waggons were to be detained there, and that the food was to
be sent into Paris as the railway authorities chose to direct. The officials
were so overcome by the extra work of the last few days, that I found all
the clerks asleep at their desks, and it was with the greatest difficulty that
I could obtain a promise that my convoy should be sent quickly into Paris.
Finding that I could do no more, and being naturally anxious to report
myself to Mr. Moore, I availed myself of an engine which was going to
the Gare d'Station du Nord, where I arrived early on the Thursday morning,
having been three nights on the road from Boulogne, during the
greater part of which time I occupied a second class compartment, subsisting upon the provisions I had most fortunately brought with me from
London. Most of the foregoing facts, which are well-known to my
friends, must have escaped the recollection of the late Mr. Moore, who,
for some time afterwards, perfectly appreciated the causes which had
delayed the arrival of my convoy, and expressed himself as being very
well pleased with my services, which, he observed, contrasted favourably
with those rendered by certain others of the convoy staff."

Mr. Moore lived during his stay, and of whose kindness he often speaks) is crowded every morning from 8.30 to 10.30. I make a point of seeing every one. I answer all letters. Sometimes I write fifty a day. I am determined, so far as I am concerned, that no one shall go away unserved. The people have been hungered for five months, and now our food is telling upon them. Their gratitude is unbounded."

Food was now coming in from various quarters. The English government sent a large quantity of biscuits and preserved beef; the Society of Friends and other private persons were also sending food to Paris and the neighbourhood. Money was supplied to enable the people to take their things out of pawn, to buy garden seeds, and for other purposes. On Wednesday, the 22nd February, the police called at Mr. Moore's depot, and ordered that the distribution of food should cease, as the crowds that assembled round the door blocked the thoroughfare. On this Mr. Moore says : "We put on all steam, and determined to keep open all night as well as during the following day. All the streets round the warehouse were blocked with people. The food was all ready for distribution. We calculated that we *ran a party through in half a minute!* The French people were astonished at our energy. They cheered me. I remained till one at night, and left them in full swing." The warehouse was closed on the evening of the 23rd. Up to eight o'clock they had distributed food to 96,500 persons. The remaining provisions were divided amongst the committees of the Archbishop of Paris, the Jewish Rabbi, and the Protestant pastors.

Mr. Moore and Colonel Wortley proceeded to vis't the villages in the neighbourhood of Paris. The poor people were tilling their private and market gardens, but they said they had no seed. All their property had been destroyed : all their money had been spent : and they had barely enough to live upon. "Upon ascertaining this," says Mr. Moore, "we decided at once to order £1,000 worth of seed to be sent to them from London. We have formed a bond of union with the gentlemen composing the War Victims Fund, and will cooperate with them as to the distribution of the seed."

To give an idea of the robbery and pillage that had been going on round Paris, Mr. Moore mentions the following circumstances: The Germans had destroyed the Graveyards, and torn up or tumbled down the Tombstones. When they took possession of a town or a village, they rooted up the ground, in order to find the treasures which, they thought, the inhabitants had left behind. Thus, the most wanton destruction was perpetrated. In one case a poor fellow who had returned to his home, found that the deed box which he had buried, had been dug up and rifled, and that all his deeds and railway scrip had been taken away. The man declared that he had been totally ruined. This was only one out of a thousand similar cases.

Mr. Moore refers in his diary to Mr. W. B. Norcott, who assisted him during this time. Mr. Norcott well remembers the occasion. He says—"It was my privilege to be associated with Mr. Moore on a memorable occasion—the relief of Paris—and I can never forget the indefatigable way in which he set us an example. His energy of purpose, early and late, was something wonderful. He was ever at his post, directing what was to be done, establishing depots of relief in different parts of the city, organising an efficient staff to carry out his plans, and personally superintending the distribution of food at each store, so as to include the greatest number of the starving poor. On one occasion we worked all through the night, with Mr. Moore at our head. I fear his self-sacrifice at that momentous time led to his subsequent ill-health. But the memory of his acts will not soon be forgotten by the poor of Paris."

The work of the commission was now at an end. The markets were becoming filled with food, and the price was falling from day to day. It is true the people were still without money, but the commissioners could not supply that. They cleared the central depots of provisions, and distributed them amongst the various *arrondissements*. They had done their best and were now prepared to start homewards. Before they left Paris, they received many thanks and congratulations. M. Thiers entered his note of thanks in Mr. Moore's memorandum-book. The Archbishop of Paris was full of gratitude. He said, in a letter to Cardinal Manning :—
" I ask them (the commissioners) to be the interpreters to the English people of our gratitude, and I should be very thankful if you made known to our friends of the Committee how much we appreciate the generosity of which we have been the object in our irreparable disaster. Physically I have not suffered much, but the moral tortures caused by the state of my unfortunate country nothing can express."

The Chiffoniers, or ragpickers of Paris, also sent in their letter of thanks.[1] But perhaps the prettiest thing was done by a French girl. One morning, when Mr. Moore and Colonel Wortley were getting into their carriage, to go the round of the depots, they found on the seat a bunch of flowers, with a little note saying that

---

[1] The letter was as follows :—

" CHERS AMIS DE LONDRES,

    " Ç'a été une grande consolation pour nous après les rudes épreuves que nous venons de traverser dans ce siége si douloureux, de voir nos frères d'Angleterre nous donner une preuve si grande de leur charité fraternelle envers la nation Française, et surtout envers nous Parisiens.

    " C'est le cœur rempli de la plus profonde gratitude que nous vous adressons nos remerciments bien sincères pour votre magnifique don, et que nous prions Dieu qu'il se souvienne qu'ayant eu faim, vous nous avez donné à manger. Soyez donc bénis. Et soyez persuadés que le souvenir de nos frères de Londres ne s'effacera jamais de notre cœur."

It was the only way in which the young girl who left them could show her gratitude to the English who had saved her mother and herself from starvation.

The commissioners left Paris on the 28th of February, and arrived in London on the following day. They were received back with many congratulations. They gave in their report to the Mansion House Committee, and received a unanimous vote of thanks. George Moore went back to his ordinary work of business and charity. He felt very much worn out. He had been sustained throughout by his pluck and energy. But the reaction had now occurred. He writes in his diary :—
"I cannot recover from my weariness. I dream all night about Paris, and cannot get sound rest. During the daytime I suffer much from aching bones."

Mr. Moore, like many others, was presented with the National Order of the Legion of Honour; though he valued far more the thanks of the Paris Chiffoniers. He was accustomed to give entertainments in London to the French exiles, both before and after the siege. In January, 1871, Mr. Moore gave a liberal entertainment to more than a hundred French refugees, in the rooms of the London City Mission, Greek Street, Soho. After the siege, the exiles presented an address to Mr. Moore at Kensington Palace Gardens ; accompanied by a blue portemonnaie made for Mrs. Moore by a German and embroidered by a Parisienne. After the presentation, about ninety of the refugees were entertained to supper.

But Paris had not yet got rid of her agony. The Germans had scarcely left the city ere the Commune broke out. Belleville was let loose. The scenes of the old Revolution were repeated. The soldiers sided with the people. Generals Thomas and Lecomte were seized and shot. The prisons were crowded. Chaplains were prohibited from offering their last services to the dying. An exception was made on one occasion. The permit allowing a priest to be passed into a prison, concluded thus—"He says he is the servant of somebody called God [le nommé Dieu]." The Archbishop of Paris, the Curé of the Madelaine, and a crowd of other ecclesiastics, were lodged in the Conciergerie. The plate and the valuables in the churches were siezed. Women were turned into furies. They broke into the Tuileries, tore down the hangings, attired themselves in wreaths of silk, and proclaimed, amidst the wildest excitement, "Liberté, Egalité, Fraternité."

The Communist organ, the *Montagne* wrote thus : "Our dogs that used only to growl when a Bishop passed, will bite him now, and not a voice will be raised to curse the day which dawns for the sacrifice of the Archbishop of Paris. . . . Darboy! tremble in your cell, for your day is past, your end is close at hand." A few days after, on the 24th of May, the Archbishop was assassinated, with six other hostages, in the prison-yard of La Roquette. Before his death, the Archbishop stept forward and said, "Do not profane the word Liberty ; it is to us alone it belongs, for we shall die for liberty and faith." After these words he was shot down.

Cardinal Manning, in writing to George Moore on the subject of the Archbishop's death, said :—"I feel sure that you have shared with us our sorrow and our joy about the dear Archbishop of Paris. It is indeed a horrible crime ; but he died nobly like a true pastor, in the midst of his flock. I thank you for all that you have done for him."

After the French army had regained possession of the city, it was necessary for Mr. Moore and Colonel Wortley to go over to Paris again to finish their work. On this occasion they were accompanied by Mrs. Moore and Mrs. Wortley. They were amazed at the destruction of property. The ashes of the Tuileries and the

Hôtel de Ville were still hot. Some seventy thousand men were employed by government to remove the ruins. Although most of the public places had been burnt, George Moore's warehouse was safe. When the crowd of Communists came up to fire the building, they were reminded that it was the warehouse of the "Anglais" who had brought the gift of food to Paris ; and they passed on. For the sake of the English, the church of Nôtre Dame de Victoire was also spared.

Frightful scenes were to be seen in the streets. Women were prodded along at the point of the bayonet to the prisons at Versailles—young girls, old hags, poor careworn-looking men, boys so young as only to be fit for infant-schools—all *déclarés*. Their hands were tied behind them with ropes, and they were driven along through the streets, which were full of soldiers. The Tuileries gardens were full of dragoons, with their horses picketed beside them. The Champs Elysées was a camp. A mass of soldiers crowded the steps of the Bourse. The churches were till closed. No priests dared be seen in the streets. Firing from the windows at the soldiers was still of daily occurrence. Every night was occupied in removing and burning the dead, who had been hastily buried where they fell,—in the squares and little patches of gardens throughout the city.

"The second siege of Paris," said George Moore, on writing home, "has been much more lamentable than the first. The devastation of private house property is double or treble more than I expected. The week's fighting has destroyed hundreds of houses in the outskirts. It is really melancholy to see the ruin that has been brought upon innocent people.

"Colonel Stuart Wortley and I are perplexed how to spend our £25,000 from the Mansion House office. We must dole it out in small amounts, as we have found out so many channels for it. The charitable institutions which abound here are drained dry, as the Government has not been able to give them anything since the commencement of the first siege, and private subscriptions have been almost *nil.* It is sad to visit Orphan Asylums, Convalescent, Deaf and Dumb Homes for old men and women, hospitals of all kinds, and many other establishments, all pining for funds.

" The cruelty and wickedness of the Commune towards them has been villainous. They would have destroyed most of them if they had been left two or three days longer. They gave the inmates of an institution called the Good Shepherd for Fallen Women ten minutes' notice to quit, and then set fire to the building, which contained 150 young women ; and there are many other cases of equal cruelty."

Mrs. Moore wrote home to her friends as follows :—
" Mrs. Wortley and I are in hourly dread of seeing some horror that we shall never forget ; for everything seems so unsafe and unsettled. We have some very kind friends,—more especially the Mallets and the Andrés ; and we wives must always feel grateful to M. and Madame Henri Mallet for being so good to our husbands on their first visit. M. Hénon has placed his carriage at our service, and it helps us very much. We spent a day at Versailles at ' Les Ombrages.' This is the country-seat of Madame André (*mère*). It was occupied by the Crown Prince of Prussia during the siege. He was much more considerate than many of his officers in the way in which he treated the contents of the house, for nothing has been wilfully damaged. He turned all the family portraits with their faces to the wall, ' feeling bored,' he said, ' at having whole generations of Andrés looking reproachfully at him.'

" Yesterday Col. Wortley had to go to St. Denis on

the business of the Fund and to make inquiries about
the needs of some institutions there.   He got out to
walk by a short cut, and Mrs. Wortley and I who had
gone with him, were driving alone in the carriage.   We
had to cross the lines, through both French and Prussian outposts ; for the Germans are still investing St.
Denis and the suburbs, within two miles of Paris.
After leaving the French sentries, closely adjoining the
Prussian lines, we drove for about a mile through a road
perfectly deserted—no grass anywhere—all, as far as we
could see, was destruction and ruin.   The place was full
of sand heaps and rubbish.   It was so hopeless that I
said, ' Doesn't it seem as if all the rubbish in the world
was "shot here"? as if it had been given up to " beating
carpets" from generation to generation ?'   Immediately
afterwards the horses reared straight up and nearly upset
the carriage.   There seemed to be no reason.   François
tried all means—strong language and stronger punishment ; but the horses swerved round, and set off galloping towards Paris.   He turned them at last, and brought
them to the same spot, when they reared and shied, as if
they saw something, and again turned round.   I managed
to get out, but Mrs. Wortley showed great pluck.   She
afterwards said that she was afraid the horses, carriage,
and driver would come to grief, and as it would be on
our behalf, she determined to face it out.   As she did
not come out of the carriage while the fight was going
on, I got in again !   The coachman three or four times
turned back, and then drove fast towards the place.   The
horses were tractable till we got back to the spot where
they had first turned ; and there they each time reared
and swerved.   At last François had to lead them on,
covered with foam and trembling all over.   In a few
moments we came upon the most awful smell of burnt
horse, and I don't know what—something too sickening.
The horses once had been finer than ours ; and I don't

wonder at their refusal to go on. Who knows? Perhaps, like Balaam's ass, their eyes were opened, and a
multitude of ghosts withstood them!

"You can judge of my horror afterwards, when Baron
A. Rothschild said, on hearing of the road that we had
been, 'You should never have been taken there ; that
is the place where every night they are obliged to bury
or burn the dead who fell during the fighting of the
Commune, and who were then so hastily buried!'

"The other night we dined at Phillipe's Restaurant,
near the Bourse, and on our way back to the Hotel
Chatham I noticed a chiffonier at work among the little
dust-heaps, which are swept out nightly into the streets.
I had never seen one busy before, and we stood a moment to watch the patience with which he probed among
the rubbish by the light of his little candle, as if for some
treasure. Having caught up a little scrap of paper, or
leather, or cotton stuff, he would, with a dexterous jerk
of his long hook, throw it into the sack on his back.
While standing by, Colonel Wortley asked the man if
he had received any of the English gift. He said, 'No ;
not any.' While we were talking to the rag-picker, a
few men, some with white aprons and paper caps, some
with blouses, gathered round, and they heard Colonel
Wortley express surprise that the man had never had
any of the 'don anglais,' as it was called. The by-
standers at once began abusing the man, accusing him
of not speaking the truth, and becoming much excited.
The chiffonier then said, '*Oui, en février! j'ai reçu le
don anglais! tout le monde en a!*' He excused himself
by saying that he thought the gentleman was speaking
of a gift come *now*. I thought it very satisfactory, as
showing that the food had filtered down to every one.
Even the stray chiffonier whom we met was made to
acknowledge it."

The remaining money was at length distributed amongst deserving societies and charities—Catholics and Protestants having their just share. The work was now accomplished, and the Commissioners finally returned home.

CHAPTER XXI.

THE strain and fatigue which Mr. Moore had gone through during the relief of Paris told upon his health. The unusual work tried him, both in mind and body. He could not get rid of the horrors he had witnessed. He would start up in the night calling out, "Do you not see that woman dying? I must go to Versailles." His face began to look worn. His hair became greyer. He looked depressed. His usual cheerful and buoyant energy disappeared, and he became listless, self-absorbed, and melancholy.

This was to a certain extent caused by a feeling of disappointment. He had formed so good an opinion of the French character, from their patience, self-control, and courage during the time of their privation, that the outburst of lawlessness and frenzy which immediately followed their relief from pressure, was to him a painful surprise and a great disappointment.

There was however a busy year before him, and he threw himself into his work as a relief from his troubles. In the beginning of 1872 he was appointed High Sheriff of Cumberland. His name had been suggested by his influential friends the Howards. Twenty years before, he had been elected Sheriff of London and Middlesex. But now that he was nearing the end of his labours, he felt proud to accept the office of High Sheriff of Cumberland, his native county.

The Queen's precept appointing him to the office required him "to take custody and charge of the said county, and duly to perform the duties of sheriff during Her Majesty's pleasure." It used to be one of the duties of the high sheriff to levy men in arms for the defence of the county against the inroads of the Scots. George Moore would doubtless have been as willing as his ancestors to mount to the war cry of " Snaffle, spur, and spear," and defend their possessions at the sword's point. But these days had long passed away. The office of High Sheriff was no longer warlike. It had become festive and social. Judging from the large number of accounts left behind, accompanied by long bills, it appears that Mr. Moore's reign as High Sheriff consisted in a great measure of lunches, dinners, entertainments, and banquets.

Mr. Moore was much gratified by the fact that the judges, Sir John Mellor and Sir Robert Lush, were his personal friends, and that they had for his sake specially arranged their progress so as to be present at the Northern Assize. It was a pleasant time to him altogether. He took much personal interest in all the details necessary to give dignity to the reception of the judges. His coachman, who had been thirty-five years in his service, took charge of everything relating to the beauty of the carriage, harness, and such like ; but Mr. Moore himself was resolute about cockades not being worn, although they are usually thought indispensable to a high sheriff's livery. He had seen nearly everybody else, so soon as they got promoted to some little honour, putting cockades on servants' hats, but he would have none of them for his serving-men, though he had been on the Lieutenancy of London for more than twenty-five years.

It may be mentioned here that though George Moore was a particularly loyal man, he never went to Court, although on one occasion he had been asked to go to a *levée* by one of the members of the Royal Family. "No, no," said he; "Court is not the place for Warehousemen."

The assizes were held at Carlisle on the 20th of February. The occasion was marked by the state and dignity with which Mr. Moore performed the office of high sheriff. There was the grand entry of the judges into the city. The high sheriff met Mr. Justice Lush on his arrival at the citadel station, and, preceded by richly caparisoned heralds and trumpeters, conveyed his lordship in a chariot drawn by four bright bay horses. Geering, the high sheriff's coachman, was master of the situation. He handled the ribbons in a manner that elicited general admiration, and if necessary, he could have turned the four-in-hand round a half-crown piece. And then, what a grand thing he was doing! He was driving in state the Cumberland lad who had gone to London without a friend, who had worked hard and made his way in the world, and had now come back to his native county to take his part among the best, and enjoy his honour and dignity. It was a combination of the story of Whittington and Warren Hastings in one! But, compared with the latter, George Moore's hands were clean.

The judge was driven to his apartments in Lowther Street. Mr. Justice Lush opened the commission in the afternoon, and subsequently attended Divine service in the cathedral. The sermon was preached by the high sheriff's chaplain and brother-in-law, the Rev. T. H. Chester, vicar of South Shields. On the following day, Mr. Justice Mellor, in addressing the grand jury, of which Lord Muncaster was foreman, said that it afforded him especial pleasure and satisfaction to revisit the

county of Cumberland when his excellent friend Mr.
George Moore was high sheriff.   Mr. George Moore, he
continued, was a gentleman universally esteemed, whose
career and, he might add, the manner in which he had
performed the duties of high sheriff, were a credit to his
native county.   The business then proceeded.   The
assize was longer than usual.   Mr. Moore had a reception, at which the gentry of the county attended.   Then
there were entertainments at Whitehall.   In fact nothing
could be more festive and delightful than the manner in
which the high sheriff performed the hospitable duties of
his office.

During his shrievalty, he summoned a county meeting
at Carlisle, for the purpose of presenting an address of
congratulation to the Queen on the recovery of the
Prince of Wales.   The meeting was crowded ; every
person of influence in the county was present.   Mr.
Moore was very nervous before making his speech ; but
he made a good one.   He rejoiced in being able to
declare his earnest convictions.   "I call the recovery of
the Prince," he said, "a miraculous recovery, because he
was on the very verge of the grave.   I believe that the
Prince's recovery was in a great measure due to the
universal prayer of all classes of the people, of all
denominations, from one end of the country to the
other.   It convinces me more than ever that God rules
everything.   When all hopes appeared to be gone, when
we waited hourly, almost momentarily, for the sad news
of his death, the Lord was with him, the gleam of hope
was shed into his sick room, and he was saved.   It may
be that his affliction was a blessing in disguise.   May it
prove so.   The Prince is anything but an idle man.   I
speak from experience.   He has taken the chair on
many occasions for institutions in which I am very much
interested, at great sacrifice to himself.   It must have
been very irksome to him to have to discharge those

duties once or twice a week, but he always came forward to alleviate distress, and he displayed an amount of charity which nobody ever knew anything about. Providence overrules everything for good. The Prince's illness has aroused a feeling of loyalty in this country that must be very satisfactory to us all. It must be most gratifying to the Prince to see that he possesses the warm love and affection of the people of this country. Such a display as that which took place last week in London has never occurred in any other country. Thousands and tens of thousands of people assembled along seven miles of streets : there were 2,000,000 of people there to welcome him and his beloved mother. What a contrast the scene of last week presented to the great hardships which I witnessed in Paris twelve months ago ! When I reflect upon the difference of the two scenes it is a perfect marvel to me. I attribute it a great deal to the fact that in our beloved country we read and love the Bible, whereas in that country it is the want of that most blessed of all books that keeps the people in their present state ! "

One of the high sheriff's duties is to take the necessary proceedings for returning members of Parliament. On the death of the Earl of Lonsdale, the Hon. Henry Lowther, who represented West Cumberland, succeeded to the peerage, and a vacancy occurred in the representation. A writ was issued to the sheriff; the necessary steps were taken, and Lord Muncaster was returned without opposition. The election took place at Cockermouth. It was the last election in England at which the candidates presented themselves and addressed the electors from the hustings, after the old usage.

The summer assizes took place in July. On that occasion the high sheriff gave a dinner to above two hundred persons,—barristers, magistrates, and friends, not forgetting his farmers and poor relations. Many of h's Cumberland friends in London came down, to be present at the parting dinner of the high sheriff.

His life was at this time clouded by the death of some of his dear friends. They were falling away from him one by one, friends who had worked with him, sympathised with him, and loved him! "When my own work is done," he says, "and my energy exhausted by reason of age, I pray that I shall not be disposed to murmur at the approach of death. To me ' to live is Christ, to die is gain.' I think upon this subject every day of my life." But even these partings from the friends who had gone before him could not be endured without human sorrow.

One ill-fated morning the news arrived at Whitehall of the death of his brother-in-law, James Wilkinson Breeks, in India, at the untimely age of forty-two. He was a man whom George Moore loved with all his heart. He was one of those distinguished men who maintain with dignity the rule of England in that far-off country. He was kind, courteous, and just. He was beloved by the natives as well as by his brother civilians. As Civil Commissioner in the Neilgherry Hills he won the respect of all with whom he was connected, by his high abilities as well as by the manliness of his character. He befriended the poor and needy ; he devoted himself, like a true Christian gentleman, to the care of the people committed to his charge ; and his death was crowned with the love and tears of many.[1]

---

[1] Mr. Moore was not singular in his regard for James Wilkinson Breeks. In India, the affection with which his memory is cherished is something extraordinary. To the natives in his own district he was, in their simple words, " a father," the soul of all that was good and useful to those about him ; he set the example of a constantly good and Christian life—a rare example of those qualities which, if commonly practised, would make this world a happier world. George Moore says of him in his diary :— "I have just heard that Jim Breeks is dead. I never loved any man more. He my relation came up to anything that I had heard of him ; and I loved him as I loved my wife from morning till night ! My faith is strong, but I cannot understand why he of all men should be taken ! When will He call me next ?"

Another friend, whose death Mr. Moore deplored, was Mr. Hasell of Dalemain. His kindness and courteousness were only equalled by his judgment and discretion. He was an ideal representative of the old county family of England. He left many a grateful remembrance in the homes of Cumberland.

But these hours of sadness did not affect George Moore's application to work. He could not be happy unless his spare time was occupied in some work of charity and benevolence. "The day is always thirteen hours long," he used to say, "if we wish to make it so." And again, "I owe nothing to genius, but if I give double the time and labour, I can do as well as others." There were a great many things that George Moore still wished to do for Cumberland, and some of them had scarcely as yet been begun.

Amongst those in which he took part that year was the enlargement of the Convalescent Hospital at Silloth. Some years before, he had sent an anonymous gift of £250 towards the hospital, but now he desired to take a more prominent part in the proceedings. On the 8th of August he took the chair at the general meeting of the society. The Convalescent Hospital owed its existence and success to the exertions and fostering care of the Rev. Chancellor Burton of Carlisle. The Hospital stands on a grassy bank on the Solway, with pleasant slopes running down to the water. It is the choicest spot in all Silloth for situation. Besides having all the day's sunshine, it is sheltered by a rising ground from the boisterous south-west gales. The building is one-storied, simple and unpretending in appearance, but suggesting comfort and snugness. It was not thought necessary to have men and women completely separated. They have separate tables for food, but can meet in the walks and on the grassy slopes, and chat together on the seats on the grounds overlooking the Solway. Mr

Moore was at this time proposing to establish a convalescent home at Littlehampton, and he always quoted Silloth Home as the model that he would like to follow.

But a still more important movement which he was the chief means of instituting in Cumberland was that for boarding out pauper children. We do not know when Mr. Moore took up the subject of poor-law administration ; but we find from his diary that on the 3rd of May, 1870, he waited on Mr. Goschen, Chairman of the Poor Law Board, to ask for powers to board orphan children out of the union. Shortly after, we find him inviting the Wigton poor law guardians to dine with him at Whitehall, in order to discuss the boarding-out system. In his diary of 14th August, 1870, he says " I had a most satisfactory day yesterday. I was accompanied by four of the Cockermouth guardians to board out pauper children. We placed twelve orphans with most respectable people." We infer from this that Mr. Moore's application to Mr. Goschen had been successful.

Mr. Moore's idea was that children should, if possible, be rescued from all pauperising influences. He held that pauperism was degrading to men, and especially to children. He desired to get children out of workhouses and bring them up in healthy homes. There they would be placed under family influences and trained like other children. They were not to continue degraded because of the faults of their parents. He held that it was necessary to separate the children altogether from pauperism and its degrading influences. To quote his own words : " The leading principle of the boarding-out system is to restore the child to family life, to create around it natural relations and natural ties. Under these conditions physical and moral health is improved, the natural affections are brought into play, and the child enjoys the liberty and variety of a home-life. Thus sympathy is produced, the true basis for religious principles in after life. Family life is the means which God has instituted for the training of the little ones, and in so far as we assimilate our method to His, so far will be our success."

While Mr. Moore was high sheriff a conference on poor-law administration was held at Gilsland, formerly a great mosstrooping centre, and there the whole subject was discussed. Poor-law administrators came from all parts of the country, but especially from the four northern counties of Northumberland, Durham, Cumberland, and Westmorland. It would occupy too much space to reprint the paper which Mr. Moore read in full, but a few extracts may be given to show his views on the subject :—

"For many years," he said, "my heart has yearned for workhouse orphan children. About three years ago I determined to build an orphanage on my estate for the reception of all the orphans in the unions in the county of Cumberland. Messrs. Cory and Ferguson, architects, Carlisle, prepared plans for the reception of fifty, and on such a scale that, if needed, they could admit of its benefits being extended so as to accommodate one hundred orphans. The ground was staked out, and I was just about to advertise for tenders for the building of the home, when I heard that the Carlisle Union had decided to adopt the boarding-out system ; and, as I had calculated upon this union as the medium for securing nearly half the supply to fill the home, I felt at once that my occupation was gone. I then resolved to see if this system could not be adopted generally throughout the county unions, and I met with a most cordial response from the Cockermouth Board of Guardians ; the only difficulty they saw being the finding of suitable cottagers to take the orphans. I was persuaded that the right people with whom the children could be placed were to be found ; though I, to some extent, realised the difficulty of fixing upon them, as they should be people whose motives had a higher aim than the mere pay of about three or four shillings per week. The discovery of suitable cottage homes to receive the orphans, and of ladies to visit them regularly, is, however, not by any means so difficult as may be supposed by some persons. This I can now assert from personal experience, as amongst small shop-

keepers, labourers of long known exemplary character, and married
servants from respectable families, many such homes are to be
found. Adhering to the resolve I had made, I set on foot a
searching inquiry for some miles around my own neighbourhood,
and I ascertained myself about those persons who from time to time
had applied for orphans; and then, on an appointed day, at my
request, the chairman, vice-chairman, and a sub-committee of
guardians of the Cockermouth Union accompanied me to each
cottage to judge for ourselves; and I think we placed about a
dozen that day. I have often thought since that it was the happiest
day's work I ever did; for I was truly thankful to help in making
so good a start. . . .

. . . . The great thing to be wished for, is to deliver these little
ones from a helpless pauper spirit. Every child that is brought up
in a workhouse seems to me in heart a pauper, and he leaves it
almost useless. Family life is God's own method of training the
young, and no other preparation can so well fit them for their lot
in life and for their dispersion amongst the ranks of honest industry.
May we not confidently hope that, if these children associate from
almost infancy with other children, share the same food, sit on the
same form at school, learn the same lessons, play the same games,
and, above all things, are cared for by some good honest foster-
mother, they will be inspired by a wish to earn an honourable and
independent living, and lose for ever the stigma of the workhouse
child. As for the girls, little need be said. The workhouse, even
under the best auspices, must be a sad place for them; for sup-
posing (which is almost impossible) that they could be kept entirely
from the worst specimens of their sex, yet they are but, as it were,
parts of a machine entirely wanting in any individual care or
tenderness; so that their love has no outlet, their feelings are
blunted, they become without shame, and in most instances, as
ruined women, return to claim a place for themselves and their
miserable offspring in the union where they passed their early and
dreary years. It is gratifying to learn that, even thus early in the
experiment, instances are not wanting of the increased brightness
and happier look of the girls, and that already there is an affection
subsisting between them and their foster-mother, and one hopes
that these children have found a friend and counsellor, some one
to love and to think of, and to strive to please when separated by
and by to work their own way in life's battle. But besides the
physical and moral training of the children being better attained
by contact with the sympathies of men and women, I am sure that
they will be better fitted to become useful servants, or good wives

and husbands, than if brought up in utter ignorance of small homes and thrifty domestic ways. . . . Finally, not to prolong this paper, and trespass further on your patience, I would remark that the aim and end of this system is to absorb these children into the general population, by having first fitted them for active life, by making them sharers in a working man's home, and associating them with his family, under the individual care of the foster-mother. I think this will make them much purer and better, more likely to become honoured members of society here and better prepared for the world to come."

This paper created much interest. A discussion took place upon boarding-out, in the course of which nearly every speaker approved of the recommendations which George Moore had made. Having once made an impression, he was not the man to let the thing drop. He proceeded at once to recommend the guardians of all the parishes over which he had an influence—and one might add, that his influence extended all over Cumberland—to carry out the practice of boarding-out the orphan girls.

Mr. Cropper of Ellergreen, who read a paper on "Vagrancy" at the conference, says that it was about this time that he became acquainted with the remarkable character of George Moore. He says he found to his surprise that whilst other people had been merely discussing the subject, George Moore had actually succeeded in finding homes for all the orphan girls of two neighbouring workhouses, and was prepared to tell of the success of his operations. "When I heard," says Mr. Cropper, "of his prompt carrying out of the work, I knew at once the power that he possessed; for it is no easy matter to induce half-a-dozen boards of guardians to carry out any particular course, or to find so many cottagers willing to accept a fresh addition to their family."[1]

[1] Those who wish to inquire further into the subject of boarding-out paupers will find it admirably treated in *Pauperism and the Boarding-out of*

The subject of pauper boarding-out is by no means calculated to increase the interest of a biography. But we could not overlook the subject, as it so completely illustrates the character of George Moore. He brought a fresh, strong, earnest, common-sense mind to bear upon the matter. "Here," he said, "is a good work to be done; let us set to at once, and do it." Up rose the functionaries of red-tape, and said it could not be done. "It would excite opposition; it was something entirely new; and, above all, it would cause great expense!" George Moore swept aside these arguments like cobwebs. "It shall be done," he said; and he forthwith began the work. He led, and others followed.

Shortly after the above meeting at Gilsland, Mr. Moore went into Scotland with Mrs. Moore and her sister, Mrs. Chester, for a change of air. This short tour was made memorable by an interview which he had with the ex-Empress of the French at Dunkeld. Mr. Moore was staying at the Birnam Hotel, and whilst there a note came to him from Count Clary, expressing a wish on the part of the Empress that he should come to see her as soon as possible. The Empress was travelling incognito, with the Prince Imperial and a small suite. When Mr. Moore arrived at her hotel, he found her ready to receive him in her apartment. She was simply dressed in a waterproof and hat, and prepared for her journey to Blair Athol. He was much struck with her great grace of manner and her beauty, though sorrow and anxiety had left their traces on her countenance.

The Empress inquired eagerly about his recent visits to Paris, as the representative of the Mansion House Fund; and she showed much feeling as he told her of the scenes and sufferings which he had witnessed. Their

---

Pauper Children in Scotland, by John Skelton, Advocate, Secretary to the Board in Scotland.

conversation was in English, and therefore limited in
extent; as she could not understand as much as she
could speak. At the last she said sadly, "Alas, they
care not for me now: they care not for me!" The
interview was melancholy. "She shed tears of gratitude," says Mr. Moore, "for what England had done
for France after the siege."

The few days which he spent in the Highlands
refreshed and cheered him. He enjoyed everything.
He was a pleasant companion to travel with. He
never raised up difficulties. While he had been a
traveller, he had to put up with all sorts of accommodation. He was the same still. He had not been
spoilt a bit. He made the best of everything, and
looked at so-called obstacles with joy and cheerfulness.

It had been the intention of the party to proceed
from Dunkeld to Braemar by coach; but when the
morning came, alas! the rain was coming down in
sheets, in floods; the wind blew in gusts and hurri-
canes. It was impossible to go out in such a day.
The outside places of the coach had been taken and
paid for. Mr. Moore got up at five, and went to the
Post Office, from whence the coach was to start. He
told the coachman that it was impossible to take
the ladies through such weather; but if any other
passengers were willing to take the places, they were
welcome to them.

Mr. Fisher, the son of the landlord, who was about
to drive the coach, gave back the money that had been
paid for the places. "You are a strange fellow," said
Mr. Moore; "you are the first Scotchman I ever met
who refused money when he had a right to it." Fisher
laughed, and rejoined, "Well, it isn't a day that I
should like to drive you and your lady to Braemar."
"Why?" "It's because you are George Moore. I
have heard of you all my life, and I wanted to see you.

I'm very sorry that it's such coarse weather that I can't drive you to Braemar!" " How did you know anything about me?" " You went into the Commercial Room last night and were recognised by some of the travellers. One of them let me know, and I saw you two or three times yesterday."

Mr. Moore asked Fisher to come and see him in London, either at Kensington Palace Gardens or at Bow Churchyard. Some time after, a tall, strong, fine-looking fellow called at Bow Churchyard and asked for Mr. Moore. He was shown to his room, and was instantly recognised as the son of the Dunkeld landlord. George Moore presented him with a pipe, which Fisher still preserves amongst his treasures.

Mr. Moore could not spend more than a fortnight in Scotland, having previously arranged to be present at a conference of the County Town Missionaries at White-hall, and to attend to other local business. The party went by rail to Inverness, then by the Caledonian Canal to Ballachulish, and from thence by Glencoe, Invernan, and the Trossachs to Callander. Next morning they went by Perth and Stirling to Carlisle, and reached Whitehall in the course of the evening.

He had a heavy fortnight's work before him. Two days after his return he attended the Diocesan Church Extension Society, at Carlisle, where he moved the first resolution. The next day he took the chair at the East Cumberland Agricultural Society, where he had to make the usual chairman's speeches. Then he attended the Carlisle Diocesan Conference, where he spoke to express his approval of a paper of the Rev. Dr. Simpson's on the evils attendant on statute-hirings in Cumberland and Westmoreland. He attended ten public meetings during the fortnight.

" After all," he said, " I should not like to live in Cumberland all the year round." And again, " I do

but little good in Cumberland compared with London."
In London he met men with larger sympathies. He
had a much wider scope of action. All the orphanages
he helped were in the neighbourhood of London. He
had seven or eight hundred young persons in his
employment for whom he considered himself largely
responsible. Then the activity and stir of life of
London interested him. All the great men of England
visited London, and many of them came within reach of
his influence.

When the Bishop of Peterborough visited London,
Mr. Moore invited him to lecture to his young men at
Bow Churchyard, and a most eloquent lecture he
delivered. On another evening the Rev. Mr. Fleming
lectured on Livingstone ; the Rev. Dr. Moffat, Livingstone's father-in-law, was present, and addressed the
meeting. Thus an immense interest was given to the
lectures, which were greatly enjoyed by the young men
of the association.

It was Mr. Moore's practice, on such occasions, to
have a large gathering of friends to dine at six o'clock,
before the lecture. He invited all the lads, in all ranks
and stations, for whom he had got situations, or to whom
he had given advice or assistance, to join these dinners
and lectures. Nothing pleased him more than to see
the dining-room so crowded that all the waiters were in
despair. Then his enjoyment was complete, and his
cheerful laughter and sunny temper spread light
amongst the guests, until they seemed to feel and enjoy
the occasion as much as he did.

The partners' lunch, or mid-day dinner, was one of
the institutions of the house. It was held in some far-
away place up stairs, and many rooms full of goods had
to be passed through before it could be reached. A
very motley congregation was sometimes to be found
there. A Cumberland schoolmaster, an aide-de-camp of

Garibaldi's, a London missionary, a noted Cumberland athlete, an Australian merchant, the chaplain of the house, a Dissenting minister, a Cumberland lad wanting a situation, an eminent bishop, and sometimes a peer, were found around the same board, mixed up with country drapers and their wives.

One who knew George Moore well gives the following recollection :—

"The most noticeable instance of pleasant incongruity that ever came under my attention happened in this way. I had been closeted with Mr. Moore for a short time in the glass sanctum where the great merchant worked, when an *employé* announced the arrival of a certain great lord of the Western country, in company with a well-known pillar of the Church. 'Ask them to wait a bit,' said Mr. Moore, and we went on with our talk. When it came to an end, the usual invitation to the partners' dinner was given and accepted, and I duly found my way up stairs. Before long the peer and the canon also put in an appearance, sitting, if memory serves, in close proximity to a Nonconformist divine and a commercial gentleman from the United States. On the opposite side of the table was the wife of a linendraper in a small way of business down in the West country. When the earl and his clerical *confrère* had withdrawn, this lady—always a favoured guest on account of her native humour—remarked, "Well, they won't believe me at home when I tell them that I dined with great Lord F——, and found him very pleasant company."[1]

Besides the various work connected with his business at Bow Churchyard, he was beset by numberless applicants for situations or for money. The secretaries of various institutions with which he was connected visited him there. Sometimes long *queues* of people waited to see him. Nearly all of them "wanted something." Some tried to force their way to his private room. It was situated at the end of a lane of inclosed clerks' desks; and before it could be reached there was a sharp turn to the left. At the end of the rows of desks his faithful secretary, Mr. Hough, was seated; and no one escaped his observation without running the gauntlet of

[1] Article in the *Globe*.

his inquiries. Some were not allowed to proceed
further; others were permitted a chance if they waited
for an audience; all who had made an appointment were
allowed admission to the private room.

Mr. Moore was forced, as it were, into punctuality.
Every minute was precious to him,—not only to him,
but to those who wished to see him. Nothing tried his
temper so much as sleepy-headed people, who did not
know the value of moments; who came languidly late,
some ten minutes behind time. One day he wrote in
his diary: "I have not a moment to call my own. I
fear my temper is not so good as it was; for I have
been twice irritated to-day. Lord, forgive me!"

He was himself most punctual in his engagements.
He was never a moment too late. It was the same
whether it was an important engagement or a visit to a
friend, or an appointment to meet his wife at a picture-
gallery. He was most punctual also in his reply to
letters. He answered them by return. He often said
that if he could not answer his letters at once, he would
" be mired, or go mad."

When an opportunity offered, he would visit his
friends in the country. Sometimes he went to Cambridge to see his friends at the University. In May,
1872, he went for a few days to stay with Dr. Guest,
Master of Caius College, the celebrated Anglo-Saxon
scholar. He had many pleasant remembrances of Cambridge. He had visited his Cumberland friend, Mr. W.
M. Gunson, there in 1853. Mr. Moore was so much
pleased with the place, that from that time he was a
constant visitor. It was by his advice that his partner's
only son, Sampson Copestake, went to Cambridge, and
passed through the regular university course.

During his visits to Dr. Guest in 1872, he met with
many kindnesses. He and Mrs. Moore paid a visit to
Professor Sedgwick at his rooms. He was then very ill,

and seldom spoke or roused himself to see any visitors ; but when George Moore and his wife called, he was delighted to see them, and began to talk of past days, and of his early life amongst the Fells of Yorkshire. His old fire rekindled ; his face glowed with enthusiasm ; and he spoke with eagerness of the North and its associations. It was almost the last spark in his life. A few weeks after, he died.

George Moore had scarcely got rid of the office of High Sheriff of Cumberland, when he was again asked to offer himself as a candidate for the representation of an important constituency in Parliament. He had already refused Nottingham, Marylebone, the City of London, the County of Surrey, the County of Cumberland ; and now he was asked to represent the County of Middlesex. His views on the latter proposal must be stated in his own words. The memorandum is dated February, 1873 :—

"Having received a letter from Lord Enfield, Under Secretary of State for Foreign Affairs, stating that he wished to see me, I was full of curiosity to know what could be his errand. He came, and to my surprise he said that he had consulted some of his colleagues and many friends in the county, and they had unanimously agreed that I should be asked to be his colleague in standing for the County of Middlesex at the next election. He stayed a long time, paid me many compliments, reminded me that I had proposed him at the last general election, and said many other kind things.

"How passing strange does all this seem to me ! When I look back upon my past life, many curious memories crowd upon me. Some forty-three years ago, when I came to London and was with Fishers, I took my half-holiday to go and see the House of Commons. I remember how I surreptitiously got into the House, and actually sat down in the seat of Canning !

I little thought at that time that I should be offered a seat for both the City of London and the County of Middlesex. But now that I can get into the House freely and openly, I do not care about it. On cool reflection, I have resolved to decline the proposition!

"My days on earth," he added, "are fast drawing to a close. Weeks and months pass away as if by magic. My old friends are dying, I myself must be prepared for following them; it may be in a moment. I cannot allow any worldly honour to be fixed upon me, to the detriment of my eternal interests.

"Then, people estimate my abilities far too highly. These are only very moderate; and my imperfect education would make me a coward in the House of Commons. I shall be sixty-seven next month. I ought to give up all worldly excitement, and prepare for another and better state."

He therefore wisely declined the distinguished honour offered to him of representing Middlesex in Parliament. He knew very well that no similar offer would again be made to him.

CHAPTER XXII.

ONE of Mr. Moore's principal reasons for declining to become a member of Parliament was because he felt it to be his duty to continue his help to the benevolent associations with which he had become identified. There were many rich and ambitious persons anxious to become members of Parliament; but there were very few who were willing to give their time and money to assist the orphanages and charitable institutions from which no honour was to be derived. George Moore therefore continued to labour at his self-imposed duty to the end of his life.

At the time when he was declining to become member of Parliament, he was one of the committee engaged in getting up subscriptions for the help of the passengers and seamen who had been wrecked in the *Northfleet*, off Dungeness. We find long memoranda in his handwriting relating to the numerous meetings held on the object. The claims of a number of persons had to be considered. George Moore occasionally differed from the committee. For instance, he objected to give to the captain's wife one-seventh of the whole amount subscribed while a comparatively small sum was divided amongst the other bereaved persons. Besides, the captain's widow had £50 yearly from the Privy Purse, and £60 of her own. Mr. Moore divided the meeting on the question, but he was beaten.

The case of Widow Stephens, described by a draper of Fraserburgh to George Moore in a private letter, was a painful one. In some respects it reminds one of the story of Enoch Arden. She had been married to two brothers. Both had served their apprenticeship at the same time. Both had courted her at the same time, and both married her—the last after a widowhood of about four years. Her life had been a chequered and eventful one. When a girl she lost her father, a ship's carpenter, by an accident in China. Then her mother died. The first Stephens she married died at sea ; and the second Stephens was drowned in the *Northfleet*, a month after her second marriage. Such are the troubles which sailors' wives have to undergo.

From an early period Mr. Moore took a deep interest in the London Cabmen's Mission. His commercial activity had early brought him into contact with the cabmen. They all knew the warehouse in Bow Church-yard and his house in Kensington Palace Gardens. These men were exposed at all hours to all weathers. They had little time to spend with their families. They were employed on Sundays[1] and Saturdays. They often bore a bad reputation, though they were perhaps more sinned against than sinning.

One day a cabman drove George Moore from his house to Euston Square. He gave the driver a shilling over the fare. The cabman returned the extra money. Mr. Moore had already discovered a Scotchman who had returned him his fare, though he had a right to it. But to have an excess fare returned by a London cabman, who had no right to it, was something still more

---

[1] As early as 1861 Mr. Moore offered a prize of £20 for the best essay on the evils connected with Sunday cab-driving. It was won by a hansom-cabman, named John Cockram.

extraordinary. "How is this?" he asked. "Well, you have paid me more than the fare, and you are George Moore!" said the cabman. Mr. Moore was in a hurry to get off by the train, and said nothing at the time, but merely asked for the cabman's number. He afterwards found that the cabman's name was Cockram, and that he had won the prize essay for £20 which had been awarded to him some years before.

On his return to London Mr. Moore sent for Mr. Cockram, and ascertained that the money he had obtained for the prize had proved the nest-egg of good fortune. First he had bought a horse and a cab. He had increased these from time to time, until he had become the possessor of about a hundred horses and of numerous cabs. He never used these on Sundays. Mr. Moore asked him, "What can I do to help the cabmen?" "Well, sir, you must do as that gentleman, Sir Hope Grant, has done, and ask some of them to supper!" "Very well," said George Moore, "they can come to the schoolroom near here, and they shall have the best possible supper." "No, sir," said Cockram; "that would not be the same thing. If you want to do any good to them, you must ask them to your own house. You must show them that every man's hand is not against them." "Very well," said Mr. Moore; "it shall be done as you say."

An invitation was issued to two hundred London cabmen to take supper at Kensington Palace Gardens, preference being given to those in the neighbourhood, to teetotallers, and to the younger men most under the influence of temptation. Not only the invited made their appearance, but a large number of the uninvited, who swelled the number to about double the expected guests.

When the cabmen sat down, their suspicions were somewhat aroused by the appearance of a tall, military-looking officer behind them serving out the beef and plum-pudding. "D'ye see the guv'nor?" asked one cabby of another, pointing back with his thumb to the gentleman behind them. In fact it was Colonel Henderson, the Commissioner of Police! No matter; the supper went on blithely. Mr. Moore was in his element, hurrying from place to place to see that his guests had plenty. The speeches which followed were short and to the point. Lots of anecdotes were told, at which the cabmen laughed heartily. Mr. Moore gave them good advice, and warned them against the evils of drunkenness,[1] which they took in very good part.

---

[1] Among Sir Wilfrid Lawson's humorous rhymes, which he sent to Mr. Moore, is the following :—

"Mr. Moore, at his banquet to the cabmen, gave them special warning against the evils of drunkenness."—*Record.*

> "Now all you young fellows take warning I pray,
> And attend to the word which I'm going to say :
> I advise one and all that you never get 'tight,'
> We merchants and clergymen don't think it right.

> "It's a very bad thing : it deprives you of wealth,
> It injures your morals, and ruins your health ;
> It's bad for yourselves, for your children and wives—
> In fact, you know well, it's the curse of your lives.

> "Then drink only sparsely of spirits and beer :
> The advice which I give you is truly sincere.
> In each street, as you know, there's a palace for gin,
> With an owner, all burning to have you come in.

> "There are publics and beer-shops set down everywhere,
> In yard and in alley, in street and in square ;
> The magistrates license these places each year,
> And the country gets rich with its tax upon beer.

> "And the brewers—how pious they are to be sure !
> They get plenty of money to give to the poor ;
> And the clergy have shares in the joint-stock concerns,
> From which every year they get famous returns.

> "And no one objects, when things go on so well,
> Except that poor idiot, Sir W. L.
> You see we're obliged thus to tempt you all round,
> For money must somehow or other be found.

Colonel Henderson satisfied them by his manner and his speech that he was by no means their enemy, but had a strong desire to improve their condition. At the end of the proceedings, after the Doxology had been sung, Mr. Moore stood at the door, tipped the cabbies each with a new shilling; gave them a copy of Bunyan, and a *British Workman* Almanac; and bade them all "Good night, God bless you!"

About two years after the above entertainment, a Mission Hall for the cabmen was established near Kings Cross Station; Mr. Samuel Morley, M.P., laying the foundation-stone. The minister and superintendent of the mission has given the following account of Mr. Moore's first visit to the hall:—"One Sabbath evening, as we were holding an open-air service, we observed two gentlemen very near to the preaching-stand; and when we gave out a hymn, they joined in singing it heartily. At the close of the meeting we gave a cordial invitation to those present to come with us into the London Cabmen's Mission Hall. In proceeding thither, the two gentlemen told the missionary who they were. The one was George Moore, and the other was his friend Mr. Stockdale. They both sat and listened to the Gospel, as we gave it in our plain, outspoken manner; and at the prayer meeting which followed the service, Mr.

> "And that rich men should pay—Oh ! that *never* would do
> When the tax is so easy collected from you.
> How well we are governed, my lads, only think !
> There's twenty five millions of taxes on drink !
>
> "And the drink keep our prisons and workhouses going,
> And asylums for lunatics fill to o'erflowing;
> It is a glorious thing, is this wonderful drink,
> At least so we merchants and clergymen think.
>
> "So, I'll only conclude the same way I began,
> With a warning most special to every young man.
> There's only one evil you're called on to funk,
> You may drink night and day only *never get drunk!*"

Moore gave us a warm address, and wished us God-speed!" He afterwards sent the mission two donations of £50 each; and a third of £100 just before his death. He provided a cabmen's rest, on the Kensington Road, close to the end of the Broad Walk in Kensington Gardens. It was supplied with every requisite for human comfort. The cabmen took their meals and coffee there. It was a snug place, and proved a cozy shelter from the winter's rain and snow.

We turn to another subject. At the beginning of 1874, it became known that the remains of the great African traveller, Dr. Livingstone, were on their way from Zanzibar to England. His numerous friends in London were anxious that his body should be interred in Westminster Abbey. This would involve some expense, but no one was willing to find the money. Mr. Russell Gurney brought the subject under the notice of the House of Commons. He said, "It had transpired that there were no funds available wherewith to give effect to the general wish of the country. The family of Dr. Livingstone were without the necessary means; and on an application being made to the Geographical Society, it had been ascertained that they had no funds which they felt at liberty to employ for the purpose. . . . The expense of interment would be very small, but there were none to whom they could look for the funds except to the Government; and he was quite sure that in incurring the small outlay which would be required the Government would be doing an act that would be welcomed by the whole community."

The proceedings connected with this affair were conducted in a rather shabby way. Why go to the Government at all, when the expenses of the interment were to be so "very small"? When George Moore heard of the difficulty, he said : "Let me bury the noble dead! What! bury him like a pauper out of the public taxes? No! Let me defray the expenses of interring the indomitable, valiant, self-denying hero!"

But this was not to be permitted. The Government at last said its say. The Chancellor of the Exchequer, in replying to Sir Wilfrid Lawson, said that the Treasury had at first promised £250 for the funeral of Dr. Livingstone,—that sum having been estimated to cover all expenses. It was afterwards found that a larger amount was required. "A wealthy merchant in the City had offered to pay the expenses; but the Treasury felt that to accept this offer would not be in accordance with the wishes of the country."

At last the remains of the hero were interred in Westminster Abbey, side by side with the great men of the country. Men of title, men of science and letters, took part in the ceremony. The Queen sent "a tribute of respect and admiration" in the shape of a beautiful wreath of the choicest flowers to deck the bier of the noble dead.

It was still left for George Moore to affix the tablet of black marble which lies over the grave of the illustrious traveller. The admirable tributary inscription was composed by the large-hearted Dean of Westminster. The Dean, in a recent letter to Mrs. Moore, says: "I well remember the circumstance of Livingstone's funeral. When there appeared to be a difficulty in carrying out the object which the nation had so much at heart, it was understood that one private person had undertaken to defray all the expenses; and though this proposal at once stimulated the Government to step in, and with a becoming sense of the occasion to supersede such an intervention, yet there was not a less grateful feeling, and I may add that there was no surprise, when it was felt that George Moore was the unknown benefactor. He afterwards laid down at his own cost the splendid slab and the long inscription which remains the sole memorial in the Abbey of the Great Traveller,—the memorial, I may also say, of one of the most generous and genuine examples of public spirit and munificence that our generation has seen."

We now return to Mr. Moore's church at Somers Town. The Rev. Mr. Worsfold was the first clergyman appointed to the charge. He had found it up-hill work. It told upon his health, and he was forced to go abroad to recruit his strength. Mr. Moore went to the church one Sunday, and found the gallery shut up. The body of the church was half empty. This was a great blow to him. "My church at Somers Town," he said, "has not yet been a success. The clergyman meets with many discouragements; we cannot get the people to come to the services." Nevertheless, the schools were successful. They were filled with large numbers of children, and were doing good.

Mr. Worsfold returned to England, and accepted a country living more easy to manage. The responsibility was then thrown upon Mr. Moore of finding a successor. From the nature of the parish, it was difficult to find the right man. He went from one church to another to hear the best preachers. He went to Stepney, Deptford, Mile End, Kennington, Kensington, Old St. Pancras, and Hornsey. At last, when he had almost given up hope, he found the man he wanted in the fashionable church of St. George's, Hanover Square. He consulted Canon Fleming of St. Michael's, and with his strong recommendation, he suggested to the trustees to offer the living of Christ's Church, Somers Town, to the Rev. Philip S. O'Brien—an excellent preacher, and an able, hard-working clergyman. Mr. O'Brien accepted the offer; and from that time has gone on labouring, in the face of many difficulties, at what is real missionary work in London.

In the month of February, George Moore was visited

by the Rev. Canon and Mrs. Ryle; he writes in his diary: "Our dear friends the Ryles arrived; very glad we were to receive them. Thank God he has recovered from his severe illness. He is one of the salt of the earth. May he long be spared to work for Christ!"

Mr. Moore continued to attend the meetings of Christ's Hospital. On the resignation of Mr. Foster White, from over-work, he was asked to become treasurer. But his hands were already full, and he could not accept the office. He however induced his friend Mr. Allcroft to accept the office, which he continues to retain. Mr. Moore was however elected one of the five almoners to meet the Endowed Schools Commissioners with respect to the future government of the institution. He accordingly went on frequent deputations to negotiate with the commissioners.

Though getting older, he felt himself as full of work as ever. "I must work as well as pray," he said; "there is no happiness in an idle life." And again, "Enable me to persevere to the end of my days." "Faithfulness in little things is a true test of character. A little thing well done proves what a man's habitual state is." "Let life go as it may, there will always be a strength underlying it, if we have come to Christ." Here is his commercial view of a Christian—"It pays to be a thorough Christian. It pays to repent and be converted. It pays to serve Christ. It does not pay in money, but it does in true happiness."

One day, after visiting the sick poor, many of them ill of typhus and scarlet fever, he writes in his diary: "How many mercies have I to be thankful for, compared with the eighty families I have visited to-day with the city missionary!" The visit was made in the middle of January, during a severe frost. He went about from door to door, distributing help and money. Again he adds:—"Outward gifts are subjects of thanksgiving, but not of rejoicing. There is a better joy,—the heart moulded unto the will of God. This was our Lord's joy—oneness of will with God. ' My meat is to do the will of Him that sent me.' "

These are merely a few of the extracts taken from his diary, which is rich in similar thoughts. The sense of duty always overcomes any personal efforts. This was characteristic of him through life. He used to say that "It wasn't that he was brave at all; but he hadn't time to think of anything but what had to be done, and what must be done, through whatever obstacles."

At length he was compelled to call a halt. Nerves of iron could not go on lasting for ever. He was beginning to feel the effects of the wear and tear of life. He consulted Mr. Erichsen, who ordered him at once to Vichy, in the centre of France. It was with great difficulty that he could tear himself away from his London work; but still he must go. He went, accompanied by Mrs. Moore and her sister, and his old friend Stockdale. He derived great benefit from the waters and the baths. He drove about the country, and sat in the open air. He was always a lover of sunshine; he never found it too hot, when other people were exhausted. His mind lay fallow, while he enjoyed enforced idleness. He made the acquaintance, while at Vichy, of the Rev. W. Gordon, the chaplain of the English Church, and of Mr. Porter, a Devonshire squire, and with them he took part in some Bible Readings. After a stay of three weeks he returned to London, greatly benefited in health.

While at Paris he called upon the friends whom he had made in 1871, during the Relief of Paris,—the Andrés, the Mallets, the Rothschilds. They always welcomed him on his arrival. A carriage, with English horses, was placed at his disposal by a French gentleman;

and more than once, when he took his seat, a rose, a bunch of mignonette, or a forget-me-not was thrown in by some poor-looking *ouvrier*. One day a lovely bouquet was laid in the carriage for Mrs. Moore, with these words attached to it: "Reconnaissance à Madame Moore et à Monsieur Moore, d'un inconnu, qui n'a pas oublié à Paris le dévouement avec lequel il à prit part à nos infortunes."[1]

Mr. Moore's first visit to Vichy was in May, 1873. He went through his ordinary hard work during the year; but with the accession of spring he began to feel seedy, tired, and exhausted. He consulted his physicians, and they again ordered him to Vichy. The baths and waters again did him good, and he returned to London once more full of health.

Towards the end of summer he went down to Whitehall. That was always a great event—to himself, to his friends, and to the people of the neighbourhood. The young people looked forward to his examinations and his tea feasts. The many charities in which he took an interest required his attention and also his support. He took his seat on the bench at Wigton, and tried to keep down drunkenness by refusing all new licences. He had his pensioners to look after, at Bolton Low Houses, Mealsgate, and elsewhere. He went on to Carlisle to visit the hospital, of which he was a large benefactor. He went to Silloth to visit the Convalescent Home, which Mrs. Moore had done much to enlarge.[2]

---

[1] The following paragraph appeared in a London newspaper in 1873:—
"A few days ago a lady who was accompanying a Frenchman in a walk ... her in ... n Palace Garden, observed that her companion took off ... cap ... g Mr. George Moore' house. She asked him the reason, ... he replied that he ... always do so whenever he passed that house. We ... her ly supply the key."

[2] In 1871 Mr. Moore gave £1,650, to the Convalescent Home at ... A ford war e tal abled, called after her name, under the direction of the Charity; and patients were sent from the Cumberland ... ary to the Convalescent Home.

Then there was his farm to look over. At first he had taken a great pleasure in farming,—when "frisking over his own soil!" But his tune had changed. He had had many losses and worries. He had discovered, as regarded the farm itself, that like most gentlemen's farms, it never paid. Mr. Moore then took to short-horns. He bought some splendid animals, and the results seemed satisfactory. But we see throughout his diary that they also caused him a good deal of dis-comfort. On one occasion a cow died which cost him £700. Other cows dropped their calves. When the beasts were so valuable, this was a great loss.

At last Mr. Moore determined to sell his shorthorns. On the 29th June, 1875, he writes :—"I lost three shorthorns worth a thousand pounds. I am heartily sick of shorthorns. They have been a great anxiety to me; I am in dread of their getting the foot-and-mouth disease." At last the shorthorns were advertised to be sold on the 9th September, 1875. The sale was a great affair. All the great shorthorn men in England were present. The Earl of Bective, Lord Skelmers-dale, Sir Curtis Lampson, Sir R. Musgrave, and Mr. Graham, with shorthorn buyers from America, Canada, Nova Scotia, and New South Wales. A lunch was given before the sale, to whet the appetite for short-horns. Sir Wilfrid Lawson presided,—Mr. Moore's nearest neighbour, and one of his most intimate friends. Moreover he is a man who knows the good points of a beast as well as of a teetotaller.

Sir Wilfrid, after drinking the health of "The Queen," proposed that of the worthy host. "Let me call him," he said, "King George. All that I will say of him is, that we know him as a good friend, kind neighbour, and a generous, I will say, a munificent benefactor to any good work which is carried on in his neighbourhood. But when Mr. Moore is in the

country he must have some amusements, as well as
attending to good works. In an evil hour a friend
came to him and said, 'Mr. Moore, take to farming!'
Mr. Moore took his advice, and rapidly began to dissi-
pate his well-earned fortune. The farming didn't pay,
and his friend came to him again, and said, 'Mr.
Moore, take to shorthorns!' Mr. Moore took his
advice, and I know from my intimate acquaintance
with him, that the shorthorns have been a source of
the deepest anxiety to him from that moment to this.
I hope that all of you, good bidders, whom I see from
every part of the kingdom, will assist in taking that
weight from his mind and transferring that weight to
his pocket!"

Mr. Moore, in returning thanks, said that at first he
had been rather intoxicated with his success in selling
his shorthorns. He thought that money was to be made
faster in shorthorns than in Bow Churchyard. But he
frankly confessed that he had not been so successful in
the shorthorn world as in the commercial world. If he
could have remained in Cumberland all the year round,
it might have been different; but as he was bound to
be in London more than half the year, things got wrong
when he was absent. He was constantly getting letters
saying that there was a dead calf or some other mishap;
and one thing and another kept him in a state of perpetual conflict. "But," he concluded, "as you are now
anxious to get to the ring, I hope you will be as blithe
there as you are here."

The sale then began. It proved very successful.
Some of the shorthorns sold at a loss; others at a profit.
A cow bought for 900 guineas three years before, now
brought only 59 guineas; whereas another, bought from
the Duke of Devonshire in the preceding year, was
sold to Sir Curtis Lampson for 2000 guineas, and her
calf, two and a half months old, was sold to the Duke

of Devonshire for 1000 guineas. The list of cows, heifers, and bulls, with their respective pedigrees, was of considerable length, and need not be given here. Suffice it to say that the sale was remarkably successful, and in one day transferred the weight of anxiety from George Moore's mind to his pocket. On the succeeding Sunday he put a hundred guineas into the plate at Allhallows church, as a thank-offering; and he gave fifty guineas to his servants at the farm for their services.

Mr. Moore had much benevolent work to do in Cumberland at this time. He was diligently assisting Miss Rye in her efforts to induce poor girls to emigrate to Canada: paying half their expenses. Miss Rye had established a home at Niagara, called "Our Western Home." The girls were carried from England across the ocean to this home. From thence about eight hundred had, in 1873, been drafted out amongst farmers and others who were willing to afford them a permanent home, and bring them up as useful and industrious members of society. Mr. Moore succeeded in sending out many of these destitute girls, and it was a great comfort to him to find that they were all doing well.

Mr. Moore continued to assist the Boards of Guardians in their efforts to board out pauper children. Another meeting of the Poor Law Conference of the northern counties was held at Carlisle in August, 1875, when Mr. Moore read a second paper on the subject. It is full of interest, and full of facts. But we can only give a few extracts :—

"My practical experience as to the working of the system since reading my paper at Gilsland, in 1872, has convinced me that the right people with whom to place the children can be found. In fact, there are more suitable cottagers to receive them than there are orphan girls to place out. My experience has convinced me that we can find a high standard of cottagers willing to have

the children,—God-fearing people, who have a higher
motive than mere profit. I feel strongly that no child
ought to be placed in any home where we do not know
the people to be not only respectable, sober, and moral,
but who distinctly make a profession of religion.

"My wife and myself have made it a duty to visit
unexpectedly those children placed out in the Wigton
union ; and we are fully capable of bearing testimony
to the healthful and happy appearance they possess,
and the tidy and comfortable homes in which they are
placed. It has interested us to observe the strong feeling of attachment that has already grown up between
them and their foster-parents. I could mention many
more places where children are boarded out, and I have
not heard of one where it has been a failure.

"I am alive to the necessity which exists for super-
vision of the homes of these children. Independently
of the regular official visits of the relieving officer, it
seems to me that the Guardians in each district ought to
consider it a part of their business to look in occasionally and see them unexpectedly ; and I am sure the
ladies in the district would cheerfully undertake this, if
so requested, for they are ever ready in works of love.
Who can overrate the good influence which their kind-
heartedness and delicacy of feeling would exercise over
the future lives of these poor orphans ? Fatherless,
motherless, and alone ! As one of the greatest writers
of this age says :—' There is no hopelessness so sad as
that of early youth when the soul is made up of *wants*,
and has no superadded life in the life of others.' We
shall always have the poor with us, and the direction
which our efforts should be aimed at, is to supply,
as best we can, the home influences which pauper
children have lost. This is the object of the system
to give the children of the parish the inestimable
advantage of home-life and home-affections which it

is simply impossible to secure to them by any other means.

"As I said in my former paper, our object is to absorb these poor children into the general population, having first fitted them for their life, by their having themselves been the sharers of a working man's home, having associated with his family in its joys and sorrows, having had the individual responsibility of being a member of it. Proficiency in reading, writing, and arithmetic is essential, but far less essential than a practical knowledge of the every day work of common life, enabling them to take care of themselves, how to be helpful to others, how to perform their part in the world upon which they are to enter. The great school of instruction for this kind of knowledge is of divine institution—the Family! So entirely do we take this for granted as a matter of course, that we are often apt to forget the wonderful *educating* influence of domestic life. In the home circle, the child learns on a small scale what he has to practice at large, in after years ; he is brought into relation with persons of different ages and sexes ; his wits are sharpened and his judgment is matured by a great variety of personal experiences ; in fact, he learns common sense."

In conclusion he said :—"I can but say, for myself, that each year only deepens my conviction of the necessity for the adoption of the system ; and I feel sure that all thoughtful men, who know something of the needs around them, if they rightly understand the boarding-out system, would be the first to bid it God-speed."

Mr. Moore's collected papers contain many letters relating to the question of boarding-out. Many of them are from persons stating that they are willing to take a pauper child ; showing that he took a personal interest in finding them out in his own district. One is from a guardian near Newcastle, stating that he has got the

B ard of Guardians to adopt the system of boarding-out. He says, " Rural Boards require a good deal of hammering before they will take up any new plan. But when once welded into shape, and the material is good, they retain the good impression." The guardian, as might be supposed from his words, was an ironman.

George Moore himself says, in one of his memoranda : " After urging the Wigton Guardians for four or five years, amidst a good deal of opposition, I have at last got them to agree to board out pauper children. I have now got my way with all the Unions in Cumberland. I have never been more in earnest in any work that I have ever undertaken."

It will thus be observed that Mr. Moore was as busily employed in Cumberland as in London—at Whitehall as at Bow Churchyard. He had no sooner got down to his country-home, and settled his books and papers, than he began to arrange the work that had to be done. He first visited the schools, and then he arranged for a meeting of the Scripture readers. He had the greatest sympathy with schoolmasters and missionaries. He thought that they had a great deal to try them, and that they were very little appreciated. Hence his visits to Cumberland were eagerly looked forward to ; as the schoolmasters knew that they would be treated with respect, encouragement, and with the honour that was really due to them.

It will be remembered with what difficulty Mr. Moore had established his first missionary in Cumberland in 1850—how the missionary was rebuffed, opposed, and hindered, not only by the common people, but by most of the persons of influence,—how George Moore himself had been twitted as a " Methodist" and sometimes abused as a " fanatic." All that feeling had now passed away. The missionaries were at work all over the country. When George Moore went down to Whitehall in 1875, he had a conference of twenty-eight missionaries to meet him.

The conference lasted for three days, during which George Moore lodged and entertained the missionaries. He combined their coming with the five or six annual Bible meetings, at which they were present, and took part in the proceedings. One of the days was appropriated to the "Whitehall feast," when the school-children, "Moore's lot" as they were called, and all the neighbours, from far and near, sometimes numbering more than a thousand, came to tea. To the young people, this was regarded as the grandest feast in Cumberland.

It was one of the first things done after George Moore's arrival at Whitehall; and sometimes before the household had become fairly settled down. But George Moore never thought anything impossible. He inspired those about him to work with a will; and the servants tried to outvie one another in carrying out his wishes. The time chosen for these entertainments was when the moon was at its full, and when the gardens were at their best. He wished the missionaries and the cottagers to see Whitehall in its glory. He never would hear of any suggestion of waiting until the fruit-gathering was over, or till the beauty of the lawn, the gardens, or the grounds, had passed.

So when the roses where in their fullest bloom, when masses of Gloire de Dijon were clustering on the walls of the house, when the lilies were shining fair and white against the yew hedge of the bowling-green,—then was the time for the meetings to be held. For some days before George Moore went round the country inviting guests. He called at every farmhouse and cottage for miles and miles about. So special was he in his invitations, that on one occasion, when the assembly had met, he observed that the grandmother of one family was not present. He at once remembered that he had not called upon her. Suspecting the cause of her non-appearance, he immediately sent off her grandchildren to bring her. When she made her appearance, he did not forget to apologise to her, and to laugh at her for being "so touchy." His thoughtfulness, his attention, to the oldest and poorest, won their hearts. His extraordinary memory helped him to remember the veriest trifles in their lives. He asked them about their boys, about their grandchildren, and how they were getting on in the battle of life. He could also tell them of many of their children, for whom he had got situations in London and elsewhere.

George Moore was always in his element at these Whitehall gatherings. The old hall was filled with long tables made for the purpose, at which seventy-five persons could be seated at a time; and the tea and cakes went on from three till seven. He seemed to be everywhere—now pressing the old women to a third cup of tea—the centre of all eyes and sympathies. Then he would be outside amongst the children at "scromallys," scattering about sugar-plums and hunting-nuts, the girls and boys running after him, and scrambling about him to gather up the sugary shower. Then he would be seen far off amongst the pastures, initiating the races. He always started the boys himself. "Off with your clogs, lads," he said; "when I was like you, I raced in my stocking feet." In the evenings, fire balloons, of curious shapes, were floated away from the top of the tower. After the boys and girls had left, a hot supper was provided for sixty or seventy friends. And thus the great day passed away.

Next day was entirely given up to the conference of the village missionaries. Mr. Bowker always conducted the meetings. He prepared and arranged suitable subjects for consideration, a copy of which was sent to

each missionary about a fortnight before the meeting.
At ten o'clock the men assembled in the Old Hall.
Clergymen and laymen took part in the proceedings.
The Rev. J. C. Ryle, Mr. Justice Lush, Mr. Wilson, the
Rev. F. Morse (vicar of Nottingham), Dr. Stoughton,
Dr. Moffat (father-in-law of Dr. Livingstone), and Mr.
Smithies, were present in July, 1875. The handling of
the meeting was ably done, and though questions of
doctrine were not excluded, the subjects kept uppermost were of daily life and practice. So minute and
searching were the questions put by the chairman, that
more than one of the missionaries afterwards remarked,
" How strict Mr. Moore was in his inquiries : he observes
things that we never expected would be noticed." In
short, the meetings were full of wise counsel, as well as
of sympathy and encouragement.

His ordinary daily life in Cumberland was almost as
busy as it was in London. He was always at work. The
only rest he took was in changing from one work to
another. He sometimes said he wished he could be
idle, but he found that to be impossible. He never had
any *spare* time. The first thing he did in the morning
was to open his batch of letters. They would amount
to forty or fifty. They were about every conceivable
thing,—about Bow Churchyard, about missionaries,
about salaries, about shorthorns, about schools, about
Bible societies, about horses, about situations for people's
sons ; but principally about money. The whole world
wanted money. Shoeblacks, convicts, schoolmasters,
clergymen, emigrants, travellers, working lads, servants,
vagrants, missionaries, scripture readers,—all wanted
money ! The Reports he received were innumerable.
The societies which sent them, like Oliver Twist, invariably "wanted more !" When it was known that
he had built a church at Somers Town, all the church

builders in England were at him. They all wanted
money.[1]

When he received his morning's post, Mr. Moore shut
himself up in his library immediately after breakfast,
and proceeded to open his budget. He went through
them all, and decided upon the answer, making a note
upon each. Then he proceeded to answer them one
by one. When he had written a letter he threw it on
the ground, and there it lay until gathered up for the
post. The consequence was that before two the floor
was mired with letters, and any approach to his table
without treading upon them was rendered impossible.
When his private secretary, Mr. Hough, was with him
the correspondence was much more easy.

Sometimes during his later years he grew tired and
weary. It required much tact on the part of Mrs.
Moore to induce him to give less time to his correspondence. Sometimes she endeavoured to get him to
lie in bed for two or three hours longer; and when he
did so he would get up and come down "like a giant
refreshed," and went to work again with his correspondence.

Then he was very much interrupted by callers; the
farmers wanted to see him about draining and manure;
schoolmasters wished to talk over the improvement of
their schools; missionaries desired to tell him of the
progress of their work; clergymen called about their

---

[1] Amongst the curious letters which he received was one from a distinguished person in Ireland no less than a descendant of the ancient Irish
kings. He, gentleman, having ascertained that the church at Somers
Town cost over £10,000, and that the clergyman's name was O'Brien,
proceeded to state his claims. He divided the cost of the church by
five, and found that there quite was £2,000. He wrote to George Moore
asking that he had concluded, that if he sent them £2,000 each he would
build up again noble living temples to the Lord, and to reverence the
race of their benefactor; but (he concluded with this threat) "if you do
not I will bring them all up as Roman Catholics; for the education
at M——— is very much cheaper than at any Protestant institution."
Of course this letter remained unanswered.

schemes of usefulness ; young men wanted advice or a helping-hand; parents came with their lads to beg him to get "spots" for them; so that his mornings were a good deal broken in upon. It is a wonder how he kept his patience; yet he was never disconcerted nor impatient. Perhaps he rather spoiled his Cumberland neighbours. They took so much for granted. They seemed as if they had a right to his services. But he knew best. He was sowing seeds of kindness which have since borne fruit far and wide.

There was a sort of routine of enjoyment at Whitehall that was regularly gone through. After all the school gatherings and public meetings were finished, the shooting began. Friends came from London and elsewhere in September to shoot over the estates, though Mr. Moore did not shoot himself. In the afternoon he usually rode or walked out; but even these rides and walks were very frequently made subservient to some purpose of benevolence and kindness. He would call upon the cottagers when they were ill, or upon some old woman to ask about her health or her comfort.

It is difficult to give an impression of the cheerfulness and brightness of his home life. In the afternoon he was always ready for anything. The clear, loud tones of his voice seemed to bring good humour and freshness. As a friend said of him, " He seems to bring a flood of life into the room." The dinner hour was very enjoyable. George Moore was a host in himself. He made every one comfortable. None were forgotten. He brought forward the shy by addressing some question to them on a subject with which they were acquainted ; and he thus not only got information, but pleased the guest, who had an opportunity of doing his best. He himself amused and interested his friends by telling them stories of his early career—his troubles, his difficulties, his obstacles,—and how he surmounted them all. When questions of religion, morals, and politics were raised, he took a keen interest in the discussion. His own remarks were racy and to the point. Before the conversation closed he would do ample justice to his opponents. If anything was said of those who were not present, he would speak of them in kindness and moderation. The Archbishop of York has told us that he never heard George Moore speak a harsh word of anybody; and he would always put in a kind word for the absent.

The hospitable gatherings at Whitehall were not limited to men of any particular station in life. Men of high rank, dignitaries of the Church, old friends and new, hard workers in the fields of benevolent labour, were alike made welcome.

It was one of George Moore's peculiarities, that whenever he had an Archbishop staying with him, he invited the clergy and curates, far and near, to visit him. On these occasions, the lawn was covered with black-coats. The clergymen were introduced to the Archbishop one by one. None were forgotten. If any curate was shy, and slunk away into a corner, George would find him out. He would take him by the arm, and bring him forward, saying, " I want to introduce my friend the Rev. Mr. So and so ;" sometimes adding, " Who knows but that he may be an Archbishop some day ? "

Mr. Moore had given up hunting for some years, but his love of horses, and of good riding, was as strong as ever. He had himself been one of the boldest and straightest riders ; and he continued to take pleasure in hearing of the Meet. The young Howards of Greystoke or Sam Foster of Killhow kept him well-informed, when he was in London, of all the runs of the Cumberland fox hound   In Nov. 1875, Mr. Moore writes in his diary, " The Prime Warden of the Fishmongers' Company has given me *carte blanche* to invite all Masters of the Hounds to a banquet at the Fishmongers' Hall on the 9th of December next." The Foxhunters came up to London accordingly, and duly enjoyed their Banquet.[1] Three days after, seventeen of the M.F.H. dined with George Moore at Bow Churchyard.

[1] Sir Wilfrid Lawson has thus commemorated the event :—

THE FISHMONGERS' HUNT DINNER, DECEMBER, 1875.

The Banquet is spread in the Fishmongers' Hall,
   And the guests are all gathered around ;
The Masters of Hounds, both the great and the small,
   Amid the gay throng may be found.

There's the Major just fresh from a run at Blindcrake,
   In the midst of the fast falling snow,
Where our fox took a line—when at last forced to break—
   Half a mile just as straight as a crow.

There's the Squire of Dalemain from the Ullswater Hunt,
   Where the hounds are as swift as young eagles ;
There's Parker who gallantly rides in the front,
   There's Harry who runs with the beagles.

There's the jovial George Moore at the head of the Board,
   At *one* time no rider was bolder ;
But in taking a steep six-barred gate he was "floored,"
   And now he's laid up with a shoulder.

But he still loves the chase in his warm-hearted way,
   Though on horseback unable to follow ;
And his pulses beat quick on a fine hunting day
   When he hears the bold Major's view halloa !

There's Sam who rides Sultan so steady and strong,
   Never known to shy, stumble, or pull ;
Ere Sam buys another 'twill be pretty long ;
   For his money's all spent on a Bull.

There's Lamplugh who steers such a swift dashing steed
   (For daring what youngster can match him ?)
That you'll hardly believe when I tell you indeed
   I myself, on some days, can scarce catch him ;

Which is strange, as you know my swift pace in the chace
   Regardless of mud, stones, and rocks ;
And how always I'm first to arrive in the place,
   Where I'm certain of heading the fox.

But though I can beat both fox, huntsman and hound,
   And leave them behind me like winking ;
At the Fishmongers' Board I don't dare to be found ;
   For I know they can beat me at drinking !

Well, well, just keep steady whatever you do,
   Shrink the sherry and stick to the soup ;
And then each will be able to ride and run through
   In good time for the Major's who-hoop !

Such is a brief sketch of George Moore's life at Whitehall. But before we conclude, we must describe an incident connected with the life of his favourite dog Jack. This was a thoroughbred bull-dog, much under-hung; and, though rather ferocious-looking, as gentle as a kitten to those whom he knew. Jack's devotion to his master was quite touching. Mrs. Moore once saw him get up a wall quite eighteen feet high, by scratch-ing up with his paws and hanging on to the projecting pieces of stone with his teeth, in order to get to his master, who was overlooking some building on the other side. But though kind to those about him, he was suspicious of strangers, and savage to other dogs that came about the place; and many were the serious adventures that took place in consequence. Jack never began the fight, but if another dog growled at him, or insulted him, he gave no quarter. Mr. Moore had been two or three times bitten in trying to separate the dogs, but as he really loved Jack, he gave him, as was his wont, "one more chance."

At length the last chance came. One day, some ladies called at Whitehall bringing a little mongrel terrier with them. The dog went into the yard, and occupied itself with barking and snarling at Jack, beyond the length of his chain. Jack was of course very much provoked, but he was tied and could do nothing at that time. He could only show his feelings by suppressed growls. In the afternoon, Jack was led to go out with his master. He first went to the lady door to make his greetings. Then he went to the bowling-green to find out the strange aggressor. He found him, and at once pinned the mongrel by the throat. No one could separate Jack from the dog. At last his master was sent for, and, with great effort, he parted them by force. He had to strike the dogs to make them loosen their hold, and Jack was terribly hurt.   Yet he crawled to lick his master's feet. George Moore went into the house quite unmanned.   He shed bitter tears over his faithful dog, and could not sleep that night.

But the order was given that he must be shot.   It was carried out next day.   He was buried, and a stone was put over his grave, with the inscription, "Faithful Jack!"

CHAPTER XXIII.

GOOD WORKS DONE IN SECRET

GEORGE MOORE had a great idea of duty. "If I have one thing," he says in his diary, "it is an imperative sense of duty." He was always possessed with the full sense of "doing his duty." He wished to do it; and he prayed to God to help him to do it. But what duty? People have so many notions about duty. They vary according to their virtue, morality, and religion.

There is a worldly-wise duty—the duty of being respectable; to work diligently all the week and go to church on Sundays; or to enjoy the self-satisfaction of a comfortable home and mix in what is called "the best society." Such is the morality on which many respectable people fatten and flourish.

This was not, however, George Moore's idea of duty. First, he knew his duty to God; but, outside of that, or rather part of that, he knew his duty to man. His prosperity in life was not due to himself. He could not enjoy all his possessions himself. There were numerous others to participate them with him. There were the hordes of neglected poor—the orphans, the sick, the destitute. Could he not help them; could he not do something to lighten their load; could he not introduce them to the light of civilisation; if not to the better light of Christianity itself? Surely this was a larger creed and a loftier code of duty than that of modern worldly-wise respectability!

In the first place, let us see what he did with those immediately about him. No man could be a more loving and affectionate husband; though this is by no means an uncommon thing. We have, however, omitted numberless entries in his diary, showing that his happiest days were those which he spent in the company of his wife. Many men may also treat their servants as well as he did; though that is perhaps still less common. He treated them as members of the same family. The bond which united them was not money-wages, but sympathy. "Sympathy," he once said, "is a word that should be written in letters of gold. It is the best word in the English language. It *must* be good for those who are about us to see that others sympathize with them."

Servants are too often treated as necessary evils. They have to bear all sorts of caprices and querulousnesses. If a kindness is vouchsafed, it is done as if from a superior to an inferior being; and servility is expected in return. It is forgotten that servants have such possessions as feelings, affections, sympathies. And yet they have within their power the thousand little atoms of which the sum of domestic happiness is composed. They are about us in health and sickness; in festivity and sorrow; ministering to our wants, our comforts, and our luxuries.

George Moore always remembered how much the well-being of his family depended upon those who lived under his roof. "Of this I am well assured," he says in his diary, "that a good master and mistress will seldom be afflicted by bad servants. The ruled are generally what the ruler makes them. Woe unto thee, oh my house, when thy master and mistress forget their duty, and when those who rule in thee care not for those who serve!"

The husband, however, cannot rule a house by himself. He must be effectually and cordially supported by his wife. And this was the case in George Moore's house. Both treated their servants affectionately, and were served honestly and faithfully. Mrs. Moore, however, gives the chief honour to her husband. "The whole household," she says, "felt his influence. Faithful service was always liberally acknowledged. All seemed to vie with one another to please him; though he always would be obeyed implicitly. Two out of three of the principal household servants, whose names he so liberally mentioned in his will, had been with him for upwards of twenty-five years."

Nor was he less kind and sympathetic with the young men and women who lived at the warehouse in Bow Churchyard. He treated them as if they belonged to the same family with himself. He often went down to meet them at family worship in the mornings. He provided religious instruction for them. He founded libraries and news-room for them. He got some of the most distinguished and influential men of the day to lecture to them. All these arrangements were made by himself, though with the consent of his partners. The following memorandum is found amongst his papers, pinned to a printed notice of the lectures, classes, mutual improvement meetings, and Bible classes carried on at Bow Churchyard, in 1874:—

"I have always felt a great interest in the souls of the people I employ. I have tried for many years to forward the objects contained in the inclosed programme. I have never been satisfied that I did my duty, though I must honestly say that I have tried to do it. I cannot get so many to prayers in the morning, or to the Bible class as I could wish. We have no drunkenness in

the house, and I believe a better conducted number of
young people does not exist in the City.

"I see every one we engage, and I specially ask them
to come to prayers, and to go regularly to church or
chapel. I give them a good book, with the rules of the
house, and a guinea card for admission to the Young
Men's Christian Association in Aldersgate Street.

"I find that many of our married men with large
families and comparatively small salaries had borrowed
money of the firm, which was a clog about their necks.
I have paid them all off out of my own pocket, with a
remonstrance not to get into debt again."

The classes, lectures, and societies, established at
Bow Churchyard proved of great use to the young men.
They furnished them with sound instruction, and gave
them a high object in life. They tended to make them
members of one family. They united them in morning
and evening prayer. Young men risen from the ranks conducted the Bible classes and devotional meetings. This
led some of them to turn their thoughts to the ministry.
Six of them became clergymen of the Church of England ; four became Dissenting ministers ; and two went
abroad as Missionaries to the heathen.

We find George Moore helping them to higher positions. Some he assisted to go to St. Bees, and others
to Cambridge. It is Southey, we believe, who says that
we know a man's character better by the letters which
his friends address to him than by those which he himself pens. If this be so, George Moore must have been
the benefactor of thousands. It would be impossible to
give a tithe of the private letters which he received from
young men whom he helped with his bounty, especially
those whom he helped while in poverty, or when at
college. It would be unwise to publish these letters,
because they are from men who are now holding high
positions in society.

We may, however, give one or two extracts. One clergyman says, "I owe a great deal to you, and am proud to acknowledge that my present position is entirely owing to what you have done for me in the past." Another, whom Mr. Moore had liberally helped while at St. Bees, and who had become a curate at Preston, says, " Thanks to you that I am now in the ministry. I trust that my conduct will be such that you shall have no reason to regret having extended your kindness and interested yourself in my behalf."

Another student, who had obtained Mr. Moore's help through the instrumentality of the Bishop of Carlisle, writes as follows :—" I beg to acknowledge with deep gratitude your very kind liberality to me, by which I am spared the necessity of continuing in my secular employment, while preparing for ordination at Christmas next. . . . . Being an entire stranger to you, I am the more touched by this act of disinterested kindness." One more extract. A student at Queen's College, Oxford, thus writes :—" Allow me to return you my warmest thanks for the cheque which you so kindly sent me this morning. I am also exceedingly obliged to you for having secured the Exhibition for me. For such extreme kindness I shall always cherish a most grateful recollection. With all this valuable help I feel stimulated to pursue my studies with increased vigour." This gentleman is now a much-esteemed rector of a parish.

It may be added, that Mr. R. H. Allpress, who first obtained George Moore's scholarship at the Commercial Travellers' School, was afterwards further educated at the City of London School, where he gained the Saddlers' Guild scholarship for mathematics. " Without your munificent gift," said Mr. Allpress to Mr. Moore, " I should never have gained the scholarship, and consequently I should have had no chance of enjoying the advantage of a university education, to which I am now looking forward."

George Moore was by no means indiscriminate in his help. The Rev. W. M. Gunson, M.A. Cambridge, informs us that he was liberal in helping young men to pass through the regular university course. "At the time of his death, I know that he was helping two present students of this university; and though I was not his almoner, he never sent the money without ascertaining through me that they were conducting themselves well, and living economically, which was a *sine quâ non* of his helping them. The very last letter I received from him concerned these two youths, about a week before the accident which removed him. This was one form of his beneficence which, I believe, is very little known."

Besides the influence which Mr. Moore exercised upon those who were students at the universities for the ministry, it was equally great upon those who entered from his house upon the practical business of life. After being trained in the firm they went out into the world to set up for themselves. They carried with them the power for good which they had received while under the instruction provided for them by their old master. They carried with them the example he had set before them. They became centres of influence, from which good seeds and kindly acts extended far and wide. One of them, writing from Edinburgh, says:—" In my very small circle and with my limited means, I try to emulate your example. I had rather be a second George Moore than a Royal Duke!"

He was never weary of helping young men. He often thought of the hard times he encountered when he first came to London; and he determined, so far as he could, to make things somewhat better for those who followed him. Crowds of young men visited him, for situations, for advice, for help of various kinds. "It is remarkable," he says, in one of his memoranda, "the number of Cumberland young men who call upon me every day. I certainly engage a great many, and those I cannot engage I try to get situations for. To-day one called who had served his apprenticeship at Wigton. He said that he had been in London a month, and must return next week, as his money was nearly done. Then he burst into tears. I sent him up to get his dinner. When he came down I gave him a letter to a house that might possibly engage him. I cheered him up by promising him a dinner every day until I succeeded. Another, from Penrith, has just come in, under similar circumstances!" Then he proceeds to set forth his own difficulties when he first came to London—his rebuffs, his trials, and his troubles, until he was engaged at Grafton House.

He obtained situations for hundreds of young men about London. He wrote to the heads of firms, or he himself went about asking situations for them. Sometimes he obtained situations with drapers, or grocers, or general warehousemen. When he failed he would apply at the Railway Clearing-house; and there he frequently succeeded. Nine young men are there at present who obtained their situations through him. One of them writing to Mrs. Moore, says, "Most of us, especially myself, owe our position, and can almost date the beginning of our real lives from the time when his influence and kindness placed us in the situations we now hold. . . . . We feel assured that no greater monument can exist to perpetuate his memory, and keep his name in lively remembrance among us, than Christ's Church, Somers Town, upon which we can daily look as we sit at our desks."

Nor did he lose sight of the men whom he had befriended. He invited them to his house in Kensington

Palace Gardens, and sometimes to Bow Churchyard, when he had much pleasant talk with them and gave them much good advice. All this tended to uphold them in life. They always felt that they had a friend in him willing to help them if needful. These evenings at Bow Churchyard must have been very agreeable. Mr. Moore generally had some distinguished speakers to address the young men. He himself often spoke. A favourite subject of his was Sympathy. On one occasion he said, " He wished particularly to impress upon them the value of time, in order to make the best possible use of it. He had no doubt that all of them might employ their leisure time more profitably than they did at present, and he admitted that this applied to himself as well as to others. He repudiated the notion that the employer, as such, was less beholden to the employed than they were to him. They were all made of one flesh and blood, and there ought to be a proper sympathy between employers and employed. If he could not feel that there was sympathy, he would not care to carry on business at all. There might be some in the City of London who did not feel that sympathy for those in their employ, but for all such a day of reckoning would be sure to come, when they would be sorry that they had not done their duty in the position in life in which it had pleased God to place them."

Although Mr. Moore was strict in business, he was always merciful. He required punctuality, accuracy, and diligence. These he thought he had a right to ask for. Of course there were failures, as there must be while men are human. But when failures occurred he was always ready to forgive. He was merciful and kind to the erring, the foolish, and even the dishonest. In two cases of large defalcations on the part of local managers, he interfered to prevent prosecution,—appearing to think only of the wives and children whom the defaulters had left destitute. The debtors of the firm often received from him that merciful consideration which enabled them to look up again in hope, and to start afresh in the hard race of life.

The recollection of his own early struggles made him very compassionate towards others. The confidence of himself and his partners was often abused; but in dealing with such cases he did not forget the painful and heartrending scenes of misery and ruin which he had seen while visiting the prisons of London. *One more opportunity!* was the decision he generally arrived at. *Give him another chance!* And in this way he saved many an erring soul from ruin.

"I feel very grateful indeed," said one person, "for the opportunity you have so kindly afforded me, of doing what I can to regain your confidence and esteem, which my recent conduct must have forfeited. I have, sir, well considered the step I now take—and though it be at your request that I take it, permit me to say that I had before resolved upon my present course. Unhappy experience has proved to me the truth of the preacher's words—'Wine is a mocker; strong drink is a delusion and a snare.' Under its influence I committed acts for which I now feel inexpressibly ashamed—acts which, but for your considerate kindness in permitting me to remain in your employment, might have ruined my prospects for life, and left a stain upon my character, which I might never have washed away. Your behaviour to me has left a deep impression on my mind, which I hope I may never outlive. These, sir, are the considerations which induce me to declare, that from this time, it is my firm intention to abstain from all intoxicating drink whatever, and may God approve and support me in my resolution."

The facts of the case were, that this young man had come from a far-off county; that, probably unaccus-

tomed to indulgence, he had taken too much drink ;
and that, in this state, he went into the streets, got into
a row, and struck a policeman. He was seized and
taken to prison. Next day he was brought before the
magistrate, and sentenced to a fortnight's imprisonment.
The notoriety given to the circumstance by the public
papers, led the firm very justly to take a serious view of
the matter. They were at first disposed to dismiss the
young man from their employment. But after a few
days, George Moore interceded. "Give him one more
opportunity !" It was granted, and hence the preceding
letter. The young man became a thorough abstainer,
and fully justified the confidence reposed in him by his
employers.

One of the greatest proofs of consideration he could
give to his young men, was to invite them to his house
at Whitehall. Sometimes he had from thirty to forty
young men visiting him during the holiday season. If
they were taken ill, he sometimes sent them down to
Cumberland, to their own homes, for a change of air.
One such visit we may mention, in the words of the
writer, who is now far away, in Dubuque County, Iowa.
After stating that no biography, however well written,
can describe the *living* George Moore, he goes on to
say : "It might almost be said that he lived two lives—
the business life and the private life. Mr. Moore at
Bow Churchyard and George Moore at Whitehall were
two separate characters. Few of the many who received
his ever-hearty welcome, and the firm, manly grip of his
hand at Whitehall, knew anything about the king he
was at his place of business—how all wills bowed to his,
what a change his presence wrought, from the basement
to the garret overlooking Bow-bells. Speaking-tubes
conveyed the magic word "George Moore" throughout
the house. Like magic, too, the house was put in order.
There was a shaking amongst the dry bones. The

loose joints rattled into their place. The sleepers awoke. Smart young men looked even smarter; and all the machinery worked noiselessly and well.

"When George Moore came round, he could scan a department at a glance. No flaw could possibly escape his never-resting eye. He was quick and decisive in action as in word. Who ever saw him sit still or stand still for a moment? His chair had a pivot, so that body and mind could swing round to the subject at once. He spoke quickly and wrote quickly. He might be said to be impulsive in his utterances, yet he seldom failed to hit the mark. Nothing like an impossibility ever dawned upon him. I remember how furious he used to be at any one who said he 'couldn't do it!' 'Couldn't,' he said, 'What d'ye mean, man? I don't know what ye mean. There's no such word. It isn't in the dictionary. Go, and do it at once!' He could brook no defeat.

"An incident will illustrate this decisive trait in his character. I had been sometime suffering from an ailment, and finally had to undergo a painful operation. Unthinkingly, I omitted to tell Mr. Moore. I left the firm, and took lodgings near the surgeon's house. About a week or so after the operation, and while I was just able to walk, a rap, almost like a policeman's, rang through the house. The door was banged open, and a quick firm step mounted the stairs, almost frightening my good old nurse out of her senses. In stepped George Moore! 'What's happened? What are you doing here? Why didn't you tell me?' 'Thank you, sir, the doctors have ordered me not to move for at least a fortnight, not to eat any meat, and to be perfectly still.' I told him this. Do you think it bothered him? Not a bit. His mind was made up. 'Doctors' orders? Fiddle-de-dee. Doctors know nothing. Get back to Auld Cummerland, my lad, and come to me at Whitehall!' That night, I dined off beefsteak, and next night I was speeding on my way home at George Moore's expense, in a carriage labelled 'Engaged,' with soft cushions and every comfort that could enable me to rest during my three hundred miles journey.

"That, sir, was the *living* George Moore, with a will of his own and a heart of gold; and faint will all efforts be to re-copy him. His hospitality at home was unbounded. That motto at Whitehall was no sham. Every one looked WELCOME into your face—servants, as well as master and mistress.

"Whilst at home for my holidays, I often went to see him. One morning, he had been very busy, and I was helping him. As we walked from the dining-room across the hall, there was an inquiry at the outside door. Mr. Moore went forward. 'Well, my friend (his usual greeting to rich or poor) what is it?' The man was long in coming to the point; and I knew by George Moore's nervous twitching of his fingers and quick glancing of his eyes, that he did not know much of anything the man said. Suddenly snatching the man's arm, he pulled him inside. 'Newbold! Newbold!' he shouted. His trusty butler was at once at his side. 'Give this man something to eat and drink!' Thus saying he passed the man on to Newbold. With a quaint, dry smile, Newbold took a firm grip of his arm, and, notwithstanding several attempts at remonstrance, marched him off to the pantry. The whole scene was so ludicrous, and yet so full of meaning, that I shall never forget it. The man was not a beggar. Who he was, George Moore couldn't quite make out. But he was a man evidently in want. Newbold took up the cue of his master, and supplied his wants. And the man went away from Whitehall with the impression that he

had at all events *seen* George Moore, and enjoyed his
hospitality.

"Years ago, on the first day of grouse-shooting, I
dined amongst a rather motley crew of Bishops, M.P.'s,
great city financiers, and poor clerks like myself;
for George Moore was no respecter of persons. He
had procured, at no small trouble, a single brace of
grouse. He said, 'Here's some grouse, and I want
everybody to have a taste of it.' There were at least
thirty of us. Mrs. Moore's gravity couldn't stand
that. But he was equal to the occasion. To use a
Yankee phrase, he never backed out. We all either
tasted grouse or stuffing.

"Mrs. Moore poked a good deal of fun at him for
speaking so loudly in church, when showing a friend
to a seat; remarking that Mr. Moore couldn't whisper
if he tried. 'No, my dear,' said he, 'I cannot whisper.
I never could whisper. I hate whispering. It isn't
honest.' Unlike most men, when speaking in public,
he had the happy knack of giving over when he had
done. He spoke concisely and to the point; and his
speech very often ended with 'Well, my friends, I
believe that's all;' or 'I think I'm done.'"

Mr. Moore did a great deal in the course of his life to
help poor clergymen. Applications came to him from
all parts of the country,—from Ireland as well as
England. He was a sort of universal referee when a
clergyman was in want. He had correspondents all
over the country. Sometimes he received his recommendations from a neighbouring clergyman. Then he
proceeded to make inquiry; and if found necessary, he
sent his help liberally. One clergyman in Derbyshire,
who had just secureed a curacy at £100 a year, had
nothing left after meeting the expenses of his ordination.
He wrote to George Moore, saying that he had nothing
to subsist upon until his first quarter's salary was due,

On receiving Mr. Moore's help by return of post, he said, "I lack words adequately to express my thankfulness for your great kindness." Another clergyman in Wiltshire, who had been injured by a railway accident, and was struggling with many difficulties, in maintaining himself, his wife, and seven children, had his case brought under the notice of Mr. Moore, who sent him some help through a friend. The clergyman's answer was—"I am indeed thankful to the anonymous donor of £10 for my private use, and £10 for the education of my children. Amidst the many cares, perplexities, and pressing needs of our children and home, these opportune gifts are to us a gleam of sunshine at this season, and they fill us with gratitude to a gracious God who in His providence disposes the hearts of his people to such deeds of mercy."

Letters such as these might be multiplied to any extent, but there is one letter which must be given, as it contains a story in itself:—"Your very great and opportune kindness has been of much service to me. My daughter has thereby been sent to Casterton Clergy Daughters' School. Without it she could not have been sent. My whole income has been derived for several years from my stipend as curate, and it has never been more than £125 a year; and were it not for the kindness of the people in making me a presentation, I could not have met the demands which a family of seven children entail. The eldest is fourteen years old, and she is the one you have kindly assisted in educating. *Yours* is the only kindness I have *sought*. I did so for two reasons. First, because of your very great bountifulness and benevolence towards every good work; and secondly, because of my very pressing need. Through the kindness of Mr. H——, your aid was readily granted, and the debt of gratitude which is due can never be fully repaid.

"As you desire it, and as your great kindness demands it, I will briefly state the reason for my present circumstances. Sixteen years ago, I commenced life on my own account, by purchasing a good business in a thriving place. I was most successful, and everything prospered with me. But it pleased God in His mercy, to bring me to a knowledge of myself as a lost sinner; and afterwards by His good Spirit to find pardon and peace in a crucified Saviour. This led me to devote myself to His work as a Sunday-school teacher, and to do everything I could do to serve Him. I was deeply impressed with the great need there was in our Church of truly evangelical ministers; and as my heart burned with gratitude and love to God for His great mercies to myself, I determined to enter the ministry, and devote myself wholly to His service.

"The step caused me a great sacrifice. My business was worth more at that time than any living I could ever hope to have in the Church. The struggle was great, and at last I sold everything, and went to college. There I was very successful, and came out first in my term. Good Bishop Waldegrave encouraged me to come into his diocese, and by him I was ordained to the curacy of ——. Had his life been spared, I should not now have needed help. God has owned and blessed my labours; and though I have had at times much anxiety respecting the education of my family, I have not regretted the step I have taken.

"The money I had saved in business I expected would have enabled me, together with my stipend, to meet the wants of my family. But part of it has been lost, and the rest I have been compelled to use. My father-in-law was so indignant at my conduct that I have not even had a letter from him since I gave up business. My own father is not able to do much.

The ages of my children will render them dependent upon me for some time. You will think my family large and my income inadequately small to meet their every want. But I have much to be grateful for, as they are healthy and intelligent. For all your kindness accept my best and warmest thanks."

At Christmas time, George Moore remembered the poor clergymen of Cumberland and Westmoreland. Many of them were very poor. They had to dress like gentlemen, for they *were* gentlemen. They were also scholars. Many of them had large families, and most of them had small stipends. Their average pay did not amount to the wages of iron-puddlers, engine-drivers, or mechanics. George Moore had a list made out every year, a few days before Christmas. His first almoner was the Hon. S. Waldegrave, while Bishop of Carlisle, who sent cheques of £5 or £10, according to the needs of the recipients, through Messrs. Williams, Deacon, and Co. His next almoner was Archdeacon Cooper, of Kendal. And lastly he sent the cheques through Mr. Matthieson, of Fuller, Banbury, and Co., Lombard Street. They were sent as from a " Lover of Evangelical Truth." George Moore's name was never mentioned. How much these Christmas gifts rejoiced the hearts of the poor clergymen and their families, may be understood from the following extracts from their letters of acknowledgment :—

One said—" Please return my very sincere thanks to the giver. It will enable me to do much which I otherwise could not do. At present there is a large influx of labourers into my parish. They are employed on the Settle and Carlisle Railway. I am endeavouring to do all that I can for these people. But schools for the children, cases of distress, supplies of books, &c., require much more than I am able to do out of my small living, which is not more than £40 per annum net. Such presents therefore help me much in carrying on this work, and especially at this season of the year."

Another says—"I never stood in more need of help than now, owing to the loss I have suffered this year through a solicitor in Carlisle. I am now in my 81st year, and am obliged to have two curates in my large parish, seven miles by four. We have four full services every Lord's Day in three places of worship; so that such kind gifts are very acceptable. May God bless the kind donor."

Some thanked their unknown benefactor for helping them to pay their Christmas bills and their doctor's fees. "This is indeed a most opportune gift, as it finds me in very straitened circumstances, mainly owing to my poor wife's protracted illness." One says, it "helps to remove anxious care at this season of Christmas for those who are already under sorrow." A joyful father says, "I accept it as a token that our little one, born on New Year's Day, will be provided for by our Heavenly Father." Another vicar says, "If I am not permitted to know who my kind benefactor is, please return my sincere thanks. *Philippians* iv. 11—14."

One says, "The contribution was a mercy laid at my door. I have need to be thankful for it. I pray, too, that the giver may have the blessing of 'the liberal soul.'" Another—"It has come to me at a time of much anxiety, as I have a large family, and my aged and infirm mother is entirely dependent on me. My wife also has been sick and under medical treatment during the whole of the past year."

One self-denying man said, "Although I have need, yet there are poorer clergymen in the neighbourhood than I am: give it to them!" Another said, "I am not above receiving this kindness, but there are many curates with large families much poorer than myself.

Therefore I will readily, with the consent of the kind donor, hand over the gift elsewhere."

These Christmas gifts were repeated during so many years that those who had been accustomed to receive them looked out for their arrival by the Christmas post. One who was overlooked says—"I was taught a bad habit in expecting to receive something every Christmas Day, when I had no right whatever to receive it. It was therefore with blank looks that my poor wife met me on my return from the morning service on Christmas Day with the words, 'No blue letter with a big red seal for you to-day!' and we sat down to our Christmas dinner with less gladsome hearts than usual." We believe that it was afterwards made "all right" with this deserving clergyman.

Nor did Mr. Moore forget the City Missionaries, with whom he had been so intimately associated for so many years. He sent each of them a bright new sovereign on Christmas Day, and they were four hundred and eighty in all. He sent two-and-a-half sovereigns each to twenty-five missionaries in Cumberland. He accompanied his gifts with a good book. He was perpetually giving books. He sometimes had as many books as would stock a bookseller's shop. He gave away about 2,500 of the Rev. J. C. Ryle's *Expositions of the Gospels.* He sent books to all the city and county town missionaries. He sent them to missionary stations abroad, and amongst others to Sierra Leone.[1] He circulated extensively *M'Cheyne's Memoir and Remains*, Dr. Bonar's *Way of Peace*, and Winslow's *Ministry of Home.*

---

[1] We find among the Whitehall papers a letter dated "Freetown, Sierra Leone, October 13th, 1875." The writer, W. J. Leigh, says, "I beg to return you my warmest thanks for the books you have been pleased to present to myself and all the local preachers of the Freetown circuit, through Mr. Walmsley. The books were distributed by him on the 11th instant at 7 P.M., when a special preachers' meeting was convened. The chapel where we met was crowded to excess. Before the distribution of

Amongst Mr. Moore's papers we find a letter from Mr. J. Robinson, one of the secretaries of the City Mission Society, thanking him for his gift of a thousand pounds for the Disabled Missionary Fund. "May I express," says Mr. Robinson, " my personal gratitude for this donation. It cheers my esteemed brethren in their labours to have some assurance that in old age and infirmity they will not be left destitute."

Mr. Moore, in conjunction with Mr. Stockdale, made a similar arrangement for the benefit of the missionaries in their native county. The following is from George Moore's diary, 26th February, 1875 :—"Gave John Martin instructions to press on a deed for the disabled Cumberland missionaries. Stockdale and I have settled three thousand on them."

George Moore's Christmases in London were full of work. "When thou makest a feast, call together the poor." He gave teas and suppers to all sorts of people. Sometimes to the poor children in Whitechapel ; sometimes to the stone-breakers at Kensington workhouse ; sometimes to poor exiles from France and Germany. One Christmas he says : " The frost has lasted for three weeks. The distress is very great amongst the poor at Kensington. Newbold (the butler) is hard at work distributing coals, bread, meat, and money." But his greatest pleasure was in spending Christmas at Field Lane Ragged School. For some years past, on Christmas Eve the Ragged School boys with their band came to serenade him at his house in Kensington Palace Gardens. But the great event was the dinner of next day. On those occasions he took part in distributing a dinner of roast beef and plum-pudding. George Moore

the book, Mr. Wahn ley gave an address relative to the duties of the good preacher, and also expressed your kind feeling to us. Such a ?? ?? we shall not soon forget. I am sure the books will be read by the ?? of our preacher, and be the means of doing much good. I am very ?? ??ful for the great kindness you have shown to our race."

was amongst the carvers, and Mrs. Moore, with many other ladies, helped to wait on the guests.

Nor were those nearer home neglected. At the house in Bow Churchyard, he gave a fine Cumberland ham to every married man in the establishment. They were upwards of two hundred in number. He also gave a book, of a religious tendency, to the seven or eight hundred employés of the firm. During the last year of his life he sent out seventeen thousand *British Workman's Almanacs* to all parts of the kingdom.

The first Christmas and the last which Mr. Moore spent in Cumberland since his boyhood was in December, 1875. He had been busily engaged in London, and went down to his country home for rest. He reached Whitehall exhausted and worn out, but "grateful to God for all His mercies." Two days after he says, "The reaction has come. I am done up, and laid in bed, sadly out of sorts. I am glad I have got back to my dearest wife; she watches over me like an angel."

The fresh country air revived him. He was soon able to go out, and attend the Way Warden Meeting at Wigton. The farmers came to pay their rent at Whitehall and have their rent-dinner with him. After a visit to Sir Wilfrid Lawson and his lady at Brayton Hall, he returned to spend a quiet Christmas Eve with his dear wife. He was very anxious that Christmas Day should be kept like "a real old one." All his nearest relations, mostly in humble life, were invited to be present.

After the Christmas dinner was over, the party sat round the hall fire, talking over the old Christmases. They looked back to the buoyant times of their youth, and reflected upon the past. After all, they said, there are no Christmases like the old ones. George Moore sprang up in his quick way, and stood in front of the fire. "Yes," he said, "we all cling to the old customs. There are no mince-pies like those I had when I was a boy! There are no old folks' nights, nor young folks' nights. Yes, we are getting too old for that. But the children can now get a good education. Their souls are cared for. That is the best of all things."

On the last night of the year Mrs. Moore had a Christmas-tree ; it was the first ever seen at Allhallows. There were a hundred and seventy-five visitors that night, consisting of the guests in the house, the neighbours, the labourers, their children, and the servants. After every one had got their Christmas gift, there were games and dances for them in the hall. George Moore seemed greatly to enjoy it. The amusements were finished up with the favourite country dance, Sir Roger de Coverley, in which every one took part.

George Moore winds up his diary for the year 1875 with the words : " Where shall I be this day next year ? I hope I shall be better prepared to die."

Alas ! he was dead before next Christmas arrived.

CHAPTER XXIV.

THE END OF GEORGE MOORE'S LIFE.

GEORGE MOORE had now reached his seventieth year. He had seen much of the world's chances and changes. He had suffered his share of the world's troubles and sorrows. He had seen his friends depart one by one. He felt that the time was fast coming when he too must die. The thought seemed to be always in his mind. " Let me be ready, ready!" he often said.

One of his friends in Scotland, whom he had never seen since he was a boy at Flint, Ray, and Company's, but with whom he had kept up a correspondence, says in a recent letter :—" Strange to say, in the last note I had from him, he said he was preparing for the great change that awaits us all. I do not infer from this that he had any premonitory notices of death, but having just attained to the period of life allotted to poor humanity, he must certainly have felt that his time was coming next,—or next."

His friend Richard Porter, with whom he had climbed the hill of perseverance, had already died. Robert Hanbury, who had been associated with him in many works of benevolence, had died suddenly. "I loved him," says George Moore, "for his simple faith." His intimate friend, Mr. Howard of Greystoke, had also departed. In one of Mr. Moore's memoranda he says : " The death of my most valued friend, Mr. Howard of Greystoke Castle, has cast a great gloom over my spirits. I spent part of seventeen summer holidays there. He took me up, and introduced me thirty-five years ago, when I was not among the gentry of Cumberland. He always behaved to me like a true friend. He was a man of rare common sense and discrimination, and I benefited much by his advice and counsel. He took upon himself the entire superintendence of the rebuilding of Whitehall." George Moore's attachment to Mr. Howard in some respects altered his life. It brought him into contact with men of a different kind and of a higher culture than those whom he had been accustomed to meet. This broadened his views and enlarged his life.

Another friend and hero departed. General Sir Hope Grant was a man after George Moore's own heart. There was the same earnestness and strength of purpose alike in both ; and this drew them together in mutual friendship. Sir Hope and Lady Grant had paid a visit to Whitehall in the autumn of 1874. He had brought with him his violoncello, and drawn forth the echoes of the old Hall with his sweetest music. In October, Sir Hope had been able to walk without fatigue over the Caldbeck Fells, and through heavy turnip field, for five or six hours a day ; but before the early springtime came the great warrior had laid him down to die. George Moore says in his diary : " We have lost one of our most valued friends, Sir Hope Grant. I never had a more manly, sincere Christian man in Cumberland home. He was the sort of man I feel God knows who is to be next. I am losing all my friends. May I be as well prepared for death as our dear friend Sir Hope Grant was." [1]

But death was coming still nearer him. In 1874 his partner, Mr. Copestake, was taken away, and in 1875 Mr. Osborne. " I shall never forget," says Mrs. Moore, "the shock he received when the sad news of Mr. Copestake's sudden death was brought to him by William Osborne on horseback." They had been faithful partners for about forty-four years. There never had been a wrong word between them during all that time. George Moore had never known a man like his partner for amiability, modesty, patience, kindness, and common sense.

Mr. Moore repeatedly alludes to his partner in his diary. He said, on the day of his death, " Indeed, I am stunned. I feel it most deeply. I feel as if I had lost my right arm ; and a severe wrench it has been. I never knew a man like him ; and yet he always kept in the shade." On the day of the funeral he says, " I have this day followed to the grave one of the best

---

[1] Some beautiful lines appeared in *Punch* at the date of Sir Hope Grant's death. We quote a few stanzas :—

> " So frequent falls the heavy hand of Death,
>   Time fails for wreathing each fresh funeral crown ;
> Men, whose own hair is gray, read with drawn breath
>   Of loved and honoured suddenly struck down.

> " O well for England that when living names
>   Pass to the death-roll in her Book of Gold,
> 'Tis rare that search finds stain to soil their fames,
>   Proudly in that proud fellowship enrolled.

> .   .   .   .

> " One whose pure life had no need to divide
>   The Christian and the Captain—well-content
> To pray with his own soldiers side by side ;
>   Yet boy for harmless sport and merriment.

> " Who lived full in the rude camp's watchful eye
>   Unblamed, beloved, respected ; who lay down
> To well-earned rest, as one for whom to die
>   Is humbly to exchange life's cross for crown."

and most aimable of men. I was his partner since I
was twenty-four years of age."

One of the present partners informs us that on the
death of Mr. Copestake the whole interest of Bow
Churchyard fell to George Moore. He had the power
of appropriating the profits of the business, subject
of course to the adjustment of the various capital
charges.

The increased value of the freeholds also fell to him.
He alludes to this in his diary. "We finally finished
our partnership to-day, I hope to the satisfaction of all.
I have volunteered to give up all Mr. Copestake's shares
to my partners. I have also given the new firm about
£45,000, the increased value of the freeholds which fell
to me at Mr. Copestake's death." George Moore was
evidently engaged in making up his own accounts.

His most intimate friend next died—George Stockdale, of the Stock Exchange. Mr. Stockdale was a
Cumberland man. He had been a commercial traveller
in the early part of his life; hence his connection with
the Commercial Travellers' Schools. Mrs. Moore says,
"Mr. Stockdale was, in some ways, my husband's most
intimate friend. Their friendship dates very far back,—
when George was the boy traveller for Fisher's. They
first met at a town in Lincolnshire, when Stockdale saw
the 'Napoleon of Watling Street,' as they used to call
the young traveller. George Moore was in a back
room, surrounded by young men from the drapers'
shops, helping him to pack up his goods. Stockdale
was struck with his energy and cheerfulness, and from
that moment he never lost sight of him. They would
appoint a place to meet some six months or even twelve
months hence; and they never once missed their meeting. Then George became a partner with Groucock
and Copestake, and Stockdale entered the Stock
Exchange.

"Mr. Stockdale always reminded me of Boswell with Johnson; for he worshipped my husband, and could never see anything but perfection in all that he said and did,—except in the matter of politics. Stockdale was a Conservative, while George was a Liberal; and yet, amidst their stirring discussions of the times, the difference never severed their friendship. In everything else he followed my husband as closely as possible. He was never happy when long separated from him. He was with us for weeks together in Cumberland, and he called upon us two or three nights every week when in London. He was with us every Saturday night. There was a special chair in the library allotted for him. He went to every public meeting where George intended to be present. He seemed to follow him like a shadow. I have heard people who knew of their friendship say—'There's Stockdale: George Moore cannot be far off.'

"George Stockdale was one of the first who joined the little band who met at Kensington Palace Gardens on Monday evenings for the Bible readings; and he attributed his interest in higher things to George's influence. So far as his means allowed, he helped in all the things that George took an interest in. He did very much for the Commercial Travellers' Schools, of which he was the chairman. He used often to say to me, 'Do get your husband to tell me what he wants to get done, and I will try to get it done.'

"The illness of such a friend could not fail to be an anxiety. In the spring of 1875 his health began to fail. My husband had joined the committee who received Moody and Sankey on their religious mission. He took the greatest interest in their work, and from the first believed in its sincerity and success. His friend insisted on going to one of their first meetings at Exeter Hall. The crowd and heat were terrible, and Mr. Stockdale increased the severe cold from which he was suffering at the time. He came to us, however, on the following Saturday as usual ; when we were shocked at his appearance. We persuaded him to go home and send for the doctor. He did so, but his life could not be saved. He sent for us only three days after, to take leave of us both. His last words were, 'I want to thank you for having made my life so happy.'"

A day or two after his death George Moore thus described him—"There are many who knew something of his character. He always took the best view of every one's conduct, and tried to attribute the purest motives to the actions of others. Through all the years of the very closest intimacy, I have never heard him say an unkind word of any one, or do anything which one would have had him do otherwise. His hand and heart were always open and ready. He was a bright example for the rising generation ; for he won a really good position entirely by his own good conduct, and the habits of self-denial and self-restraint which were early learnt in his Cumberland home, and which he afterwards carefully practised."

These deaths of his old friends could not but affect George Moore. They did not alarm him, for he was ready to die. He begins his diary of 1876 with the following entry :—"It may be that I have entered on the last year of my mortal career. If so, what have I to rescue me when stripped of all that I can now call my own ? I do believe that Jesus will go with me through the dark valley, and that I shall have abundant entrance into the presence of God."

On the following day he adds: " I have felt this New Year's entrance with more reverence and awe than I ever did before." The opening of the New Year had always affected him, but this year more than any other. He had never written any entry like this before, though there are abundant records in his diary of self-examination, and one might almost say of exaggerated self-condemnation. He spoke of not serving God more, and not giving up his will to serve Him more entirely. But from this time the shadow of his speedy death begins to fall upon much that he said and did.

"The New Year," he said, "must always seem solemn. It comes with the unknown, untried future. It brings back the memory of vows broken, of promises to one's self unfulfilled. How fast time flies! Months pass away as days did formerly. I may be taken away at any moment!" He usually began the New Year as he had ended the old, by some munificent bounty. "I have started this year," he says, in 1874, "by giving a thousand pounds each, to Christ's Hospital for prizes, to the Bible Society, to the Missionary Society, and to the Carlisle Infirmary."

At the end of January, 1876, he returned to London. He occupied himself as before. He divided his time between business and beneficence. Four days after his return he informed the Committee of the Royal Free Hospital that he had bought a Convalescent Hospital at Littlehampton, partly for the use of their patients.

A little later he says, "I am much troubled about the Convalescent Hospital that I bought at Littlehampton. They will not confirm the purchase because they object to the building being used for such a purpose."

Nevertheless the house was purchased, a suitable matron was chosen, and the hospital was almost ready to be started, when the Duke of Norfolk refused to transfer the lease to the trustees of the Convalescent Hospital. Being bent on his purpose, Mr. Moore nevertheless set apart in his accounts a sum of £15,000 to

establish a convalescent hospital somewhere, if not at
Littlehampton. It remained there at the time of his
death; but the law of mortmain prevented the money
being applied to the purpose for which it was intended,
and it went to the estate. The house at Littlehampton was sold by George Moore's trustees, so
that his desires in this direction were eventually
defeated.

There was another matter that George Moore desired
to accomplish before winding up his accounts with the
world. It was to reward those who had been so long
in his service at Bow Churchyard, and who had so
zealously helped to make his fortune. "I am proceeding," he says in his diary, "to make large presents
to each of our employés that has lived above five years
in our service. I have long wished to do this, and
Mr. Copestake (the son of his old partner) willingly
joins me in giving away between thirty-five and forty
thousand pounds out of our private money, to our old
servants. They have done much, by their industry
and probity, to enable us to do so. It is one of the
best acts of our lives."

All who had been with the old firm for five years
received a donation of £50, and an additional £50 for
every other five years' service. In more than one
instance the gift reached £1,000. No distinction
was made as regards position in the firm. That had
already been acknowledged in the usual way by successive rises of salary. The reward was for fidelity
of service. Even the porters, with one or two exceptions, received the same measure of acknowledgment
as the heads of the different departments. Nearly
£40,000 were thus disbursed. This was the last act
George Moore did for those employed in the firm at
Bow Churchyard which he had loved so well.

In April, 1876, another old friend of Mr. Moore's

died—Mr. Nicholson Hodgson, M. P. for East Cumberland. As before, great pressure was brought upon George Moore to come forward and represent the county. But no! He had firmly made up his mind not to enter Parliament. He suggested however that the younger son of Mr. Howard of Greystoke should be requested to stand. Mr. Stafford Howard consented. George Moore proposed his nomination : he diligently canvassed for him ; and his satisfaction was great when his friend was returned by a considerable majority.

He returned to London, ·and dined at the Royal Academy Banquet on the 29th of April. He had often done so before, and he appreciated the honour very much. He presented to the Academy Cope's picture of " The Council," which had been painted for him. This picture had much interested him, and he was delighted when it was transferred from his friend Mr. Cope's studio to form part of the permanent collection of the Royal Academy. It represents the " Hanging Committee " in conclave, accepting and rejecting the pictures sent in for exhibition. The portraits of the leading R. A.'s are excellent. Mr. Richmond, R.A., observed of the gift, " It is pleasant all round ! "

In May 1876 the Government appointed a commission to inquire into the money-order system of the Post-office, and Mr. Moore was requested to become a member. Although his hands were full of work, he consented When the commission met he was immediately appointed chairman. He writes in his diary, " Whatever I undertake I like to do well. But what I do now costs me all that I have. I cannot take things easy. This Post-office business has cost me much labour and thought. The object is to reduce the expense and make the work equally effective."

Mr. Moore proved, as usual, an excellent chairman.

He was short, sharp, and decisive. He kept the witnesses to the point. Whenever they rambled away into unnecessary talk, he at once brought them back to the question. Much time was thus saved. Mr. Moore attended every meeting. The first was on the 4th of May, and by the 17th the committee were ready for arranging the report.

In the meantime he was occupied with many other things. He was still anxious about the success of his church at Somers Town.

On the 22nd of May he enters in his diary:—"Found eight hundred children in the schools at 'No Man's Land,' Somers Town. The church is better attended. I cannot but feel that I did a good work in building the church and schools. It has been a great anxiety to me, but I am getting my reward." And on the 23rd:—"Every day I live, I feel more and more my responsibilities. God has given me means, and I want to give them back to Him. I am pledged for £6,000 to assist Evangelical curates, and £12,000 to improve education in Cumberland."

On the 25th of May, he says: "I have not a minute to call my own." On the following day he enters these words:—"I attended a meeting at Portman Chapel at 9.30; the Fine Arts Gallery at 10.15; the Industrial Dwellings at 11; the Post-office Commission at 2; the Little Boys' Home at 4; and the City Mission at 5. Thankful to be home to my dear wife at last. We had to go out to dinner after all." Mrs. Moore says that this was to Mr. S. Morley's. "It was the *last* time we were out in London."

The strain of work began to tell upon his health. He consulted Mr. Erichsen and Sir William Gull, who ordered him at once to Vichy. This cast him down a great deal. "But," he says, "I am most grateful to God for all His mercies. When I look within I am

humbled." And again, "All is for the best: but it is
a gloomy prospect for me and my dear wife to be exiled
at Vichy for three or four weeks. But I cannot refuse
taking my doctors' joint opinion. We had our *last*
Bible-reading. A great company was present."

Before he left for Vichy he took an acitve part in
organising the Clerical Education Society. He had
often heard clergymen of different views deploring
the increasing difficulty of finding curates of religious
views. The Keble College at Oxford had opened
the way for earnest High Churchmen to study and
have a University training at less expense than
usual; and Mr. Moore desired that there should be a
similar opportunity for young men of Evangelical
views. The opinion of Canon Hoare greatly commended itself to him : "That they must be men taught
of God, and of good common sense and vigorous under-
standings."

There were then two societies little known, and
languishing for want of funds. Mr. Moore determined to
persuade them to amalgamate. He visited the trustees
of both societies, and at length they agreed to take his
advice. He assembled them at his house to dinner ;
and it was resolved that the united society should be
called "The London Clerical Education Aid Society."
He gave £6,000 towards the enterprise; but he did not
live to work out the experiment. A few days before his
death he was occupied in sending out letters to young
men whom he thought likely to be serviceable in the
Church.

Mr. and Mrs. Moore set out for Vichy in the company of the late William Longman and his family.
They reached Vichy on the 6th of June. George Moore
formerly disliked the monotony of life at that place.
But on this occasion he was more content. He used to
sit for hours having what the doctors called "*bains*

de soleil." He admired the blueness of the sky and
the slanting of the sunbeams through a golden mist
between the branches of the trees near the Allier.
What he could not bear was the croaking of the frogs,
which on dry hot nights was simply deafening. The
Longmans lived in the same hotel. Mr. Longman had
often hunted with George, and they had many talks of
old times. Mr. Moore was sometimes very much
depressed, but the powerfulness of the waters in some
measure accounted for this.

At Vichy he began an innermost sort of diary, principally on religious subjects. On the 19th of June he
wrote as follows :—" I must not forget that I am three-
score years and ten. My time here below must be
short : still I feel an unwillingness to die. I suppose I
shall be plucked away against my will at the last. I
believe I shall be with Christ, which is far better." And
again : " This unwillingness to die is spiritual rebellion.
I ought to be free from this. Can I not trust God for
the future? I ought to be free, I can be free, I *will* be
free. I have no doubt of my Heavenly Father's love.
Christ says, ' Him that cometh unto me, I will *in no
wise* cast out.'" On June 24th, he says, " I have
thought a good deal about death lately. I have tried
to realise in my soul that there is nothing to fear, if one
is certain to be with Christ. Wherever or whenever I
may die, may I know that Death is a vanquished foe,
and that I may not fear."

Mr. Moore reached London again on the 27th of
June. The report of the money-order commission was
agreed to on the 29th, and sent in a few days later. At
this time everything seems to have been done by him
once more. He had had his last Bible-reading. He had
paid his last visit to Vichy. Before he left London he
paid another last visit. " I took a long drive," he says,
" to Finchley, where my first wife lived. I saw the house

which I once loved for its inmates. Then I visited the churchyard, where my father and mother-in-law lie buried. It brought back many strange feelings to my mind."

He went down to Whitehall, and arranged for a conference of thirty Scripture-readers at his house, and for the five Bible-meetings that were to be held in the neighbourhood during the following week. The usual entertainments were given. When the Missionaries left, he says, "I gave them all a new hat, a bundle of tracts, a copy of Baxter's *Saint's Rest* and Cecil's *Remains*, and bade them all Good-bye. Some of us will never meet again." It proved indeed a long Good-bye!

He had a great deal of work to do. He was still full of vitality. "I have no sooner," he says, "got out of one class of work than I have to prepare for another." On the 27th of July he got together at Wigton a conference of deputations from all the Young Men's Christian Associations in the North of England. Mr. Moore took the chair, and occupied it from ten in the morning until ten at night. The meeting was occupied with discussions as to the extended usefulness of the associations. Mr. Moore was much pleased with the result.

Visitors came and went. Whitehall was full, fuller, and fullest. Sporting friends came in August to shoot the grouse on the Cumberland fells; and in September to shoot partridges in the Whitehall covers. In the midst of his company, George Moore attended his various meetings. On licensing day, he sat on the bench at Wigton. He attended the Board of Guardians, and continued to take an active interest in the boarding-out system. He went to Carlisle to take the chair at a public meeting in support of the workshops for the blind.

Among the various visitors to Whitehall in August were Mr. Moore's young partner Mr. Copestake, who, with Mr. Tarn, had many a long walk in pursuit of grouse on Caldbeck fells. For the first time since he had had possession of Whitehall his brother-in-law, Charles Ray, had been prevented from paying him a visit. To the last he had retained the warmest affection for each member of that family, and he alludes to the disappointment it was to him, that not one of the Rays or Sievekings had been at Whitehall that year.

Mr. and Mrs. Thompson came to him from his Leeds branch,—"a most faithful servant," he says, "who has been with the firm for twenty-five years ;" Mr. Routledge the publisher, one of Mr. Moore's staunchest friends ; the Rev. Henry Chester, his brother-in-law, and family, from South Shields; the Rev. Canon Ryle ; and Mr. Spurgeon, the famous baptist preacher, from London. It was a singular mixture. Many of the visitors at Whitehall were High Church, Low Church, Broad Church, and sometimes No Church. "Ryle and Spurgeon," says George Moore in his Diary, "got on capitally. Indeed Spurgeon gets on well with every-body. Henry Chester is quite in love with him ; they have found out many things on which they agree. There is nothing like getting men of different opinions thrown together. Spurgeon is a remarkable man. He has such a memory, such good humour, and such spirit ; and he is a giant for work."

Mrs. Moore says—" Mr. Spurgeon interested George greatly. His wit and humour delighted him. One day, on my what influence he had on the farmers and people about, Mr. Spurgeon said to me, ' You are a queen, for your husband is king of Cumberland.' ' Oh! no,' said I, 'he is not that!' 'No,' was his quick reply, 'he is Moore.'"

On the 2nd of September three of the young men from Bow Churchyard arrived, and spent the day at Whitehall. "I took them," says Mr. Moore, "a long drive by the fells and the mountains. We have had fifty Cumberland men from Bow Churchyard this year, and these were the last." Again, *the last*.

Towards the end of the month (20th September) he took the chair at the meeting of the Agricultural Show at Wigton. He occupied the place against his will; but being there, he had to make his speech. It was a sort of lamentation over the decay of the class to which he originally belonged—the statesmen and yeomen of Cumberland. He said, "he had a very warm side to his native county, and it grieved him not to see farmers in greater force there. If for nothing else, they might have come to support a poor feckless chairman like him- self. He had been proud of the 'grey coats' of Cum- berland; but where were they all gone? In his parish there were only two or three of the old yeomen left. Railways, telegraphs, and other affairs were driving things to such a pitch that we were all going wild, and if people did not keep pace with the times they must go. He supposed that the grey coats had not been keeping pace with the times, and that they had been obliged to sell their property. It gave him much con- cern to see that farmers now are not in so good a posi- tion as they once were. He hoped he had done his duty as a chairman." It was the last occasion on which he was to occupy the chair.

He went to London for a few days—his last visit. He was advancing salaries during the day, and inviting old friends to dine with him at night. He went to Christ's Church, Somers Town, to see how it was getting on. He invited the secretaries of the benevolent institutions in which he was interested, and the nume- rous young men for whom he had obtained situations, to dine with him at Bow Churchyard.   There were over fifty in number on that occasion.

He visited the Christian Community Hall, which he had helped to build.   He saw many of the City Missionaries, and encouraged them in their work.   He was still paying the marriage fees of poor persons who were living together without the necessary ceremony.   The City Missionaries found them out for him.   The number had of late years considerably decreased.   During the last year, only eighty-four couples had been married. He wrote across the paper containing the names of the married couples, with the receipt for his cheque, the words, " I have paid for more marriages than any man in England, and it is well-spent money."

Mr. Moore left London on the 30th of September, and went home by Warcop, Kirkby Stephen, Holker, and Barrow.   He visited Whitehaven and Cockermouth, and reached home on the 7th of October, "right glad to get back again ; Home, sweet Home!"

One of the last subjects that occupied Mr. Moore's mind was his desire to organize some method by means of which poor boys of Cumberland and Westmoreland might enjoy the benefits of a higher class education. The system of national schools, while it improves the primary education of the whole mass by bringing all up to a sort of level, actually represses the real genius of a very clever boy.   Under the old system, a learned schoolmaster took pleasure in pushing a boy upwards. To him the clever boy was a source of special delight and interest.   He taught him Greek, Latin, and Mathematics at bye hours, which often elevated him to a high rank at the grammar school or the university.

But now the certificated master has no time for special instruction.   He is paid by results, and these depend upon the standard education of the mass of his scholars. George Moore saw this ; for he was constantly thinking

about education. He had, three or four years previously, wished to do something by himself. He had
asked many persons of high educational authority for
their suggestions. They all gave him good advice, and
took much trouble about his suggestions for a scheme.

It was, however, to Dr. Percival, head-master of
Clifton College, that Mr. Moore owed the working out
of a practicable plan. Dr. Percival's early life, his distinguished honours, and the high position he occupied
in the educational world, enabled him to ascertain the
weak places and the difficulties of the proposed scheme,
and how the money endowed might prove of the best
possible use. At length, after much time and pains
had been given, and many consultations and meetings
had been held,—after Dr. Temple, Bishop of Exeter,
had been consulted and given his advice freely and
fully,—the plan was at length determined on. It was
drawn up in a rough draft by the Education Department and printed. All that was wanted was the final
settlement and George Moore's signature. Twelve
thousand pounds was the amount of money which he
had set apart for the purpose. And thus the matter
rested.

In the beginning of November, Mr. and Mrs. Moore
paid a visit to Muncaster Castle. When the invitation
was received, he said : " Yes, let us go : it will be our
last visit." The "nearness of eternity" was constantly
referred to in his diary. It was forming the under-
current of his thoughts. He was parting at this
time from his old friend and neighbour, Mr. Foster, of
Kilhow, and he felt it much. Mr. Foster had, on
account of ill-health, been ordered to a warmer climate.
On the 2nd of November George Moore writes :—
" I have seen Foster, the companion of my youth, for
the last time. I shall never see him again in this
world."

On returning from Muncaster Castle, he arranged to pay a visit to Mr. Thompson, of Whitehaven. He writes of him as "one of the men for whom all my life I have had the greatest respect. I have often tried to get him to come to see us at Whitehall, but have not succeeded; so I was determined to go and see him." This was his last visit, and he now returned to Whitehall for the last time.

On arriving at Whitehall he found, as usual, a number of letters requiring an answer. On the 11th of November he writes in his diary:—"A long day of letter-writing. Heaps of letters awaiting me—as usual a good many begging letters. At first these letters rile me, but after a little thought, I feel it is God's money I have to give away."

One evening Mrs. Moore was playing the Schlummerlied of Schumann. It was one of George Moore's favourites. He was sitting opposite the piano. Mrs. Moore looked up, and saw an expression of intense melancholy on his face. He was wrapped in thought, and seemed to be looking far away. She stopped playing, and spoke to him: "Come and sit in your own chair. Is anything the matter?" He answered: "I never felt so melancholy in my life." He afterwards said, "An indescribable feeling came over me. I never felt anything like it before. Perhaps it was your playing. You must never play that song again." Was it the shadow of the parting that had fallen on his heart, unconsciously to them both?

Mrs. Moore says that about this time he often spoke of this and that having been finished, done with, and "ended." There seemed to be a tenderness and a meaning about all that he did. One of his last letters was to his sister-in-law, Mrs. S——, who had lost her only daughter under peculiarly sad circumstances. His last words in the note are: "It is just when all seems dark

and broken down that God's help is needed, and if you
pray for it you will be comforted. . . . . We do not
meet as often as we used to do, dear A——, but you
know my love is as strong as ever, and as one grows
older, one perhaps thinks *most* about early happy
days."

He sometimes spoke suddenly and unexpectedly to
people, asking them abruptly, " Are you ready to die ?"
At other times he would say, " There is really nothing
worth living for, but working to do good.   He never
talked much about religion, nor of doctrines nor denominations.   In one of the entries in his diary he says,
" I always thank God that I am no sectarian.   I belong
to all the Christian people in all the world.   I heartily
wish that they all belonged to one denomination—the
universal Church of Christ."

" By their works ye shall know them."   He never
forgot *that.*   He thought that a man's *life* should tell
what he was.   And yet, if any one had faith, he had.
He lived, as seeing One that is invisible.   He writes—
" I seem to have got rid of all the doubts which once
troubled me.   I see, though it be in a glass darkly."
He had faith too, as a moral quality ; and this enabled
him to see all that was noble in others.   He always
believed in the motives of others being good.   He
never had anything but a kind word to say for the
absent.   Of him, as of few, could it be said, " He
thinketh no evil."

On his last Sunday at Whitehall, he attended Allhallows Church in the morning, when the Rev. H.
Harris preached.   As he went down the garden, he
called the faithful Potter to him, and said, " Be sure
to look after the poor people when I am gone."   Next
day a meeting was to be held at Carlisle about the
Nurses' Home.   Mrs. Moore, being a member of the
committee, intended to be present.   But Mr. Moore

E E

at first declined to go, having an engagement at Aspatria. Mrs. Goodwin, however, had again urged him to be present. She sent him the first annual report. He then saw that the object of the meeting was to consider the question of having one or more nurses in connection with the institution, set apart for helping the poor who were without help. This settled him to alter his plans for the day.

Early on Monday morning he said to his wife, "I have been thinking about that Nurses' Home, and I think I ought to go. I felt no interest about it so long as I thought it was only to have nurses for the rich, but now it is different." Mrs. Moore tried to dissuade him, saying that "he was not expected to be there." But he went down stairs, and sent away the groom to put off the other engagement. At breakfast he said, "I *must* go; it will be the last time I shall be in Carlisle." "Don't talk nonsense!" said Mrs. Moore; "what *do* you mean?" "I mean that I shall never be on a platform there again."

The post came in. There was a letter from G. F. Watts, R.A., to whom he had been sitting for his portrait in London. He intended it to be his wife's birthday present. He had sent the cheque for the portrait before it was finished. Mr. Watts expressed his surprise at being paid for the work before he had had his final sittings. George Moore gave the note to his wife. "There," said he, "you've got your birthday present before the day!" He proceeded to say, "I want you to write to Percival, and ask him if he can arrange for a meeting next week. I must have one more reading of that scheme (the scheme for the higher education of poor boys in Cumberland); then it will be possible, and we can get it fairly launched." Yes, this desire of his, which he had so often thought about, and which had become stronger and stronger in his mind, was to become possible,—but not as he thought. It was the offering which a multitude of mourners were to lay upon his grave.

There was also a short letter which he had himself to write. It was addressed to Mr. Hough, his private secretary at Bow Churchyard. It was written on the back of a doctor's certificate, certifying that a young man was suffering from acute rheumatism, and "unable to obtain the requisite amount of nourishment required." Mr. Moore's note was very short: "Please call upon Fursman, and give him a sovereign or two for me. Also a bottle or two of wine from B. C. Y., if it will do him good."

The aid, which was sent, proved most seasonable. It helped to save the young man's life.

Mr. Moore remained in his library to prepare some brief notes of the speech which he intended to deliver at the meeting of the Nurses' Institution at Carlisle These are the notes :—

Metropolitan National Nursing Association.

Dr. Sieveking is the Chairman of the Medical Sub-Committee. Has the support and sympathy of the Medical profession. Mr. Rathbone a great helper.

The Association does not work in connection with any particular Church or denomination.

We have engaged Miss Lees, a friend of Miss Nightingale, who was at Metz with the Germans.

We are going to have three Homes—Bloomsbury for centre.

The Report. To have a trained nurse to attend exclusively to the Poor at their own homes, FREE.

Make moderate charges for the middle classes, artizans getting good wages, and small shopkeepers. Rich to pay £2 a week.

To receive patients into the Homes who wish to remain in Carlisle under medical attendance.

It is well to be afflicted if we can believe it.

It is our duty to work as if all depended upon us, and to think that all depends upon God.

I was sick and ye visited me, and inasmuch as ye did it unto one of the least of these my brethren, so you did it unto me.— MATTHEW XXV.

There is a divinity that shapes our ends, rough hew them as we will.

The carriage was now at the door. Before entering it, Mr. Moore called to his wife descending the stairs, " What is that passage in St. Matthew ? " " Do you mean, ' I was sick and ye visited me ' ? " " No ! " he said, " I remember : ' Well done thou good and faithful servant, enter thou into the joy of thy Lord.' " These were the last words that passed between husband and wife in that happy home.

They drove off to the station, and reached Carlisle about mid-day. George Moore had £50 in his pocket, probably to give as his contribution to the fund. The meeting was to be held at two. About half-past one Mrs. Moore and her sister went shopping, while Mr. Moore with Mr. Steele, of the *Carlisle Journal*, proceeded down English Street. While standing opposite the Grey Goat Inn, two runaway horses, which had escaped from a livery stable in Lonsdale Street, came galloping along at a furious pace. Mr. Steele had left the causeway, and was upon the pavement when the first of the two horses passed between Mr. Moore and himself. The second, a few yards behind, was close upon Mr. Moore. He made a step towards the channel to get out of the way ; but it was too late. He was struck by the hinder part of the horse, and knocked down. He fell on his right side and struck the ground heavily with his head and shoulder.

He was taken up insensible, and carried into the Grey Goat Inn. It will be remembered that fifty-two years before, George Moore had slept in the same house. He was then a mere lad, on his way to London. He had stayed at the Grey Goat during the night, and started by coach on the following morning. Many years had passed. He had worked his way onward and upward. He had returned to his native county, a prosperous, noble, benevolent man. He had now come to his death by this fatal accident, and was taken into the very same place where he had slept before, and where he was now to die.

It was ascertained that four of his ribs were broken— one of them in such a manner as to have necessarily injured the lungs. There was also a comminuted fracture of the right collar-bone. He was severely bruised about the head, and his system had necessarily sustained a severe nervous shock. He experienced great difficulty of breathing, and complained of severe pain in the back.

In the meantime Mrs. Moore and her sisster had gone to the Town Hall, where they expected to find him, and to attend the meeting of the Nurses' Institution. "I was struck," says Mrs. Moore, "with the strange way in which people looked at us, and the kind of awe there seemed to be on the crowd outside. Dr. Barnes came up to me, looking very pale, and said, 'Mrs. Moore, I want to speak to you.' I said, 'Is anything wrong?' 'Mr. Moore has had a little accident, and is asking for you.' I said, 'Oh, those horses!' 'Yes,' he answered. He took us to the Grey Goat Inn. It seemed that when George left us he went to a music shop, and asked for a song for me. He could not remember the name, but he whistled and hummed the air till they recognised it. The song was, 'The Harp is now Silent,' by Kücken. Messrs. Scott, of Carlisle, afterwards sent it to me, as showing me the last thing George had done.'

" When I reached the inn there was great confusion. They took me from room to room, and at first they would not let me see him. There were present the doctors, Mr. Page, Mr. Leckie, and Dr. Barnes, and many other gentlemen, showing great concern and alarm. Presently, Mr. Page came and said, ' Can you be very quiet, and not excite him?' I don't know what I said. I was not likely to excite him. I was turned to stone. Then I heard him calling very loudly, 'Wife, wife, where's my wife?' When I was admitted to the room, he kept on saying, 'My wife would take me from these men if she would come.' He did not recognise me at first. He knew my voice, and kept saying, 'I hear her voice, why does she not come?' Thank God! a conscious look came into his eyes at last, and then he knew that I was with him.

"I believe that from the first, the doctors knew there was no hope. They did not say so to me. They only said his ribs were broken. Nothing could have been more devoted than the attention of Mr. Page and Dr. Barnes; but, as we knew him best, I proposed that Sir William Gull should be sent for. I proposed it to himself also. He said, 'Not unless the doctors think it very serious.' Sir William Gull was sent for, and so was Mr. Copestake. Both arrived at four o'clock next morning. By that time he had become colder. His breathing was very laboured. I began to have no hope. He could not speak much. It was cruel to ask him a question. The doctors gave him ether constantly, and Brand's essence of beef and brandy, but he could scarcely swallow. They said, 'You had better ask him if he has anything to say to you.' I did so, and he said 'Yes, a great deal, but I must wait till I can breathe.'

"He had so often talked of death while in health, and of wishing to be told he was dying, and that he hoped I would say three texts to him;[1] so I felt that I must tell him. At first I said, 'George, darling; we have often talked about Heaven. Perhaps Jesus is going to take you home. You are willing to go with Him, are you not? He will take care of you.' He looked wistfully in my face, and said, 'Yes! I fear no evil . . . He will never leave me nor forsake me.' Several times after, he said a word or two, expressive of

[1] The texts were St. John iii. 16; Psalm 23; and 1. John v. 24.

the same trust. He was soon past much speech. But he knew perfectly that he was dying, and his faith failed not.

> " Rest in the Lord ! although the sands
>   Of life are running low ;
> Though clinging hearts and clasping hands
>   May not detain thee now ;
> His hand is on thee—Death's alarms
>   Can never work thee ill ;
> Rest in His everlasting arms ;
>   Rest and be still."

" Sir William Gull was very kind.   He sat with him and me alone, from nine till nearly twelve o'clock.   I think he was quite conscious.   He knew his sister, and his old servants when they arrived, though he could not speak much.   By and by the terribly laboured breathing grew quieter.   He was fast nearing the end of earthly life.

" Meantime, when it became known throughout Carlisle that the accident was of an alarming nature, the sympathy became very manifest.   Crowds blocked the square in front of the Grey Goat all night.   Policemen were placed by the Mayor to keep them quiet, and to prevent them coming under the window of the bedroom where he lay.   The people seemed stunned—that the one Cumberland man universally beloved, perhaps more than any other, should be dying in that room, of an accident received in the streets of Carlisle.

" The Grey Goat Inn was to have the sanctity, as it were, of comprising two of the greatest events of his life.   He had slept there in 1825 ; and now, in 1876, he was brought to die there.   Neither of his homes was to have the memory of his death.   From the little dark room, looking into the court of the small commercial inn, George Moore's spirit passed away into the hands of God who gave it.   He died at twenty minutes to two o'clock in the afternoon of the twenty-first of November, just twenty-four hours after the accident."

The feeling in the City of London, during his death-stroke, was intense. Telegrams conveyed hurriedly the news of his condition. When the last telegram arrived "George Moore is dead," strong men broke down and wept. Bow bells were tolled on that November afternoon from three till four, and spread the mournful news far and wide.

An inquest was held on the body in the course of the afternoon, when a verdict of "Accidental Death" was returned. The fees of the jury were presented to the Nurses' Training Institution. Mrs. Moore, accompanied by her sister, Mrs. Chester, and the Rev. Henry Chester, returned to Whitehall in the evening. The body shortly followed, accompanied by Mr. Copestake and Mr. Newbold. It was laid in the large oak-room, forming the central floor of the old Border Tower, in which George Moore had taken so much pride.

The funeral took place on the following Saturday. Friends, known and unknown, attended unbidden from all parts of the country. It was the last honour they could pay him. The coffin was borne from the oak-room to the courtyard. It was taken on twelve men's shoulders and carried up the gravel walk leading to the church of Allhallows. The crowd was something quite unequalled. Rich and poor, old and young, thronged the walks. The churchyard was quite full, so that numbers could not enter the church at all. The wind and rain were terrible, as if the very elements were troubled.

The pall-bearers were the Archbishop of York, Sir Wilfrid Lawson, Colonel Henderson, C.B., Mr. F. J. Reed, Mr. S. Copestake, and Mr. S. P. Foster. On reaching the churchyard, the body was received by the Bishop of Carlisle, the Rev. Canon Reeve, and the Rev. H. H. Harris. The burial service within the church read by Canon Reeve, George Moore's old friend

and pastor. That at the vault-side was conducted by
the Bishop of Carlisle, who also pronounced the
blessing. The assembled multitude then sang, "Safe
in the Arms of Jesus." The coffin was completely
hidden with wreaths of rare and beautiful flowers,
sent as loving memories. The body was afterwards
placed in the mortuary chapel, within the church of
Allhallows.

After the funeral, men whispered to each other about
the great loss they had sustained. Each felt as if he
had lost an individual friend,—a man who could help
him in time of need as nobody else could. Yet they
were all different, in character, in education, in social
position. The Archbishop, the Bishop, the High
Sheriff, the Lord Lieutenant, the Squires, the clergy,
the farmers, the labourers, mourned alike over their
common friend. Each recognised something in him
different from others. His benevolence was naturally
the first point in his character that touched the crowd of
mourners. "How much has he done for Cumberland!"
said one. "No," said another, "it is not merely for
Cumberland : he was a *national* man and a *national*
worker." Another spoke of his originality, which broke
out in so many ways of generosity and liberality. Then
he was as humble as the humblest. And with this
manner of talk, the vast crowd of mourners separated,
and went to their respective homes.

Funeral sermons were preached on the following
Sunday ; at Carlisle, at Wigton, at Allhallows, at
Bromfield, at Christ's Church, Somers Town, and
elsewhere. A few days after Mr. Moore's death, the
Bishop of Carlisle preached a sermon in connection
with the Mission Services in the Cathedral. He
could scarcely speak for tears. He said, "We have
lost one whom, according to human estimate, we
could least afford to lose : an earnest-hearted servant

of the Lord Jesus, who devoted his clear head, his
mighty energies, and the princely wealth which, by
h's own power and industry and God's blessing on
them he had earned, to the furtherance of godliness
and to the welfare of his brethren : a man standing
almost by himself—at least I never saw any one like
him ; a man whom all will miss, from the very highest
to the very lowest : a man whose place it seems
almost impossible to fill : a man, I may add, concerning whom it is the less necessary I should say
much, because all here knew him well. Yes, George
Moore has been taken from us ! He rests from his
labours, and his works do follow him ; and he leaves
to us all the noblest and best of legacies—the memory
of a holy life and the precious possession of a good
example."

The French Journals referred to the death of Mr.
Moore in terms of deep gratitude for the services
which he had given five years before, when Paris
was stripped of food. The *Journal des Débats* said—
"C'est avec un regret profond que nous enregistrons
la mort d'un homme dont les Parisiens reconnaissants
n'avaient point perdu le souvenir. Pendant plusieurs
semaines après la levée du siége de Paris, M. G.
Moore ne cessa de présider, dans ses bureaux de
la rue de Notre-Dame-des-Victoires, aux distributions
de vivres faites à des milliers de pauvres gens affamés.
Beaucoup d'entre eux ont dû la vie, tant à ses
généreuses donations qu'à son zèle dévoué et à l'habile
administration dont il fit preuve dans ces circonstances
pénibles. Ce serait donc de la part des Parisiens faire
acte d'ingratitude s'ils ne payaient pas un tribut de
regret à cet homme de bien."

Letters of condolence poured in upon Mrs. Moore.
They came from all parts of the kingdom ; as well as
from France and America. The institutions which he

had helped during his life, thirty-eight in number, sent copies of the resolutions passed by their respective boards and committees. The united secretaries of the Commercial Travellers' Schools, the Home for Little Boys, the Warehousemen's and Clerks' Schools, the London City Mission, the British Home for Incurables, the Field Lane Ragged School, the Cabmen's Mission, the Reformatory and Refuge Union, the Deaf and Dumb Asylum, the Female Mission to the Fallen, the Pure Literature Society, and the Orphan Working School, sent in their words of condolence.

The British and Foreign Bible Society warmly acknowledged his merits. He had been an unfailing supporter of that great institution. The letter of the secretary said : " Earnest in purpose, frank and free in the expression of opinion, firm and unshaken in the maintenance of what he deemed essential principle, prompt and vigorous in action, and deeply moved by the conviction of his personal responsibility in the appropriation of the resources God had entrusted to his stewardship, he was foremost in every enterprise calculated to ameliorate the physical and spiritual wretchedness of his fellow-creatures ; never failing, however, to place the British and Foreign Bible Society in the front rank of those institutions to which he accorded the largest measure of his sympathy and help. His place in the wide field of enlightened philanthropy and Christian effort will not be easily filled ; and in many circles it will be felt that a power and an influence has been withdrawn from the Church which to human view could ill be spared in such a period as that through which the world is now passing."

Public meetings were held in London and Carlisle for the purpose of erecting a suitable memorial to the memory of George Moore. At the meeting held in London, his Grace the Archbishop of Canterbury occupied the chair. Bishop Claughton, Lord Hampton, the Hon Arthur Kinnaird, M.P., Sir Sydney Waterlow, M.P., Mr. S. Morley, M.P., Sir A. Lusk, M.P., the Rev. Dr. Stoughton, Colonel Stuart Wortley, Colonel Henderson, Mr. Alderman McArthur, and many others were present. The room was so crowded that the meeting had to be removed to a larger hall. The Archbishop feelingly referred to his intimate knowledge of the life and character of Mr. Moore, and gave utterance to the general feeling that it is well to commemorate such excellences as those of which he was so illustrious an exemplar.

Mr. Morley, in moving the second resolution inviting subscriptions, observed that he looked with great doubt on memorials. The greatest monument that could be erected to George Moore was, that he maintained to the last the simplicity of his character, and that any memorial should be simple and genuine like himself. All knew Mr. Moore to be a sincere, ardent, and liberal supporter of the Church of England ; but his generosity was not confined to that. All that he required was that his money, as he often playfully said, should have "a good return."

The public meeting at Carlisle was presided over by Lord Muncaster, M.P., the Lord-Lieutenant of Cumberland.

At this meeting the question of the memorial was discussed. Was it to be a statue, a monument, a tower, a building, an institution ? No, it was to be none of these. It will be remembered that George Moore had completed a scheme for the purpose of helping the poorer boys of Cumberland to a higher education. The scheme had been arranged with the help of Dr. Percival, and only wanted Mr. Moore's signature at the time of his death. Twelve thousand pounds had been set aside for the purpose of carrying it out. It was one of the last desires of his life to bridge over the gap between the elementary schools and the higher class schools. Death only prevented his carrying out his project. And now was the opportunity for his friends to take up his unfinished work, and carry it out to completion.

The Bishop of Carlisle clearly pointed out the necessity for such a memorial. It should be something which tended to help his poor brethren onward in the world which George Moore had just left ; something that would be entirely in accordance with George Moore's own feelings of what should be done for the poor boys and girls of Cumberland. "When we consider," he said, "what Mr. Moore's intention was—the last monument which he himself, as it were, intended to erect as a memorial to himself, and which he was only prevented by death from erecting—and when, as I shall show you, the memorial has the express approbation of Mrs. Moore, I think that really we need not argue the matter any further."

And this was the form that the memorial assumed. The subscriptions amounted to about £8,300. It was to be appropriated as follows : Sixteen scholarships of £5 each, tenable for two years ; eight exhibitions, four for £50, and four for £40 each, tenable for four years, subject to various conditions. Such was the scheme which Mr. Moore intended to be carried out, and such was the scheme which the memorialists carried out, in conformity with his intentions. It was the proper crowning of the life and labours of a good man.

There were other memorials. A marble tablet, containing his medallion likeness, was erected in Carlisle Cathedral, " to perpetuate his name and example, and as a tribute of love." The epitaph was composed by the Bishop of Carlisle. The people of Silloth, in recollection of his good works in the neighbourhood, placed bells in the church, every ring of which reminded them of George Moore. The chimes were to peal a hymn which was one of his greatest favourites. At Wigton a beautiful window was placed in the church in grateful remembrance. He is there represented as the good Samaritan ministering to the man who was wounded and distressed.

The employés of the firm at Bow Churchyard also presented their memorial. The subscribed upwards of five hundred pounds. They first thought of erecting a marble tablet in St. Paul's Cathedral, but they finally determined that their memorial should be something that George Moore himself would have admired. They presented a lifeboat to the National Lifeboat Institution. It was placed where it was likely to be of the greatest use—at Porthdinllaen, near Pwllheli, on the wild and rocky coast of Carnarvonshire, North Wales. It is named the "George Moore Memorial Lifeboat."

By a strange coincidence the first crew saved by the "George Moore" lifeboat was that of the schooner *Velocity*, bound from Silloth in *Cumberland!* It was on Sunday evening, the 24th of March, 1878, in a heavy gale and blinding snowstorm, that the crew of the gallant little boat succeeded in saving all the lives in the schooner, which was in great distress off Porthdinllaen Bay.

The supporters of the Commercial Travellers' School could not forget his services. About six weeks before Mr. Moore's death, Mr. Hughes, his partner, had consented to take the chair at the following anniversary dinner of the institution. As it was found necessary to enlarge the school-buildings, by adding above fifty beds, and also an infirmary, laundry, and swimming-bath, Mr. Hughes proceeded, with great vigour, to collect subscriptions. As the institution had already proved itself to be one of the most successfully managed schools in the country, he was received by his friends

in the most generous manner. The result was, that
he was able to announce at the dinner the largest
subscription (£17,000) that had ever been made for
an institution of the kind. The committee then decided to call the new erections the "George Moore
Memorial Buildings."

The infirmary stands near the road from Pinner to
Stanmore. In its central gable stands a bust of Mr.
Moore, executed in Della Robbia ware. It is of an oval
form, with blue background, and a surrounding of fruit
and flowers in colours. Beneath is a bas-relief, representing Mr. Moore seated, distributing prizes to the
children.

Dr. Montague Butler, Master of Harrow, was present
at the annual dinner. He was an old and faithful
friend of the schools. He had conducted many examinations there. He said that "from his heart, as one
who resided near the schools, he could testify to the
great ends which they were calculated to promote. The
institution seemed now possessed of all the elements
of strength and prosperity. He would not dwell on
that topic, as he wished to say a few words of admiration for the character of their late treasurer. George
Moore was not merely an active and enterprising
worker, but he was a rare man in other respects. He
had never met one so true in life's simplicity, or who
so well carried out the Christian principle of doing
good to his fellow-creatures. Often when in his presence, the eulogium of Burke on Howard had occurred
to him; for he inherited the spirit of philanthropy in
almost an equal degree. Mr. Moore was one of those
self-made men of whom the English nation might well
be proud. He always acted with great self-denial and
with a gentleness and amiability towards those with
whom he came in contact which was particularly note-
worthy. Sometimes it happened that philanthropic

men, busy with great schemes, were irritable in little
things.   But George Moore was always found self-
sacrificing and amiable to the humble, as well as to the
great ; and his ability always to sympathise with others
made him more than ordinarily noble.   He would thank
God for having known a man of his simplicity of
character, and yet of such a largeness of heart.   As
the head-master of Harrow, he could not forget that
that institution owed its foundation to a humble yeoman, and it had now celebrated the 300th anniversary
of its birth.   It would, no doubt, be the destiny of
their institution to survive through the ages, and count-
less thousands would look back with gratitude and
admiration to George Moore as its founder."

There were many other more humble memorialists,
men and women, who could give their tears but not
their money.   Allhallows Church is not far from the
high road.   It was easy to reach George Moore's tomb.
Many came from long distances to look at it, and to
think of the man that lay below.   His good acts, great
and small, had left living influences in their hearts.
They could not see him any more, but they could linger
where his body lay.

> " Only the actions of the just
> Smell sweet and blossom in the dust."

CHAPTER XXV.

GEORGE MOORE'S CHARACTER.

GEORGE MOORE'S character is best known by his life and works. Everything that he did was part of himself.

His life was a succession of growths. At first he was in no respect different from the other country boys at Mealsgate and Bolton. The education he received at the village school was of the slenderest kind. The first thing he did, when he had the power, was to introduce what has been called the "educational revival" of Cumberland.

His apprenticeship at Wigton was a period of trouble and sorrow, and yet it was full of trust and responsibility. His knowledge of men increased, and with it his knowledge of character. Afterwards, in passing through Wigton, he would say, "This town reminds me of the many careless, thoughtless days I spent here, all for the world, for I never thought of God."

Wigton was too small for him. He went to London to seek his fortune. He slept on that memorable night at the Grey Coat Inn, where he afterwards died. He started next morning by coach. He was two days and nights on the road. He little thought that in about thirty-four years he should return to Carlisle in less than eight hours, to buy the lands on which he had played when a boy.

F F

A young man accompanied him on the coach. It was one of the features of his character never to forget those who had been his friends in youth, however poor they might be. This young man got a situation in London like himself. But he went down in the world, and George, who had risen, helped him to raise himself up again. We have a letter before us written about five months before George Moore's death, in which this companion of his youth says, "I am quite at a loss to express my thanks to you for your kindness to me, not only on the present but on previous occasions. You have now placed me in a position that I trust, if I am spared for a few years, to be able to keep for the remainder of my life."

We have already related the account of George Moore's difficulties in obtaining a situation in London; his engagement at Flint, Ray, and Company, and the resolution he early formed of marrying his master's daughter. Perhaps this early resolution contributed to save and raise him. He worked on with diligence, application, and sobriety, in the meantime improving his education by attending a night-school. He went from one situation to another, always commending himself by his vigour and energy, until at length he became a partner, and actually married his master's daughter.

From this point all was clear before him. He built up a business, which constantly widened and extended. But a serious misfortune befell him. His partner became seriously ill and died. Wealth, omnipotent in life, is useless in death. So the dying man felt, and Mr. Moore felt it too. Time had now new interests and duties, and life new purposes and hopes. Shortly after his wife died, after a long and lingering illness. He had loved her, and grievously mourned her death.

These two events, coming so close together, opened an entirely new phase in Mr. Moore's character. After earnestly seeking, he at length found comfort. He had thought little of religion before, but now it became the mainspring of his life. He found that Christianity required of him love, joy, peace, longsuffering, gentleness, goodness, faith, meekness, temperance, and, above all, charity. "Though I bestow all my goods to feed the poor, and though I give my body to be burned, and have not charity, it profiteth me nothing." "Pure religion and undefiled before God and the Father is this, To visit the fatherless and widows in their affliction, and to keep himself unspotted from the world." This formed the key to George Moore's future life.

Sir Arthur Helps wisely says—"After a certain age, when the character is formed, there are only two things which can greatly affect it, sorrow and responsibility. If one could weigh the motive power that affects the mind, it would be found that one ounce of responsibility laid upon a man, has more effect in determining his conduct, and even his character, than tons of good advice, lay or clerical, or hundredweights even of good example." George Moore had had sorrow enough, and he now discovered his responsibility.

He looked to those of his own household. He regarded the young people who served him as belonging to his family. They had left their homes. Their characters were in course of formation. He considered it his duty to do for them that which their fathers and mothers would have done. Hence the beginning of the family prayers at Bow Churchyard, and the meetings, lectures, and personal attention which he constantly gave, to ensure the proper up-bringing of his young men and women.

He next instituted a Benevolent Institution for the Porters in his employment. In his memoranda we find a reference to this work. "All true Christians," he says, "whatever their denominational distinctions may

be, are bound to one another by ties of the most sacred
and enduring nature, and are conscious of a natural
interest in each other's welfare, which gladdens this
earthly life and renders the prospect of a life to come
more pleasing and blessed."

Then he went outside of his own household. He took
an active part in establishing schools for the orphans of
commercial travellers. He had been one of them
himself, and well knew their trials and temptations
Lord Lytton said of him at one of the anniversary
dinners, that George Moore threw himself, heart and
soul, into services of that nature, with as much ardour as
if he were building up a fortune for his own children !

He next went on to reformatories for released
prisoners and to refuges for fallen women. He became
connected with twelve different orphanages, of which he
was a liberal helper. He helped the ragged children of
the streets, the diseased, the blind, and the forgotten.
But above all, he helped on the work of Education.
"We must begin at the beginning," he said ; "every
boy and girl born into the world is entitled to a fair
start in life." Hence his great efforts to help on
Education in London, and more especially in Cumberland. This was long before the Education Act was passed.

His goodness became extensively known. One of the
first questions asked about any proposed charitable
scheme was this :—" Has George Moore been spoken to
about it ?" His name was almost a passport to success.
If the scheme was such as to approve itself to his judgment, he went into it with his wonted vigour and
determination. Whatever he believed in, he was full of,
and must pour out to all he met. His friends knew that,
meeting him, they would have a clear-cut impression of
what was on his mind at once before them. He
went direct to every matter he had in hand,—business,
philanthropy, or education.

The first elements in his character were simplicity and directness. As in hunting, he "rode straight," so he was in life. He was prompt, energetic, earnest, concise, —doing at once what he had to do. He never cavilled about trifles. There was no shuffling about him—no humbug. The only thing he could not tolerate was the *drone.* He held strong opinions on most things, and he adhered to them firmly. He never did anything by halves. He went into it body and soul, with the whole of his nature. He went straight to the point. When he had settled a thing, he left it as *something done.* When two sides of a question were presented to him, he was quick to decide ; and he was usually right in his decision.

The successful merchant is not merely the man who is most fertile in commercial combinations, but the man who acts upon his judgment with the greatest promptitude. Mr. Crampton, George Moore's partner, says, " I never knew him make a mistake in judgment."

He was abrupt, spoke loudly, and sometimes so rapidly that people who did not know him asked if he was a foreigner. His physique was, to a certain extent, the counterpart of his character. His keen brown eyes had a dauntless look ; they were eager and penetrating. A Cumberland old woman, in her curious dialect, said that "His eye would fetch a duck off a pond." A tender look would sometimes come into his eyes in moments of feeling, which showed how sensitive his heart was. His mouth was firm and powerful. The form of his head, with its abundant hair, was refined, though indicating much strength of will.

Towards the end of his life, the lines of his face became very much softened down and refined, as may be seen from the portrait prefixed to this volume. One, who knew him early in life, said that he should not have known him from his last photograph.

He was of sturdy Cumberland build, which had been tried in his youth in many a famous "worsle." His short, sudden manner, and his decided tone of voice which never lost its grand Cumberland accent, gave one the impression of a man of uncommon energy. His whole aspect was expressive of the frankness and strength of his character. It was impossible to be in his company without the sense of being in the presence of a remarkable man.

He was a man of power, and yet he used it bravely and wisely. He was daring, yet prudent. His manner was cheerful and frank, yet often very impressive. Many who thought they knew him the best, yet knew him the least. He exhibited great self-control, not only over his habits, but over his feelings.

He never tried to attempt what other men could do as well as himself; but when a charity was in difficulties, and seemed to be falling to the ground, he then stept in, and raised it up again by his vigour and determination. In this way he bore up the Field Lane Ragged Schools and the National Orphan Home. "Never attempt what is impossible to carry out," he said; "but if you have decided that it is possible, then never give up—then death or victory!"

His individuality was quite unique. His manner, speech, abrupt gestures, characterised only himself. He sometimes asked strings of questions with a naïve simplicity. The sharp-pointed utterances indicated an impatience to get at the object he had in view. His power lay in direction and organisation. Then he had a wonderful faculty in getting others to work for him and with him. "He seemed to me," says one who knew him, "to dwell but little on details, perhaps losing thus some of the enjoyment of his work as well of its benefit to himself. He seemed to have always something fresh before him, and to be ready very quickly to turn the page."

The Hon. Charles Howard, M.P. for East Cumberland, says of him:—"It always seemed to me that Mr. Moore was the most thorough man I knew in all that he undertook; and whatever was the object, whether it was business, fox-hunting, canvassing at elections, acts of charity, or services of devotion, his heart was always in his work. He was never satisfied until he had accomplished all that he had proposed to do. I have no doubt that this quality of earnest perseverance and shrewdness of character accounted for George Moore's success in life; but they would not have gained for him the love and affection that all felt for him, were it not for his warm heart and his genial nature."

Some people misconceived him. They called him a Fanatic; others called him a Methodist. They said he was running after other people's business, and not minding his own. But he never neglected his business. If he did not do it with his own hands, he had the gift of insight into character, which enabled him to select the men best fitted to do his work.

He was sometimes rebuffed when going about to collect money for the charities he was interested in, though his persistence usually carried all before him. Sometimes the money-getting merchant would look up from his desk and growl, "What do you want?" "Well, my friend, I want £10 for the Field Lane Ragged Schools." "Ragged Humbugs! Let people work for themselves, and there would be no need for ragged schools. I began without a penny—" "Stop! let me go; I have called upon the wrong man." And away he went to some more charitable soul.

These rebuffs did not baffle him; his enthusiasm was too great for that. Difficulties did not daunt him. His life had been a long conquest of difficulties. He was one who never shrank from duty when it was difficult, nor refused it because it was trivial. This was one secret of his progress. "Do your best," he would say, "do your best always; do your best in everything." This was the lesson of his life. Besides, he was never ashamed of being in earnest. Nor was his enthusiasm confined to any pet project. It was large, and embraced a thousand objects, yet they never clouded his common sense.

The power of his name became more valuable than the power of his money. The prudent were at once convinced of the worth of that which he had taken in hand. His name brought to his assistance the time, labour, sympathy, and money of a crowd of friends and helpers. Mr. Morley said of him :—"In a city where wealth was accumulating so fast, it is refreshing to see a man who, not by giving only, but by hearty personal service, recognised the responsibility which was thrown upon him." The Bishop of Carlisle said, "His loss to this diocese alone is simply unspeakable ; but it may be hoped and believed that his memory will long be found a tower of strength to the many good works which for so many years had his countenance and support." And Captain Bayly, of Trinity House, with whom he had been associated in many good works, said of him :— "There are thousands who feel that life is sadder and the world poorer, because he is no longer in it."

It was a marvel how he found time to attend to such a multitude of interests. An extraordinary capacity for business, as well as an exact attention to punctuality, with an aptitude for grasping the leading principle, and a wonderful memory, enabled him to do an amount of work with cheerfulness and composure, which would have overwhelmed many a more gifted but less persevering man. "I think his memory," says Mrs. Moore,

" was quite unusual. He never seemed to forget the smallest thing that he said he would do. Yet he kept no regular memoranda. Very few things were written in his pocket-book. But instead of this, he would write a word on the back of an envelope, anyhow, sometimes upside down, curiously, irregularly ; and the envelope would be used for days, until it was a complete network of black strokes and hieroglyphics. I really never knew him forget anything, or any engagement."

Having so many people under him, he had often occasion to find fault. Unpunctuality, loss of time, negligence, laziness, galled him exceedingly. Hence his reproof was firm and strong. But when any one got into trouble he was always ready with an excuse. " Give him another chance, he will do better next time." " Nay, nay," he would say, " never turn your back upon a friend, however far he may fall down, for then you lose all chance of doing him good : stick to him, and then perhaps you may be able to make him better at some time." When dealing with others he would say, " Never seek to *mak nought into summat.*" He was absolutely fair. His fault-finding never left a sting. He was not carried away by feelings or prejudices, by likes or by dislikes.

He was a man of great promptitude and coolness in emergencies. One night he heard a hansom cab driving up to his door in Kensington Palace Gardens. He had been dreaming that Bow Churchyard was on fire, as it really was. Before the hansom stopped he had got on his boots, and in two minutes he was in the cab. Before starting, he asked the butler for a cigar, and drove off as cool as if he had been going to break-fast,—though such tremendous risks were at stake, as the premises could not at that time be adequately insured.

He was also a man of enthusiasm. " I recall," says one who knew him, " his excitement of interest in the

relief of Paris after the siege. 'I think I should have
died,' he said, 'if I had not been the first man into
Paris.' The whole story of his visit at that time filled
up one of the most interesting evenings I have spent
with him; and it added, I think, though he was so
much the worse for it, a permanent enjoyment to his
life. When in Paris, he said the 91st psalm contained
his 'marching orders.'"

It requires a good deal of moral courage, in these
days of doubt and unrest, to avow boldly what one
thinks, more especially as regards religious matters.
The divorce of mind and speech, between thinking and
saying, is very prevalent in modern society. It is considered the "hall-mark" of modern civilisation. Yet
George Moore was never at fault in this respect.
When such subjects were introduced, he spoke out
clearly and distinctly. He unhesitatingly avowed his
religious faith, whether in society, business, or amusement. To some it might seem inconsistent. But be
that as it may, it was in him to tell out, in due season,
his sense of dependence on God's Word; and whether
agreeing with him or not, men liked, as they always
do, to meet one so true to his convictions, and so
unfettered in his avowals.

"The foremost feature in George Moore's character,"
says one of his intimate friends, "was the admirable
simplicity of his faith in God's Word. There was no
ostentation or prejudice about him. He was a bright
example of a brave, uncompromising religious man.
He had a firm grip of the Truth as it is in Jesus; and
he commended by his catholic consistency the cause of
the Gospel, which he so dearly loved, to all those with
whom he came in contact. The guiding principle of his
life obviously was to occupy the talents committed to
him, as one who would hereafter have to give an account
of his stewardship."

"There was much," says another, "in George Moore's progress through life, to foster arrogance or even vain-gloriousness. I like, therefore, to recall his remarks to me one morning in London, on some meetings where Christian Perfection was the topic. He said he could not get hold of it at all, as the speakers did; but he added, that he was going to take lodgings in their neighbourhood for a week, and humbly trusted that he might learn something of what they knew."

Mr. Moore valued money at its proper price. "The parsons," he once said to a meeting of children at Wigton, "will tell you a good deal about money. They will tell you that it is the *root* of all evil. But my opinion is that it is a good thing to make plenty of money, provided you make a proper use of it." This is what he himself did. During some years, he gave away more than he made. In other years he gave away more than he had spent upon himself. During the last three years of his life he gave away an average of sixteen thousand pounds a year; and, at his death, he left a large sum to various orphanages and hospitals.

He entered in his diary that he did not wish to die a rich man. "The money," he said, "belongs to God; let me give it back to Him." He made a fortune, he gave away a fortune, and he left a fortune. As he used to say, "Whatever I give in good works, it all comes back again." "There are many in these days," says Mr. Rathbone, M.P. for Liverpool, "who have achieved making a great fortune, but few know how greatly to spend one. Mr. Moore ever spent liberally, and, what is far more valuable, he gave with sympathy and conscientiousness,—not to do harm, but assured that he should do real good, while gratifying his own warm feelings and ardent generosity."

"There was one thing," says the Rev. Mr. Schnibben, vicar of Wigton, "with which I was especially struck in his character, and that was his utter forgetfulness of self in the arrangements which he was continually making for the good of others. It always seemed to be a great source of happiness to himself when he had an opportunity of making others happy. He never grudged any trouble or inconvenience in seeking to advance the welfare of others. Rich and poor were alike welcome at Whitehall. The house seemed to be open to all comers, and all went away happy and contented. He was very large-hearted in his sympathies; and his thoughtful character and business habits manifested themselves in the bestowal of his princely charities."

George Moore was utterly unspoiled by prosperity. He refused many honours which others would have clutched at. He was elected Sheriff of London, and paid the fine rather than accept the office. He twice refused to be alderman for his ward. He six times refused to be member of Parliament. All these might have led to titles. Once he says in his Diary, "I am sadly cast down by hearing that an injudicious friend has applied to get me made a Baronet. I have stopt the application."

One of the Royal Princes specially invited him to attend a levee, but he did not go. He would never consider himself anything but a statesman's son. "You may think yourself," he said to a friend, "belonging to the Upper Ten; but I do not." Perhaps he was, like Diogenes, too proud of his humility. At all events he was quite content to be known as GEORGE MOORE. "The people in Cumberland," he said one day to a friend with evident pleasure, "always call me George Moore." "Yes," said the other, "except that they often leave out the Moore."

Nothing pleased him better than to go into a widow's cottage, sit down in her chair, "sup curds," or partake of her bran bread and milk. When alone at Whitehall,

he cared for nothing so much as cock-broth, potato-
pot, herb-pudding, or some other old-fashioned Cumberland fare—things which *bon vivants* would have turned
up their noses at.   Of course, when visitors or strangers
were present, the best of everything that could be procured was bestowed upon them lavishly.   He altogether
disliked display, either in his house, his dress, or the
dress of his servants.   The latter never wore cockades,
even while he was High Sheriff of Cumberland.   That
office was one, indeed, that he could not refuse ; perhaps
because it gave him more influence among the people,
and enabled him better to carry out his views with
respect to the boarding-out of pauper children.

He was a lover of nature, but he specially loved the
hills, and fells, and dales of his dear Cumberland.
While sitting in his London office, he would often dream
of them, and wish he was back to them again, and to
the haunts of his early boyhood.   When he summoned
his friends about him at Whitehall, he would take them
up to the top of his old Border tower to survey the
wide-spreading prospect.   He took them to Harbybrow
to visit the old Warriors' tower.   Or he would drive
them to Caldbeck Fells, or over the Derwent to Bassenthwaite lake, where he would tell them the local traditions of the places, learnt in his boyhood, and remembered ever afterwards.   Nothing was without interest
for him among the scenes of his youth.

He liked having young people about him.   He
said they had always a softening influence upon him.
The little children used to cluster round him at the
Whitehall feasts.   He knew them one by one.   He
not only knew them, but he helped to educate them.
He did all that he could to give them a fair start in
the world.

He was fond of flowers, especially wild flowers.   He
introduced cottage gardens in his neighbourhood, and

tried to induce the cottagers to grow the old-fashioned flowers. The sweetwilliam, southernwood, mint, and lavender, were his favourites. His prizes for flowers were among the great events of the summer days at Whitehall. He did a great deal in the way of quiet unostentatious kindnesses. Wordsworth says that these are the best portions of a good man's life—

> "His little nameless, unremembered acts
> Of kindness and of love."

The Archbishop of York said of him:—"George Moore was benevolence at every pore." He also added, "He never said an ill word of anybody. When anything severe was said of his opponents, he was always ready to find an excuse for them." Another friend, the Rev. Mr. Puxley, of Kimbolton Vicarage, says, "What struck me, not once or twice, but invariably, in my intercourse with him, was his settled purpose never to speak ill of any one. I knew instance upon instance where his kindness had been met with ingratitude, and where he had been unjustly maligned; and when others were sneering at and abusing those who had done him injustice, he refused to join in the conversation or encourage those who were blaming his opponents, even though he had just cause for indignation. This struck me over and over again. I used to ponder over it, and wished that I could imitate him."

George Moore used sometimes to speak about his position in the Church. At a meeting of the Clerical Education Conference at Carlisle in August, 1874, the Bishop said that "if a man was a Churchman, he did not understand how he could help being a High Churchman. If a man called himself a Churchman, and then qualified it by saying he was Low, it was to take away the benefit." George Moore immediately got up and said that he himself was a Low Churchman, some people called him a *horrid* Low Churchman, and a very weak brother in the Church. But his faith was much wider than his creed. In fact he sympathised with all who loved Christ, and preached Christ.

On one occasion, when a lady of distinguished family had left the English Church and gone over to the Roman Catholics, some of her friends complained, in Mr. Moore's hearing, of the great pain she had caused them by the course she had taken. " Yes," said he ; " but you speak as if all the pain belonged to *you*. Do you ever think of the agony which it must have caused *her* to leave the Church in which she was born ? I have often thought what pain that poor woman must have suffered before she could have brought herself to take the step. Don't you ever think of that ?" There was certainly great insight into character and great human sympathy in these words of George Moore's.

" Sympathy," he used to say, "is the grandest word in the world." It overcomes evil, and strengthens good. It disarms resistance, melts the hardest heart, and draws out the better part of human nature. Sympathy is the old truth on which Christianity is. based : " Love one another." It contains within it a gospel sufficient to renovate the world. Judge Talfourd lamented the want of sympathy with his dying breath. "If I were to be asked," said he, "what is the great want of English society, so as to mingle class with class, I would say, in one word, the want is *the want of sympathy*." Hence sympathy was George Moore's grandest word. He showed it in everything,—in his kindness to his servants, to his young men, to orphans, to the poor and the destitute. Frankel has said with truth, that the truest sympathy with suffering is often found in the man who does not himself suffer.

He was always ready to help a poor friend. A little help given when a man is on his beam-ends, and thinks the world is utterly neglecting him, is the best help of all. It lifts him up again, and gives him a renewed belief in the worth of human nature. It often sets him on the right track again. But George Moore was not satisfied with that. He invited the friend he had helped to his house, gave him the best advice, and watched over his well-being nd well-doing. Thus while he helped others, he was adding to his own happiness. For kindness may be regarded as a moral savings' bank, in which a man may store up happiness for others as well as for himself. In the words written in his pocket-book :—

> " What I spent I had,
> What I saved I lost,
> What I gave I have."

He felt that what he gave he *had*, for it was turned into the treasure of affection which was given back to him from many hearts.

Remark, also, how this conduct on his part affected the characters of others. " The influence of his character," says one who knew him well, "has had a lasting effect upon mine. But this is a mere drop in the ocean compared with the blessing his life has been to his day and generation. I have called my eldest child after him. I have hung his portrait over my study mantelpiece, and also over my dining-room. How much more shall we all value his memory!" Another says, " On the occasions when I was brought face to face with him, his common sense, his ability, his unpretendingness, and his practical godliness, made a great impression upon me; so that I thought that I had never met with such a Man as that before."

Another friend of Mr. Moore's, Mr. Bowker, said, His heurty of purpose and singular transparency of mind were striking features in a character combined of no ordinary materials. And this was the charm of his life—causing him to be respected and beloved by all manner of people, from the highest ranks to the most humble. Men and women of intellect and culture, of rank and station, as well as those of less-known walks of life, all thought and spoke well of him, all respected him. How many will miss his liberal help, his generous assistance, in all the forms of helplessness and misery! We may bless God that his life was so effective, and so permanently useful."

The United Teachers' Association of Wigton laid their memorial upon his tomb. They said, " A gap has been made in the ranks of Christian heroism ; and who shall fill it up? What a proud claim to admiration to know, that he turned aside from the splendid attractions of civic and parliamentary honours which were pressed upon him, and chose rather to devote himself to works of charity and benevolence in a less brilliant sphere ! And how clearly do we trace in every action of his life the grand outlines of his estimable character— his singleness of mind, his largeness of heart, and his all-embracing charity. In his deeds of kindness he knew no creed nor caste. Above all, however, we as teachers proudly call to mind his fervent zeal, unflagging energy, and untiring labours in the cause of education. He deemed no trouble too great, and no expense too much, to spend in the high endeavour that sound learning and true religion might abound and flourish. And now that his career of usefulness is ended, and his kindly voice is hushed for ever, we, who are working in the cause he loved so well, desire to be permitted to record our humble tribute of respect and veneration to the memory of departed worth—the noble philanthropist, George Moore !"

Though still strong and healthy in his seventieth year, he seemed to have many forewarnings of death. He saw the end drawing nearer and nearer. The foreshadowings which Mrs. Moore relates, are very remarkable. "I shall never stand on that platform again," he said, when starting on that fateful journey to Carlisle. He advanced step by step to the verge of the unknown land with awe and wonder, but with supremest hope. And then the fatal blow came. But he was not unprepared. He was thoughtful and calm in the full face of death. He had committed the safe-keeping of his life to his Redeemer; and he knew that God would take him to Himself.

George Moore died before his intended works of benevolence were completed. He had many things in his mind that he meant to accomplish. One of these was to benefit the clever boys in the Northern elementary schools, and help them on to higher class schools in England; and the other was to erect a Convalescent Hospital at Littlehampton. The first of these has been accomplished by the memorial subscription of his friends. Is there no rich London merchant to take up the other and carry it out to completion?

Indeed, George Moore, like everybody else, could only make beginnings. Where he left off, others begin. We can finish nothing in this life; but we may make a beginning, and bequeath a noble example. Thus Character is the true antiseptic of society. The good deed leaves an indelible stamp. It lives on and on; and while the frame moulders and disappears, the great worker lives for ever in the memory of his race. "Death," says the Philosopher, "is a co-mingling of Eternity with Time. In the death of a good man, Eternity is seen looking through Time."

Theodore Monod said that he would like the epitaph on his tombstone to be " *Here endeth the First Lesson!* " Brief but happy! But the epitaph on George Moore's tombstone could not be dismissed so briefly. It was erected in Carlisle Cathedral by the Moore Education

Trust, established by public subscription, " to perpetuate his name and example, as a tribute of Love." George Moore is thus described :—

"A MAN OF RARE STRENGTH AND SIMPLICITY OF CHARACTER,

OF ACTIVE BENEVOLENCE AND WIDE INFLUENCE.

A YEOMAN'S SON,

HE WAS NOT BORN TO WEALTH,

BUT BY ABILITY AND INDUSTRY HE GAINED IT,

AND HE EVER USED IT

AS A STEWARD OF GOD AND A DISCIPLE OF THE LORD JESUS CHRIST

FOR THE FURTHERANCE OF ALL GOOD WORKS."

APPENDIX.

"IT is not easy," says the Rev. Daniel Moore, "to single out, from the group of George Moore's many-sided excellences, that which especially made him a power among men. But a power he unquestionably was, and all felt it. A great work taken in hand, with George Moore at the head of it, was an assured and achieved success. In the presence of his sharp and incisive words of confidence, men of fearful and misgiving hearts could speak only with 'bated breath;' and, as fast as they cropped up, the difficulties were laid low by the strong arm of his energetic will. Who shall say to what extent at the root of this success, - of firm self-reliance on his part, and of strong confidence on the part of those who were to work with him—was the knowledge that, whatever our dear friend undertook, he undertook for the Divine glory; and, what was more, that he always took the All wise into counsels, by secret prayer, before he ventured on a single step.

"Of course, there were present the human elements of success also. A wide and varied experience of men and things, a keen and discriminative insight into human character, a watchful and cautious heed-taking to the prevailing tendencies of the age, - like the men of Issachar 'who had understanding of the times' – and withal a fertility of resource and expedient equal to any new emergency : - these are qualities often honoured of God to the success of an undertaking, even though there should be wanting, in its authors, those higher religious considerations which, in all important projects, ever actuated our dear friend.

" With regard to the forms of good works to which Mr. Moore gave a uniform preference, if I were to describe them by one expression, I should say that they were those which put within the reach of fortune's less favoured children *the means of self-elevation.* He had no faith in the inevitable permanence, in any of God's creatures, of a low and dust-trodden condition. The reptile state was not a normal state of Humanity, and if man, woman, or child had the misfortune to be born in such a condition, he would have them lift themselves out of it as soon as they could. Hence the heartiness with which he threw himself into the Ragged School movement, Mothers' meetings, Lectures for Working Men, meetings of Cabmen at his own house, with any other exceptional scheme that might be suggested for benefiting those whom our older and more established agencies for ameliorating the condition of the humbler classes, had either overlooked or at least failed to reach. With the late Charles Kingsley, he felt that there was no human 'mud' which was not worth caring for, or which would not abundantly repay the pains and cost of husbandry for noble uses. Enough for all of us, who hold his memory in honour, to know, that to few more than to our lamented friend, could those words of the patriarch be applied—' When the ear heard me, then it blessed me : and when the eye saw me, it gave witness to me : because I delivered the poor that cried, and the fatherless, and him that had none to help him : the blessing of him that was ready to perish came upon me, and I caused the widow's heart to sing for joy."

INDEX.

THE END.

www.ingramcontent.com/pod-product-compliance
Lightning Source LLC
Chambersburg PA
CBHW052345110726
47901CB00005B/1360